S0-AJH-136

**IT WAS A MIDNIGHT WORLD
OF LOVERS AND LOSERS—
AND "SILENCER" HATED THEM ALL.**

He drove north to Sunset Boulevard. It was late enough for traffic to have thinned out, but there were still cars and pedestrians aplenty. They'd be there all through the night, because it was summer and this was the Strip.

A young woman in bright, revealing clothing—dress slit to her upper thigh, blouse open down to her middle—crossed in front of him at a traffic light. She looked at him and ran her tongue over her red lips in an obvious solicitation. His face twisted and he gunned his engine in sudden need to run the filth down. She leaped out of the way and shouted, "Fag bastard!"

People turned to look, and he jumped the light and turned south off Sunset at the very next corner.

His nerves were stretched taut. He couldn't go on this way. He'd do something foolish.

He needed the tranquilizing effect of the gun.

BOOKS BY HERBERT KASTLE

ONE THING ON MY MIND
KOPTIC COURT
BACHELOR SUMMER
CAMERA
COUNTDOWN TO MURDER
THE WORLD THEY WANTED
THE REASSEMBLED MAN
HOT PROWL
THE MOVIE MAKER
MIAMI GOLDEN BOY
SURROGATE WIFE
   (pseudonym Herbert d'H Lee, with "Valerie")
MILLIONAIRES
ELLIE
CROSS-COUNTRY
EDWARD BERNER IS ALIVE AGAIN!
THE GANG
DEATH SQUAD
LADIES OF THE VALLEY
SUNSET PEOPLE

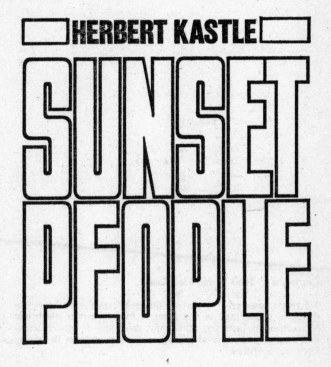

HERBERT KASTLE

SUNSET PEOPLE

A JOVE BOOK

First Jove edition published May 1980

10   9   8   7   6   5   4   3   2   1

Printed in the United States of America

Jove books are published by Jove Publications, Inc.,
200 Madison Avenue, New York, NY 10016

For Raines & Raines & Korman & Buck,
comrades in arms in the longest battle.

"The fox knows many things, but the hedgehog knows one big thing."

—Archilochus

"Death, that is the most important of all ideas."
—*L'Enfer* by
Henri Barbusse

PROLOGUE

One night in July of 1966, in a clearing beside the ferocious jungle called the Annamese Cordillera, not far from Danang, a special three-man squad was deposited by helicopter, and settled down to wait for daylight. Two were American civilians, CIA men in their late twenties. The third was Vietnamese, an ARVN specialist, a guide who'd once farmed on the fringes of the Cordillera and had as good a chance of finding his way through it as any man did. Which wasn't saying much.

Dressed in standard Marine fatigues, they entered the jungle at break of day. According to a map and a briefing given them at the American Embassy in Saigon, a high-ranking Viet Cong political officer would be at a clearing x-marked on the map between eleven and twelve today, which gave them five to six hours. The clearing wasn't more than two miles away, but exactly where was the question.

Four hours later, fatigues drenched in perspiration, they came upon a trail, on either side of which were signs of a nearby VC staging area—pangee traps, the impaling stakes fresh, and spider holes for snipers. They paused for a quick meal, and the smaller of the Americans, sporting a pencil-line mustache, unslung his rifle, a Remington 7.62mm with scope and tubular silencer. He was the sharpshooter, the hit man in this execution squad, and he had to be ready.

They set off again, following the path, peering at the soggy soil and damp growth before their feet, trying to pick up the gleam of mine trip wires. Abruptly, the jungle darkness broke before them: a clearing. A subdued chattering of Vietnamese indicated that it was *the* clearing.

On the path about fifteen meters to their left was a VC sentry shabby in patched pajama clothing. They dropped to their faces in the dampness, the dankness, and the sharpshooter tapped the guide on the ankle. The Vietnamese looked back. The sharpshooter jerked his head right, to where another sentry was just visible some twenty-five meters off through the brush.

Voices rose in the clearing. Both VC guards craned to see what was going on.

The three-man squad inched along on their bellies in the slime. The sharpshooter eased a shell into the chamber of his rifle. He was now able to see directly into the clearing.

Perhaps twenty-five VC stood there, thirty at the most, their backs more or less to the assassination squad, their voices growing louder, taking on a cheering, greeting sound. The guards edged closer to the clearing to see their celebrity.

The sharpshooter also edged closer, and saw a man in a North Vietnamese uniform and cape rising dramatically up and over the VC, being lifted onto some sort of platform.

He stood alone, small, slight, aging; nodding and smiling. He was clearly in view.

The sharpshooter adjusted his scope. As the old man opened his mouth to speak, he fired.

There was a whisper of sound, not enough to alert the guards; certainly not enough to alert anyone amidst that crowd of VC. The man simply fell backward and

10

out of sight. The sharpshooter was satisfied that the dum-dum had entered his chest, and that no one could survive that spread.

He was already turning and crawling. In the clearing behind him, there was a hush.

He saw that the guide was now well ahead of him, rising and moving off in a crouch. The sharpshooter rose and followed, glancing back at the other American, just now jogging toward him, smiling. But the smile disappeared, along with the entire face, as a heavy burst of automatic rifle fire raking the brush caught him. The fire continued—wildly, the sharpshooter realized—from the clearing, then ended in screams of rage and further firing on the other side of the clearing.

The sharpshooter waited a moment, not wanting to go back there. But his orders were explicit, and he sprinted to the nearly decapitated body and grabbed the submachine gun.

The guide was already moving into the jungle.

The sharpshooter hurried to catch up.

The guide turned, waving him on . . . and suddenly went down and out of sight. A brief scream told the sharpshooter what had happened, and he confirmed it when he reached the man. The guide was in a narrow pangee trap, impaled on a stake that had entered his stomach and come out through his back. He shook his head feebly as the sharpshooter raised the sub. *"Tai Sao?"* Why?

After finishing him, the sharpshooter reached down and got the guide's long pistol. Rifle and sub slung over his shoulders, and holding the pistol, he began following the trail. He glanced back often, praying that the VC hadn't picked up on him.

When the trail ended, he used his pocket compass. And swore to God that if he got out of this alive, he'd find a way to quit the Company.

At four-thirty, exhausted, dehydrated, ready to begin discarding the special weapons in defiance of A-priority orders, he broke out of the Cordillera and stood dazed and blinded by intense sunlight.

The chopper came at dusk, and returned the sharp-shooter to the kickoff point—the Marine airport perimeter base at Danang. He showered, changed into fresh fatigues, and ate at the officers' mess. Back in his tent, he glanced at the two empty bunks, and thought of the weapons. High-priority orders or no, he could say one had been lost. This would strengthen the image of an agent whose nerve had begun to fail, and help him get back home.

He speculated on what such a silenced firearm would bring in the States. Ten times the actual value of the gun would be a modest price; double that would be possible if Maxie, a Syndicate chieftain the Company had dealt with, was still filling contracts out of Frisco. Maxie would want handguns only . . .

He went to the locker and took out the guide's Hi-Standard HD: lean, hungry, beautiful to anyone who had ever staked his life on a firearm. A ten-shot .22 automatic as deadly as a .45 because of its special hollow-point dum-dum load, and far more accurate. A target pistol in its civilian role, and not markedly reduced in range or accuracy by the superb MAC silencer. Hit men swore by it in urban situations.

Maybe he should keep it for himself?

But he shrugged and put it away. He was finished with such passions. He would return to law school. He would find the right woman and begin to live the good life.

And the pistol would help finance that life.

12

BOOK ONE
Today

ONE: *Friday, July 28*

The cab sped west on Olympic, carrying Frank Berdon home from his shop. It was almost ten o'clock. He stayed open late Fridays, and had also taken his time closing up. He much preferred work to home lately.

It had been a hot day, but in typical Los Angeles manner had cooled rapidly at dusk. Now it was mild and pleasant, and Frank sat away from the direct whip of air from the open window.

He was flung to the side as the cab turned sharply north, toward the Hollywood Hills.

He righted himself, a heavy man of thirty-six, on the short side, which made him look even heavier. A balding man with a round, pink, almost cherubic face who smiled often, as he did now, catching the driver's eyes on him in the rear-view mirror. A man who rarely meant his smiles, as he certainly didn't now. The cabby was big and surly and drove with an aggressiveness which seemed directed as much toward his fare as toward the traffic. And there was very little traffic.

Especially on this side street, one lane in each direction, along which the cabby sped, before braking to a sudden stop for the traffic light. Frank was flung forward, and back. Again he smiled for the pugnacious eyes in the rear-view mirror, but they jerked left, toward the window. Another car, traveling in the same direction, was pulling alongside them, half in the opposite lane.

"Excuse me," a voice called. "How do we get to Santa Monica?"

The car held two men in the front seat; the passenger was doing the speaking.

"City or street?" the cabby asked, and inched the cab forward against the soon-to-change light. The other car inched forward even more.

"Street," the man said, and put his arm out the window. The cabby said, *"Jesus, no!"* and twisted the wheel toward the car. Frank saw a long shadow at the end of the man's pointing hand, and then it jerked. The cab jerked too, into the car, but too late. The cabby slumped over the wheel.

Frank was jolted; there was a brief grinding of metal; the cab stalled.

Headlights were coming toward them.

The two men in the car were arguing. The passenger was opening his door, or trying to since the cab had jammed it. ". . . fell on the street," he was saying. The other snapped, "Fuck it!" and backed up, freeing his vehicle with another brief rending of metal; then he screeched forward and out of the way of the approaching auto.

Frank watched it speed off, and watched the approaching car pass without slowing. He got out and leaned toward the driver's window. The man's face rested against the steering wheel. It dripped blood. But it was the back of his head which made Frank jerk away. There was no back; just a big wet hole.

Frank stepped on something that almost turned his ankle. He bent and picked up a pistol, unnaturally long.

Another car was coming, this time from behind the cab.

Frank hesitated an instant; then stooped low and ran

16

around the front of the cab and across the intersection. He put his hand with the gun inside his jacket, and kept running until he saw the alley.

He turned into it, panting, and looked back. The approaching car simply pulled around the cab and kept going.

Another car came up and stopped behind the cab; the traffic light had changed to red again.

Frank began walking through the alley. He would try to find a cab, but he was close enough to walk home in about half an hour.

A horn blew several impatient blasts back on the street. Frank was startled, and came to a stop. He took hand and gun from under his jacket, and stared at the weapon. His face was oily with sweat.

The horn blew again. Frank loosened his belt and jammed the gun under it, on the left hip, butt forward. He buttoned his jacket and began walking again, carefully, differently, because of pressure on that left hip and thigh.

He came out of the alley and turned north on the dark street. He was alone. People didn't walk in Los Angeles at night. Only an occasional prostitute.

He began to feel ill.

Footsteps sounded. His head jerked around. A woman was strolling on the other side of the street: young, dressed in tight pants, blouse, and very high heels. She was blonde and pretty, and glanced across at him.

He heard heavy breathing. His own.

The girl turned and began walking the other way.

Strolling. Walking the street. Up and back.

He opened his jacket and stepped into the street. He was ready to cross . . . when headlights flared and a car pulled to the curb beside the girl. The driver said, "Sorry I'm late. They tried to make me work another shift. How's that sweet mother of yours?" And they were gone.

Frank buttoned his jacket and walked north. Nausea tickled his gullet. His head throbbed.

17

Near the corner he gagged, bent to the curb, and threw up.

Tacos and enchiladas for dinner. And that cabby's head . . .

He wiped his mouth with a handkerchief and stood still. The little eyes in the big face blinked. Then, slowly, he continued walking toward Sunset Boulevard, the Strip, the Hollywood Hills.

TWO: *Saturday, July 29, a.m.*

She had taken the midnight-to-eight-a.m. shift because she wanted a rest. She'd handled too many men the past month. Tourists were fattening the customer list, and her bank account. But enough was enough.

She also wanted to read. Nice reading at the desk in front, being both receptionist and staff. Nice reading with the place quiet, the city quiet.

Nice being alone, except for the occasional customer who spotted the Grecian Massage sign while driving up Grover half a block from Sunset. Most of the Sunset Boulevard massage parlors had been closed in the recent crackdowns. Bad for other businesses, the citizens groups and police said. Brought crime and violence to a neighborhood. Same on Santa Monica and Hollywood boulevards.

Perhaps. She doubted it, but perhaps. She didn't really pay much attention to the other girls and their men. She herself had no man, except for her customers.

And she wouldn't have a man until she was through

with this scene. And until she met someone she rather doubted existed.

She turned the page, smiling at Philip Roth's sexist insanity, and heard the bell tinkle. She put the book down, marking her place, and glanced at her wristwatch. Two o'clock. Only then did she look up.

The man was old: late sixties or early seventies. He was a little drunk, and very nervous. He'd once been big—tall and husky. You could see the bone structure, the sagging folds of flesh. He was now gaunt, rawboned. He had a few gray wisps of hair, a grayish stubble of beard.

She stood up. His eyes went over her, quickly, guiltily, and he cleared his throat. She was five-five, dark-haired, full-breasted, full-bottomed, long-legged, serious and pretty and dressed in a mini toga, a pale pink wisp of nylon with matching bikini panties from Fredericks of Hollywood. Arthur insisted all his girls wear the same outfit.

"I'm Diana," she said, smiling easily. "Would you like a massage?"

He cleared his throat again, and laughed. His laugh was very deep. His voice, when he said, "Yes, a massage," was a basso's, suiting what had once been an impressive physique.

She liked that. She liked his suit, a blue pinstripe, a good suit, even though his jacket was rumpled and his tie pulled awry and his shirt wilted at collar and cuffs.

She walked around the desk, which brought her close to him. He smelled of alcohol and tobacco, and while she neither drank nor smoked herself, she didn't mind it in some men.

She took his hand, something she didn't always do. "This way, please."

She took him all the way to the back, even though the other three booths—little alcoves, side by side, holding a massage table and chair, separated one from the other by curtains—were empty and closer to the front where she could hear the bell. Only the back booth had solid walls and a solid door. It was the one

20

the girls used when they thought they saw a full trick—coitus—shaping up.

She didn't see that, though it could be. She only wanted the privacy that would relax him.

She opened the door, throwing the wall switch. He stepped past her, glancing around. He looked at the massage table, the chair stacked with towels, the ceiling fixture.

"Why don't you disrobe and lie down on the table? Cover your middle with a towel." She turned to go.

"Uh . . . on my back or stomach?"

"Stomach, to start."

"You're leaving?"

"Just to get some lotion."

"You wouldn't happen to have a drink here?"

"We used to serve wine, but the police and ABC used it as a means of hassling us, so we don't anymore. I think you'll find you won't need it."

He began to speak again, but she went out, closing the door behind her. She wondered how far age had gone in ruining that fine man. She hoped not too far, at least in performance, so he could come away with the victory that an orgasm represented for most of his generation.

She didn't think of age in relation to herself, but knew that twenty-eight was no longer young; not in this business. And she felt a good deal older than twenty-eight.

She took the squeeze bottle of lotion from the locker, and the credit-card machine from the drawer. She did it this way whenever possible, reducing the obviousness of payment. In the Lotus Massage they had made her run the credit cards through at the reception desk, a distasteful operation for both her and her clients.

When she entered the room, he was lying on his stomach, face pressed into the little pillow. He had a towel across his bottom, and one across his back and shoulders too.

She put bottle and machine down on the chair and removed the top towel. He shifted weight a little.

21

She stroked his shoulders—broad, the bones showing through. Freckled skin and some muscle tone. Not a bad torso.

"You're built well. Are you a police officer?"

He turned his big head and stared at her. She said, "We have to ask that of each client. To avoid entrapment."

"Do I look like a cop?"

"Like a chief, a commissioner."

He smiled, putting his face down again. "I'm Harold Lowndes, general insurance, retired."

She got the machine. "Can I have a credit card, Harold? We take Master Charge, Visa, and American Express."

He looked up. "Now?"

She nodded.

"In my jacket. Breast pocket."

She got the wallet from the jacket draped over the chair. He gave her his card and she ran it through and explained that the charge was twenty dollars for a basic massage. "The rest is between the two of us. The free-enterprise system."

"Let's wait and see if I'll want more than a basic massage."

She put the wallet and machine away and spread lotion on his back and began to knead the flesh. Some of the girls barely stroked their clients, getting down to the genitals as quickly as possible, raising the question of masturbation, or more, for a price. The price varied with the girl, the client. You tried for as much as you thought the traffic would bear. For masturbation, anywhere from an additional ten on up. For fellatio, or "head" as the girls called it, an additional twenty on up. For coitus, if the back room was free, whatever the traffic would bear, but often the same as for head.

Diana gave head only when the spirit, and the man moved her.

She could count the times she'd laid a client.

She had lean, delicate hands. Most times the client reached orgasm before he could ask for anything more. She had a list of regulars who preferred masturbation

22

with her to coitus with other girls. She made between eight hundred and a thousand dollars a week, working seven days most weeks. Except when she took a "vacation" on the late shift.

She was now stroking his waist, reaching under the towel to brush his buttocks. His face remained in the pillow, but he sighed a little. She pushed the towel down, and felt him tense. He had long buttocks that were still hard to the touch.

She probed them, stroked them, massaged them.

He sighed again, and relaxed.

She ran a little lotion down his legs, kneading the calves. She went back up and did the same to his arms, his biceps—big biceps, but much soft flesh before she could find strength, hardness.

She asked him to turn over, and was pleased to see that there was strength and hardness where it counted. The towel, which she'd arranged as he'd turned, tented high.

She smiled into his face. He wet his lips. "What was your name again?" the deep whisper asked.

"Diana."

"The huntress. What are you hunting now, Diana?"

"Pleasure."

The ruin of age was far more evident in front, despite that erection. She kept her eyes from the looseness of pectorals, the sagging of fleshy breasts, the weak flab of stomach. She looked at his face, liking it, the vestigial handsomeness of it, the questioning need of it. She slipped her hand under the towel, and lightly touched his penis. "A beauty," she said, without artifice or whorish guile.

"So they used to tell me."

"Bet they still would, if you gave them a chance."

"No. My wife died last year. Don't want her friends, my friends, those widows and old ladies. I'm a dirty old man . . ."

She grasped his penis to stop the negative talk. Also because she was curious and excited.

She bent over him, brushing the towel to the floor. She kissed his mouth, stroking his penis, a big one,

23

perhaps eight inches and thick, though not really in full erection; not gorged and rigid with blood; not yet sensitive enough to make him lose all pain, all care.

She decided to change that. She decided to forgo the business preliminaries, the dealings. She held his organ with her right hand and touched his face with her left and kissed him, eyes closing, smelling the whiskey and tobacco and maleness, dreaming of this man as he once had been, as he might have been for her: the right man, the great love that she no longer believed in but yearned for as much as any schoolgirl.

Then she moved her mouth to his penis. She knew she was supposed to wash it first, in the hospital-aseptic manner of prostitutes, but she felt a turn-on, a passion, a need to suck it . . . and did so. The smell of him was the smell of man, of genitals. The taste of him was salt, which disappeared and left a non-taste, an erotic feel in her mouth.

When she paused, he said, "God, Diana, more."

She gave him more. She gave him whatever she had to give, which was considerable though she wasn't a brilliant head artist like some of the other girls.

And finally felt his hand running along her thighs, under the little toga, grasping her bottom through the panties. Felt his other hand fumbling for her breasts. And liked it.

"Can you get on here with me?" he panted.

She liked that too. She removed the panties and climbed on top of him and rode him and bent for his kisses and heard the explosion of breath and cry of near-pain that was his conclusion. She rode him a little longer for her own conclusion, which she marked by a sobbing sound vented with head back.

The first thing he said was, "It really happened for you?"

She was off and heading for the bathroom. "Yes." She pointed at the ledge under the table. "There are moist towelettes."

She took her time douching, wondering what he would do. He could rush and leave. It would save him money.

24

But when she returned, he was waiting, fully dressed, sitting on the chair.

"It was great," he said, voice quiet now. "What do I owe?"

She could say a hundred. It had gone that well.

She shrugged. It had gone too well. She couldn't price it. "Do you live in town?" she asked.

"No. New Mexico. I'll be here another three days. I'm staying at that little motel a few blocks east on Sunset. I forget the name. I forget most things lately. Don't seem important. But I'll remember Diana."

Which made her smile, though it was all over and her natural cynicism, her need to withdraw, was on her.

He handed her a bill. It was a hundred. He wasn't *that* well off if he was staying at the Sunset Strip motel. A hundred was important to a retired insurance man from New Mexico. It put a seal of truth to his words.

She walked him to the door. She said, "Come back," and had to add, "I can't promise it will be as nice again," because it never was.

When he'd gone, she returned to the desk and her book. *The Breast* seemed frantic and thin now. But it would fit right in with the world in an hour or so, when the glow wore off.

She had another customer, a young Oriental, who carefully reviewed the prices and dickered for a "hand job" for ten dollars over the twenty. She said, "Why not?" and gave him a leisurely massage, concentrating on brushing his testicles and penis for perhaps five minutes. Then she grasped his organ and with a few quick strokes brought him to climax.

He was disappointed at not lasting longer. A lot of young men were, which was why she'd been especially certain to get payment in advance. He hung around, asking if she was available "for functions." She said no, she worked only here. She began to read, and after a while he was gone.

She'd enjoyed him. He'd been quite beautiful: a small, lean-muscled youth with a waist narrower than hers and a rigid little penis that tilted back toward his naval. And lovely tan skin that was no more yellow than her own. And a voice that would do credit to an altar boy.

Physically, there was much to be said for men.

The doorbell tinkled. She closed her book, checking the time. Four-ten. Seven customers since midnight, which was busier than usual for this shift. Of course, it was Friday night, Saturday morning.

She looked at the man in the doorway: in his thirties. Tall and hard-looking in his work-a-day gray suit. Faded blond hair cut medium-short; less-faded mustache worn medium-full.

She couldn't be wrong about this one. She'd seen them come in flashing badges too often.

She didn't have to ask the question.

"I'm a police officer. Are you Diana Searls?"

She was surprised. Unlike some of the other girls, she had no record to speak of, and wasn't known by sight. "Yes."

"Did you have a sister named Carla Woodruff?"

Woodruff was their real name, which she'd dropped in order to keep it out of the parlors.

"Yes. Is there anything wrong?" (And he'd spoken of Carla in the past tense and she began to fear . . . but most cops were such illiterates.)

He came inside. He didn't answer her.

"I haven't seen any credentials," she said, fear for Carla growing. She knew what this world was. She knew what it could do.

He showed her a badge and card. She read the card aloud: "Lawrence Admer, lieutenant. What about my sister?"

"She was in the same business as you, right?" His eyes flickered over her body.

(The past tense again.) "Wrong. She works in a dress shop."

"Only she lost the job and was looking for new employment, on the street maybe eleven, maybe twelve tonight, right?"

"Not right. She didn't work weekends. You can check with her employer. Did you bust her for prosti-

26

tution because she was walking along the street? Did she give me as a reference?" (She hoped, hoped, and didn't believe.)

"Why? Has it happened before?"

"Never!" She sat down, knees suddenly weak. "Is she outside in your car?"

"No."

"Then why all the questions, the implications that she's a hooker?"

"Because someone killed her and it fits the pattern of pimp justice or hooker haters."

He was looking around.

"What?" she whispered.

He moved to the small plaster Venus near the rear curtain and began examining it closely. "I'm sorry," he said. "She was found dead, gunshot wound, on a side street off Sunset, not far from here."

He lifted his eyes to the curtain and reached out as if to pull it aside; then turned and met her stunned gaze. He said, "It'll help us find whoever did it if we get the nonsense about her profession out of the way. Get us talking to the right people . . ."

"Goddam you!" And having nowhere to go with her agony but at his bland, blond, uncaring face, she lunged up and around the desk, reaching with her nails.

"Take it easy," he said, grabbing her wrists, finally showing some emotion. He was angry.

"You asshole!" she shouted, hating him.

"What the hell, lady! I'm not responsible."

She stopped struggling. "Oh yes you are. God, are you ever."

"Now how do you figure that?"

She tugged her wrists, and he freed them. She went to the closet, got her clothes, and turned to the curtain.

"You're not going to run out the back, are you?"

She was thinking of Carla and trying not to cry and she kept going.

He followed her. He examined the toilet before allowing her to enter.

27

When she came out, he was using the desk phone. "Local call," he said.

She released the automatic snap-lock on the door, and went out to the parking lot. She saw the other cop leaning against a dark, four-door sedan, the only car there besides her Fiat. She walked over, and he nodded, and she opened the door and got in back.

He was a short, powerfully built man, older than the other, and he got in front and turned to her, smiling. "Hey, honey, you're pretty. You gonna help us?"

She looked out the side window, away from him.

Which was when his attitude changed radically. He lunged over the seat, grabbed her arm, and jerked her toward him. "I'm speaking to you, cunt!"

She kept her face turned away.

And the other detective was there, looking in at them. "Marv, it's the deceased's sister."

"So the dead whore's got a live whore for a sister. So when I speak to her I expect an answer." He shook her savagely.

"And when I speak to you," Admer said, opening the driver's door, "I expect you to remember who's the lieutenant and who's the sergeant."

"Shit," the short detective muttered, but he flung her arm away and turned in his seat.

Admer got behind the wheel.

Diana didn't cry. Not until she had to identify her baby sister at the morgue.

Frank Berdon slept as late as Lila and his mother would allow him to, which was a little past noon and better than usual for recent weekends.

The two women had "discussions," as Lila called them. Though his mother was partially deaf and partially senile at seventy years of age and how Lila could discuss anything with her was beyond him. *He* certainly couldn't do anything with his mother but nod at her constant instructions, lectures, diatribes which no one could interrupt. Except Lila. Her powerful soprano got through even those dulled ears to that dull brain.

And through to him in the master bedroom. The stucco California cottage south of Sunset, a few blocks east of La Cienega, was small, and there was no place to hide but under the covers.

He tried it, and Lila opened the door. "She's impossible! It gets worse every day!"

He stuck his head out. "I know."

"You know," she mocked. She was a big woman (a "whale" as Martin, his young clerk, called certain large, unattractive women) with reddish hair worn short and fluffed, making her face look even larger. That hair was rapidly flecking with gray, and the large face picking up wrinkles. She was forty-one, five years older than he, also far better educated and from a better family, a wealthier family, a family that considered her marriage beneath her, as she reminded him often enough.

"*How* can you know," she asked, "when you're either at the store or under the covers?"

He sat up, chuckling, though she wasn't joking, had practically no sense of humor.

"What are you cackling about?" she snapped.

He looked at her then, none too kindly. "I was *laughing*."

"Ah, the grammarian wants to indulge in semantics." She put her hands on her broad hips, ready to engage in combat. "What were you *laughing* about?"

"Just glad it's the weekend," he muttered, and went into the bathroom. He took his time showering and shaving. Only when he heard Lila leave did he come to the bedroom to dress.

She returned as he was finishing, and asked what he wanted for breakfast.

He said he felt like eating out at the IHOP.

"I've eaten," she said. "And I'm not driving you."

"I'll drive myself, dear."

"After ruining your car's transmission you want to ruin mine? No thanks."

"I'll walk to Schwab's," he said. "I can use the exercise."

She was silent a moment, and when she spoke her voice had changed. "Frank, have you considered what can be done about your mother?"

He made himself look puzzled, but his heart began to thump.

"I mean a nursing home."

"That's ridiculous." He moved toward the door.

"I understand how you feel. I felt the same way when they put Edith into Clairmont." Edith was her mother. "But it was necessary."

"Because Edith was wandering away from home,"

30

he said, "forgetting who her children and grandchildren were, losing control of her . . . her natural functions." His heart hammered. He knew from the way her eyes flickered that she was going to tell him something awful.

"Your mother has been fouling her bed the past two weeks."

"That's a lie!"

"Frank! You forget yourself! I do not lie!"

"Then you're mistaken!"

She began to speak, and he whirled on her. "Shut up! I won't hear any more! Fucking whale!"

She stepped back, and he realized his fist was drawn up before her mouth.

"Frank," she said weakly, and burst into tears.

He dropped his hand. "I'm sorry."

"You called me . . ." She wept. "You never used to say such things. And I hid what your mother did . . . other things too . . . I wanted to spare you as long as possible." She sank to the bed, big body shaking, hands over her face.

He sat down beside her, his heartbeat quieting. The more she wept, the calmer he grew. Until he was able to draw her hands from her face and kiss her cheek and tell her he appreciated her above anyone on earth and couldn't do without her.

She dried her eyes.

"We'll talk of it again," he said, "later on. Just give me a little time."

"All right. But she wandered away last Wednesday and I had to call the police. Luckily she was only—"

He rose. "Later on," he said firmly. And still firmly, "I'm going to take your car."

She looked up then, gaze hardening. But he met that gaze, and she nodded.

He went to the kitchen, to the counter-top bowl where she kept her car keys. His mother was sitting at the table, so small, so very fragile-looking lately. He turned his eyes from her.

She said, "Well, Frankie, how did you like your father's singing in the shower last night?"

31

He was shocked into brittle laughter.

"His favorite," she said. " 'Red Sails in the Sunset.' "

"C'mon now, Mom. You know Dad's gone. Six years . . ."

"He still doesn't know all the words," she said, shaking her head.

He walked past her . . . and caught the distinct scent of urine.

Lila made no further protest when he took the car. He drove to the IHOP, listening to the all-news station on the radio, and heard about the "pointless killing."

Before entering the restaurant, he bought a newspaper from the machine out front. But it was too early for the story to have made print.

He ate hugely—a large order of pancakes, two eggs over easy, a ham steak, home fries, double order of toast, and coffee.

The aging orange-haired waitress asked if he wanted anything else; pencil poised to total his check, she let her eyes flicker to the front where people were waiting for tables. But he said, "Yes, a piece of cherry pie, please," and poured himself a third cup of coffee from the thermos pitcher and lit a cigarette. The smoke felt wonderful, even though he was down to six or seven a day and planning to quit within the month. He ate his pie slowly and had another, leisurely cigarette. Lila could wait for her car and the waitress for her empty table and the cheap Sunset Boulevard crowd for their lunches.

When he did leave, he drove to Fairfax Avenue and a great delicatessen, to make certain that his dinner wouldn't be one of Lila's diet plates that did neither of them any good since they both cheated. And Mom loved that thin-sliced roast beef . . .

Later, at home, watching the news on TV with Lila as his mother napped, he learned that the cab driver had been identified as Arnold Latrile, once a blackjack dealer in a Las Vegas casino. Latrile had been sought by Nevada authorities for questioning in a robbery of that same casino . . . but his employers apparently had found him first.

He chuckled a little. Lila glanced at him and began to speak. He tried to hear what the announcer was saying about Carla Woodruff, but Lila was going on about his mother again. And he was getting a headache again.

Lila had to stop when his mother came in for dinner. But sitting at the table with both of them ruined the joy of deli cuts, pickles, and potato salad.

He left them still eating, saying he was going for a walk.

Outside, he turned away from the street, going up the driveway and around to the back yard and the bushes near the master bedroom windows. He dropped to his knees and felt beneath the bushes and found the gun in its plastic bag.

Still kneeling, he removed the bag and held the long automatic in both hands. He stayed that way for quite awhile.

Then he went for his walk.

FOUR: *Sunday, July 30, a.m.*

Arthur called Diana at one-thirty. She wasn't overly fond of the Grecian Massage's owner-manager because of his AC/DC action and his numerous attempts to drag her into it. But yesterday had been the worst day of her life, and now she was into the black morning hours, and there was no one to turn to. Certainly not Mom and Pop.

Arthur said, "I've been in La Jolla since Friday afternoon, y'know?"

"I know."

"I just got back about an hour ago and Lori's filling your shift and she tells me what happened and I can't believe it, right?"

"Right," she whispered.

"You need anything?"

"I can't sleep."

"Quaalude'll relax you. I'll bring a few. And a friend so we can talk."

"No friend, Art."

"A lady, hon. A doll."

"Please. I'm a sick girl tonight."

35

He was silent. She knew she'd spoiled his plan to dope her and comfort her with hetero and lesbian sex. To Arthur Dumont, sex was the answer to all pain, all loss and anguish, his main, perhaps his only reason for living. And he wasn't alone. The Strip was loaded with what street people called "come freaks."

When he still said nothing, she said, "I'd be glad to pick up the pills at your place if you don't want to bother coming here. I really need something to knock out the thinking mechanism, the memory banks."

"What about your books?" he mocked, having resented her withdrawal into reading as so many of the parlor people did.

She answered straight. "Can't read, Art. Can't concentrate. Can't do anything but remember." Which disarmed him.

"Yeah, well, a tragedy like that—" He sighed. "You don't know how to live, Diana. I'll bring 'em over." He hung up.

It would be at least half an hour, probably longer. Arthur was in Hollywood; Diana lived in a condominium in upper Malibu, inland side of the Pacific Coast Highway but with a good view of the ocean. One of a row of attached two-level apartments called townhouses in L.A.—two bedrooms and bath upstairs; living room, kitchen, dining area, and shower-bath downstairs—it had cost more than she'd felt she should spend. But she'd needed a place away from the action, a place with some sense of the natural world, with the peace that the ocean provided, and she'd sunk just about every dime into buying and furnishing it. That was three years ago, and the townhouse had turned out to be the best investment she could have made, more than doubling in value. A neighbor had recently sold a similar apartment for two hundred thousand.

Another reason she'd bought the townhouse was so that her beach-loving sister would spend weekends with her. Her friend. Her lifelong playmate . . .

She was crying again, and there was no sense in that. Better Arthur's way, with drugs and repeated orgasms. Better *any* way than to remember Carla, remember childhood.

St. Louis. Mom and Pop and Carla and Diana. And for fifteen years, their brother, youngest of the brood, Jackie. Like Carla, doomed. Like Carla, struck down by violence. But unlike Carla, it was violence of his own making. He'd wanted a car. He'd stolen two before taking the Corvette from the dealer's lot, and being chased, and dumping the car, and running.

And being shot when he ignored the officer's repeated commands to stop.

"I swear I thought I would hit him in the legs," the officer had said at the inquest, looking at her parents. "But he tripped . . ."

So he'd been struck in the back, the bullet passing through his heart. So he'd been buried near Grandma's, in St. Anne's township, where he'd been happiest.

Not that they hadn't been happy enough as kids. Poor, yes, but no one mistreated them too badly. An occasional slap in the face from Pop, who saved his real anger for Mom. Her he beat up. And that, along with Jackie's death, had sent Diana out of the house, out of her sophomore year at Washington University and plans to teach English, to Los Angeles and a brief attempt to break into the movies.

Being pretty, being involved in amateur theatrics, had led to a good deal of attention from men in St. Louis, and to a certain amount of sexual experience. Which increased during her year of acting classes and auditions in Hollywood. Also, her own appetites had been strong and steady.

Still were, though her cynicism had matured and altered the way she looked at men. A stiff penis was one thing; it could be enjoyed on the very simplest of terms without involving your mind, your future, your freedom. Love, long-term affairs, and marriage were other things entirely, being weighted, it seemed to her, so heavily in the male's favor that fewer and fewer intelligent women were willing to involve themselves. Careers were the answer for these women. And Diana

37

felt her career was to earn as much money as quickly as possible with as little involvement as possible.

Which the massage parlors had offered, with the big plus of satisfying her sexual appetites. She got ten percent of the money Arthur received from her basic twenty-dollar fees, plus everything else she could make. Other parlors had paid less, but she hadn't stayed long where she wasn't getting her just share. Now she was content.

Or had been.

She'd had her condominium and her reading and an occasional play or movie. Had a weekend or two each month with Carla when they cooked for each other or ate out at a good restaurant. And watched TV. And talked, talked, always talked about home and Jackie and their parents and their old friends. And this link to the past had kept them both—but especially Diana— sane and stable.

It was Diana who had suffered most at Jackie's death. With Mom so hard on him, saying he was "just like his father," Diana had become surrogate mother. It was she who had known how bad he was turning, how dangerous his life was becoming. It was she who had planned to get him away from St. Louis as soon as possible. And it was she who had sat up with his body all night in St. Anne before allowing the morticians to have it.

A strange night, that one. A night of healing as well as grieving. A night during which she had grown in a way that few people her age grew.

She'd known her own mortality that night. She'd lost her true virginity that night. She'd understood life in a certain way, and while Carla had continued to look for love, for marriage, it had somehow ended for Diana.

And now what? Now her sister was dead and she hadn't been able to make herself call her parents. Her embittered parents who kept asking when she and Carla, who had followed her to L.A. within eight months, were going to "come home." Her mother who explained the continued beatings by saying, "It's your fault. Yours and Carla's. Your father takes his grief, his loss, out on me."

Which was bullshit! Her father took his failure at work, at being a man, out on her. Her father, who talked of having been scouted by the major leagues when he was a high-school baseball star. Who said her mother had "planned to get pregnant with you," looking at Diana, "so she could trap me into marriage and make me quit school and lose my chance to pitch for the Cardinals. Oh, Christ, what I could've been if it weren't for you and your mother!"

He would have been just what he was now. He'd worked hard enough at the Anheuser Busch Breweries. He was about to retire.

But he was nothing in his own eyes, so he was nothing.

And he'd never been able to enjoy his wife, his children, make them part of the fabric of his life. So *they* were nothing . . . when they were with him.

She and Carla had escaped. Her mother was trapped by habit, history, an inability to conceive of making it on her own.

She was standing near the phone. She simply had to inform her parents!

But her mother would shriek and both would blame her for—as her mother had once put it—"influencing your younger sister to follow you in a life of sin." And that was without having any idea about the massage parlor.

What if the story hit the *St. Louis Post Dispatch* which her father read faithfully for crime and sports? What if they had already found out? What if the phone rang . . .

It did ring! It sent her stumbling backward, trembling. It kept ringing until she had to pick it up to stop the awful clangor.

"Diana?"

"Who is it?"

"Lieutenant Admer." He paused. "Call me Larry."

She was silent.

39

"I'm sorry for the way I informed you of your sister's death."

He didn't sound sorry to her. He sounded glib.

"Has anything come up about the case?"

"Not yet. But I promise I'll do a job."

"Like the job you did releasing my occupation to the news media so that everyone thinks my sister was a streetwalker?"

"That I had no control over. The reporters get all the infomation we get, with the exception of a few facts about the modus operandi, the killer's technique . . ." He interrupted himself. "Anyway, we can't hold anything back from newsmen these days."

"Newspersons. Or haven't you ever met a woman reporter?"

He chuckled. "Push women's rights, do you? Chop down the macho?"

She thought of giving him an answer, but she was sick of him and said, "Unless you get to the point of this call, I'm hanging up. And don't ever bring that other officer, Marv, near me again."

"Take it easy. I only want to apologize for the way I broke the news. I've never been good at things like that." He was more convincing this time. But then he said, "As for Sergeant Rodin, he's an experienced detective and he'll work as hard to solve this thing as I will."

"Don't let him come near me."

"C'mon now, Diana. I've warned him not to repeat . . ."

"Or else I'll file a complaint."

His voice hardened. "I wouldn't recommend that, lady. You know what you're worth in front of a judge, the D.A.?"

She hung up.

In half a minute, the phone rang again.

"I lost my temper," Admer said. "I'd like to come over and talk about your sister, her habits, the people she worked for, her dates . . ."

"I gave you everything yesterday."

"Why can't we be friends?"

40

"At two in the morning?"

"So what? You deal with men all night, don't you?"

"For a fee," she said, despising him.

"Okay. What is it? Twenty? Twenty-five? I'm curious enough to pay. Once."

"I only do business at the parlor."

The man's temper blew. "You're a real bitch, you know that? If I wanted to apply a little pressure, you'd never work again!"

She continued as if he hadn't spoken. "Of course, I'm not allowed to deal with a cop. I'm required to ask the question, 'Are you a police officer?' of each prospective customer, to avoid entrapment. I've never had a yes, but should the answer *be* yes, I'd ask that customer to leave. With you, I already know the answer."

It was he who hung up this time.

Probably not smart to antagonize a police lieutenant. But the uncaring nerve of the man, trying a make, with her sister still on ice at the morgue!

She decided to speak to Arthur about transferring to another of his four parlors. Or to check on the Taj Mahal in Santa Monica . . . though that was a little too close to home. She'd always kept her professional life and home life far apart.

But what home life could she have now? Carla's visits had been family. Without family, what did she have?

No man in her life besides her clients.

No real girlfriends, though she occasionally saw one of the less freaky parlor girls.

No one at all, really.

Quite suddenly, grief was overshadowed by panic.

Dear God, she was alone in all this world!

And there wasn't even any dear God for her.

The doorbell rang. Gratefully, she ran downstairs to answer it.

Arthur was a small, dark-haired man with sharp, ferret-like features and a pair of the purest, widest, bluest eyes she'd ever seen. Looking into them, you would never think he pushed dope, women, men, children, pornography. Even an occasional murder-for-hire, she'd heard.

He came inside and looked around. "Nice." He pressed a small plastic jar into her hand.

"How much?" she asked, turning to her purse on the coffee table.

"You owe me." He sat down on the couch. "Why do you live way the hell out here?"

"I'm an ocean freak."

He nodded, accepting that. To Arthur, everyone was some sort of freak.

She went to the kitchen and took one of the large tablets. She came back and sat down beside him and raised his hand and kissed it. "Thank you," she whispered, and knew she was falling apart.

He stared at her. "Hey, nothing." He was about thirty-five, whipcord-lean, dressed in tight brown pants and loose maroon velour shirt. He wore a small gold spoon on a gold chain around his neck, decorative and also quite functional for snorting coke.

She held tight to his hand. It was all she had this black, black night.

He kept staring. Then he said, "You want a straight scene? Like a missionary fuck or something?"

She laughed, tears pushing at her eyes, and shook her head. "If you'd just sleep with me."

He pulled his hand away and stood up. "Can't see it. If I sack you, I'll fuck you. At the least."

Again she laughed, and this time the tears rolled down her cheeks. No help from Arthur of the purest blue eyes.

"Listen, you're falling out of it, you know?"

"I know," she whispered thickly.

"You need something." He thought a moment. "Remember Chrissie, the redhead? She was turning hard junkie. Scientology was her out. You oughta try Scientology. Or maybe Hari Krishna. Or the Jesus freaks. Something to latch onto, Diana, because fun isn't your bag." He walked out the door.

She sat there alone, and nodded. Fun wasn't her bag. But neither was religion.

42

Still, he was right about her needing *something*.

A smart man, Arthur Dumont. A man with friends high up in city government. Which was why he'd retained four of his six massage parlors when most other such entrepreneurs had folded completely. A rich man too, and she respected the self-made rich. They generally knew what they were talking about.

Not like the wailers, the complainers, the failures: her father.

Not like the make-out cops: Lieutenant Lawrence (call me Larry) Admer. Who was in charge of finding the animal who had blown her sister's life out the top of her head. Who couldn't care less because he obviously classified Carla, along with Diana, as a hooker, a non-person. Carla, who hadn't been robbed, hadn't been sexually assaulted, hadn't been touched at all . . . simply murdered.

She got up, fists clenched . . . and staggered. She'd never taken Quaalude before, or any of the mind-altering drugs that people popped like candy, but it was obviously beginning to work.

The super-relaxant was taking her out of it, at last.

She went upstairs and undressed, dropping her clothes where she stood, and got into the king-sized bed. Where she and Carla had spent so many nights giggling together like kids, talking far into the morning.

And Quaalude or not, she again clenched her fists, again saw her sister's waxy face and matted hair—matted with blood and bits of brain. Again wept. Again despaired of life. Again panicked. Again knew Arthur was right and she had to find something to live for; her "out."

Had to find it *soon*.

She had wanted, for an insane week, to kill the cop who had shot her brother. It was her out at the time. But he'd been transferred and no one would say where and she'd known it was impossible. And also known it wouldn't have satisfied her even if it had been possible.

Now she wanted to kill the animal who had taken Carla from her.

And this too seemed impossible.

43

But if it *were* possible, it *would* satisfy her.

Her eyes closed. Her fists unclenched. The drug took stronger hold.

And still, she knew she had to have a course of action, a *raison d'etre,* something to hinge her life on.

An out.

She forced open lips and eyes, which seemed glued shut now, and said, "I swear, baby," speaking to Carla, "I'll find whoever did it. I swear I'll punish him."

The next time that cop phoned her, he'd get a surprise—a cordial reception. Because whatever it took, she had to learn how to find the murderer, had to know everything the police knew.

With this, she could finally surrender consciousness.

FIVE: *Sunday, July 30, p.m.*

Larry Admer spent Sundays with his five-year-old son Larry Junior, whom he called J.R. Gloria had remarried. Almost seemed as if she'd been waiting for him to cut out. Two months after the final decree she was at the altar with a new guy, partner in an Orange County real estate company with his name on the for-sale signs. An older man, maybe forty-five, but in good shape and so together and friendly he made Larry sick.

But what the hell, he was good to J.R., no doubt about that. Good *for* him, too, and Larry hadn't been, and wasn't. Not that he hadn't tried.

Just not the daddy type, he thought, driving back from Huntington Beach and the expensive sea-view house. Not the husband type either.

But he didn't envy Roscoe Green of Green Realty Inc. Sure, he would've liked some of that heavy bread, and wouldn't have minded the classic Jag convertible either. But Green wasn't what he considered a real man, a blood-and-guts man, the kind that won the wars and made the country what it was . . . or had been. Like George C. Scott playing Patton. Jesus, the world's greatest movie!

Larry Admer had been a damned good soldier—got his Silver Star to prove it—but Vietnam had been the wrong war. He hated thinking of the way they'd pulled out. God, the wasted American lives! The fine lives. And the ones who had copped out and stayed home, who *bought* their way out with college courses, had run around the streets making shit out of those sweating, bleeding, dying men.

Well, it was long finished and no one wanted to remember, so fuck the great American public that had sat on its ass and watched the war on television. Just another show and the ratings had gone down so cancel one war. Catch Larry Admer enlisting in the next one!

Still, he'd been a helluva soldier. And parlayed his Silver Star and a lifelong ambition into becoming a helluva cop. And that meant a helluva man, which Roscoe Green, whatever else he was, could never be. Which few men could ever be.

He smiled. Everything going along well. He had Roberta and sometimes a new chick and he could've moved in with a dozen chicks in the two years he'd been separated from Gloria. He'd gotten his B.A. from Los Angeles Community College, and then his lieutenant's bars—had to give Gloria credit on both, as he was a lousy student—and the bread wasn't bad at this level. He was doing exactly what he wanted to do . . . if he couldn't quarterback the L.A. Rams.

He came off the freeway, and opened the glove compartment for his cigarettes. He didn't smoke when he was with J.R., because neither Gloria nor Green smoked and she'd asked him not to "give the child bad habits." Right. But he made up for it on the trips home.

Lighting his third unfiltered Camel of the evening, he saw the massage-parlor sign. And immediately thought of that victim's sister. And tried not to.

Small, neat sign, this one. Blue letters on a white background lighted from underneath: A-1 MASSAGE. No more blinking arrows and bright neons and all the rest of the attention-getters of two, three years ago. The few that had managed to renew their licenses tried not to draw too much attention to themselves. (The regular customers knew where to go. The tourists who searched long enough would find a place.) Vice still hassled them, and he'd spent five months on Vice and hated every day of it. No job for a real man.

Some of the girls were good-looking. Some were hard. Some were junky kids trying to feed their habits without using the streets and a nigger pimp. Some were just pathetic.

He wondered again how a girl as knockout as Diana Woodruff had sunk so low.

And how a girl who had sunk so low had the nerve to treat him the way she had!

He was raging on the instant.

He could drive over to her house right now and take her in her own bed and what the hell could the whore do, yell rape?

He laughed aloud to hear the sound, to show himself what a nothing the whole scene was. And stopped at a gas station and entered the phone booth to call Roberta and say he'd be over by eight. And dialed Diana Woodruff's number instead.

The ring sounded six times before she answered, and her "Hello" was thick, groggy.

"It's Lieutenant Admer. I've got some questions to ask. Either I come over to your place, or you come down to the Central West Station." His hand was sweating on the phone. He was upset, and annoyed with himself for being upset.

She mumbled something he couldn't make out.

"What's wrong with you?" he snapped.

She cleared her throat. "Doctor prescribed a sedative. Lieutenant Admer, you say?"

He began to feel lousy. "We can do it another time."

"That's all right. Just have to shower and clear my mind of sleep. Sleep that knits up the ravell'd sleave of care." She made a laughing sound. "Shakespeare obviously didn't have a murdered sister."

"I don't really have anything important to ask, Diana."

She was quiet, and he began to say goodbye, and she surprised him. "I haven't eaten in almost two days. I'm either going to die or grief and starvation, or I'm going out to dinner. Want to take me?"

"Yeah, sure," he said eagerly, then was embarrassed and tried to cover. "Maybe you'll show me some of those massage-parlor moves, so I can use 'em on my girlfriends." And winced because the remark sounded so gross, so stupid. "Erase that," he muttered. "I can't seem to say anything right with you."

"What difference does it make?" she asked, and he regained his balance and said, "Yeah, see you in about half an hour."

A whore, he kept reminding himself as he drove toward the coast and Malibu, with a bunch of good looks and some style and . . . and shit, a murdered sister, like she said, which made him sorry for her.

But when she answered the door to her condo, he had no thought of feeling sorry for her. Red-rimmed eyes and all, she was the best-looking woman he'd ever seen. And she knew how to dress—a long black skirt and black high heels and a satiny deep-green blouse and thin silver chains around the neck of that blouse and her hair hanging long and dark and a delicate hand that moved out to take his. He didn't want to think of what that hand did at the parlor, and couldn't help thinking of it. At the same time, she was about as far from cheap and whorey as she could be.

He raised her hand and kissed it.

She said, "Rather gallant for a cop."

"Fuck my being a cop," he snapped, angered by her patronizing manner.

"That's more like it, Lieutenant."

He sighed. "Sorry. Had a long day. I meant, I'm not a cop right now, with you."

"But you are," she said firmly. "The cop who's going to avenge my sister."

"Well, avenge . . ."

"That's the word."

He shrugged, and she kept looking at him, and he finally said, "Okay."

She directed him to a seafood restaurant set on pilings right over the water. There were tables available, but not the one she wanted so they waited at the bar. He had a Chivas and water. She had plain water and asked if he ever experimented with alcohol—martinis, Manhattans, Margaritas, some of the more exotic drinks. He said, "No. Booze is booze."

"Then you should drink straight domestic vodka. That way you'll get the most effect for your money. With Scotch, bourbon, brandy, you pay for the congeners, the color and flavor elements that are as superfluous as the fruit juices, flowers, and coconut shells of exotic drinks."

"You lecture this way all the time?"

"With friends, yes. Not that I have many." She looked away and tapped her long, slender fingers on the bar. She wore a silver and jade ring in the shape of a curled serpent holding the Earth in its mouth.

"Nice ring," he said. "Gift?"

"No. I bought it myself, at an auction in Beverly Hills. An extravagance, but I wanted it."

He raised her hand for a closer look. It was as knockout as she was. And looking past her, he realized that a man at the other end of the bar, with a pretty woman of his own, was sneaking glances at Diana. And the bartender, young and bushy-haired, passed by more often than necessary. And other men at tables along the wall looked at her occasionally.

And they only saw what he had first seen. They didn't know her voice, soft yet incisive; her obvious intelligence; her poise . . .

He was proud to be with her. Still, he heard himself saying, "I wouldn't think you'd have to buy jewelry. Men must give you presents all the time, trying to make contact outside your place of business."

"Carla was wearing two of those presents when she died. I sold all the others. Most were costume pieces. A few were genuine. None were to my taste."

The *maitre d'* was there, smiling at Diana, saying,

49

"Your table is ready now, Miss Woodruff," barely including Larry in the sweep of his arm.

But that was okay. That was part of the pleasure of being with this surprising woman.

Their table was in a corner where two glass walls met. Sitting down, they were suspended over black, rolling water which gave a shattered reflection of moon and stars. It was incredible, and he looked from the view to her, wanting to comment but afraid his words wouldn't be right, would disappoint her. He waited for *her* comment.

She said, "Tell me what you're doing to find the man who killed Carla."

He lit a cigarette. "We're just starting."

"Tell me how you're starting. How many officers are working on the case. How they're chosen." She leaned forward. "Tell me everything."

He sighed. It was simple enough to explain to a cop or reporter or anyone who knew the Los Angeles Police Department. But explaining it from scratch was another matter. He'd have to shorthand it.

"When there's a homicide, it's given to an S.I.T., a special-investigations team. Some teams have as many as six detectives, some as few as three. Mine has four. Teams are headed up by a lieutenant, and mine operates out of the Central West Station. We were assigned the case because your sister was found in our area. My men are Marv Rodin, Vic Chasen, and a detective who hasn't been designated yet, who'll report tomorrow.

"When your sister was discovered Saturday morning, the information was relayed to DHQ—Detective Headquarters—in Parker Center. They phoned me at home, and I phoned Marv. If we hadn't been available, DHQ would have sent a man of their own, who'd have filled us in the next day, then left the case. Right now we're waiting for the autopsy and lab reports. No weapon was found, and it's doubtful whether any fingerprints will be either—no surfaces on which to find them."

"What," she asked, "can you expect from the autopsy and laboratory reports?"

"Not much. We know she was killed by a twenty-two caliber firearm. We found the casing and fragments of the bullet on the sidewalk. Looks like a hollow-point load, also called dum-dums, which struck the brick apartment house wall after passing through the victim's skull."

She winced.

"Sorry. That's the trouble with explaining these things to relatives. Should I stop?"

She shook her head.

"The fragments are too small to be of much use, though we'll try to match them up with larger fragments found in the cab of the driver who was killed a few streets away. His was definitely a gangland execution. If we can tie him to your sister . . ."

She was shaking her head. "I knew her life. It was remarkably free of entanglements. She had a steady boyfriend from her job. No contacts with gangsters." She paused. "And no one on that street where she was found."

He'd heard parents, husbands and wives, sisters and brothers and lovers, insist they knew everything there was to know about a victim's or criminal's life. And from long experience had learned that no one knew everything about another person; that in fact, people knew remarkably little about each other.

Diana Woodruff was a smart woman, but she fit the surviving-relative pattern . . . which gave him a badly needed shot of superiority.

He said, "She might have been a passenger in the cab, or witnessed the shooting from the street. She might have been chased by the killer; gone several blocks before she was caught and killed. That's our best hope for a solution."

"Why? I thought gangland executions were rarely solved."

"Oh, we solve a few. Because we can use snitches—police informants—who are often underworld figures themselves. But if it's a random killing, then we're in big trouble. That's why I thought . . ." He stopped, and she finished for him:

"That Carla was a prostitute. Because psychopaths

51

often pick on streetwalkers, or those they classify as such. From Jack the Ripper on. But would such a man be satisfied with one victim? The Ripper wasn't. The Hillside Strangler kept killing; so did Son of Sam."

"There's no way of telling. For every repeat killer, there might be a thousand one-shot psychos who never get identified as such, or even caught. But one thing is certain: Here in Los Angeles, we've had no recent killings that match your sister's."

"Have you interviewed the tenants in that apartment house near where she was found?"

"More than half, and we're still in the process. So far, no one saw a thing or heard a sound."

"Not a sound? How can that be—a gun going off on a quiet street at night?"

"Small calibers like twenty-twos don't make all that much noise. And then there's the possibility it's a silenced weapon. Professional killers sometimes use them. A professional killer wouldn't go out hunting hookers—those he thinks are hookers. Which is reason to believe your sister witnessed the driver's death and was eliminated because of it. Then again, there's no law which says a psycho can't get hold of a silenced weapon."

"Any other prospects?"

"We're hoping the lab comes up with skin, hair, or cloth under your sister's fingernails. If she struggled with the killer . . ." He shrugged. "It's not likely she got the chance with a pro. And if it was a random killing, the odds aren't good that we'll find him."

"Unless he kills again."

"Right. Then the odds begin to narrow."

"Though Jack the Ripper was never caught."

He spread his hands, apologizing for the failings of his profession.

"I guess it was simpler in Chaucer's day," she murmured. " 'Murder will out,' he said. Cervantes said it too."

He remembered Chaucer from an English Lit course. "Maybe they were talking about religion, not detection. Some people believe a murderer is punished by God and his conscience, no matter what the law does."

She was looking at him, surprised . . . which both insulted and pleased him. "Do you believe that?" she asked.

He would have liked to comfort her. But then again, he doubted she would believe such crap. He said, "Unless we kill them or jail them, they get away with it. And even when we jail them, I don't think I've seen one killer in ten who's sorry for anything except that he got caught."

She nodded, and their food came. He enjoyed his fresh snapper, looking from the sea to her every so often, trying to get her to share the experience. But she kept her head down, eating quickly. Maybe too quickly, because she suddenly stopped, pressing her hands to her stomach.

"Excuse me," she said, and left the table.

She was gone about five minutes, and returned holding a tissue to her mouth. "Would you mind if we went home?"

He called for the waiter.

At her door, he said, "Don't bother asking me in," because he was sure she wasn't going to. Also, he wanted to make some sort of impression on her. She'd certainly made one on him!

At the same time, he couldn't help wondering if her stomachache was real, or an act to dump him early.

He began to turn away.

She said, "Will you call me again?"

"Or drop in at the parlor," he muttered.

She opened her door.

"Forgot. No cops allowed," he said.

She went inside.

He wondered why the hell *he* should feel ashamed, and stalked off. But he turned back before he reached his car.

She answered the bell. He said, "Sorry. I'll call again."

She said, "I'll look forward to it. And to holding my dinner down next time." She smiled.

53

He wanted to kiss that beautiful smile. Wanted to very badly. But he nodded and walked away.

He used Sunset to drive from the shore to Laurel Canyon, then took Laurel north past Mulholland into the Valley to Studio City. It was better than an hour's trip, and he never traveled that far for a chick.

But as he entered his apartment, he realized he could hardly wait for the next time.

SIX: *Monday, July 31*

Mel finally got her on the phone at two in the afternoon, which wasn't all that late for his beautiful honky wife to sleep when she'd been dancing at the club till three and screwing around with Chris, the manager, till God knew what hour. Chris was now her main man, though he wouldn't last any longer than the others; not any longer than her husband.

Anyway, she sounded reasonably awake and not yet stoned, and he said, "Hey, love, are we gonna have that reconciliation?"

So how does she answer ole black Mel layin' his heart on the line? "Glad you called. I need a lid of Columbian, lightly dusted."

"Yeah, and how *you* been?" he muttered. A real user, Beth-Anne. A real cunt. He'd known it from day one, and no way could he fall for her when she was just another nude dancer and the Sunset Strip was full of them and he'd had his way with so many he was certain he was immune to anything as cube-like as *love*. But he'd surprised himself by being the john of

55

johns—ended up marrying her after a week in Vegas, in one of those plastic quick-job chapels.

"We'll talk tonight," she said. "You might as well bring the pot."

"Might as well," he mocked. But his pulse had picked up speed and there was a stirring in his pants. She'd almost fucked him to death during their five months of togetherness. At fifty-six, he wasn't quite the man the twenty-three-year-old stripper needed, though he had never let her know this. He performed whenever she snapped her pussy—and, man, could it snap! Also taught her a few things about vibrators, big and rectal size, she hadn't known.

But it wasn't only sex he'd wanted from her. And it was *only* sex she'd wanted from him: sex and bread and dope, which he'd provided in unlimited quantities. Which meant he'd had to take chances he normally wouldn't take.

He was a dealer, yes, but only in a small way, more to get the girls than the bread. When a dancer was broke, he worked a trade—what she needed for what he wanted. Before Beth-Ann, he had paid the rent and the grocery bills, and given away as much as he sold. One pickup a week, and then he used his phone to arrange meetings with the chicks, or with the rare male he supplied—who in turn supplied him with chicks.

It was a neighborhood business, like your friendly Mom-and-Pop grocery. It was nothing much to interest the *poh*lice.

But, baby, now was different. Now he made three pickups and now he pushed the real thing and now he was loaded and ready to buy back his wife. He had five grand, a nice round figure; had been saving until he could flash it on her. If she came back, he'd make more to hold her and try not to think of the slammer and what it had been like when he'd done what the cons called "an easy dozen."

He was sweating as he thought how far from easy that year had been. How his mind had almost cracked. Because Mel Crane wasn't made for the tough stuff.

He was a lover, not a fighter. He was a pussycat, a pushover for most pretty white chicks, and especially for his young wife.

She proved it by dropping her voice—probably so the guy in bed with her wouldn't hear: "You been thinking about your little Beth-Anne, Mel? You been thinking how you'd like to crawl into her?"

"Among other things," he said, but she had his number. He was her ole black patsy. "Can I come to your pad?"

"Someone's sharing it with me."

Guess who, but he wanted no hassles. "Then my place."

"Well, maybe." She was playing little-girl cute. "First, we'll have dinner. Then we'll talk about reconciliations and your pad."

"Dinner? You have to be on stage by nine, and it's three before you're done."

"Night off, baby. Don't play with that cute black dicky too much. Save some for Beth-Anne. *If* you bring the pot and we get along without arguments."

They'd get along without arguments, once she saw the bread.

"Tarpon's Fishery?" he asked.

"Right! I haven't had a good seafood dinner since we split. Chris . . ." She paused. "Almost all my dates eat steak and Italian over and over, maybe a little Chinese. You know how to keep a girl's figure for her, Mel."

There was a voice in the background. She said, "Eight. Tarpon's. 'Bye."

He told himself he wasn't square enough to feel jealousy . . . but whatever the feeling was, it hurt.

Frank Berdon hadn't picked up his Chevy until noon, though Lila drove him to the garage at nine. "A few last-minute adjustments," Gallico had said; then Frank had waited three hours. People were always doing that to him.

He'd been carrying his briefcase. He often did, when he was going to call on his steady customers, checking

57

them for shortages, showing them whatever was current in the lines he carried.

Berdon's Stationery and Business Machines specialized in such personal service. His father had started the practice in a more gracious time, and Frank had carried on so as to survive in an era of big discount stores.

But his briefcase hadn't held stationery today, and while he'd waited for his car he'd taken it with him to the garage's toilet. It was a dirty, smelly, closet-like room and he would no more have considered sitting on that grimy seat than drinking from that foul bowl.

What it did have was privacy.

After locking the door, he'd opened the case and taken out the gun, examining it in the light for the very first time. And noticed another unusual feature besides the obvious one, the silencer: the entire weapon, including the custom wood grips, was finished in dull black.

He'd found the catch on the base of the butt, fiddled with it, and felt it give as he pushed it toward the rear. Then he'd pulled out the magazine, and smiled his cherub's smile. Because there were eight rounds in the clip, and since this was an automatic that reloaded itself on firing, there was another round in the chamber. Nine in all.

Now, at seven-thirty, closing up the store, he looked at the counter on which the briefcase rested, and again smiled. He'd been given a bonus. Whoever had loaded the gun had inserted a shell into the chamber in addition to a full clip of ten in the butt. Eleven to start with, two fired, nine remaining—one more than he had expected.

And when those rounds were finished, so was he with the gun. No purchases of shells to connect him to the killings. Nothing at all to connect him to the killings.

He left the store, drawing the grilled metal gate closed behind him, and locking it with the heavy chain and padlock.

Crime was a real problem in this town.

* * *

When Mel reached the restaurant, he saw Beth-Anne standing outside. Which surprised him. True, he was twenty minutes late—he'd had to cover half of L.A. to get angel-dusted pot on such short notice—but why wasn't she waiting inside in comfort?

Then he realized the Tarpon Fishery's parking lot was empty except for Beth-Anne's Javelin and his Mustang.

"Damn," he said, running over to her. "Forgot they're closed on Mondays."

She wore a sour expression along with her tight knit dress, and the way she was standing, hand on hip, showed she figured him for some sort of con.

No matter what her expression, her attitude, he loved the way she looked. God, but the broad had everything! In that wild pink knit, in spike heels that brought her a little over his five-eight, she was the prettiest blonde on the Strip.

He smiled, drinking her in. "Hey, baby, I gave up kiddy scams like running out of gas and hitting on closed joints a long time ago. Besides, we can choose from a dozen seafood places."

She nodded, but he could tell she was still pissed. So he decided not to wait. He took her arm and hurried her to his car, where he handed her the brown paper bag with the thick plastic bag inside.

She sniffed it, beginning to smile. "Dusted?"

He nodded. "Three full ounces."

She leaned toward him from the passenger's seat. Her lips brushed his cheek.

"And then there's something a little heavier," he said. He reached into his breast pocket and took out the bulging wallet, and from it the thick, rubber-banded sheaf of crisp hundred-dollar bills. He riffled it under her nose.

"Ummm!" she exclaimed, reaching. "Smells like two or three grand!"

He let her take it. "Five. For our second honeymoon. Vegas or wherever. Right here in L.A. if you want. Clothes and jewelry and anything that makes you happy."

59

"Great!" She began to put the money in her purse.

He laughed, and took it back and put it away. "First the reconciliation."

"All right," she murmured. "Let's pick up some Chinese or fried chicken and go to your place."

"How about picking up your clothes? I'm talking about a permanent deal."

Her green eyes were on him, and they were warm. "One step at a time, black beauty." She leaned over and kissed him again, on the mouth this time. "Step one," she said, and her hand pressed his thigh and began to slide upward.

He hadn't kissed her, held her, in almost three months. He was so hungry for her he was trembling. But he pushed her away. "Not in the parking lot."

He began to drive, saying they'd pick up her car in the morning. He drove two blocks, reaching out to touch her short-cropped platinum hair, her soft cheek, telling her how much he'd missed her, how much he loved her . . . and her hand returned to his thigh.

He went another block before she reached his crotch.

"Remember our first time? On your lap in the Fairfax Drive-In movie? You couldn't wait, black beauty. I'll bet you can't now."

He wanted the comfort of his bed. He wanted the pleasure of her naked body stretched out beside his. But she began squeezing, and he just had to stop.

They were on a side street somewhere between Santa Monica and Fountain, and it was very dark. She rolled a joint and they shared it. It was heavy junk because of the dust, and they lost all restraint. He had her boobs out and was kissing them. She had his cock out and was stroking it.

And then she bent her head and took him in her mouth. He grasped her head with both hands, pressing down, making her deep-throat him, loving her gargling sounds, loving the sight of his woman sucking him . . .

The voice said, "Filth! You're forcing her! Black filth!"

Mel jerked his head to the left, to his open window.

Beth-Anne straightened.

They both saw the fat man. And the long gun.

"He wasn't forcing me!" Beth-Anne said. "If that's what you're worried about, forget it!"

"She's my wife, Mel said, shoving his wilting penis back inside his fly. And knowing what he knew about Whitey, added, "She's Negro too, but it doesn't show," Negro because some nuts hated the word black.

The gun was in the window, but the man didn't seem sure what to do. So Mel reached for the ignition, still talking: "Too much wine with dinner. Spur of the moment. Married folks on a lark. You got every right to be disgusted. Never happen again."

Beth-Anne was frozen, eyes glued to the gun. Her big show-girl tits were hanging out, and the fat man was staring at them. Mel didn't know if that would help or hurt and was ready to burn rubber.

"Get your hand away!" the fat man said, and Mel let go of the key. The fat man looked around quickly, and so did Mel, and there was no one there, no one to help.

"Show me your licenses," the fat man said. "If your last names match, I'll let you go."

Mel smiled, relief washing over him like a cool wave. He turned to Beth-Anne. "Make yourself presentable, dear."

She said, "Presentable?" and then, "Oh!" and began stuffing her boobs back inside her dress.

The fat man leaned closer, breathing loudly. The gun moved inside the car, right in front of Mel's face, which wasn't very professional. Mel could grab it . . .

But he was the wrong guy for heroics. Besides, it could go off in Beth-Anne's direction.

And why bother when the licenses would prove they were married and the freak would let them go?

Mel took out his wallet, and only then remembered the five thousand. He began to sweat. If he lost the money, he knew he would lose Beth-Anne. And Christ, he hated to wait more months!

The gun hiccupped and jerked in front of his face, then drew back out of the window. Mel turned to Beth-

Anne. She was falling over against the opposite door. There was a sharp smell, a burning smell, and Mel remembered it from Italy and Monte Casino where he'd been a cook in Mark Clark's Eighth Army and there'd been no need for cooks during three terrible days of assault when the burning smell and dead men had been everywhere.

Beth-Anne had a small spot close to her ear. It leaked a little.

Mel said, "Dear Jesus," and turned to his window; turned directly into that extended barrel. He wanted to beg and grovel and live. And said, "Dirty white fuck!" and reached for the gun.

As soon as he walked into the house, Lila went at him.

"What were you doing in the back yard just now? And don't play dumb . . . I heard you clearly. And where were you anyway! I called the store and it was closed two hours ago!"

Before he could begin to answer, she said, "Just *look* at you, Frank Berdon! Your hair . . . your face!"

He stepped quickly from the kitchen to the foyer mirror, expecting blood . . . and there was nothing. His hair was slightly mussed in front; he was somewhat sweaty, somewhat pale.

He stepped back into the kitchen, to where she sat at the table, a cup in her hand. "I'd like some coffee too," he said. He spoke quietly, to make sure his voice would remain steady.

"Then get it!"

He went to the electric coffee machine and poured a cup. His hand shook, and he blocked it from her view by turning away. He took several long sips before facing her. "That lilac bush in back is dying."

She began to say something about it being dark out, and he interrupted: "A little water in the morning, a little at night, and maybe we'll save it. It takes only a moment to turn on the hose."

"Idiocy," she muttered, but she was subsiding.

"As for being late," he said, raising his cup, his hand

steadier now, "I drove Martin home. His car wouldn't start." He came to the table and sat down. "We pushed it, and I guess I over-exerted myself." He brushed at his hair, his face. "Could you get me something to eat?"

"Over-exerted yourself," she muttered, rising. "You were deathly pale."

"Short of breath. Comes of being overweight. We really must stick to our diets, dear."

She worked around the stove. "I exerted myself a bit today too." Her voice had softened, and he recognized that sudden change of tone.

"My mother?"

She turned. "That's why I was so testy just now. I needed you tonight."

He sat waiting, the blood beginning to pound in his temples. When she hesitated, he said, "I'll just go to her room . . ."

"She's not there. She's at Cedars-Sinai Hospital, Intensive Care."

He was standing without knowing it, "Oh, God." He started for the foyer.

"There's no point in going now, Frank. She's in a coma. They'll call when she regains consciousness."

She made him sit down and served him dinner. He ate a lot, gulping, asking for more, as he always did when upset. She told him what had happened.

At four, she'd been preparing the lamb stew he was eating. His mother had come into the kitchen and begun making herself a sandwich. Lila had stopped her, saying it would spoil her dinner. His mother had been in an "irrational mood," and stormed out of the house. Lila had followed immediately, but before she could catch the old lady, there was an accident.

"She walked right in front of a car."

Frank soaked up gravy with a fifth slice of bread, and groaned. "Christ, couldn't you have let her have her sandwich?"

"It's too late for that, Frank! I blamed myself enough while waiting here for you!" She wiped at her eyes.

He muttered, "Yes, sorry. What did the doctors say?"

"Really, she was lucky. It could have been much worse. She has a broken hip. In falling, she also fractured her skull, and that's causing the coma. But they feel there's a good chance she'll regain consciousness . . ."

The phone rang. "Maybe that's the hospital," she said, and ran to the wall unit near the foyer. He took another slice of bread.

"This is Mrs. Berdon," she said. "Oh, wonderful! We'll be right over. I know it's late, but Dr. Meade promised we could see her, if only for a moment. Yes . . . thank you!"

She hung up. "She's regained consciousness! We can go now, Frank."

He was sagging in his chair. He was stuffed with food, emptied of emotion, eyes heavy, truly exhausted.

"What is it?" she asked.

"Have to lie down a moment," he mumbled, and pulled himself out of the chair and stumbled to the bedroom, where he fell face forward on the bed and into a deep sleep.

The man and woman had been found at about eleven p.m.; the first black-and-white had arrived at eleven-twenty, the ambulance almost immediately afterward. Larry Admer had been called at home, and pulled up to the scene as the ambulance was disappearing down the street, siren winding into high gear. He took the two responding officers aside to get whatever information they had.

"Middle-aged male Negro," one young officer said, tilting his notebook toward a street lamp, "and young female Caucasian, both shot with a small-caliber weapon." He pointed at a dark Mustang parked at the curb, an officer standing guard over it. "They were seated in that car, the black behind the wheel, the girl in the passenger's seat. They might've been making out because the girl's dress was open and disarranged at the top, the black's fly unzipped. Neither was robbed."

"Head wounds?"

"Correct. The girl in the left temple. The black in the upper jaw, obviously a missed headshot."

"A bullet in the jaw killed him?"

"He's not dead, Lieutenant."

"Way to go!" Admer said, thinking of being able to show Diana that justice *could* triumph.

"But he's in bad shape, according to the ambulance intern. Looks like bone and bullet fragments entered the brain. Anyway, he wasn't conscious to tell us anything."

Admer sighed. "What hospital?"

"I didn't get that." He looked at his partner, who was as boyish as he was. "You get it, Matt?"

"Nearest hospital to here: Cedars-Sinai."

"Who found them?"

The first officer turned toward the entrance to a two-story, motel-like apartment complex, where an elderly woman stood holding a small white dog. She was hugging the animal and crying.

"A Mrs. Clausen. She was taking her dog for a walk. Came out of that entrance and passed the car and heard what she thought was a groan. She didn't stop, but on the way back she again heard the sound, and this time she glanced in."

"ID on the victims?"

"Get the stuff," the officer said to his partner. Matt hurried toward a black-and-white parked across the street.

"Anyone hear the shots?"

"We haven't canvassed the neighborhood, but no one's come forward. Mrs. Clausen lives in that ground-floor apartment right off the street." He pointed at an open window almost in a direct line with the Mustang. "She says she was resting in bed beside the window, wide awake. But old ladies get hard of hearing, right?"

Admer glanced over at her. "Doesn't look *that* old. And two gunshots almost in her ear. She heard your questions all right, didn't she?"

The officer nodded.

Admer looked up and down the street. A civilian male stood watching them from across the way. Three more were clustered half a block north, near the corner.

"Gunshots on a quiet street like this . . . we should have had a mob scene." He made some notes, did some thinking.

Within the last three days, four people had been shot in the head, counting the black's wound as a missed headshot. There'd been no robbery. No sexual assault, though he wanted to ask the black about the girl's disarranged dress. No discernible motive in three of the four killings, the cabby cum Vegas-dealer being a possible professional hit.

The two in the Mustang had been found four blocks from Diana's sister, who had been found six blocks from the cabby, all in the West Los Angeles area, not far from the Sunset Strip.

No gunshots had been heard in any of the four assaults, and this was beginning to worry him . . .

Two cars pulled up, coming from opposite directions. Detectives Marv Rodin and Vic Chasen got out of the one across the street. A fingerprint specialist from Forensic named DiLorca got out of the other, indicating DHQ was also beginning to worry.

"Go talk to them," Larry told the young officer, giving his men a wave and pointing at the Mustang.

The other officer, Matt, was back with a large, white plastic bag. It bore a department-store logo, and Larry said, "L.A. County issue, right?

"Since Prop Thirteen, Matt said, "we even provide our own toilet paper.

They were both joking. The police had done well, despite shrinking funds. This town, like New York, like Chicago, like any large American city, was always in a criminal state of siege, and no one was willing to cut defense funds too deeply.

Larry reached into the bag.

"Wait'll you see the loaf that jigg was carrying. You can *really* write off robbery in this case!"

Larry took out a bulging wallet. He handed the plastic bag to the officer and counted the bills. "Five thousand rubber-banded, and eighty loose." He put the money back in the wallet. "Lucky you weren't alone," he said, smiling to show it was another joke.

"That's what you call lucky?"

Larry read the driver's license. "I certainly hope Mr. Melvin Crane lives. I'd like to meet a man who carries five grand in pocket money."

The woman's wallet held considerably less cash—eight dollars. Her name was Beth-Anne Crane, indicating she was related to the black. Which blew a possibility he'd been shaping up in his mind: that she was a hooker and the man was a customer. It figured, didn't it, she being young and white and he being older and black? At least in and around the Sunset Strip it figured, especially in light of a possible psycho hooker-killer.

"If you're wondering how he could make that kind of bread," Matt was saying, "this might give you a clue." He handed over a brown paper bag. Inside was a smaller plastic bag, and inside that a considerable quantity of marijuana. "The pocket scale shows over three ounces," Matt said. "My nose says PCP, angel dusted."

"You wouldn't happen to have personal experience smoking that dust poison, would you?"

Matt smiled slightly. "If it was as bad as they tell us, half a million or more in L.A. rock audiences would be dead or crazy."

"You like rock concerts?"

"They still legal? If so, I confess."

Larry handed him the dope, nodding sourly. The officer walked back to his black-and-white, and locked the plastic bag in the trunk. Young, maybe twenty-two, twenty-three, and like many of his contemporaries, in as well as out of the department, with a fine contempt for the drug laws. Always comparing them to Prohibition; always asking him if he'd have given up his beer, his Scotch. What really griped him was he didn't have an answer. And what griped him even more was that he knew, rationally, that alcoholism was a bigger problem than drug addiction, and felt, irrationally, that drugs were *filthy*.

He wondered whether Diana was into any kind of drugs.

Marv called from the Mustang. Larry walked over. The stocky detective held up a flattened piece of metal. "Lodged in the door jamb. Twenty-two, for sure. Now we'll look for the other slug."

"From what I hear, it's in the survivor's head, in bits and pieces."

"Tell the doctors to save it, if not the spook."

Larry gave him the mandatory chuckle, and headed for his car and the hospital.

The moment he flashed his badge at the Emergency desk, the young and attractive black nurse showed that prejudice worked two ways. "What did he do that you had to shoot him in the head?" she asked coolly, "pass a traffic signal?"

He smiled, and explained that Melvin Crane had been shot by an unknown assailant, and that in order to find that assailant the police had to interview Mr. Crane.

"I'm sorry," she said, opening a folder, "Mr. Crane won't be allowed visitors, police included, for *quite* a while. We're here to save lives, not conduct investigations."

He nodded slowly, saying nothing, until she finally looked up. He handed her a card with his station telephone number and said, "The moment he regains consciousness, someone is to call me. Or else you might have more Melvin Cranes for Intensive Care and the morgue."

Since she *still* didn't seem impressed, or cooperative, he asked for the doctor on duty . . . and began repeating it all again to a young, bearded character who heard him out with one ear, while the other was tuned to the pretty black nurse's murmured comments about Melvin Crane's "very critical" condition. "All right, Lieutenant," Kevin Riley, boy-doctor, said abruptly, and walked away.

Larry stood there another moment wondering

whether to call his commander at home, or to file a complaint with the Chief's office at Parker Center.

But official channels had never been effective for him, and he went out to his car. He would return tomorrow morning, but not to Emergency; he'd walk into Intensive Care to see Mr. Crane's condition for himself.

He had been about to shower when DHQ had called him on the mislabeled "double killing," and as soon as he reached his apartment he stripped and stepped into a strong, hot stream. He completed the relaxing process with a Scotch and water, and reached for the phone, thinking to call Diana and discuss the possibility of a solution to her sister's murder.

But he didn't dial her number. Nothing to say yet, really. And he wanted to give her straight dope, no bullshit, no con. Just Numbah One info, as they used to say in 'Nam.

Instead, he called Roberta. The little blonde secretary was eager, and drove over from Studio City in twenty minutes. She was wearing a green slicker-style raincoat, which surprisd him since it hadn't rained since June. But then she took it off and was nude underneath.

He was surprised again, when it didn't mean a hell of a lot.

SEVEN: *Tuesday, August 1*

Mel awoke, twitching, trying to shove that long gun aside, cursing the fat man for what he'd done to Beth-Anne.

And the fat man was gone. The car was gone. There was a milky haze. And a heavy, deeply felt drumming sound.

And a smell. Like his mother's room after a customer had left and she'd been cleaning up. A medicinal douche.

No. It was more like her room at the hospital when she'd been dying . . .

He remembered then! He'd grabbed at the gun in the window and felt a sledgehammer blow to the head.

He'd been shot. Like Beth-Ann.

He moved his head, trying to see beyond the milky haze.

Oh, God, the granddaddy of all headaches!

He tried calling for help: "Someone, anyone, come here!" And realized that while he was *thinking* words, and while his vocal chords were thrumming under the

71

correct thrust of air from the lungs, his mouth wasn't moving.

Slowly, to avoid pain, he reached for his lips.

At least he *thought* to move his right hand up to his mouth.

And couldn't feel his right hand. Or left hand. Or legs. Christ, he couldn't even feel his cock and he'd never ever lost awareness of *that!*

The heavy, drumming sound increased. He thanked God for it. At least there was *something* getting through to him. Rock music, maybe. Or machinery . . .

But then he listened more carefully, and recognized the sound. His own heart, pounding away. The only sound in all the world.

Why couldn't he see clearly?

The panic came then, so quickly he couldn't fight it. The hysteria and insanity caught him and tried to overwhelm him and he jerked his head back and forth and pain joined horror.

He'd been shot in the head like Beth-Anne, and hadn't been lucky enough to die like Beth-Anne. He was paralyzed and he was deaf and he was dumb and he was blind except for a milky white haze.

He shrieked his horror, his pain.

And heard the shriek. It was blocked at the mouth, it was held inside, but he heard it.

So he wasn't deaf. And he wasn't dumb, just unable to speak words.

Beats a blank, baby. Now wait for someone to come. Wait for input, information, salvation.

But his eyes. Christ, he could take almost anything if he could only *see.* A pretty chick. A newspaper. A TV screen.

And he saw. A *gorgeous* chick! Who was really a chunky, middle-aged nurse who lifted what he now saw was a plastic oxygen tent off him—removing the milky haze—but who looked like Monroe and Farrah and Beth-Anne put together, because he wasn't blind!

He wasn't deaf or dumb or blind, and he laughed and opened his mouth to say, "Hey, hon, when do I get outta here?"

And said nothing, grunting instead, because his mouth still wouldn't work. And neither would his arms or legs.

He looked at her, trying to thank her with his eyes for coming to him.

She said, "You're in Cedars-Sinai Hospital, Mr. Crane. You've been shot in the face. Your head and jaw are bandaged, so you can't speak. But you're all right."

He flickered his eyes at her.

"Are you thirsty? Hungry? We can give you nourishment through a tube. Or do you need a bedpan?"

He shook his head, even though it made him groan.

"Please don't move," she said. And then she looked at his body, at his arms and legs. Because he hadn't moved *them*, not even a little bit. Because he lay there like a stone, except for his bandaged head.

He saw the understanding cross her face, and she said, "I'll get the doctor. Just remember you've suffered severe shock. Just remember that it takes time . . ." She ran out of comforting things to say, and hurried from the room.

He waited. He tried to hold onto the joy he'd felt at having eyes and ears and vocal chords. He tried not to think of anything else.

But he *did* think of Beth-Anne falling over against the door, and of the fat white face in the window. The fat white face belonging to the fat white fuck . . .

Incredibly, in the midst of so much hatred, he felt himself losing thought, drifting away, being enveloped by heavy sleep.

And gave himself to it gratefully.

Sleep might be the best thing left in his life.

At nine a.m., Frank and Lila were at the hospital, waiting to be admitted into the Intensive Care section. His mother was being cleaned up now, the nurse at the desk explained. She was doing well, "though she might be a little fuzzy, you know." He nodded and asked for a phone and was directed down the hall.

He was in a state of shock . . . and not just because

73

of his mother. On the way over to Cedars-Sinai, he'd turned on the car radio, tuned to the all-news station, and learned that the black was alive. And somewhere in this very hospital.

The man had seen him. The man could describe him.

He fumbled for a dime, hands sweaty, and dialed the store. He told Martin he wouldn't be in until later, and hung up. He tried to think of what to do.

Get rid of the gun; that was the first thing. Maybe, somehow, get rid of the black . . . if he didn't die on his own.

He was in "a deep coma," the radio said. "In critical condition."

He began walking back to Intensive Care. He walked slowly. What if the black was in one of those rooms? What if he regained consciousness and saw Frank?

He was sweating heavily now. He paused to wipe his face and neck with his handkerchief.

He should run from this place, go home, get rid of the gun.

Lila was waving at him from the desk. He went over, reluctantly. "We can go in now," she murmured.

He walked behind her and a nurse. The rooms in Intensive Care had their doors closed, but the walls facing the nurses' station had clear glass panels so that these critically ill patients could be under constant surveillance.

Frank took one look at all that glass, and dropped his head. And kept it down. Until they entered a room and he was able to relax a little.

If you could call talking to a woman who didn't remember her own son relaxing.

"I know you," she said, propped up in bed, her body bulky under the blankets (due, the nurse explained, to a hip cast), her head bandaged. "I'm sure I do. But I can't quite remember who you are."

Lila said, "It's Frank, Mother. Your Frank."

"My Frank?" Her voice was weak, uncertain. "But

74

we had a funeral, didn't we? Though he does keep singing 'Red Sails . . .' "

"Your *son*," Lila said impatiently.

Frank chuckled a little. "It confuses everyone when you name a child after his father."

His explanation had no effect whatsoever. His mother continued to blink puzzled eyes at him.

Lila sighed, pulled up a chair, and plumped herself down.

His mother looked at her. "Lila? What are you doing here? I thought you were in Los Angeles."

Frank said, We're all in Los Angeles, Mom. You moved from Agoura when Dad died. You live with Lila and me now. You'll be getting better and coming home soon."

"You're married to Lila? My memory . . ." She closed her eyes and began to weep. "The car hit me. It's terrible being old. So humiliating . . . a sandwich . . . not even a sandwich . . ."

Lila began to say something. Frank said, "That's all right, Mom. Things will be different when you come home. You'll see."

She opened her eyes; her red, weak, streaming eyes. "I know you. I'm sure I know you."

The nurse must have been right outside, because she stepped in and said they'd better leave. "Give her at last one full day before your next visit. She'll remember much more then."

When they reached the front desk, Frank said to the nurse, "Oh, forgot my sunglasses," and turned back. He'd left them, deliberately, on the bedside table.

The nurse said, "I'll have to go with you."

Lila said she'd wait in the hall.

In his mother's room, he got the glasses; then bent over the old lady and kissed her cheek, which he somehow hadn't been able to do a moment ago with all the confusion, and with Lila present. "Love you, Mommy," he whispered, as he had as a child.

"Frankie," she said, and touched his face. "Of course, my little Frankie."

He turned quickly away so as not to cry.

The nurse smiled. "There. Clearing up by the minute."

He nodded and said, "I heard that the Negro who was shot last night is here."

They were walking into the U-shaped room that was the nerve-center of this Intensive Care Unit. The open end of the U wasn't open at all—a wall with a counter and a door, facing the hall where relatives waited to be admitted. Rooms opened off each of the three sides of the U; his mother's was the second of four on the first side; the glass panels looked out on a nurses' station dead center of the room.

"Yes," the nurse said. "The woman with him died." She pointed at the central section of the U, at the first door of three. "But he regained consciousness a short while ago."

"Ah," Frank said, and followed her, face averted from that one glass panel.

As he was opening the door to join Lila in the hall, he heard a man at the counter identify himself as a police lieutenant and ask to see Melvin Crane.

Frank thanked the nurse. She said, "Not at all," and turned to listen as the nurse at the desk answered the officer:

"He can't speak, Lieutenant. We haven't allowed newspersons in . . ." She pointed down the hall to where a cluster of people, one wearing camera and harness, was just entering an elevator, "and we can't allow you . . ."

Lila was waving her hand. "Frank!" she whispered.

He stepped through the door.

"I have to go grocery shopping," she said, "and you have to get to work!"

He said, "Yes," and they went to the elevators.

He parked his Chevy on the street in front of the house and went inside, ostensibly to use the bathroom. And stayed there until he heard her back her Plymouth down the driveway. Then he came out, in time to let her see him entering his car.

As soon as she turned the corner, he got out, carrying his briefcase, and hurried to the back yard.

Where with repeated glances around to make sure no one could see him, he put the plastic bag into the case and started for his car. He could go to the shore, to a pier, and dump it in the water. Or to one of the more remote canyons, like Latigo.

He turned into the house. He sat at the kitchen table and took the gun out of the bag. He held it, stroked it, marveled at the precision of it, the beauty of it. He sniffed it—smelled the oil, the gunpowder, the marvelous odor of a killing machine. He remembered what it could do.

And knew that risk or no, he couldn't throw it away.

Not until it was empty.

Because without it, *he* was empty . . . of purpose, of pleasure, of power.

He put it in his case and carried it out to his car. He drove down the street.

He could find another hiding place for it, far from his home, his business. So that the connection would be severed as completely as if he'd tossed it into the sea. And he would wait before using it again. Wait and see what developed with that black animal.

He reached Sunset and stopped for a traffic light.

A young woman, nineteen or twenty, in tight blue jeans and tee shirt, strolled lazily across in front of him. At the corner behind her, two young men were laughing and making loud comments. Frank heard ". . . enough for both of us, man!"

The girl turned her head at that. But instead of being outraged, she was *smiling*.

The light changed. Frank began to move forward. The two youths ran out in front of him, following the girl. Frank slammed his brakes, and his horn. One boy stopped in front of the car and jerked his finger up and down obscenely, saying, "You got objections, step out here, turkey."

Frank didn't answer, but heard his breath rasping.

"Hal, c'mon!" the other youth called.

The one in front of the car sneered, and ran to join his friend, who was standing with the girl. Then all three strolled away together.

77

Frank was trembling and sweating. He had his hand on his briefcase, at the clasp.

A horn sounded behind him. He realized he was blocking traffic, and turned east on Sunset.

He put his hand back on the briefcase, and grew calmer. It was better than Valium. Even if he couldn't use it, he had to keep it close by him. And he might have to use it . . . on the Negro.

Larry Admer finally got in to see the victim, but it was a real hassle. He'd kept his temper, and his smile, but inside he was seething. It was getting worse and worse, the way people looked at police in this town. Especially blacks and Hispanics. Even the Orientals were beginning to lose respect.

Just another sign of the disintegration of American society. Let them lose *sufficient* respect, and restraint, and the wise-guy liberal middle class, blacks and Hispanics included, would find out what it meant to have the shit of the world come down on them. Then they'd be yelling for the National Guard.

He said, "Thank you," oh-so-sweetly to the nurse who'd given him such a tough time at the counter, and followed another nurse, Chicano and with a great ass, but with hard eyes for him, to the room.

"We told you he was sleeping," she whispered.

"So he is," he said in his normal voice—which was loud and clear.

Before she could shush him, the man in the bed opened his eyes. He was bandaged about the head, and bandaged over some sort of metal brace about the jaw. His eyes and nostrils showed, as did a small hole where his mouth would be. Except for the eyes, he was absolutely still.

Larry said, "I'm Lieutenant Admer, L.A.P.D." He brought his credentials in front of the man's eyes. "Congratulations on fooling that bastard who shot you. Was the woman your wife?"

"He can't speak," the nurse said. "And he can't write, as we told you. She spoke to the man in bed. "The doctor will be back late this afternoon, Mr.

Crane. He'll have the results of those X-rays and tests we took earlier."

"You can blink your eyes, Mel. One for yes, two for no."

The man's eyes blinked once. And he grunted.

"Or grunt once for yes, twice for no."

The grunt was loud and clear.

"Fine. Was the woman your wife?"

One grunt, and the eyes closed. Larry murmured, "Sorry," and waited for them to open.

"Did you see your attacker?"

A pause, and a sigh.

"Saw him but not clearly?"

One grunt.

"Clearly enough to give a description?"

Long pause. Two grunts.

Larry couldn't hide his disappointment, and a muttered, "Damn." Then he said, "Well, when you're able to talk, we'll get more from you than you think you know. You'll remember more as you recover."

A little nod, and a groan.

"Let's get some basics. It was a male, right?"

One grunt.

"White?"

One grunt.

"Young? Say twenty?"

Two grunts.

"Middle-aged? About forty?"

A pause, then one grunt.

"Facial hair? Like a mustache or beard?"

A pause, and a faint grunt.

"Not sure? Face in the dark, in shadows, or made you turn from him?"

One grunt, then a sigh and the eyes closed.

"He's not ready for this," the nurse said.

Larry spoke quickly. "The gun, you saw it, didn't you?" He didn't wait for an answer. "Just tell me if it had a silencer at the end."

Crane didn't open his eyes, didn't answer.

"An extension, thicker than the barrel. You know—you've seen them in movies."

One weak grunt.

"Did the hand holding the gun have any special characteristics? Like a scar, a deformity, missing fingers?"

No response.

"A ring?"

"I really must *insist!*" the nurse said, voice climbing.

Larry said, "All right; sorry." And to Crane, "Take it easy, Melvin. I know you want that creep, and we're going to get him for you. And don't worry about your money." The eyes flew open. Larry smiled. "Safe, the whole five thousand. And your other possessions."

The eyes stayed on him.

"I've been a police officer for some time, Melvin, and I've never met a man, a real man, who didn't want to avenge a loved one's death himself. We all know how lousy the court system is, and how light the sentences are, even for murder. But the police and the courts are all you've got. Remember that. And remember that we'll not only help you nail that killer, but we'll be grateful if you really extend yourself, if you push yourself to remember every last bit of information that might be hiding in your memory. Grateful enough, Melvin, so that one of your possessions, in a bag, might get misplaced."

The eyes closed. Larry turned to the door. He'd gotten a feeling about Crane while questioning him: halfway through the interview there'd been a change, a holding back. Sometimes rage and hatred made citizens, especially men, feel they could do the law's job themselves. It usually didn't last long, a few days after the tragedy, but in this case he didn't want to waste a single hour. And in this case the bag of dusted pot would provide leverage.

If his instinct about Crane holding back was correct. If he wasn't getting paranoid about being a cop!

A sharp dude, the lieutenant, Mel thought. Because sometime during the questioning, Mel had decided not to give everything he knew on the fat white fuck. Had actually given some *mis*information. And the cop's expression showed he had guessed Mel was holding back.

Because the courts *did* stink, and even when they convicted murderers they let them off easy, out of jail and on parole in seven to ten years. And Beth-Anne would get no parole from her hole in the ground; and old black Melvin might get no parole from this bed or, at best, a wheelchair.

So he'd made a quick decision and grunted "Yes" when Admer had said middle-aged and forty; and the fat white fuck was younger. And said yes to facial hair when that fat white face was baby clean and baby smooth. And wouldn't be able to say it was a fat white face; would claim he'd barely glimpsed it.

But Admer had a lid of marijuana treated with angel dust. The PCP made that a heavier rap than usual for three ounces of pot, which could be a good rap anyway if they nailed him for pushing, for dealing. And the five grand made it a natural for dealing.

Still, the least of his worries. What the doctor had to say was the main event. What he'd already said was no Bob Hope special—fragments of bone had "touched" the brain; "minute fragments" that might not be removable. Sometimes such fragments "ceased being a problem" with the passage of time. Then came the bad news: "Sometimes, however, they continue to cause problems, with the motor centers for example, as in your case."

Which meant paralysis, baby. Which meant being dead from the neck down.

Though he thought he'd felt something when the doctor had jabbed his upper right arm with a pin. Nothing anywhere else, but *something,* maybe, in the upper right arm, like a grain of sand falling there.

They'd wheeled in machinery and taken more X-rays in addition to those taken while he was out cold. And taken blood and made other tests, "Now that you're conscious and strong enough to withstand them."

He didn't know how conscious he was. He kept falling asleep every ten or fifteen minutes. And didn't mind.

81

But he got the idea that the doctor minded; that the doctor was worried he might fall asleep and not wake up, ever.

If it meant death, Mel wasn't afraid of it. He didn't *want* it, but he wasn't afraid of it. In his condition, it wasn't that big a deal.

But if it meant being a vegetable, lying here for months and years, like that girl in New Jersey who'd been plugged into a machine, "fear" was a weak word for his reaction.

Or if it meant waking up for a few minutes each day and being out the rest of the time and having his body wither, shrivel, rot . . .

There was much to be afraid of, and he breathed heavily and told himself not to think of those things, to think only of finding the fat white fuck.

He could do it, too, even from here.

He closed his eyes. He ran names, faces through his mind. Dangerous people whom he'd hoped never to have to see again. People who could be his arms and legs. And fists. People who would see to it that the fat white fuck didn't live to go to court.

If he could keep from helping Admer.

Which might not be too easy.

Mel Crane knew when someone was good at his job. And this cop was good.

He waited for sleep, which was overdue according to the every-ten-or-fifteen-minutes schedule. And it wouldn't come.

He thought of when he himself had been good at a job. For a short while, true, but that was because pimping was a lot harder than popular myth and rumor had it, especially in little old New York. And after his year in Ossining, up the Hudson—his "easy dozen" that had shown him exactly who he was, and wasn't—his days of imitating Iceberg Slim were numbered.

After the slammer, the only part of pimping he'd liked was breaking in a new chick. Holding them in line and knocking them around wore him down, and he'd left Manhattan and his East Side clientele at age twenty-nine and fled the width of the country to get away. And gone from well-heeled but miserable user to broke but contented john. Not exactly in one easy lesson, since he'd been in L.A. some twenty years.

Twenty-*one* years, he calculated, his mind clear and unclouded. Twenty-one years since he'd run that string of hard-as-nails broads in Manhattan. But every so often there'd be a cutie, a softie, a girl bound to be a loser at that tough trade in the long run. He would be touched and try to help her, because he knew they had something in common. And they would make beautiful music together for a brief time.

In fact, it was one of these he had helped to escape, a little Italian knockout named Anna, innocent deep down where it counted despite falling for the scum who'd sold her to Pell-Mel. That was how he had been known in those long-ago days, the nickname coming from his crazy way of fighting when he was forced to, a mad confused attack (covering his fear, his distaste for his way of life). Anna, with bright eyes that believed too much, whose light would be extinguished, he was sure, trying to survive in a world without tenderness— Anna had touched him so deeply he had taken her with him when he'd run from the trade, the racket overlords, the goddam ugliness. Dropped her off at her brother's in Cleveland and told her, "No more pills and no more *bums*, got it?" and hoped she could make it in the straight world.

As he himself hadn't been able to, becoming a small-time bum himself. But one who'd never hurt people.

And now someone had hurt him.

And now look at yourself, nigger . . .

He didn't have time to hit bottom again, because sleep grabbed him.

At eleven, Cloris left English class, but didn't go to study hall in the auditorium. Instead, she left the school and walked to the shopping center, about ten minutes in the Valley heat, and met Verna Tomlinson and her boyfriend Buddy at the coffee shop. Verna and Buddy were both drop-outs from Granada High. They were secretly married, but the secret wouldn't hold too much longer. Verna was pregnant, and so she and Buddy had decided to leave Granada Hills for Los Angeles. And Cloris had decided to join them.

It wasn't a long trip, maybe fifteen, twenty miles (she was lousy at geography and maps), but the San Fernando Valley suburb and the Big Town were *worlds* apart in the things that counted to Cloris. A movie career. Discos. Roller boogie rinks. Lots of dates. And no mother and no Uncle Bert!

They had burgers and fries and coffee, and relaxed over cigarettes. Verna was a chunky brunette, pretty face but much too heavy. Still, Buddy seemed happy enough, and with his slouchy, skinny build and bad skin he was no bargain himself.

Cloris wouldn't have dated him in a million years, though she'd been curious after Verna had said, "His thing's a foot long and thick as my arm!" So at the party in Christofer Bayshore's house, when Buddy got drunk and grabbed her playfully in the kitchen, she'd unzipped him and made it hard with her hand. And discovered Verna had been bragging about nothing. Then she'd had a job calming him down.

"You sure, Cloris?" Verna asked, leaning across the table conspiratorially. "You know Buddy and me can't put you up or anything. We're staying with his cousin Elma and her husband, and they only got two rooms in Echo Park."

Cloris said she had a hundred sixty dollars saved from her part-time job at the supermarket checkout, "and before that's gone I'll have a job and I'll move from the motel to a good apartment. I'm going to dramatic school and modeling school. Maybe take voice lessons too. I want a career in *film*."

"You got the looks all right," Verna said. "Don't she, Buddy?"

He nodded. "Sure do."

Cloris said, "Thank you, thank you," bowing her head as if on a stage, and they all laughed together, but she didn't need *them* telling her what she had. She'd

84

looked in the mirror a few times. "A teenaged American Charo," that football player had called her.

Well, maybe, though she felt she had more class than cootchie-coo. But she *was* blonde with long hair and she was built on top and all the rest of it. And she had the sexy moves.

She smiled to herself, thinking how worked up the football player had been when she'd left him in his car in the drive-in movie to go to the bathroom. Instead, she'd gone to the snack-bar and called Freddy and said, "I can't handle him, honey! Please come and get me," and made crying sounds.

Freddy had raced over and she'd hopped into his car and they'd had a beautiful time that night.

Her smile faded.

He'd gone East to college last fall and hadn't called or written since, and one of the kids said he was home on vacation but she'd heard nothing. Mom said he'd "used" her, and Uncle Bert nodded with that Holy-Roller look on his face, the bastard! He was jumping Mom twice a night in the bedroom just across the hall from Cloris in the small condo that had been fine when it was just Mom and Cloris and had become awful when Bert moved in.

Mom said he was going to marry her "soon." That was nine months ago, and he'd never marry her and maybe she was lucky he wouldn't. Because with all his lectures about "late hours" and "saving yourself for some fine boy" and "wearing less-revealing clothing," just two weeks ago he'd shown what he really was. He'd come home early and Mom wasn't back from work yet and Clois had been watching TV. It was hot; she hadn't expected anyone; she'd been in her panties and bra. And there he'd stood, hands on his hips, face sour, eyes stern behind those teacher-like glasses.

But then, when she'd gotten up to go to her room for clothes, he'd suddenly grabbed her! What a shock, and she'd screamed, but it hadn't stopped him. He'd been a wild man and she'd had to hit him in the face three times before he'd gained control of himself. By then, her pants and bra had been torn off and she'd backed away, naked. He'd stared and spoken in a hoarse, shaky voice: "A hundred dollars for what you give every schoolboy . . ."

She'd locked herself in her room. Later, he'd come to the door and said he'd "gone beserk" and begged her not to tell her mother. "It would only hurt her," he'd pleaded.

It would also get him out of here, Cloris had reasoned.

She'd been wrong. Mom had slapped her, accused her of *tempting* him—"I've seen how you flaunt yourself, you little slut!"—then burst into tears. They hadn't talked much since then. And things were cool between Bert and Mom too, with Bert sleeping on the couch. So that the apartment was like a penitentiary, with everyone in a separate cell. Cloris couldn't take it anymore. Nor could she take school, which she'd *always* hated!

"Let's get going," she said to Verna and Buddy.

Behind a locked door she'd packed two bags last night, moving quietly so as not to be heard. They would drive by the house to pick them up now . . . then onto the freeway and off to Hollywood! She had made a reservation at a motel on Sunset Boulevard; picked it out of the Yellow Pages. The rates were low compared to places like Holiday Inns or Howard Johnsons or other big chains.

Sunset Boulevard! Tonight she'd be walking along Sunset Boulevard! On her own! With the whole world opening up before her!

She jumped up. "We're off to see the wizard!" she sang, and ran to the door, her long yellow hair swirling, her ripe figure rippling inside the tight white linen pants and tighter blouse. So that the counterman paused to stare and wet his lips. So that Verna and Buddy laughed and ran after her.

Later, half-dozing in the back seat of the car, her luggage jamming her into one corner, she thought of how someday Freddy would go to the movies in Massachusetts where his college was, and he'd see her dancing and singing and acting. Then he'd come home on vacation and try to visit her at the studio where she'd be working, but her agent wouldn't let him get near her dressing room. Her famous actor sweetheart, or maybe a rock star like Rod Stewart, would walk out with her, past Freddy, who would look at her, tears streaming down his face, and whisper. "I've always loved you, Cloris darling, you know that. My parents forced me to go to school so far away, and forbid me to write or call you. I meant all those things I said on your Sweet Sixteenth, when you gave your virgin self to me. I want to marry you, if you'll only accept me."

She would turn to her famous escort and say, "Did you hear that, Rod honey?" and walk off, pealing laughter.

Or maybe she would forgive him, a little, and allow him to date her once in a while.

She remembered her Freddy. She remembered loving him. And her seventeen-year-old heart ached and she wanted him more than Rod Stewart or Burt Reynolds or anyone on God's earth. Wanted him as she had once wanted the father who had used his officer's status in the Army Reserve to run away from a marriage that had stifled him to a "small war" that had killed him.

She put her head down in the seat so neither Verna nor Buddy could see and cried very quietly.

EIGHT: *Wednesday, August 2, a.m.*

Larry Admer knew it was part of his job, a recurrent illness that went with the territory. Still, he tried to duck it, turning back to the parking lot when he saw the thirtyish woman with plasticized gray-blonde hair and club-like microphone, known to local news fans as Wyona Wise, and to police as The Mouth, standing near the station-house entrance, waiting for Guess Who.

With her was a bushy-haired guy with harness-held camera, an older, balding guy with lights and sound equipment, and a young tan woman who was their resident black and Mouth-in-training.

The Loathsome Foursome, as Captain Cohen had dubbed them; just a little harder to take than some of the other news crews, such as the Hells Angels, who were into Levis and leather, the Count and Igor, a team that showed a lot of teeth, and the ever-popular Quinn's Quims, Lester Quinn and his two sex-pot assistants.

He'd turned into the lot, was almost at his car, when

the Mouth-in-training called, "Lieutenant Admer! A moment, please!"

He considered jumping into the Dodge, as if he hadn't heard, and burning rubber the hell away from here. But then he sighed and turned. He had to resign himself to facing them every day or two until this case was solved. And a frequent comment of "declined to be interviewed," had made many an official sound like a secret Mafia *capo*.

He leaned back against the car, stroking his mustache, glad that he'd worn the good tan suit. He planned to see Diana later in the day. Now the first part of that day was spoiled, because these four were of the same breed who had come to Vietnam, and by their "compassionate reporting" for everyone involved but the grunts, had made shit out of American sacrifice.

The Foursome approached, and at the same time Larry saw another network's mobile unit pull into the lot and stop in a spot reserved for officers of the Central West Station. He considered ticketing them for illegal parking, but it was only a delightful fantasy.

The Foursome had reached him. The cameraman adjusted his lens. The sound and light man put his lights down on the pavement, since they were filming in bright sunshine. The Mouth got their nods and cleared her throat. "Lieutenant Admer," she began, half-smile on her lips, gray eyes twinkling, expression *devilishly* clever as per her usual opening, when she appeared on screen as Crisply Attractive Feminist Seeker After Truth.

Truth be known, she was a muckraker to delight the heart of Grandpa Hearst.

Larry held up his hand, smiling his own plastic smile. "Forgive me, but I believe we should wait for the competition."

He was beginning to speak in the stilted, unnatural way he and other officers used before the cameras. After seeing himself on a hundred newscasts, he no longer blushed at the crap flowing from his mouth.

Even as he pointed at the crew piling out of the van,

two more vans pulled in, one from the third network, the other from a Los Angeles station.

"I don't see why *we* should have to wait," Wyona Wise said sharply, "because *they* aren't prompt."

Larry looked apologetic. He put his head down and stared at his shoes.

One thing they didn't teach at the Academy was the amount of time a detective or ranking officer had to spend with the news media, especially TV, but including the two all-news radio stations and two newspapers, and occasionally the newspapers in the Valley and Orange County. But mainly the television hounds who stuck their cameras and mikes in the faces of half-dead victims, grieving relatives, stunned and demoralized men, women and children, and using compassion as a cover said such things as "Tell us how you felt on learning that your daughter was raped, murdered, and thrown in a ditch?"

Still another two vans had arrived, leaving only the two smallest local TV stations unrepresented, and they often skipped film and used the press services for still photos and stories.

The noise around him grew considerably as the newcomers set up their equipment, but he continued to stare at the pavement. This kept him from having to see too much of them and risk wearing his patience thin over too long an interview. Because he resented their intrusions into the lives of the unfortunate, and resented even more the way they could screw up a police action by digging where they weren't supposed to and revealing what might blow a case or conviction. And occasionally lead to injury or even death for an officer.

But what was a cop anyway? Let some junkie under the influence of heavy PCP flip out on the street and with the strength of a madman pose a threat to citizens. Let officers try and restrain him before using their batons on his skull or their guns on his body. Let a choke-hold result in death when the madman struggled too violently. And every Mouth on the air would report the parents' assurances that their son had

91

been "a good boy" and that the officers were "cold-blooded murderers," and dig up witnesses who insisted "the poor guy" was just "having himself a few beers." And when the police ran their investigation and cleared the officers for doing what they were paid to do, protect the public good, the Mouths would raise hell, crying whitewash. It happened so often, it made some officers hesitate in their duty—which was dangerous for all concerned.

"Can we begin now, Lieutenant?" the Mouth asked acidly.

Larry nodded, and told himself that today was a bad day; that he had to remember he was prejudiced against television reporters and had been since Vietnam. Not fair to them, really, or to Walter Cronkite, whom he watched religiously.

He looked around at a full-fledged mob scene, with people stopping on the sidewalk to watch. A cluster of mikes was thrust under his nose, and one jabbed his chin. He was backed up against his car, so there was no room to spare. He pushed the mike back an inch; pushed *gently* because it was in the hand of an ex-Ram tight end who, like many sports figures, had been adopted by the news shows. Dubbed "the Jock" by Captain Cohen, he weighed in at two hundred and forty pounds, and when *that* mass of muscle stuck a mike in your face and asked how you felt, you damn well tried to answer him . . . even if you'd been shot three times!

Larry chuckled, then realized some of the cameras were rolling. "That was very funny, Jess," he said to the ex-footballer, who smiled blankly at him. Larry knew his remark would get the chuckle and line cut from every show, with the possible exception of the tight end's. You learned self-defense with these people real quick, especially after seeing yourself on the small screen, leading off a discussion of some horrible crime with what appeared to be a heartless laugh. There'd been lots of calls the only time he'd committed a similar goof, and a little lecture from the captain.

The Mouth was beginning a question. Larry held up

92

his hand as he saw two reporters—one newspaper, one press service—jogging from the station. One good thing: he would get most of them, maybe all of them, out of the way until the next murder in West Los Angeles. There'd been occasions when he'd had to give six separate interviews on the same subject in the same day, losing three or four hours and ending with a hell of a headache.

The Mouth began the questioning. He didn't answer her directly, but responded to the entire group, looking from camera to camera. Some officers secretly lusted after show-biz, and you could spot them by their unctuous, "That's an interesting point, *Wyona*." or "*Jess*." Or whoever the questioner was. It ingratiated the cop with the interviewer. It got the cop good close-ups on that one camera. And some cops did it for each and every camera.

"Lieutenat Admer, I've learned that Parker Center considers four killings to be the work of one criminal." She named the cabby, Diana's sister, Mel Crane, and his wife.

"Mr. Crane has survived . . ."

"Four *shootings* then," she interrupted, not too pleased at being corrected on camera. "Are you in charge of a task force comparable to the one that worked on the Hillside Strangler?"

The mob seemed to shiver then; with delight, of course, since that case had provided them with grist for *years*.

Using his stilted, on-camera delivery, he said, "There is some indication the cases might be connected, but at the present we can't so state."

"The weapon used," a male voice said—the Count, grinning toothily, with Igor filming at his elbow—"was the same in all four shootings, wasn't it?"

"We don't have the weapon. The caliber was the same. Twenty-two. And indications—from the spread and high degree of disintegration of the bullets—are that all were hollow points, known as dum-dums."

"And no noise from the gun?" Jess asked, leaning

93

forward eagerly. Which caused his mike to again bump Larry's chin.

Larry moved his head a trifle. "No witnesses have been found who saw or heard anything. That, of course, doesn't include the surviving victim, Melvin Crane. He's not able to communicate freely because of his wound, but he *has* given us some important information on the man who shot him."

"He saw the killer?"

"Not clearly. Though as he recovers, he should remember more. At the moment he's unable to provide us with enough for a composite drawing." He paused, and gave them what they wanted: the revelation a news conference needed to make it a success. "The important information I referred to could explain the lack of noise connected with the shootings. At least during the attack on Crane and his wife. Crane believes the weapon had a silencer."

That created a stir, and the Mouth showed why she received both the highest ratings and the largest salary (as reported in the *Times*). "Then this killer—we might as well call him Silencer until we know his real name—then Silencer can shoot anyone, anywhere, anytime, even on a crowded street?" She jerked her thumb at the street behind her, where pedestrians stood watching. "Shoot even you, right here, without drawing attention to himself?"

"I wouldn't say it was quite that easy." He made no jokes about her statement, as a rookie might have. Didn't grin and say, "Me? Let's hope not," or something equally natural. Because oh how bad it could look on that small screen; how foolish it could sound, especially if cut and taken out of sequence. No, you played it very straight, almost dumb, and kept to that stiff, official language.

"Assuming Silencer killed the first two victims," the newspaper reporter, a top man from the revitalized *Examiner,* asked, "couldn't we say he's attacking in one small area only? West Los Angeles in the general vicinity of the Sunset Strip?"

Silencer. The Mouth had coined a name.

"You could say that, though we don't believe he killed Arnold Latrile, the cab driver. That appears more like a gangland slaying."

But they weren't to be denied. They had their new Hillside Strangler, their own Jack the Ripper. They couldn't wait for more killings, conclusive evidence that a mass murderer was on the loose. They needed their big stories by air time this evening—five or six p.m.

"There haven't been any obvious motives," the press service reporter asked, "like robbery or rape, have there?"

"No," he said, feeling the interview was at an end, that he'd told them what little he could, that they were now asking him to project, to guess. "But it's far too early to establish any pattern, such as a psychopathic killer's."

"Without motive, you would almost *have* to assume it's a psychopath, wouldn't you, Lieutenant? Someone who hates certain kinds of people. Prostitutes, for example, as indicated in the death of Carla Woodruff."

"Carla Woodruff," he said smoothly, "has now been established as a salesperson in a good women's dress shop." Which should help him with Diana, if she saw this on television. Though he was far from convinced himself as to the victim's true profession. Things were developing . . .

The Count had his hand up. "But her being out on the street at night, especially in that area—we all know that prostitutes work on and around the Sunset Strip —could lead Silencer to classify her as such. And Beth-Anne Crane danced at a nude club, also on the Strip. She could have been followed by Silencer, who would certainly consider her a fallen woman. Her husband's shooting would then be incidental to hers."

Larry simply nodded, because they were beginning to interview each other. From here on, with the hard evidence used up, the questions would be more important than the answers, allowing them to make their points, do their projections, weave their stories of might-be.

95

And from long experience, he knew that most of this would end on the cutting-room floor.

"Do you think," the Mouth asked, "that Silencer might stop his attacks, leave the area, perhaps even the state or country, because of that survivor and possible eyewitness, Melvin Crane?"

"That's what a sane man would do," Larry said, a bud of irritation beginning to flower in his gut. He wanted out of this bullshit session.

The Mouth began to respond.

Larry said, "I think that's it, ladies and gentlemen. We'll keep looking for him, sane or not. And keep you informed."

There was some grumbling, and a few more questions which he treated with smiles and shrugs. One by one the mikes withdrew, along with their owners. Until only one was left. That one dipped low as the ex-Ram moved alongside Larry and put a heavy arm around his shoulders. "Between us honkies," he rumbled confidentially, "any chance that black dude killed his white wife and tried suicide? Pretty funky couple, you got to admit."

Larry said, "No chance at all," and slipped from under the arm, into his car.

He drove two blocks to a coffee shop.

He loved football, especially the Rams. One of his favorite fantasies had him quarterbacking them in the Super Bowl. But he had to admit he preferred the Mouth, with all her plastic bitchiness, to this locker-room cracker who never failed to make some negative reference to blacks.

There'd been few football heroes in 'Nam. College boys had been deferred from the draft. The first war since the Civil, as one college-boy enlister had told Larry, that allowed men to *buy* their way out of service. Maybe not as blatantly as by hiring a substitute, which had been the practice in the Civil. But if you had a middle- or upper-class background, you simply enrolled in college, whether or not you had intended to before the draft. Which bought you a deferment.

That was why there had been lots of blacks, Hispanics, rednecks, blue-collar kids in 'Nam. That was why Lawrence Admer, despite dealing with black criminals more often than he wanted to, and the same with Chicanos and all the rest of the poor folk, never lumped good and bad guys together in racist remarks the way so many of his fellow officers did. He'd served with those men. He'd seen them die. He regularly visited two in the Westwood Village Veterans Hospital; two who would never get out. Maybe he wanted to forget Vietnam, but he couldn't. It colored his thoughts, his opinions; made him far more complex a man than he would otherwise have been, highly conservative in some ways, just as liberal in others.

It was the strongest single experience of his life.

Sipping coffee, smoking a Camel, he watched a long-legged girl in black go by his booth. And remembered that he'd planned to see Diana.

He spotted the phone on the wall near the restrooms, and walked there, digging change from his pocket.

He was no longer thinking of Vietnam.

She heard the phone ringing, but she needed sleep.

It kept ringing, eight, nine, ten times, and who else would be so persistent, and so thoughtless, but a policeman?

It rang twice more, and ended. She curled up, eyes closed determinedly against the world . . . and found she couldn't get back to sleep. Maybe it hadn't been Larry Admer. Maybe it had been her mother, her father . . .

She sat up, and her head swam and nausea gripped her stomach; a reaction to the drugs she'd been taking lately. She remained still and quiet until it passed, then looked at her bedside clock.

Only ten, and she'd been up until three a.m., killing time with television, not really seeing the shows, waiting for the Quaalude to knock her out. She'd taken *two* tablets, and even though she'd spaced them out over a five-hour period, two was dangerous. But her mind had been running away with her . . . out of control . . . she hadn't been able to turn it off.

Carla, of course.

But herself too. Her life. What had led her—and through her, her sister—to Los Angeles and this dismal point in time.

That cop thought she was a prostitute. His attraction to her, she was certain, was that of a john to a whore.

Was she a prostitute?

She gave men various kinds of sex for money. She fit the dictionary definition. But she had never thought of herself that way . . . until, perhaps, these past few days, when she'd grown shaky, vulnerable.

She went downstairs. She made coffee and sat sipping and thinking. How could a woman become something as obvious in society as a prostitute, and not know it?

The sex in her life had begun innocently enough. She'd been almost eighteen before her first coital experience, and judging by what her friends in high school divulged about themselves, among the few virgins left in the graduating class of 1968. And so in love with her steady, John Kleiser, six months her senior and class valedictorian, that when he had taken her outside the gym on prom night and told her he was enlisting in the Army "to fight the reds," the issue was resolved. Filled with compassion for him, she'd soon found herself in his home, on the playroom couch, losing what her mother termed "a girl's most important organ." And in such a passionate, fumbling, tearful rush that birth control had been forgotten.

Luckily, they'd gotten away with it, and Diana had vowed never again to give herself so carelessly to any man. But give herself she would—that she'd known—because a truly lusty appetite had been awakened . . . along with recognition of something strange and disturbing: Her love for John had faded bit by bit with each sexual encounter. Her *lust* had survived and she was pleased to continue seeing him, but the romantic attachment had become irrelevant. She no longer dreamed of marriage, of children, of a life with him.

Why this should have been so, she hadn't known at the time. Later, she'd realized she was that way with most men. And after her brother's death in early 1971, she'd become that way with all of them.

In the fall, she'd begun classes at Washington University. She'd dated several students and, secretly, one instructor. The instructor had become her heavy love affair; and then, in the same manner as with John, simply an affair. A small, intellectual man in his thirties, married and with no less than four children, he'd written poetry for her, introduced her to the pains and pleasures of anal intercourse, and, at about the same time that she had begun to find him a bore, had fallen madly in love with her.

He had attempted suicide after she'd stopped seeing him. She'd found it difficult to believe anyone could be that idiotic. "I die for love of the Huntress," he'd written in a poem mailed to her home, where she still lived with her parents, her sister, and her brother Jackie, who was becoming more and more troubled and troublesome, more and more dependent on Diana for help.

The English instructor had survived a jar of sleeping pills, and left Washington University for a private secondary school. He'd written to Diana several times, enclosing small poems with his letters, and one had called her "The cruel killer of the heart, the cold mortician of the soul." She'd found herself laughing; then wondered which one of them was the freak. From all that went on between men and women, she'd realized it might easily be *her*. But she'd continued to enjoy sex, often, with a variety of men.

Around that time she'd been involved in an amateur theatrical company, and during the early part of her sophomore year, she'd opened in her first stage role playing the Judy Holliday part of the dumb blonde— complete with wig—in *Born Yesterday*. Her co-star, playing the Bill Holden role, had been gay. But in the Broderick Crawford role of the junk dealer turned political manipulator had been a man of about fifty, who, when he'd put his hands on her, had made her feel

99

something other than the simple lust she'd become accustomed to.

Opening night, she had gone to bed with Axel Mandel in a suite at the old Forest Park Hotel. He'd been skillful, and thoughtful, placing her atop him because of a thick-set body that weighed almost two hundred pounds. He'd asked if she could stay the night. She'd said yes, surprised that *he* could, since men of Mandel's caliber—he was a wealthy clothier with two large shops in St. Louis and three in the suburbs—were invariably married. "Widower," he'd explained, and taken her in his thick arms and fallen asleep.

The show had run for three consecutive weekends. They'd spent all but one of those six nights together in their suite, and by the time they'd taken their final bows, she was hooked on show business, and him. But still, she had said goodbye to him after that final night, because he had said goodbye to her. She hadn't asked to see him, because he hadn't asked to see her. Despite a terrible emptiness, she hadn't considered trying to manipulate him in any way. Because she was certain that if the relationship were to continue long enough, she would tire of him.

The next day she'd received her first expensive gift from a man; from anyone, for that matter: a beautiful watch with platinum case and jeweled band. And a goodbye note from Axel Mandel.

The following week, her brother Jackie had been shot and killed, and her heart had turned to stone. And when she'd consented to see Axel, who'd thought to comfort her, he'd been a fat old man with coarse ways. Still, looking at the beautiful watch on her wrist, she'd agreed to go to bed with him, feeling it was expected of her. Which might have been the first time she'd made love for profit.

She'd taken the watch to a jeweler, and when he said he could give her a thousand dollars, had known that it must have been worth three or four. A generous man, her Axel.

She'd used the thousand to finance her move to Los

100

Angeles. She'd tried to break down the studio doors for about a year, while she'd worked in an office as secretary-typist, and lived in a tiny apartment in a cheap neighborhood just off Hollywood Boulevard west of Vine. Full of junkies, pimps, prostitutes, and runaway kids, the neighborhood was dangerous, but she'd stayed there in order to save money for acting classes. Occasionally she'd gone to parties thrown by fellow students and lower-level studio people, and at one of them she'd met Anthony Loretto-Suise, from Lugano-Paradiso, Switzerland.

Tony Swiss, as he was known, was wealthy, was educated, was bisexual. He'd laughed when she'd used the "breaking down the studio doors" expression, and replied, "Breaking in the studio casting couches, you mean."

She'd been angered, and moved to another part of the crowded room in the cliffside house high above Los Angeles. She'd sipped her soft drink and wondered where she would get the rent money due next Friday. This had been a bad month, as at least half of them were, with extra expenses such as a tooth that had to be capped. And Tony Swiss had caught her eye and shaken his head, smiling. A hawk's face, his, the mouth thin, the eyes glinting, the nose beak-like and narrow. A hard-looking man . . . and he had turned out to be one of the most helpful she'd ever met.

After she'd failed to persuade her date, who'd grown stoned on pot and wine, to take her home, Tony had offered her a ride. She'd been a little afraid of him, but had accepted because tomorrow was work and it was after midnight.

In the car, he'd revealed he knew something about her. "From your boss, Adam Revere. He's an old acquaintance of mine. You're far too beautiful, and not nearly talented enough, to be draining yourself in this foolish life. You're also far too intelligent, from what Adam has said, and from what I can gather."

She'd defended her way of life, and wondered when he would make his move.

He hadn't moved. He had *mocked* . . . mocked her

101

job, her casting-couch encounters, and mocked her for "working like a slave when what you give away could make you comfortable."

"You're a pimp?"

He'd laughed. And nodded. "Amateur status. When I see a sensual woman, or man, wasting life in a particular fashion, I offer education."

"And your reward?"

He'd glanced away from the winding road, to her. His smile remained, and his face didn't seem that cold and cruel any more. "Having that sensual woman, or man, for a brief period. I don't need money, Diana."

Since they'd been driving in a thirty-thousand-dollar Mercedes, and he was wearing what could have been another thirty thousand in jewelry, she'd believed him. But still had said, "No, thanks."

He'd said, "Being comfortable and independent is all-important, unless you are dedicated to something, such as an art—painting, music, writing—something that might justify poverty, humiliation, and general discomfort. But you . . . are you dedicated to being manipulated by men, Diana?"

An intellectual pimp's pitch, she'd thought.

What had made it difficult to ignore that particular evening was that he had struck a nerve. Not only wasn't she dedicated to acting any longer, she had lost enthusiasm and pleasure in just about everything. She was tired of being pursued in her underpaid office job by half a dozen men, the most persistent being Tony's friend, Revere, who thought that promising her a ten-dollar raise, or threatening her with unemployment, would change her no-office-dating policy. Tired of the so-called producers who had fooled her for a while with Hollywood fantasies. Tired of empty checking and savings accounts. Tired of her younger sister doing better than she in a simple salesgirl's job because she didn't waste her energies in studios and acting schools, and enjoyed life because she was always in love.

And then they'd reached the shabby side street, the dingy apartment house, the place she was beginning to dread returning to each evening. "All right," she'd said. "Show me."

He'd U-turned and headed for Beverly Hills. On the way, he'd stopped at a service station and made a phone call; then they'd continued into the park-like township that deserved its reputation as one of the richest and most delightful places to live in all the world. He'd taken her to a beautiful home and introduced her to a handsome, graying man who, she later learned, was married to a famous singer. The handsome graying man had introduced himself as Barnet; then thanked Tony and said he would return Diana home himself. She'd begun to protest. Tony had taken her aside and said, "Be trusting, just this once." She'd looked into his cynic's face, and nodded.

Barnet had taken her on a tour of the house and grounds—seventeen rooms, a pool, and a tennis court. H had then shown her to a small gymnasium, and told her he was going to strip and lie down on a high table, the kind used by masseurs. "I'd like you to strip too, Diana, except for your shoes. I'd like you to massage me, do you understand?"

She had, of course, but had wanted to ask him *why* she should do this for a perfect stranger. Still, Tony must have known what he was about . . .

As she'd hesitated, Barnet had pressed two one-hundred-dollar bills into her hand, and said, "Use the baby oil, please. Would you like a drink first?" She had looked at the money, and shaken her head. She still hadn't believed she was going to do it, even as he'd stripped. She'd thought how well-conditioned he was, cleanly muscled and flat-stomached, especially for a man in his mid-forties. And had begun to undress, watching him as he leaned against the table, watching her. Watched as his penis grew turgid, lengthened against his thigh, and rose.

She'd approached him. He'd waited, expecting, she thought, an embrace.

She hadn't embraced him. She'd said, "On the table, please," calmly, professionally. He had hired her for a job and she was going to do it.

He'd gotten on the table, on his back. She'd taken the baby oil from a shelf and applied some to his penis. He'd groaned, and his hand had stroked her bottom, her thighs, brushed at her pubic hair.

She had concentrated on *him*. For the first time in her life, she hadn't been concerned with achieving orgasm when dealing with a nude, aroused male. And when he'd begged for "just a little touch of the mouth," she'd bent and kissed his glans and stroked and murmured how big he was, how strong he was, how he was going to "come gallons," all calculated to get him off quickly so that she would have earned two hundred dollars in a few minutes.

It had worked. His hand had clutched her buttock. He'd arched himself upward, groaning deeply, and shot semen into the air. She'd continued stroking . . . and found herself kissing his mouth, sucking at his mouth. Job or not, her sensuality couldn't be turned completely off.

After they'd washed and dressed, he'd suggested they go to an all-night steak house on La Cienega. She had been about to plead weariness, when he'd said, "There are generally some friends of mine there, and I think you should meet them."

Which had turned out to be the case, and had led to a series of massages and recommendations.

There was, she had learned, a group of well-to-do married men in Los Angeles who sought out beautiful young women. They were careful of their reputations, and therefore rarely asked a woman back a second time. They were also careful of their health, fearing venereal disease, which explained their preference for the hand over the vagina.

After two weeks, during which Diana had earned two thousand two hundred dollars, her client list had suddenly run out. She had called Tony Swiss, and he'd said not-to-worry and that she could now take a few days off to pay him for his services.

She'd been glad of the opportunity for some mutually satisfying sex, and had enjoyed Tony thoroughly. At the end of three days, during which they had rarely left his giant waterbed, he'd said he would line up a new group of clients for her, also wealthy, but mostly single and more interested in coitus.

At that, the word *prostitute* had popped into her mind. Also, like the married men, she preferred the immunity from disease provided by massage. And the degree of remoteness, separateness it had offered. And so she had said no.

Tony hadn't been surprised. Other women had reacted the same way, he'd said. No reason she couldn't continue along the massage route, except that it would have to be done in the parlors. If she was interested, he'd be glad to contact several friends in the trade.

She'd said yes . . . but in the weeks that followed, kept putting off actually going to any of the three addresses he'd given her. She'd continued to hope for the less involved method of visiting wealthy men's homes. The fact that she could make as much money working the parlors hadn't enthused her, since she would be working a regular shift of four to six days a week, dealing with many men each day.

But finally, after spending half her two thousand and realizing Tony was no longer interested in either seeing or speaking to her (he'd begun living with an eighteen-year-old boy) she had gone to a place in the Wilshire district called The Island Paradise . . .

The phone was ringing again.

She raised her cup, drank, and shuddered. The coffee was ice-cold. She checked her watch.

Almost noon.

And now she was ready to *do* something, get out of here, answer that phone and whoever was at the other end. If it was Arthur, she'd say she was ready for work. Larry Admer, she'd ask for dinner and find out if he'd learned anything new about her prey. Her parents, which she'd feared for days, she'd play it by ear, and survive.

It was Larry. He said her sister's body would be released to her on Friday. "It won't be fit for an open coffin, so make your plans accordingly. If you'd like some help . . ."

"Yes, I would. I haven't the faintest notion of how to arrange a funeral."

"Forest Lawn is easy. We can drive over there about three-thirty, four. Seeing you comes under the heading of investigation. You can make all the arrangements, and keep the cost down."

"Thank you." And for once she meant it. The funeral had frightened her. "It's in Glendale, isn't it? Should I meet you there?"

"No, we'll have plenty of daylight. I'll pick you up about six."

"Will you have time for dinner?" she murmured.

"Yes," he said warmly.

She waited. He made no wise-cracks, no pitches, committed no gaucheries.

She nodded slowly, and said goodbye.

The john was learning how to operate. "Treat a lady like a whore, and a whore like a lady," the old street saying went. Lots of truth in it. Except that she'd always considered herself a lady.

106

NINE: *Wednesday, August 2, p.m.*

Cloris had checked into the Caravan Inn at two-thirty the previous afternoon. It was a lot shabbier place than she had expected—her room was a dingy closet with old furniture—and the black guy at the desk had hit on her for a date. But she'd handled the guy by saying her brother was coming to stay with her. And why should she care about the room? She wasn't going to spend any time in it, just to sleep, because one flight down was Sunset Boulevard and the rock clubs and the discos and the restaurants! And not far away was Hollywood and the studios!

Cloris had bought a special map of Los Angeles showing the studios and the historical sites like Grauman's Chinese Theatre, the place with stars' footprints in cement, and how to get to these places. After settling in at the motel, she had gone to Paramount, using the buses, which had taken forever. But then again, she *had* forever—no school and no hassles with Mom and Uncle Bert and she wouldn't look for work until next week.

She'd gone right up to those big Paramount gates

and asked if she could take a tour of the place. "I'll pay, of course," she'd said to the guard, an old guy but one she figured might let her in for nothing the way his eyes were checking her out. She'd been wearing cut-off jeans; not her turn-on short-shorts, but with the tight blue tee shirt and semi-heeled walking shoes, she'd known she looked okay.

The guard had laughed and said the tours were at Universal. She'd said, "I know that!" embarrassed because she'd mixed up the two studios. Then she'd asked him how to get there.

Easy, he'd said, even though Universal was in Studio City, which was in the Valley. Tour buses left from most of the hotels, and she could go to the Roosevelt on Hollywood Boulevard.

Like everywhere else in Southern California, you needed wheels to survive in L.A., and she'd decided she would look for a car the day she got a steady job.

She'd taken the bus to Hollywood Boulevard, but it was almost five by now, and across the way from the hotel was that wild-looking theatre with the sign reading Mann's Chinese, which her special map explained was the new name for Grauman's Chinese. So she'd changed her plans, figuring to do Universal tomorrow, and had gone over to the theatre and read all the names that were with the prints in the concrete.

A real great day, not too hot, and lots of people dressed like Yogi Bear on vacation, with cameras and funny hats and godawful Hawaiian print dresses and shirts. She'd left the theatre and walked along Hollywood Boulevard, looking down at the metal stars set in the sidewalk squares, reading the names. Some she'd recognized, but most she'd never heard of, like John Gilbert and Leslie Howard and Olivia De Havilland.

She'd stopped for a chili dog and cola, and while she was eating, guys kept coming up to the stand and hitting on her. Some she hadn't minded, though she hadn't been in the mood, but some were real scrounges, hair all over their faces and down to their shoulders and torn Levis like it was the old hippy days. Those she'd minded plenty, especially one asshole

108

who'd stroked her arm, stared straight at her breasts, and said, "Like, you know, you got the equipment to make me happy, right?" She'd walked away in a hurry, thinking he had junkie eyes, and a girl had to be careful.

Besides, she'd promised to meet Verna and Buddy for dinner.

They'd taken her to a Love's Barbecue, and Buddy had ordered a carafe of wine. No one had carded her and she'd ended up stuffed and sleepy. On the way out, Verna had gone to the bathroom, like she did so much since getting pregnant, and Buddy had stood with Cloris in a corner, talking. "Man," he'd said, "you look like the million-dollar jackpot!"

Before she'd been able to slide away, he'd given her ass a good feel. "Remember the party at Christofer Bayshore's when we got loaded and you massaged my cock?"

She'd told him to clean up his mouth, and Verna had come back, and they'd taken her home. But later, in bed, she'd envied Verna a little, at least for sleeping with a man's arms around her. Buddy hadn't looked bad at all tonight. And while it hadn't meant anything at the time, she *did* remember the party at Chris Bayshore's.

She'd ended up thinking of her Freddy, of his great body, of the way they'd made love three and four times in a row. Or how his penis felt throbbing inside her. How it felt in her mouth . . .

Finally, she'd had to masturbate.

She'd slept late this morning. After an Eggs McMuffin at the arches, she'd headed for a hotel down the Strip, and from there had taken a bus to Universal. The studio tour had been *great!* Fired up her ambition to make it as an actress. Also, her ego had gotten a lift when a tall, good-looking man, maybe thirty-five, maybe more, dressed *fantastic*, had kept giving her the eye during the tour; then followed her to the bus stop and asked if he could give her a lift.

She would really have liked a ride home instead of

waiting an hour for the damned bus, but he'd been checking her out too heavy and a girl would have to be braver than Cloris, and dumber, to risk it. So she'd said, "Thank you, no," very sweetly. He'd tried to talk her into it, but an old lady had started giving him hard looks and he'd walked back to the Universal parking lot. A minute later, he'd driven slowly by in a big, white Mark IV, still trying.

Oh, yes, little Cloris was going to make it!

Now it was seven-thirty and getting dark. She'd showered and dressed in her best skirt suit, egg-shell white and fitted like skin, and brushed her freshly shampooed hair, and had changed shoes twice before settling on the high heels even though they weren't all that comfortable. They gave her the height and the moves, and she felt ready for anyone, including Robert Redford! Man, if he was down there, he'd look twice!

She stepped through the door, onto the outside walkway, and heard the sounds of that swinging street. And hesitated. She was suddenly scared—a little girl, alone, facing a strange scene.

But then she thought of the book she'd read about Hollywood; of all the girls that had come here and "fought for fame and fortune." Of those that had "the looks and the ability, but not the courage." Of those "who in spite of being alone and friendless, persisted and eventually attained stardom." Of needing "*heart* more than anything else" to make it in show-biz.

Right! She had the looks and she had the heart! She'd go down there and show them all!

Besides, she reminded herself as she started for the staircase, she was only going to walk around a little, scout around a little, look into clubs like the Whiskey and the Crazy Horse Saloon and the Roxy, check out the record shops like Tower which sometimes had rock stars walking around in them. Maybe eat in one of those restaurants with outdoor tables like the Old World. But only if it wasn't too expensive. Or if some nice guy asked her. She wouldn't mind meeting someone, maybe a college man, or better still an actor who could give her advice about dramatic schools and employment agencies.

She was walking down the stairs toward the courtyard, toward the Strip. "Here I come," she murmured, thinking that Farrah and other actresses all the way back to Monroe must have said the same thing. She walked as gracefully as she could, carefully on those spike heels, and hummed the song from the Miss America Pageant. She turned right, and came onto Sunset Boulevard. And stopped.

People *thronged* the sidewalks. Cars jammed the street in both directions, headlights glaring, horns honking, radios blaring through open windows on this balmy summer night. Voices talked, shouted, laughed. And almost everyone, on the sidewalk and in the cars, was in twos.

Well, stars came in *ones!*

With that she began to walk east, toward the brightest lights, the greatest congestion and noise. Two boys coming toward her went wow and hey and wanna-have-a-burger? But they were real kids, maybe younger than she was, and she ignored them.

A minute later, a black Trans-Am with hood flame-mural pulled to the curb and a Spanish-looking guy said, "Hey, you know the Palladium? Can you tell me where it is? Maybe show me? They got a great concert tonight."

He didn't sound Mex, so she smiled a little because she knew when she'd been hit on. But there were two more in the car and that wasn't safe. Besides, she wanted to stay right here on Sunset.

She kept walking and noticed there were other women alone on the street. The way then were dressed, the way they kept checking cars, they reminded Cloris of hookers on TV shows.

God, she hoped no one thought *she* was a hooker!

Suddenly feeling exposed, she fled into the next store—a record shop. She walked along the aisles, glancing around from the corners of her eyes, and when no one bothered her she began to feel better.

111

And then she bumped into a guy who was bent over a file of records. "Oh, gee, I'm sorry!"

He muttered, "All right." Then he looked at her. "My fault, miss. I get carried away when I'm buying records. My big weakness. Do you like Pink Floyd?"

He wasn't too tall, but he had nice brown hair, cut neat, and a nice face, cute rather than handsome, and he was sort of shy because he muffed a few words while trying to act cool. He was at least twenty-five, dressed casual in tan slacks and a short-sleeved sport shirt, not with-it but *safe*, which was important to Cloris.

"Pink Floyd's all right," she said, "but I'm into softer music, ballads, like Barry Manilow."

He agreed fast, muffing another few words, that "Manilow is the best, super, you know, in his category. It's just that I enjoy all kinds of music, even the classics like Sinatra and Crosby."

Wow! She wondered if maybe he wasn't older than he looked! But he bought the Pink Floyd, so she figured he'd just been trying to impress her.

They walked out together. He said, "Look, don't think I'm forward or anything, you know, but would you like to have something to eat?"

She said, "Well . . ." and made herself look doubtful; then asked if he liked the Old World.

He said, "My favorite restaurant!" and took her arm, smiling a real nice smile.

His name was Andy Harty—"Almost like the old TV movies with Mickey Rooney." She laughed and introduced herself and they started walking.

A little later, eating a fantastic health-food plate, looking down from the little outdoor balcony at all the people and cars and lights, she listened as he told her he lived just a five-minute walk from the record shop, on Larrabee; that he worked at the Broadway department store in Century City while he—*get this!*—studied acting at the Sunset Theatrecraft Workshop.

Cloris couldn't believe her good luck!

* * *

112

Larry had helped Diana make the arrangements for her sister's burial at Forest Lawn, and promised he would be with her all through the Saturday funeral.

He'd taken her to dinner at the Malibu fish house, and they'd waited for the same table, and she'd ordered the same entree, broiled snapper, holding it down this time.

They'd gone for a walk along the beach, and he'd talked and talked, as he had ever since they'd left the Glendale mortuary-cemetery. Mostly about the four West L.A. killings. Because she never ran out of questions.

"How could Melvin Crane," she now asked, "have been shot in the face and not have seen his assailant?"

"Many ways. Too dark. Told not to turn his head. Too frightened. And the strongest possibility—that he doesn't remember what he did see because of his physical disability. He was shot in the jaw, and the bullet slanted upward, shattering a hell of a lot of bone. Silencer tried to shoot him in the brain."

"Have you considered that he might be lying?"

"Of course. His wife was killed. Men often want to beat the police to a criminal, to avenge a crime themselves.

She began to say something. He quickly added, "I didn't mean *males* when I said men. I meant *people*. You, for example, might want to put a bullet into the man who killed your sister."

She didn't answer right away, and he looked at her; at the beautiful face in starlight. Then she said, "I don't think that way. Besides, there are more logical reasons for Crane lying, for not wanting Silencer—what a melodramatic name!—not wanting him caught and tried."

He continued to look at her as they walked along the shore. As he'd looked at her on and off all day. Yet he hadn't made a personal overture—not even touching her hand—all those hours. And God how he'd wanted to! And he wanted to now.

He said, "Like what?" and knew she was going to refer to what he'd told her—but hadn't told the media—about the Angel-dusted pot. Knew that what-

113

ever she said, he'd have thought of it before, long before. But she was a survivor, as in "Carla Woodruff is survived by her sister, Diana Woodruff." Survivors always had theories. Survivors were pains in the ass. Though he was willing to listen to this one.

"Like Crane and Silencer being involved in the drug trade together. Or in other criminal activities. Anything linking the two men that would mean prison for Crane if Silencer were caught."

"That's good detective-story stuff. But if Silencer isn't a psychopath, if he kills with such logic, with such motive, then he'd have to have motive with your sister too."

She stopped walking and looked out at the sea. "Maybe Carla *did* know him. Maybe it's someone in her shop, someone I might have met, someone she'd discovered doing something illegal."

He sighed to himself, and said nothing.

"Someone who lured her to Lakeland Street . . ."

"Lakewood," he interrupted, hoping to stop the nonsense.

"You sound impatient, Lieutenant."

"Sorry." They began to walk again, and he explained that survivors almost always wanted some logical reason, some solid motive, to be connected with a killing. And survivors often included the followers of a political or religious leader. Which explained why so many people believed in the existence of involved plots, of complicated conspiracies, in the deaths of John Kennedy and Martin Luther King.

"Random killings, psycho killings, are the hardest of all to accept. I remember one woman whose husband was killed by a freeway sniper. She said, 'It can't be that! God wouldn't allow such a *pointless* thing, such a waste!' I could have told her about pointlessness and waste multiplied by the thousands in what became a pointless, wasteful war."

"Vietnam," she murmured. "The Holocaust. Genghis Khan and the mountain of skulls. Reverend Jones and Guyana."

"Slipping on a banana peel," he said. "Falling in the

114

bathtub." And when she smiled, he took her hand, smiling too.

She pulled away and turned back.

He was deeply shocked. He stood still for a moment, then followed, trying to control his anger.

He wasn't altogether successful. "I guess you're not used to holding *hands*."

She slowed. "You're right. I'm not."

Her face and voice were serious. He said, "Are you telling me I should put my cock in your hand, and then you'll act human?"

"Then I'll act professional. If you still want that, as you said you did Sunday, I'll consider the chauffeuring and the dinner the fee, and when we get to my place . . ."

"Christ!" He looked away, afraid he was going to hit her. And why? Why not take her up on the hand job? Why not try for some head too?

He looked at her again. He read something in her face; felt she was making a point. And suddenly got it. "You're right. I don't know what I'm doing with you, what I want with you. It's all fucked up. Holding hands!" He laughed harshly.

They walked toward the restaurant. The sea was on their left, slick and black with rolling white crests. Its sound was a subdued crashing. It smelled as only the sea could smell. After a while he felt something, and glanced at her.

She was looking at him.

He felt something else: she was touching his hand with the back of hers, lightly, timidly.

"If you want me as a person, a friend, you'll have to convince me of it. I don't know how you can do that, Larry."

She'd never used his name before, and his hand opened and enfolded hers. The feeling was much the same as when he'd been a kid in San Fernando High, in love with Adele Jergenson, and they'd sat in the movies holding hands. He'd been fourteen then, and the next year he'd fucked her and forgotten her.

115

He'd held hands with Gloria too, before they'd bedded down for six months, then married because they'd had to, Junior being on the way. And look what had happened to *that* love story.

And it had happened with every girl before, between, and since.

So maybe going past hand-holding was the death of this incredible feeling, this tight-chested, cry-in-the-throat feeling. Maybe it was the same for Diana—not possible for her to go past hand-holding without getting into what she did in the parlor.

Maybe. A very dismal maybe, and he didn't want to believe it. Now they were looking at each other and he stopped. He pulled her close and kissed her, sweetly. He kept her hand in his and kept his other hand, his other arm, around her waist and nowhere else though it wanted to go everywhere else. And released her almost immediately.

He said, "What one straight vodka, domestic, without congeners, will do to a guy."

She laughed then, hard, the first time he'd seen her do that, because he'd followed her advice about the no-frills, cut-rate drink.

He drove her home. He couldn't believe the wonderful feeling! He walked her up the blacktop path. And tensed, because they were at her door again and here was where he felt dumped, rejected. "Goodnight."

"I think you'd better come in."

He was startled.

"Otherwise, you'll get uptight again."

"And if I come in?"

"We'll hold hands and watch TV. I'm about talked out for today."

He was still uptight, even though she gave him a vodka and held his hand and leaned her head on his shoulder as they watched a variety show. And didn't complain, as she had in the car, when he lit a cigarette.

He still didn't know what he was doing with her. He still wanted his cock in her hand, her mouth, between her legs, up her gorgeous ass! Wanted it so intensely

116

when she crossed those lovely legs and the dress hiked above the knee and the sweet, rounded thighs showed, that he was sure she would notice. He stood up quickly, turning away at the same time. "Have to go. Tough day tomorrow. I'm putting together all the interviews on Lakewood and maybe I'll spot something. Maybe we'll find out why Carla was there."

"All right. And thank you."

"My job, ma'am," he said, mocking himself, mocking his teen-age blue balls, and went out the door.

Diana had known what he'd wanted. She'd felt how strong a wanting it became after she'd put her head on his shoulder and crossed her legs, allowing a bit of thigh to show. Larry Admer was a lusty man. He'd had a lusty bump in his trousers. And she'd begun to feel a little lusty herself, just before he'd left.

Nor was it simply lust that kept him coming around . . .

She cut that thought, and went to the kitchen. She busied herself with cleaning what had been left uncleaned since Carla's death.

She refused to admit to herself that she could understand the non-lust that Larry had felt, or remember John and Prom Night and the nights before that when they had held hands and her heart had filled to bursting. Refused to admit that most males, perhaps *any* male, including this make-out cop, could feel that way, especially about a woman he'd met in a massage parlor; a woman who jerked penises for a living. And occasionally sucked them. And sometimes fucked them . . .

All confused. Had to get back to normalcy. Which meant back to work on penises.

Had to continue earning the thousand a week as long as she could, which meant while youth and beauty lasted and customers asked for her above the other girls. Once they stopped asking, she would stop working, then enjoy the freedom from dependency on jobs and men that her savings would bring.

117

Had to forget confusion and non-lust and memories of non-lust, and remember why she had taken up with the cop in the first place.

She had learned much today. She would learn more, as Lieutenant Lawrence Admer learned more. And perhaps she would learn things he hadn't, and couldn't; things Melvin Crane would tell her and not the police.

Because she had recognized the nude dancer, Beth-Anne Crane—her name; her picture on television. Because Beth-Anne Crane had been in the parlor a month or so ago for a *ménage à trois* with the owner of the club in which she'd worked and a big-bottomed Oriental girl who'd made the night shift just for this "three-freak act," as street people called it. Which turned into a four-freak act when Arthur showed up to join them in the back room.

Beth-Anne had wandered out once, saying, "The boys're sixty-nining," and offered Diana "a snort" of cocaine "worth a hundred bucks, easy, but I get it from my ex, only he's not yet ex and maybe I'll never let him *be* ex." She'd been high and talked about her "nigger-baby" and said he would "eat my shit, if I asked him to. Or any other foxy white chick's if she went at him one on one. A real lonely heart, my black beauty . . ." And so on. And then tried to get her to come into the back room "because Arthur has a nut for you and he's the boss, right?"

Wrong, and Diana had taken care of a customer, which was business and compartmentalized and therefore not a freak act of any sort.

Now she finished in the kitchen, thinking *she* was a foxy white chick.

Now she went to the phone and dialed Arthur's number. It took a while, but he finally answered, voice low and thick. "Yeah."

"It's Diana. I want to go back to work."

"When?"

"Tomorrow night."

"Still nights? After what happened? All the girls are jumpy about nights with this Silencer crap."

118

"For a while longer." She needed her days for Admer and Crane and a funeral.

"Right. Gotta run. People waiting."

She could imagine. People, and maybe an animal or two. Arthur had done it all.

She took her Quaalude and went to bed.

She stopped thinking about everything but Carla. She gave herself to memories of Carla. And to fantasies of avenging Carla.

Silencer, they called him.

She considered methods of breaking his silence, of making him shriek . . .

Frank was tired. He'd put in a long day, not only at the store, but visiting offices. As Martin had pointed out, he was behind in those contacts that kept Berdon's Stationery profitable. And having personal problems meant nothing in the business world. There were too many cut-rate outfits ready to snap up his customers.

He was also depressed. He hadn't visited his mother today, taking the nurse's advice to give her fuzzy mind a chance to clear. But that wasn't why he felt so low. It was his decision to stop using the gun; it was the resultant lack of goals, of enthusiasm for any project, and that included business.

He hadn't taken time to listen to the radio or read a newspaper all day. And after a large dinner—with Lila commenting on how much he ate, just about bite by bite—he'd napped two hours, and awakened even more lethargic and depressed than before.

Now he turned on the television for the eleven o'clock news, and sank into his easy chair, glad that Lila was moving around in the kitchen. But as soon as the sound came on, she entered the living room, wiping her hands on a towel, talking about the "horrendous" price of meat and that "this nation is in for a depression."

He nodded, trying to hear the newscaster's voice over hers.

She sat down on the couch, still talking.

He answered her with nods and no's during the commercial, but then a filmed interview with that detective he had seen at the hospital came on, and he tried to shush her. She wouldn't shush, saying, "Why anyone would want to listen to that awful garbage about murders and prostitutes, *I* for one can't understand."

He was too lethargic to fight her, and said he was going out for some air.

Also, too lethargic to walk, and got into his car, opening the windows, hoping to chase away the dullness of body and spirit.

He was parked facing north, so he drove north, to Sunset Boulevard. It was late enough for traffic to have thinned out, but there were still cars and pedestrians aplenty. There would be some cars and pedestrians almost all through the night, because it was summer and this was the Strip.

A young woman in bright, revealing clothing—dress slit up the right side to her upper thigh; blouse open down to her middle—crossed in front of him at a traffic light. She looked at him and ran her tongue over her red lips in an obvious solicitation. His face twisted and he gunned his engine in sudden need to run the filth down! She leaped out of the way, and shouted, "Fag bastard!"

People turned to look, and he jumped the light and turned south off Sunset at the very next corner.

His nerves were stretched taut. He couldn't go on this way. He'd do something foolish.

He needed the tranquilizing effect of his gun.

He drove home, parking up the street from the house. He walked to the driveway, and the backyard, and got the automatic. He jammed it in his waistband, under his jacket, doing it quickly, almost professionally.

He told himself he wasn't going to use the weapon, was carrying it just for the comfort, and returned to his car.

He turned on the radio as he drove off, tuned to the all-news station. He drove up and down the streets be-

120

tween Sunset and Santa Monica; the dark, quiet, residential streets. A few people walked dogs, or walked briskly, purposefully, for exercise. It was after eleven and time for bed. Soon, no decent person would be outside his home.

The report of Lieutenant Admer's interview came on. "Silencer," they called him. He smiled, his heart leaping. But then came something to make his heart sink. The Negro lived. The Negro appeared to be recovering.

Frank had tried and tried since Monday night to remember if that woolly head had turned all the way toward him before he'd fired. All he remembered was the hand rising toward the window, the face coming around from looking at the whore, the voice beginning to shout an obscenity.

But if Crane had seen him, a description would have been given the news media. The police might hold back some things, but not the description of a wanted man. They depended on the public's help in such matters; handed out composite drawings and the like.

So no one knew about him, yet.

So there was no reason to fear discovery, yet.

And even if a description eventually came from Crane, there was no reason to believe it would be accurate. And even if it turned out to be reasonably accurate, time enough to stop then, to dispose of the weapon and go back to normalcy then.

Normalcy.

He and Lila and Mom.

Mom sicker, less his mother, than before.

Lila as repellent . . .

Just a stage, a phase they were passing through. He and Lila would come back into loving contact again. Mom would recover and there would be no need of nursing homes.

He was sweating. He would have to visit Mom tomorrow. With that Negro lying just a few doors away.

No matter how he tried to block the concept, he began to feel that waiting to act on the Negro was dan-

121

gerous. That he should try to kill him as soon as possible. Take the case and gun to the Intensive Care unit tonight—*right now!*—and visit his mother and leave her room before the nurse came to escort him back to the desk. Watch for the right moment and walk to that other door and step inside and open his case and, blocking it from the glass wall with his body, shoot Crane through the head. Then back to his mother's room, or directly to the desk.

He could do it! With a little luck, it was quite possible!

But then he thought it through again, went over his earlier reasoning, and wondered if it was quite necessary; whether it wasn't more dangerous to act than to wait.

A horn blasted, making him jump. He realized he'd strayed to the right, cutting off a vehicle behind him.

He reached the corner, where there was room for the other vehicle to come alongside on the left. It was a small pickup truck, and the man at the wheel was dark, *Latino*, full of anger. Frank tried to say, "Sorry," but the man leaned toward him, shouting, "*Idiota!* You want I bust your fuckin' face?"

Frank glanced quickly around.

No one.

He put his hand to the gun. He began to answer, "Try it, Spic," so that the man would get out to attack him. Then a bullet would smash that detestable, foreign face.

He dropped his hand. He said nothing. The pickup roared by, cutting in front of him closely, viciously. He managed a smile.

He was beyond wasting time, and bullets, on such ordinary trash. He had a mission. The news media knew it. Everyone knew it.

And remembering that mission finally decided him against trying to kill Crane, also ordinary trash.

He remained at the corner. To the left was home. To the right was the westernmost portion of the Sunset Strip area; its side streets. He hadn't tried there yet.

He turned right.

And thought that tomorrow he could see, hear, and read more about Silencer.

Silencer!

His heart was leaping again.

TEN: *Thursday, August 3, a.m.*

Cloris had thought she would return to her room early, maybe ten-thirty or eleven, allowing Andy to walk her there, maybe giving him a goodnight kiss outside her door, maybe even inviting him inside for ten minutes.

But he'd talked and talked about acting; said he had "a real library" of books on the subject and would lend her "a few of the best." And his apartment was only three or four blocks away.

He'd held her hand in the Old World and said, "*Please*, Cloris?"

She'd had to smile. He was such a straight guy, almost a nerd, and she couldn't see any problems developing.

Besides, she'd wanted him to stay interested in her; wanted him as a friend even if she couldn't see him as anything more than that. So she'd said yes, and prepared herself for some makeout on the couch.

But what had happened was that she'd fallen asleep! They'd been listening to Bob Dylan and sipping white wine, and even though she'd had only one glass, she'd zonked out. She'd felt it beginning to happen, and laughed, and was gone.

Now she was awake, and heard voices.

She tried to look around, and found she was lying in bed on her stomach, her face in a pillow. And then she felt pain. In a very private place.

She cried out and tried to roll over. She found she was groggy, a little sick to her stomach. And hands shoved her back.

A man's voice, deep, said, "I thought you gave her a full Lude?"

Andy's voice said, "I did, right before I phoned you. She was out a good two hours. It's not my fault you showed up at midnight!"

There was the sound of a slap. Andy said, "Oh, Georgie!" but he didn't sound hurt, or even angry. "Let the smelly bitch go. You don't really want her."

Another slap, and Andy began to cry just like a kid. "Too hard, baby!"

"Hold her down," the deep voice said, "or I'll use my fist."

"Why do you treat me this way?" Andy wept. "I get them for you whenever I can. If you'd been here on time, she'd never have known what happened."

Cloris twisted her head around. She was being held down by two men, one Andy, the other a bigger, bearded man. Who was naked from the waist down and had an erection and was just lowering himself onto her. And she too was naked from the waist down, her skirt pushed up, her panties gone, her shoes still on.

The man began to shove his tool into her—into her rectum!

Again she felt pain, and again she yelled.

Andy said, "Take it easy, Cloris. It's just . . . sex, honey. You invited my friend . . ."

"I was drugged," she said, words slurring. "Let me go and I won't say anything."

"You won't say anything anyway," the bearded man said, lifting himself up. "You asked for twenty dollars and I paid you."

"I never . . ." she began, and he shoved her head

126

down, hard. She tried to clear her mind. *Lude* he'd said. Short for Quaalude. Some of the wilder kids had used Q's . . .

"Hand me the baby oil," the man said to Andy. "She's still too tight."

"Listen, George, seriously, I think it's dangerous. I'll take care of your sweet cock . . . ummm . . . don't risk our necks." Again he made the "ummm" sound, and again Cloris twisted her head to look back.

Andy was stroking the bearded man's penis and kissing his mouth. Then he dropped to his knees and began sucking.

The bearded man's head went back; his eyes closed; he began moaning.

Andy made a motion with his hand, jerking his thumb at the door. Cloris realized it was for her, and moved to the edge of the bed. She fell rather than got off, and tried to climb to her feet. But she felt so dizzy, she decided to crawl out.

And kept crawling, stopping in the living room when she saw her purse on the couch; then continued to the door. Where she pulled herself to her feet, swaying, and managed to get the door open.

She was in the pool courtyard, onto which all the apartments in this house opened, and so she was safe. And so she wasn't terrified anymore; she was *enraged!*

If Andy thought she was going to keep quiet about this . . . if the older guy thought his saying she'd done it for money would stop her from going to the police . . . well, they were in for a surprise!

She let go of the door. She stumbled as she moved past the pool, but with each step her head cleared a bit more.

She reached the gate, grabbed it, and rested, taking deep breaths.

She decided she'd better keep moving—couldn't tell what those two animals might do.

She opened the gate, got down three steps by holding tight to an iron railing, and reached the street. It was dark, and empty of people. She looked both ways, and couldn't remember in which direction was Sunset. But she *thought* it was left.

She began to walk. She staggered once or twice, but the clearing-up process continued, and by the time she reached the corner she was doing okay. She paused, trying to see ahead, trying to spot the lights and action of the Strip. But from here, all she could see was another long, climbing street.

Climbing. The streets climbed toward Sunset, and beyond into the hills. She was going in the right direction, thank God!

Now that she was out of danger, she found that she was trembling, was close to tears.

She fought it. She'd cry later, after finding a cop . . .

She realized she couldn't go to the police. She was a runaway. Mom would have reported her missing by now. The cops would arrest her, take her back home, to school and Uncle Bert and everything she hated. Andy Harty or not, she still wanted a job, a good dramatic school, a career in show business.

She crossed the street and started up the second, steeper incline. She was gasping before she'd gone a third of the block, the drug slowing her system, weakening her muscles. She looked around for a place to rest, and there was nothing except the curb.

She'd sat on curbs before. Not so long ago, because she was still a kid. She stepped over and sat down, stretching out her legs, groaning with the pleasure of it.

There was a street lamp about fifty feet further along. She examined her arms, her legs, to see if she was hurt. Nothing, but she felt slightly sore in the behind. Cool there, too, because she was without panties.

A car drove by, slowly, and she realized that her legs were spread out and apart and someone passing by might be able to see up between them. She quickly brought them in and together, but the car was gone. Still, she felt it was time to move on.

She got up and began to walk. What she wanted right now was a shower, to rid herself of the dirty feeling, and then bed. Tomorrow she'd call Verna and Buddy; maybe tell them what had happened. Buddy was pretty tough with his fists. He might pay that queer bastard Andy a little visit and put some lumps on his oh-so-sincere face!

But she knew she wouldn't tell them, wouldn't tell anyone, because she'd been a real fool, been taken like a clown. Luckily, it hadn't cost her too much, hadn't led to anything really serious.

She'd be a lot more careful from now on . . .

Someone was coming down the street toward her. She slowed, straining to see more clearly. Then the figure passed under the street lamp and she saw it was a short, fat man. Looked sort of old.

She relaxed.

But still, she was going to cross to the other side of the street. She'd had enough problems with men for one night!

Except that he called out, "Good evening," and she couldn't just turn away, couldn't just *ignore* him. So she kept walking and mumbled, "Hi," without really looking at him.

A moment later, they were abreast of each other.

He said, "So young to be showing your wares!"

She didn't understand. She turned her head. Into something dark and cold that pressed her forehead.

He said, "I'm Silencer," and the world blew up and she never did understand.

Vivian Garner couldn't sleep. The hotel was quiet enough, being well off Wilshire on the otherwise residential street. And her room was on the fourth floor, the top floor of this small, well-kept Beverly Hills hostelry. Everything was conducive to sleep, and yet she kept twisting about in bed, kept thinking.

She hadn't slept well last night either, after arriving at L.A. International Airport from New York. She'd sat right down to call Harold, since he was the reason for her being here, second-cousin Louise and her husband and three children notwithstanding. Harold, whom she hadn't seen in over seven years; hadn't heard from but once in the last two years. A man who had loved her, as she still loved him, when they'd both been married. A man who had divorced in order to marry her, according to their plan . . . and then she'd panicked, using her daughter Ellie as reason for not going through with the plan. "She's only six. Let's go on as before, and when she's thirteen, fourteen . . ."

He hadn't made a scene, as he'd had every right to do. He'd simply nodded, walked her to the door, and been out of his apartment, and New York, within the week.

He might never have told her where he'd gone. So after six months, she'd had a lawyer make up some papers relating to a mythical debt, and the ex-Mrs. Harold Braeden had kindly forwarded the "legal papers."

Obviously, he'd understood, and hadn't answered for another six months. Then she'd received a letter, saying he had settled in Los Angeles, "am lucky, for an old man of forty-three, to have found a job in a New York agency's West Coast branch, and am currently writing the Great American commercial for bathroom tissue, which is an advertising euphemism for toilet paper." He'd gone on to say that his two sons had visited him during the summer, would visit again at Christmas, "and I expect I'll be a better father from a distance of three thousand miles than I ever was from down the hall."

She'd always loved his speech, his writing, so different from her husband Marty and his garment-industry ways. She'd written back, immediately, that she knew now she'd made a mistake. If he would send for her, she'd file the divorce papers.

He hadn't answered.

She'd written again and again, obsessively, and tried to call, over a period of eighteen months.

His number hadn't been listed and no operator would get it for her.

She'd waited about a year, had written again, and this time received a brief note in reply. She could remember it word for word:

"Dear Vivian: You keep saying you made a mistake

with me. You didn't. People change. I've changed very much since coming to Los Angeles. I'm seeing several women, and enjoying them all. I don't think I'll ever consider marriage again. Yours, Harold."

After a month of stark depression, during which Marty had suggested she see a psychiatrist, she'd taken herself in hand. She was, she had reminded herself, only thirty-nine years old, and from the attention she'd received from men all her life, knew she was an attractive woman. "Goddam *gorgeous!*" as Elliot Freed, her dentist, had exclaimed during their first meeting at a New Jersey motel. He'd kissed her breasts for half an hour. He'd given her cunnilingus for longer than that. She'd had her orgasm . . . and ached for Harold.

She had continued seeing other men—because Harold's "I'm seeing several women, and enjoying them all"—was branded on her brain. Though *she* didn't enjoy them all. Enjoyed fewer and fewer, as another year, then two, then three slipped by.

Still, she'd needed them, needed their attention, their adoration. She was delicately boned, but richly curved in hip and bosom. Her hair was auburn, and while it began needing "rinses" to maintain its highlights, was still her crowning glory, rippling almost to her shoulders in a cut that some people considered too youthful for a woman in her forties.

A woman who had finally asked for and, in a surprisingly low-keyed scene, received her husband's permission to divorce. Marty, it seemed, had long felt he had lost his wife's affection, not to say her love, and was involved in a serious romance with one of the ladies'-wear buyers.

That had been two months ago, and Vivian had written Harold a long letter. She had ended with:

"Whether or not I hear from you, I intend to see you when I arrive in Los Angeles. If you send me a phone number, I will call. If not, I will visit you at your home. I wish only to convince myself that what we once had is completely lost. I can't otherwise accept it, dearest H. *Love*, Vivian."

He had answered the following week. She had the

letter in her purse. It had chilled her . . . but she'd taken comfort from the fact that he had given her his phone number.

"Dear Vivian: I'm now fifty years old. I date—if so innocent a word can be used for what I do—young women in the movie, television, and modeling lines. I *swing*, as that and that alone can stimulate me into a proper physical response. This is partly due to my having been ill with both a kidney and blood disease. I'm not interested, dear girl, in Love. Harold."

As an apparent afterthought, his phone number had been printed underneath.

She'd waited six weeks. Then, having convinced herself he would catch fire once he saw her, she'd made a flight reservation Monday and flown out yesterday, all in a rush, without allowing herself time for further thought.

But fear and doubt had caught her as she'd stepped from the plane. Now, at two in the morning, turning on the lamp and looking at the phone, she said, "For God's sake, call him and be done with it!"

Knowing it was much too late an hour, knowing she was in much too emotional a state, knowing it could be handled far better tomorrow, she picked up the phone and dialed.

The ring sounded six times at the other end. She panicked and began to hang up. And heard the voice say, "Who is it?" *angrily*.

She could still hang up.

She said, "Hello there, Harold. It's Vivian. Hope I didn't wake you. Just flew in on a red-eye flight. I spared you the chore of picking me up, but wanted to make sure I could see you this weekend." She was proud of how cool and certain she sounded.

He said, "Ah . . . Vivian? This weekend? Well, I'm having a little gathering tomorrow night."

"I would think that after persisting for all these years, I've earned an invitation." She tinkled laughter.

"It might be better if we got together Sunday."

"Why not the party too?"

132

"I'm going to be with someone. It would be difficult to talk."

"I won't mind."

He sighed. "I would. Tell me where you're staying, and I'll pick you up Sunday evening at seven."

"Only if you promise to let me see your home. In the Hollywood Hills, isn't it?" She'd looked it up on a street map, which she'd gotten from the Auto Club in New York. She'd fantasized living with him there, her daughter in a good prep school.

"All right," he said, and his voice and attitude seemed to lighten. "It's quite a nice place. Like nothing you can get in Manhattan. Up Sunset Plaza Drive, which is a canyon. Overlooking the entire city. Remote, yet only minutes from the Strip. New Yorkers really don't know how to live."

She was tempted to say, "I'll buy that," but didn't, for fear it would be moving too fast. He'd already begun to loosen up. Just let her get close to him, establish a little body contact, and it would start to come together. He'd never been able to resist her kisses traveling from his lips down his body. He'd never been able to resist her climbing atop him and riding him, breasts dangling before his eyes.

And she'd never been able to resist his large hands gripping her thighs, her backside. His thick organ filling her more completely than any other man's ever had, though she'd had larger organs since. His eyes, brown and bright and compassionate, looking up at her. His voice whispering, "Love you, Vivian, love you, love you," over and over until it ended in orgasm.

She was breathing quickly. She had tears in her eyes. How could she have let him get away? And was she insane to stay in love seven empty years?

"Vivian?"

"Sorry. I'm at the Beverly Hills Stratford. Let me check their stationery for the address."

"I know the place," he said. "We've had clients stay there."

"Sunday at seven," she said, and hung up before the weeping overcame her.

133

She cried for quite a while; then decided she would call Louise in the morning and spend Friday, Saturday, and part of Sunday with her at Malibu. The weather was clear and warm. She would, as Louise had written, "be able to lie around the beach and get a great tan." She would also play with Louise's children, the oldest only five; she had loved her own child most during those precious, pre-school years.

That made her smile . . . and she was finally able to sleep.

Larry Admer sat in his office, four folders on his desk, awaiting delivery of a fifth. That would be Cloris Hendryx's, which would contain only the Preliminary Investigation forms, now being typed up from material he and his men had gathered since discovery of the juvenile's body at two-forty this morning. Damned distressing discovery—little seventeen-year-old high-school girl on the Missing Persons lists only one day. Ran off Tuesday; dead Thursday.

He lit a Camel, drained a container of tepid coffee, and blocked out the ache of compassion. Lots of little runaways, boys as well as girls, died in this town, which was a Mecca for them.

Fucking Hollywood!

He rubbed his eyes. He'd managed to catch four hours of sleep after leaving Larrabee Street, the scene of the crime, but it wasn't enough. Especially since he hadn't gotten back from Diana's place until midnight, and the three hours before being called to Larrabee had been restless ones.

He still didn't know what he was doing with that woman. He only knew he was compelled to go on with her. "At least for a while," he added to himself, as a sop to his pride.

He opened a folder; the one marked Carla Woodruff. It was the thickest, because his men had done a thorough canvass of Lakewood Street. On his orders. And not just because the surviving sister was important to him, but because she insisted Carla

134

Woodruff had no reason to be on that street, especially at that hour.

His instinct was that she was wrong. He felt he was going to prove her wrong, possibly today. And he wanted no accusations that he hadn't looked, and looked hard, for other answers.

He reread the Preliminary Investigations Report: the body had been discovered lying on the sidewalk at a few minutes before midnight, Friday, July 28th, by a young married couple returning from a movie. They had called the police, and when the body was examined half an hour later by ambulance attendants, it was still warm. That and other bodily evidence had eventually led the coroner to estimate time of death at somewhere between eleven and eleven-thirty of the same night. Cause of death was one bullet which had passed through the brain from left rear of the skull to right front. No witnesses had been found, and the Preliminary Report concluded with a description of the victim's identification and possessions.

Larry read this part carefully, as he had the first time he'd seen it Saturday morning. Yet he hadn't mentioned it to Diana. Because she would probably accuse him of sexism, prejudice, whatever label applied to the unproven suspicion that her sister was a hooker.

Carla Woodruff had been wearing what the responding officer had called "a short-skirted, cowgirl-type outfit." When Larry had examined the bloodstained clothing, he'd found it to consist of white boots, a white skirt which had reached to about mid-thigh, dark brown sweater blouse with deep-cut frontage, and underwear with Frederick's of Hollywood labels and very interesting features. Such as a fringed fly-front on the panties and nipple openings on the brassiere, both items in flaming red lace. (There was a notation here in Marv Rodin's spidery hand: "See first Follow-Up Form 314 on Coroner's info.")

Larry flipped ahead, and read that the victim had "trace elements of semen in the vagina." Only traces because she had used "a popular pre-packaged douche

135

shortly before her death, a container of which was found in her purse."

End of note and a referral back to the Preliminary Report, which went on to say that also found in her purse was identification such as a driver's license, and a wallet card listing her nearest living relative, a sister, Diana Woodruff. Diana's home and business addresses had been included, which had led Larry to the massage parlor.

Carla was twenty-six and three months at the time of her death. She had Blue Cross, belonged to the Auto Club, and lived in an apartment house off Franklin Avenue in North Hollywood. Investigators described the house and apartment as "lower middle class." Still, she had been carrying five crisp, new one-hundred-dollar bills in her wallet, but not even one small or normally-worn bill. Which had caused Rodin to write another spidery line:

"Must be a pro, right?"

At the victim's apartment, detectives had turned up a savings-account pass book with deposits totaling three thousand-some odd dollars. Larry had urged them to look for keys—safety-deposit box keys—and included in the Forms 314 this morning was a report stating one such key had been found, along with payment slip from a commercial bank on Ventura Boulevard. Responding to detectives' inquiries, the bank had reported that two names were on the signature card: Carla Searls . . . and Diana Searls.

Searls was the name Diana used at work. Obviously, it was a complete phony, unregistered to her anywhere, and as such would protect not only her reputation but her income.

In this case, it would protect Carla too. And keep a surviving sister from the clutches of the IRS, which audited death in many ways—medical certificates; morgue, police and hospital records; obituary columns—in their never-ending search for inheritance-tax dollars. Unless, as a loyal servant of the law, he himself turned informer.

Another thing occurred to him—Diana had *signed*

136

the card, not just been listed as beneficiary. Which could mean she had known all along what her sister was.

The thought made him rub his eyes again.

But then he thought it through, and it didn't make sense for Diana to create such a fuss over "aspersions," as she'd put it, "cast on my sister's character." The *less* fuss she made, if she'd known Carla was a hooker, the better it would be. The police weren't inclined to smear murder victims, with the possible exception of Mafia hoods.

The media, yes . . . but even they let go after an initial period of sensational revelations. Except in certain kinds of mass murder cases, such as this one, in which they would refer time and again to the killer's taste in victims, and try to fit every victim into that category. Which wasn't going to do little Cloris Hendryx any good either, especially with that initial Coroner's report stating that there was "considerable lubricant and irritation in the rectal area, indicating at least a possibility of anal intercourse."

Well, he'd see what he could do to rob the Mouth and her buddies of that particular tidbit. It had nothing to do with Silencer, just as Carla Woodruff's intercourse had nothing to do with a psycho killer who didn't have time, maybe not even the inclination, to have sex with his victims.

If Cloris Hendryx had had her ass fucked, it was her own business. As for Carla's sex, it was business, period, and he was going to prove it . . . for his own satisfaction if for no other reason. So that Diana couldn't blame *him* for the "aspersions."

He wanted that safety box opened. But unless he could give the D.A. a damned good reason—and that meant something leading to the killer—he doubted he would get a court order.

The easiest way was to ask Diana. He was willing to bet that she had never seen inside that box. It was common enough for boxes to be held in false names, two or more, allowing the survivor to empty it out

137

without disclosing the contents to the tax people. And what better place to keep illegal earnings?

Which brought something else to mind; something that might help him get Diana's cooperation in this matter, if the D.A. said no. Where would *Diana* keep all earnings except those declared by her employer? Where would she keep the tips massage-parlor girls earned for "additional services"?

He didn't want to pursue that line of thought, and picked up the phone. He dialed and asked for Assistant District Attorney Roger Vineland, a man with whom he had established a good rapport over the years. Vineland would get the writ, if anyone could.

The secretary said Vineland was in court. "Can I help, Lieutenant?"

He'd dealt with Mary Cleaver for years, also, as she was half Vineland's efficiency. He said, "Maybe, Mary," and explained his problem.

"I'm afraid not, Lieutenant. They haven't okayed such fishing expeditions since I was a child, and I'd hate to tell you how long *that's* been."

Larry gave her the required chuckle, and hung up. He lit another cigarette and threw the empty pack into the basket. Diana disliked smoking. When he was with her, he smoked very little. Bet she could get him to do something he'd never considered doing—quit. Thinking that she found his mouth, his breath, offensive, made the pleasure of those unfiltered little coffin nails less intense. In fact, it made him stub out his freshly lit Camel and get back to the Follow-Up forms.

One report commented on the fact that the victim's car had been found at her home parked in the basement space allotted to it, and raised the question of how she had gotten to Lakewood Street and how she'd intended to leave. This kind of question-raising was standard procedure, since it concentrated detectives' efforts on finding the friend, the lover, the whatever who had given her transportation—who might either be the murderer, or know who the murderer was. A married lover, for instance . . .

But in the case of Carla Woodruff, this methodology

was, he felt, a waste of time. Because everything could be explained if one simply assumed that she was what all the evidence pointed at: a prostitute who had kept a cover job at a fashionable La Cienega dress shop, and also kept her sister in the dark. A discreet whore who had been picked up and delivered to her client . . . or clients, as the five hundred fresh dollars indicated. Who had been waiting to be picked up and either delivered to another client, or taken home. Who had been killed before her ride arrived; before her pimp or his assistant came to get her.

And why was Vice finding that more and more top-grade hookers were being handled this way when they had cars of their own, or could in many cases be chauffeured by their johns? Because just as in other businesses, inflation and white-collar crime had hit the oldest profession. And with fees reaching two and three hundred a trick, and the hustlers looking to pocket an extra hundred whenever they could, the pimps had to have a sure way of collecting their twenty-five to fifty percent. The surest was to *be* there, and to take their cut of *everything* the girls had on their person. So that hookers were carrying no cash of their own. So that they were being arrested with large, even sums; money fresh from the wallets of their customers.

And this profile the late Miss Woodruff fit in every way.

He continued on through the Follow-Ups.

Carla Woodruff had filed a will and talked about it to the woman who was designer and partner in the dress shop . . . and maybe even her pimp, as women's lib was reaching to great heights, and depths, in Southern California. Diana was the beneficiary of Carla's $25,000 life-insurance policy, and of whatever else was in her estate. Carla had also mentioned that she was, in turn, Diana's beneficiary.

All this reportage was part of standard police procedure—the attempt to establish motive.

Which was of no importance here, considering Silencer and the developing, emerging case against him.

What *was* important was that Larry now could get Diana to open that box for him. And have lunch with her. And, if he handled a delicate situation very carefully, even score a few points as Mr. Nice Guy.

He gave it some thought, and used the phone. She answered sleepily. He said he needed her help and explained about the box.

She said, "I'd rather check it out myself. If there's anything in it to help your case, I'll let you know."

He said, "Right." And then, blandly, "Because of your reciprocal wills and insurance policies, we'll have to search Carla's effects for the key to another safety box."

"Another?"

"Yes. Yours. Under the name of Searls, of course. It's standard that close relatives exchange such services."

"I see."

"Internal Revenue can be sticky about such things." He paused, giving her time to comment. She didn't, and he continued: "If you help me, I'll do my best to help you. I mean, my job should extend only to the victim and *her* effects. I see no reason why *you* should be harassed."

She startled him with a quick laugh. "You'll go far, young man."

He flushed and began to protest. She said, "I never thought about it, but I guess I should have. Carla does have a key to my deposit box. It's on her chain, along with house and car keys."

"I'll have it for you when we meet at the bank."

"I'll dress right now. Say an hour?"

"Make it one o'clock. I have another Silencer murder to work on. Looks like our sick friend is really beginning to roll. A seventeen-year-old girl this time."

"That's horrible." She paused. "But it does bring those odds you talked about into play, doesn't it? With each additional crime, he makes himself more vulnerable, doesn't he?"

"That's the theory," he said, but without much enthusiasm. Because he had a possible eyewitness who

140

had refused to see him yesterday afternoon, insisting he was too sick to be interviewed. Who through his doctor had said he remembered nothing more than he'd already told. Who failed to convince Larry, and strengthened his cop's hunch that he was holding back.

So he'd have to squeeze Mel Crane; begin loosening up that shattered jaw. The D.A. wouldn't be inclined to prosecute a man whose wife had been murdered and who had barely survived a bullet himself—not for a few ounces of pot. But Larry could push him on the PCP content, angel dust being a dirty word in official circles . . .

"You still there?" Diana asked.

"Just making a note to get that key off Carla's chain. In such a way that I won't have to put it back." Which was easy enough, though she couldn't know it. None of the victim's personal effects were important in a psycho-killing case.

"I'm running up quite a tab with you, Larry. Let me know when you want to collect."

She was being playful, and he chuckled—but he would have liked to "collect" right now!

She said goodbye. He reached into his bottom drawer for a fresh pack of Camels; then decided against it. He'd try to stay kissing sweet for lunch. Which made him grin . . . but briefly, since the Preliminary on Cloris Hendryx arrived, complete with pictures. And this was a little girl, a child, and where that hollow-point bullet had exited, her head looked like a smashed tomato.

All the reports and all the detection wouldn't do her any good; probably wouldn't do the next victim any good either. Because what he really needed was the one element that solved more crimes than vital clues, fingerprints, forensic medicine, lie detectors, computers, and brilliant cops: a snitch. A stoolie. An informer.

Though in cases with lone-wolf psycho killers, informers were almost useless.

Which was why a Hillside Strangler or Zodiac Killer or Son of Sam took so long to find, if he were ever found.

141

But still, there might be somebody out there—a wife, a friend, a relative—somebody close to Silencer; somebody who could begin to notice things, realize things . . .

The phone rang. It was The Mouth, asking for an interview on Cloris Hendryx. He said he would try and set up a general press conference for tomorrow. The leader of the Loathesome Foursome said, "Lieutenant, I spoke to Captain Cohen and he said you would make the arrangements for whenever is convenient for *both* of us."

He heard the implied threat of her returning to the captain with a complaint. He said, "I just don't have the time today, Miss Wise."

She said, "I really have to *insist*," her voice crackling.

For a moment his temper flared, and he hunched forward, ready to tell her what he thought of her goddam insistence and her fucking profession.

But he gained control and leaned back, reaching into the drawer for cigarettes.

"Lieutenant? Must we go through this *all* the time?"

He tore open silver foil and tapped out a Camel. "I'll try hard for five o'clock."

"That won't be any good for my show, the early news."

He lit up and inhaled deeply. And there went his kissing-sweet breath.

"Lieutenant! Can I at least have the courtesy of a reply!"

"It's the best I can do, Miss Wise. I'll have the other stations alerted."

She was saying she wasn't concerned with the other stations, when he hung up.

He looked at the photos of the next media sensation—the kid with the hole in her head—and the phone rang again.

"Jess Burdine, Larry."

Larry began reaching for another Camel, to light off the first one. The jock reporter was just what he needed!

"Yeah, Jess."

"Got time for a drink? And a chat about the teen-aged victim?"

"Five o'clock, Jess. A general news conference."

"Between us sodomists . . ." He chuckled, and waited.

Larry groaned away from the phone. He'd asked everyone to keep the lid on that. He'd even made it sound like an important part of a secret M.O.

"You got a nose for news, Jess." What he *really* wanted to say he swallowed, though it had almost emerged.

"And young ass. Remind me to tell you about the football groupies. Beautiful cunt, some even younger than the sodomist . . . what's her name again?"

"Cloris Hendryx. And your information isn't quite accurate. Sodomy is only one possible explanation for her condition. Another could be medical treatment."

"Hey, it's *all* medical treatment, baby."

Larry laughed along with him, and said, "Heavy schedule, Jess. We'll have that drink another time."

"I hope so, man. I'm beginning to think you're dodging this old honky."

"No way. See you."

He was grim-faced as he returned to the Cloris Hendryx folder.

Ten minutes later, Captain Cohen ambled in, big and gray and bear-like. He leaned against the doorjamb and puffed his pipe, filling the room with the sugary aroma of Rum and Maple.

Larry said, "Cal, honest, I just don't have the time . . ."

"Learn to live with it," Cohen interrupted. "I've told you this before—a few times too many, Larry—we have to be media men as well as policemen."

"Police *persons*," Larry corrected, mock-serious.

Cohen smiled. "Right. I'm still learning. We all are. It's a changing world. Almost by the minute, it seems." He tamped his pipe with a little tool. "Five is okay for today's briefing. But try to help them meet their dead-lines from now on."

143

"The Mouth was flapping?"

"And the Jock. He thinks you don't like him."

"I don't."

"Try to. They're going to be with the department every step of the way on Silencer, and it's your case. They're going to be with us on *everything, always.*"

"God help us."

Cohen wasn't smiling any longer. He was nodding. "One reason I'm not too saddened by my impending retirement. But you're staying, Larry. And you can be murdered if your attitude doesn't change. Go back to school. Take some courses in Public Relations."

"How about Public Lying?"

The captain looked up from his pipe. "I'm worried about you, Lieutenant. About your career."

Larry got back to work. He made notes on a long yellow pad. He piled facts in columns, trying to make some sort of police sense out of them.

There was no sense.

It came back to Silencer; to a psycho killer.

Which he'd felt from the first killing—Carla Woodruff's.

But he had to look for alternatives anyway. He was the head of this S.I.T. He had to cover all bases. Including the media.

He wondered if Diana made enough money to keep him in high style. So he could escape this growing pile of shit.

Frank was alone when he stepped off the elevator and walked toward Intensive Care. He'd told Lila he had sales to handle this morning and would visit his mother later in the day. He'd told her to go ahead with her morning visit as he wasn't sure just when he'd be free. "Please call," he'd said, "to let me know how she is."

She called at ten. She'd been careful in her choice of words, but Frank knew his mother wasn't any better.

Still, he'd left immediately for the hospital, his purpose accomplished—to be certain he wouldn't run into

Lila. They'd had a bad night last night. She'd wanted to make love.

He shuddered, coming up to the nurses' desk.

He hadn't been able to.

He hadn't wanted to for a long time, perhaps a year, perhaps longer. But he'd forced himself, done his duty. Until a month or so ago.

He didn't remember the exact date, but he remembered the exact circumstances.

They'd been in bed. She'd come up against him, having stripped off her nightgown. He'd tried caressing the big body, the massive buttocks cold with fat, the flabby thighs rippling with cellulite. She'd pulled his head down to her breasts. He'd found the nipples with his mouth, and this had always been his major point of excitation: her big, solid breasts.

But over the years, they had become as flabby and unattractive as the rest of her. And that night, a few days before the Fourth of July, he had failed for the first time to attain an erection.

He'd asked her to help him by kissing his penis, but of course she'd said no, as she always did.

She'd jerked it, impatiently, and the more she'd jerked the limper he'd gone. Until she'd twisted away, saying, "God knows what you do to waste your energy! I wouldn't put it past you to be hiring some slut! Or to be playing with yourself!"

He'd left the bed then. He'd been humiliated, and terribly angered. Humiliated because she was so sure no woman would give herself to him except for money. Angered because something in him knew his manhood was being twisted, destroyed by this woman, by this life he led, by this home with wife and mother in awful combination against him.

Later, he'd reasoned anger away.

Later, he'd talked to her, shamefaced, apologetic, saying he hadn't been feeling well. She'd taken him to see Dr. Beiner.

It would all come around, the elderly GP had assured him. They now knew a good deal about human sexuality, through Masters and Johnson. The important

145

thing was not to press the issue, not to allow a sense of strain and failure to develop.

Beiner had then called Lila in to join them, and advised their taking "a little vacation from sex, say three or four weeks. Then try again, with a lot of foreplay . . ."

The "little vacation" had lasted until he had returned to the house at one a.m. last night, this morning, and Lila had been waiting, in a rage. She'd ranted about his "gallivanting about, and don't tell me there isn't a prostitute involved!"

So he'd tried to "prove" he hadn't been with a woman. And drained of that *other* need, satisfied by that *other* explosion, he'd had nothing left for her.

Luckily, she'd reacted in a different manner this time: she'd run weeping to the bathroom and locked herself inside.

Luckily, because he didn't know if he could have tolerated another insulting attack on his manhood. Didn't know if he could have resisted the temptation to get the gun and rid himself of her forever. Which would have destroyed him too.

And he had much to live for now. More and more to live for with each of Silencer's triumphs.

He smiled at the nurse, and asked to see his mother. She said, "In a moment, Mr. Berden, when Nurse Hayes returns to escort you."

He nodded and looked at his watch. Ten-thirty. But he was ready for lunch. He'd had only a cup of coffee this morning. Because Lila had been too upset to cook, and he'd been anxious to leave her presence.

Still, they'd made up. He'd promised to see Beiner again and take vitamin E and do whatever else the doctor recommended to "revitalize" himself. She'd nodded, and said she was sorry she'd accused him of seeing prostitutes . . . and then, just when it seemed they could part amicably, she'd burst forth with a bitter laugh.

"What would you want with a prostitute when you can't *do* anything?"

He'd contained his own bitterness, his need to reply

that he could *do* with any reasonably attractive woman, but not with a *whale*.

And had driven dangerously fast, erratically, trying to leave behind that bitterness . . . and also the deeply hidden fear that she was right.

The nurse was opening the door for him, and he followed her into the U-shaped unit. And forgot Lila; forgot everything, including his mother, as he saw that door, first along the U's central section, where the Negro was. Where the man who should've been dead was. The only person who could menace Silencer.

He wanted to ask about Crane, but they had reached his mother's room—the second along the first wing—and he felt it might seem strange to show too much interest.

"They told me you were dead," his mother said, raised in a half-sitting position, head still bandaged, fluttering her hands, eyes wild-looking.

"She's been very excitable this morning," the nurse murmured.

"What lies is she telling you, Franklin?"

That was what she had called his father. Her son had been Frankie, and was now Frank.

"So please be agreeable to whatever she says. And stop by the desk before leaving. The doctor has asked to speak to you."

"I won't have it!" his mother said, voice shrill. "Whispering in corners! I want to go home, Franklin!"

"Soon, Mother," Frank said, steeling himself as the nurse left.

"Mother?"

He came to the bed. He pulled up a chair and sat down. "We'll have a nice chat. We'll discuss your coming home and how Lila and I can make your recuperation as pleasant as possible."

"Lila and you?"

He leaned forward and took her hand; her shriveled, speckled hand. There was a fetid odor about her— urine and feces and deteriorating flesh.

Oh, God, that age should rob him of someone who'd always been there, strong and sure and supportive!

147

Someone whose love had made this world bearable; this world revealed as ugly when he'd first left her for school and a progression of defeats. Whom he'd lost when he'd married. Whom he'd regained when his father had died and he'd insisted she come to live with another part of his defeat, Lila. Who had again brought him joy, briefly, before age began taking her mind from him. Who had then slowly started to become part of the ugliness and defeat.

Who was now the worst part of this ugly world.

"You're not my husband?"

He dropped his head. He couldn't speak. It was too much.

"SILENCER STRIKES AGAIN!" the front-page headline of his morning newspaper had read.

He brought the big black letters before his mind's eye. He held to them. He gained strength and purpose from them. And looked at his mother.

"I'm Frank, your son," he said. "Please remember that."

Something in his voice reached the old woman, and frightened her. She drew her hand away. "All right. When can I go home?"

"Soon."

"Not today?" Her voice trembled.

"No, not today." He felt his power over her. "When I say so. But soon, I promise."

"Good, good," she muttered, and kept her eyes on him, and said, "My little boy was always gentle, easily startled. You're sure you're my son?"

He said, "Give me your hand."

She hesitated. He half rose and leaned over the bed, holding his breath against the odor. He took her hand and drew it toward him, firmly, against some resistance, until he could sit comfortably.

"Your little boy is finally growing up, Mother."

He held her eyes with his. And smiled.

They sat there. She breathed heavily at first, and her eyes kept blinking, and he knew she was afraid. But he kept smiling, kept holding her hand, firmly, and soon

148

her breathing slowed and her eyes closed and her hand lay loosely in his.

She slept.

He released the hand.

And was released by the hand, rising and standing over her, freed finally of his mother.

He took a deep breath, and went to the door. No more Mommy. But that was all right. He no longer needed her. He had something else.

He walked quickly, eyes and face averted from the Negro's room and glass panel. At the desk, he said that the other nurse had mentioned something about the doctor wanting to see him.

"Oh, yes, Mr. Berdon. Just a moment." She used the phone, murmuring into it, and hung up. "The doctor will be here in a moment. Why not take a seat in the waiting room?"

He went outside and took one of the plastic chairs. He sat still and empty. His mother was gone. But he would honor her shell, her dying body. He would take her out of here soon and so avoid the Negro's room. And with that would no longer be endangered.

A tall, darkly-bearded man came along and looked at him. "Mr. Berdon?" Frank nodded. "I'm Dr. Herrera."

Frank nodded again, slowly, mouth pursing a little, because a Captain Herrera—or some such Hispanic name—had adjudged him UNSAT thirteen years ago after he'd mistaken the village couple for Vietcong and done what he'd been taught to do to Vietcong.

But he never thought of that brief period of his life. Absolutely never. Because it was full of foolishness, and the usual defeat.

"We can't do much more for your mother here," Herrera was saying. "Her concussion was a mild one, and in a physical sense is healing rapidly. Her broken hip is more serious, but doesn't require Intensive Care. We'll move her to a regular room in a day or two . . ."

"Then I can prepare to take her home? Say in a week?"

"I think you should consider a nursing home."

"Oh, my wife and I are quite willing to nurse my mother until she recovers."

"If you mean until she recovers the use of her limbs, that's one thing. And not a simple thing, since her hip will take months, and then she'll need therapy before she's fully ambulatory. If you mean until her mind clears, that's something else entirely. The concussion seems to have accelerated the onset of senility."

Frank stood up. "That's a guess, Doctor."

Herrera must have sensed antagonism, because his voice sharpened. "Yes, but an educated guess. And here's another: you won't be able to handle her."

"It's an American tradition to care for one's own."

"Is it? Then why do we have more nursing homes than any nation on earth?"

Frank began moving past him, toward the hallway.

"Mr. Berdon, I know you're upset. And you're to be commended for wanting to help her. But the best way to help her is to let professionals do it."

Frank nodded, to cut the nonsense short.

"At least until she's able to walk again. Because bedpans and sponge baths are a severe strain on the family. Think of your wife. Think of the daily details."

Frank said he would, and "Thank you," and walked away.

But he couldn't think of those things.

They made him sick.

And how could he abandon the person who had once been the most important in the world, to strangers?

What other choice did he have if he considered "the details"?

He was starving.

He drove to Canter's in the middle of the old Jewish community of Fairfax. He had a huge lunch. He read his newspaper. The details of the murder of Cloris Hendryx "were still sketchy," but he savored what little there was. And thought ahead to the radio, and better still the television.

SILENCER STRIKES AGAIN!

He tipped the waitress more than she deserved. He

walked along Fairfax, looking in the strange little shops that sold Jewish religious articles. He was in no hurry. Martin could handle things. He burped covertly, and smiled at the funny Jewish accents. He chuckled at one bumptious old woman jabbering away at a caftaned little man. But then a voluptuous young woman swung by, full breasts quivering beneath a bright blouse, laughing at a bushy-haired boy. And he whispered under his breath: "Watch out, *whore!*" and went to his car.

ELEVEN: *Thursday, August 3, p.m.*

Mel was having lunch, which consisted of beef broth and chocolate milk with an egg beaten into it, both sucked up into the tiny opening in his facial cast through a long glass straw. There was always the backup nourishment provided by intravenous feeding into his arm, but he was getting less and less of that and more stomach food.

He was definitely feeling better. Sensation and movement were returning to his limbs; to his entire body.

Including his cock, he discovered, when the knockout chick appeared at his door. She was escorted by a nurse, the Chicano with the big ass, whom he'd begun to notice, but the chick with her was the real thing, hot from the Strip or he didn't know fox from hound! His eyes drank her in, from spike heels to long, dark hair, and what lay between was much more than Tits and Ass, as the show-song went. And caused a stirring in his groin that he welcomed with joy, then sweated down as he wondered whether he would be able to move so as to hide a hard-on.

The nurse said, "Your friend said you'd want to see

153

her. Since she's so much nicer-looking than that detective, I thought so too." She smiled.

The chick also smiled—*stunning!*—and said, "Hello, Mel. Feeling up to it?"

He said, *"Ohoho!"* to himself, meeting those wise eyes, and didn't give a damn that he'd never seen her before. He nodded in the slow, careful manner he'd cultivated so as to avoid pain. He also grunted, once, loud and clear, in the "yes" signal the cop had established, that he now used with everyone here.

But he could also form a few words—he'd practiced in private—and with this visitor he might take the wraps off his communication skills. Maybe one of his friends had sent her as a get-well present?

The nurse said, "It's twelve. I'll give you until twelve-fifteen. That should be long enough."

He grunted, thinking that a week ago it would have been long enough for more than she'd ever dreamed of! The chick smiled her wise smile and they were on the same wavelength and he wondered if she danced in a club or worked a massage parlor or what. She didn't look the type to work the streets. In fact, she had too much class for the nudes and the parlors . . . but there was that eye contact, that street-wise aura. And what the hell was she doing here?

The nurse left. The chick came over and sat in the bedside chair. He turned his head and looked at her. And enunciated with very minor lip movement, "One . . . grunt . . . yes."

"Thank you for seeing me, I'm Diana Woodruff. My sister, Carla, was the first victim . . ."

He grunted sharply. He'd read everything the papers, and the latest issue of *Newsweek* given him this morning by his doctor, had on the fat fuck. His heart began to beat strongly. He and this fox were on the same wavelength, all right, but not the way he'd first thought.

Her eyes followed his to the table; to the papers and magazine. "I read everything too." She glanced around the room. "No television. *That's* a treat. When they

154

move you out of Intensive Care, you'll have a set, and get a lot more about Silencer than you'll want."

He waited; they looked at each other; then she leaned forward and spoke softly. "I want to find that animal. I want to punish him. Not the way the law would, which could be as little as ten or twelve years of actual prison time, if he has a good lawyer."

He grunted. Oh yes, the same wavelength.

"Or a mental institution, since the more he kills the more likely they are to judge him insane."

He nodded. He said, straining for clarity, "Kill . . . bastard."

"Yes. But you're in a hospital bed, and you might be immobile for months. While I'm in a perfect position in regard to a psychotic like this one—out there on the Strip, in a massage parlor, just what he wants. If I knew who to look for, I could set up a situation where I'd seem an easy victim . . ."

He sighed. He dropped his eyes. Classy chick, but dreaming a game she wasn't equipped to play. Movie game. TV game. It didn't happen that way.

It happened through the cops. In which case what she said about Silencer not getting enough punishment came true.

It happened through a contract. If he could get word to the right people, and feed them enough information, and they got lucky.

It happened through Mel Crane—if that was the only way—searching forever, watching faces, waiting and hoping. And spotting the fat fuck one day and doing him in very slowly, very creatively.

It didn't happen through foxy chicks and their fantasies.

She then proved she was not only foxy but smart and intuitive. "I know it seems silly. But consider that Lieutenant Admer is a friend of mine."

His eyes snapped back to her.

"He wants to become a *close* friend. He's keeping me informed of every development. From what he *hasn't* told me, and from the news media, I know you

155

haven't given much of a description of the man who killed your wife. And I think I know why."

He didn't bother grunting or sighing or trying to speak. She was making more sense than he'd expected. He waited for her deal.

"Why don't we help each other? Neither one of us wants the police to find Silencer. It just won't satisfy us. Why don't we exchange whatever information we now have, or will get in the future? We can work separately, each in his own way. Whoever finds him will certainly do what will satisfy the other."

She paused. He nodded, but very slightly.

"Even if you think I'm not equipped to do such a job . . ."

His eyes slid, then, over her breasts and legs.

She nodded. "It'll help, considering what Silencer seems to hate most."

"What . . . I . . . love . . . most."

"Bravo," she said. "You'll soon be able to tell me what he looks like, won't you?"

"May . . . be."

"I'll be visiting again, in the hope that you'll change that maybe to a yes."

He held her eyes . . . and then, once again, but very slowly, slid his over her body. And the stirring in his groin grew, pushed against the hospital gown and thin sheet.

She glanced at the glass panel, and half rose, speaking loud enough for anyone passing the door to hear:

"I'll adjust that for you, Mel." She bent over him, lips touching the oval mouth opening in his cast . . . and gently squeezed the bump in the sheet. As he gasped, she murmured, "I'll come prepared next time."

He said, "Now . . . please!" though he didn't expect she would trade for nothing.

She surprised him.

She looked around, went into the bathroom, and came out with a white washcloth. She sat down and began talking in that loud, cheerful voice. He didn't understand a single word, because her hand was under the sheet, inside the nightgown, grasping his penis. Be-

156

cause she was stroking him and he was feeling the good feeling, the great feeling, and finally the greatest feeling in the world.

She caught his ejaculation in the washcloth, folded it, and put it in her purse. She adjusted his gown and the sheet. When the nurse came to the door, she was sitting back quietly.

"Afraid your time is up. Say goodbye now." She turned away from the door, giving them a last moment of privacy.

He said, "Owe . . . you."

"Not necessarily. I can't bargain with some people. For example, a man trapped in a hospital bed, attacked by passion."

He stared at her. Was she too slick? Was she psyching him?

She touched his hand, and rose. "I'm sorry about your wife." She started to go.

He said, "Dian . . . ah. Thank . . . you."

She kept walking, and was gone

Maybe slick. Maybe psyching him. But he didn't feel it in his street-wise gut.

There were good and bad chicks on the Strip. Class and low chicks on the Strip.

He'd loved Beth-Anne, but had known she wasn't much good; known that he outclassed her.

Diana Woodruff was something else again. Diana was a class act, beyond him in some ways. And above all, a good chick.

The old pimp knew it, no matter how badly he wanted to tell himself she was trying to use him . . . because then he could follow his plan to keep the fat fuck's description to himself.

The old pimp knew he couldn't play a good chick for a sucker.

Of course, the old pimp also knew *he* was a sucker, when it came to white foxes.

He moved his arms a little, his legs a little. A little each half-hour. A little more each hour or two.

He'd slept only once since awakening at seven this morning, and that for a brief fifteen minutes at ten. He was staying awake longer and longer periods of time. But now his eyelids grew heavy and the shadows rolled across his brain.

Still, it was less like passing out; more like a sweet nap after a good piece . . .

They stood together in the booth off the bank's vault room. Diana opened the double-sized safety box; Larry Admer looked over her shoulder.

She let out breath in an explosive sigh.

The box was packed with sheafs of bills, mostly hundreds, a few fifties.

She pulled out the chair and dropped into it. "I didn't know her at all."

She felt his hand on her shoulder, and said, "Aren't you going to say, I told you so?"

He didn't say anything.

She reached into the box, as she'd often reached into her own. She began to count the money, and said, "Help me."

He bent over her, taking out several sheafs.

Later, he said, "I've got thirty-eight thousand some-odd."

"Thirty-five . . . a little more," she murmured, stunned. "Seventy-three thousand total. A busy girl, my kid sister. Probably hooking since she came to join me in Los Angeles. Maybe even before I started at the massage parlors."

But what she was thinking, what was stabbing her heart, was that Carla had followed the example big sister had provided. And that it had eventually killed her.

"Oh, God!" she said, realizing again that she *had* to find Silencer, and no longer only for a *raison d'etre,* or revenge. But to expiate her culpability in her sister's way of life; to stop guilt before it could grow and take over her mind. She had enough going against her without *that!*

Admer's hand was back on her shoulder. She looked up at him. She waited for him to say something about all this money. All this illegal money.

He began putting it back in the box. She joined him.

"What happens now?" she asked, closing the lid.

"Now we have lunch."

"With *this*, I mean?"

He shrugged. "You're sole owner of the box. Anything in it is yours."

"What about you?"

"Officially, it's none of my business and I don't know anything about it. I don't love the Internal Revenue Service any more than anyone else does, so why do their work for them?" He paused, "Unofficially is something else again."

"Ah," she said, and waited.

He bent close to her. "You're paying for lunch."

She stared at him. "That's it?"

He straightened, and she saw the flush moving into his cheeks. He blushed easily for a cop.

"You're a rich woman now, Diana. A hell of a lot richer than I'll ever be. If I'm out of your class, let me know!" He opened the door and left the booth.

She was richer than he could guess. Her own safety box held only forty thousand, but that had been placed there in the last three years, and she'd lived and spent liberally off the contents, unlike Carla who'd lived tight. She had another fifty thousand invested in her condominium, which had just about tripled in value. With Carla's seventy-three, and her *declared* earnings over the years, she was worth well over two hundred fifty thousand.

Which meant that if she could find Silencer, if she could do what her insides demanded she do, she could leave this town, maybe even return home to St. Louis and start over again. With a quarter of a million, she could go back to school in leisurely fashion, train to teach literature as she'd once planned . . .

She sighed. Daydreams. She was a long way from finding Silencer, despite being sure she could get Mel Crane to tell her whatever he knew.

And Mr. Straight-Arrow cop waiting outside might have a change of heart once he realized she wasn't going to fall madly in love with him, no matter *what* he did, no matter how old-movie-hero he played it. She might yet have to part with a good-sized piece of Carla's money, or face the IRS in court.

Which was why she smiled at him as she came outside, and murmured, "Don't be angry. You're too good to be true."

He flushed again, but with pleasure this time.

She followed the attendant into the vault room and waited as he locked the box into place. She looked back at Larry Admer, tall and hard and fair . . . handsome, you could say. And thought how naturally she'd reacted with Mel Crane. How easy it had been to relieve him, despite feeling nothing besides compassion. How simple it was when dealing with street people, or customers, or anyone with simple needs.

There was far more excitement in her relationship with Larry Admer. She'd become aware of it on their last date. And yet, despite wanting to keep him firmly on her side, she couldn't visualize doing to him what she'd done to Crane. It would have to be artifice, stratagem, planned from stroke one. Because his need for her wasn't simple, and she would have to pretend more than a simple response.

She thanked the attendant as he handed her the key. She followed him to where Admer waited, fiddling with one of the unfiltered cigarettes he smoked . . . smoked more often when he was tense or nervous, she'd observed.

They walked outside onto Ventura Boulevard, the San Fernando Valley's super street. They walked a little further to an Italian restaurant he said was among the best, and entered the dimness of a large, leather-and-darkwood room, a type of place popular in Los Angeles and especially the Valley.

It was her experience that such places concentrated more on liquor than on food. And from the waiter's near-shock at their both refusing cocktails, she thought this would fit the mold.

But the linguini with white clam sauce was excellent, and her taste of Larry's Lobster Fra Diavolo showed they knew how *not* to bury shellfish in tomato sauce.

When she complimented him on his choice of restaurants, he nodded sourly. "I know. Surprising for a cop, right?"

She shrugged. "You could say the same about me and my taste. Surprising for a jerk-off artist."

He stopped eating, staring at his plate.

She hadn't meant to be so rough. Things just seemed to pop out of her with this man.

He reached into his jacket and came out with cigarettes. She said, "Could you wait until I finish?"

He stood up, muttered, "Men's room," and walked away.

She continued eating, enjoying the pasta more now that she was alone.

She was accustomed to eating alone . . . except for those weekends with Carla.

Carla.

She discovered she didn't feel like being alone right now, and sipped water and waited for Larry Admer to return.

Carla was to be buried this Saturday.

She wanted to make certain Admer would be with her.

When he returned, he picked up his fork and said, "Sin to waste good food. My mother would force us to finish everything. When I see the amount of food people leave on their plates, it makes me sick."

"We never had that trouble at home. Portions were always small. Except with pork and beans, and spaghetti. We got as much of those as we wanted." She too picked up her fork. "I liked everything, except prunes."

He chuckled. "My father said he hated prunes as a boy. But become an adult, he said, and you get to need them."

"Your parents live in L.A.?"

"Dead, both of them."

"I'm sorry. They must have been relatively young. Was it illness?"

"The Southern California disease, as a buddy in Traffic calls it. Three-car collision on the San Diego Freeway—four fatalities. Seems my father was

161

speeding. I was in boot camp at the time, or I might have been with them. We went everywhere together."

Before she could ask about his military service, he said, "Tell me something about your work. I can't believe you're very involved with your . . . customers."

"I'm not, most of the time."

"Then you get to feel something *some*times?"

"Yes. Though even when I feel something, it's gone the moment the customer is gone."

He looked at his plate. He moved his fork around, but he wasn't eating. "You ever been in love?"

"Of course." The question annoyed her, seeming to indicate she was somehow less than human. "Hasn't everyone?"

He looked up quickly. "I didn't mean . . ." He shook his head.

He had red sauce on his mustache. She reached out with her napkin and dabbed it.

As she withdrew her hand, he caught it and kissed the wrist. "I don't think I've ever been in love," he said. "And I've been married. And I have a son."

"You love your child, don't you?"

He kissed her fingers, and let go. "Not really. Not as I imagine loving should be."

She was surprised.

He changed the subject back to her. "You must get some awful freaks at work. How do you handle them? You didn't even have a bouncer, a guard, when I came to tell you about Carla."

"Mostly we do have a guard. It just so happens I'm not fond of the types my boss hires. They're more trouble than the rare freaks. *Very* rare, in my experience."

He was eating, his eyes on his plate. He said, through a mouthful of food, covering whatever emotion he was experiencing, "What kind of freaks have you had?"

She could have laughed off the question, changed the subject, refused to answer. But somehow, she didn't.

"Well, I was reading *Portnoy's Complaint* some

162

years ago, and a college-boy client began discussing the book with me. He asked if I'd reached the part where Roth's hero masturbates into a piece of raw liver." She paused to sip water, and to look at Admer. His eyes were buried in the ruins of his lobster. "I said yes, and he asked if I would do that for him."

Admer looked up. "Do what?"

"Masturbate him into a piece of raw liver. I said he'd have to supply the liver." She laughed, both at the memory, and at Admer's expression. "So he did, and I did. Then he wanted me to come to his apartment for dinner. He offered a hundred-dollar tip if I would share that same piece of liver with him broiled just as it was."

Admer said, "Christ, Diana." And, "Did you?"

She laughed again. "I make it a policy never to meet clients outside the parlor."

He shook his head.

She said, "He was absolutely harmless. I've had a few that weren't so harmless. For example: The distinguished older gentleman who suddenly tried to tear my breasts off. I mean, *literally*. And the man who turned out to be a woman who turned out to have a bayonet taped to her side and used it to force me into my one and only lesbian experience. And a popular rock singer disguised with a wig and putty nose who brought his dog along and asked me to have sex with it and choked me when I . . ."

"Okay," Admer said, hand rising. "Enough."

She resumed eating. She had almost cleaned her plate, and wondered if he would notice. He seemed to be having trouble cleaning his own.

She laughed a little . . . but then she remembered Saturday, and was afraid she had gone too far with him. And couldn't understand why she seemed compelled to upset him, annoy him, hurt him. When she needed him, and not just for Saturday but until Silencer was destroyed.

She touched his hand. "You really shouldn't ask about my work."

"I know. But I thought that if we could talk about it . . . if I could learn to accept it, at least a little . . ."

"You'll never accept it."

"Probably. And now that you have enough money without it, why not quit?"

Because she had to be bait for Silencer.

But she couldn't tell him that.

She said, "I'll consider it. In the next few weeks."

He took the hand that was touching his. "Something's happened to me, Diana. I . . ."

"Larry," she said, stopping him. "I'm burying my sister Saturday. I can't think of such things yet."

He nodded, and checked his watch. He said he had to get back to the station.

And she had to see Arthur about working tonight.

Late this morning, after she'd finally gotten a decent night's sleep, Vivian Garner had made her call to Louise, arranged with the hotel to check her out tomorrow and check her back in Sunday, and then done some sightseeing. Utilizing the limousine service her hotel provided, she'd gone to Universal Studios, because friends had described the tour as interesting.

Perhaps, but it hadn't provided *her* with much interest. She'd considered the sets and stages worth looking at and hearing about—for fifteen or twenty minutes—but the main attraction, the "special effects" from films and TV shows, were cheap and tawdry to her way of thinking. As had been the films and shows that spawned them. Space monsters, mechanical sharks and plastic avalanches were nice for children, or those who had never experienced the pleasures of truly adult entertainment—the films and plays, the ballets and operas, the symphony concerts and fine books, that opened the emotions through the mind, not the lower intestines.

And looking around at her fellows on the seemingly endless trip through the studio, she'd realized she was indeed out of place. There'd been no one she could relate to, except perhaps the wide-eyed children. There'd been camera snappers and loud guffawers and

Gee-whizzers. And two very young women in practically no clothing at all—the so-called disco-look of shiny shorts and slit-to-the-waist skirts, of nipple-tight tee shirts and plunging-necked blouses, of heels that climbed toward the heavens and threw legs and buttocks into sharp relief.

It was these two girls who had most annoyed her. They'd flirted and flaunted on the open bus, breathlessly approached every non-tourist male while walking through the sets and stages, and eventually managed to pass on some information—obviously telephone numbers—to no less than three men near the studio commissary. Mature men, who should have known better . . . or at least had better taste!

She'd thought then of Harold's last letter, of his reference to "young women in the movie, television and modeling lines." And told herself there was no way a man of his education and intelligence would be attracted to trashy hoydens such as *these!*

She had finally been released from growing tension when the tour ended and she hurried to the hotel limo. My God! No wonder they had a woman-killer in L.A.! Some of these little *demi-mondes* deserved it!

Back at the hotel, she'd had a quick martini at the bar, and gone to her room. Where she'd called the desk, giving in to an impulse. Not a sudden impulse by any means; the thought had been with her since she'd stepped off the plane yesterday. The thought that had urged her to rent a car and drive past Harold's house . . .

Now, showered and dressed in one of her best summer chiffons (Harold might just happen to step out of his home), she ate a room-service dinner of chicken sandwich and iced coffee, waiting for the desk to call that her rental car was out front. Which happened, as promised, at precisely five-thirty.

She hurried downstairs, where she received detailed instructions on how to use the Ford's accessories from an aging black attendant, and even more detailed instructions on how to reach her destination. "You're just a couple miles away, on main surface streets."

"Surface," he explained, was Los Angelese for any non-freeway road. She chuckled and tipped him and thought that this city would turn out to be charming, wait and see. And with a good deal of excitement, drove to the corner, which was Wilshire Boulevard, and turned right . . . into considerable rush-hour traffic, something she hadn't considered.

But she'd experienced worse in Manhattan, and after a few moments of adjustment, proceeded coolly enough. To Doheny, where she made a left and began climbing toward distant hills, dramatically etched by sunlight and shadow, something you couldn't find in New York City, even if you somehow could manage to see through the grimy skyscrapers.

She was smiling. She was building her liking for Los Angeles, because Harold lived in Los Angeles. And because she might too, some day.

She reached Sunset Boulevard and made a right, into even heavier traffic. She had to concentrate on the road, but she was also compelled to look around. So she pulled to the right and, despite an occasional blare of horn, reduced speed to a minimum.

She looked at billboards extolling movies, Vegas hotels, entertainers, and especially rock stars and groups. At club signs promising "Topless-Bottomless Totally Nude Dancers." At a surprisingly high percentage of exotic automobiles: Rollses, Ferraris, Mercedes-Benzes, Jaguars, classic vintage cars . . . almost all headed in the opposite direction from hers, which was to say west, toward Beverly Hills. And especially at the glut of pedestrians, some obviously tourists, but far more young men and women, flamboyantly and revealingly dressed, at least by her Saks's and Bloomingdale's standards.

She tightened inside at this last observation.

The large green sign she'd been told to watch for appeared, and she turned left off Sunset and into the Hills, up a road which was at first wide and comfortable, lined by large houses, some of them true mansions. Then it began climbing steeply, narrowed, and twisted in S's and hairpins, reminiscent of Swiss mountain roads. And the view from Sunset Plaza Drive was as good as those Swiss views, in its own way: an enormous, spread-out, sun-washed city stretching to the gray-glinting Pacific.

She continued climbing. The houses grew smaller and more contemporary in design, hanging to cliffsides, composed in great part of sundecks and slabs of glass, exciting her with their lack of Eastern conventionality.

The addresses had reached the high two thousands. And as she came around a turn, she saw it: A small, cantilevered house, all redwood and glass walls and doors. A heart-catching house . . . and her heart caught and she whispered: "Here I am, darling H. A few years late, but here anyway."

She drove slowly past a carport just off the narrow road. And there *he* was, getting out of a green Jaguar sedan!

She wanted to race away. And she wanted to look at him.

Slowing to a crawl, she looked. At a man leaner, with much more gray in his hair than seven years ago. At a man whose smile brought out lines of age; a man who made her heart catch far more than a house, or any other man, could.

She also found herself looking at a woman who was just emerging through the car door he held open.

No, not a woman. A *girl*, perhaps nineteen, perhaps a little more, but far too young for him. A beautiful, theatrical girl with long, jet-black hair, wearing tight silver shorts, a black blouse with plunging neckline, and silver sky-high shoes. A girl who came upright from the car, and against him, laughing . . .

And Vivian was into another hairpin turn, losing sight of them.

She stamped on the gas, accelerating dangerously, and reached the next house. She used its driveway for her U-turn, and sped back. But there was only the Jaguar. They'd gone inside.

They. Her dearest H, and one of his Hollywood "dates."

She drove back down to Sunset Boulevard, far more

quickly than she should have on the twisting road, and saw the cluster of fine clothing shops near the canyon's entry. She made a sudden decision, and went into a parking lot. She walked to a shop; then to another. She was amazed at how much a reasonably good, reasonably stylish, sexually oriented outfit could cost.

She put seven hundred dollars on her American Express Card, and found a phone booth. She called Louise to say she would have to be back at her hotel earlier than she'd planned—by noon Saturday—because that was when her dress would be ready for final fitting. She then followed a salesgirl's direction to a "knockout shoe store" on Santa Monica Boulevard that "carries everything in heels, platforms, klunkers." From there she was directed to a shop on Hollywood Boulevard that specialized in "theatrical undies"—what Vivian immediately classified as *whores'* undies. What she laughed at, blushed at . . . even as she selected and purchased.

But once out of the store, she stopped laughing. She drove directly to the hotel, went to the bar, and sat solemnly for half an hour with two martinis. She was engaged in a serious business. The black G-string panties, the matching mesh brassiere, the garter belt and design-woven black stockings, the shorty nightgown of wispy pink that revealed all that standard nightgowns were supposed to hide; these along with the sexy dress and shoes comprised her uniform, her armor for a war that would determine the remainder of her life. A war scheduled to begin on Sunday night.

When she would enter into combat with Harold's "dates."

The eleven o'clock news carried an interview with that lieutenant in charge of the case . . . *his* case, Frank thought, watching television with Lila. There was also an interview with a sobbing woman—the young slut's mother—who said, "Cloris was an innocent child, a confused runaway," and similar garbage.

"Poor thing," Lila said. "Times like these, I'm glad we never had children."

She'd blamed that on him too, though they'd never really tried to have a child. And when in shame and anger, he'd been forced to defend himself by suggesting they take tests to determine who, exactly, needed help in the conception process, she'd somehow put it off.

Which had suited him fine, since he'd dreaded being named the guilty party.

Not that he'd ever wanted a child with her.

And not that she'd ever wanted a child with him.

So what were they doing together?

The story on Silencer ended, and he turned to another channel and picked up their film of the interview. Lila said, "Must we hear about that frightening maniac over and over?"

"Frightening, yes," he murmured, "but what makes you think he's a maniac?"

She stared at him. "He's killed three women for no reason! What would *you* call him?"

"We can't say he has no reason. We don't know . . ."

"He didn't rob them. He didn't molest them, sexually. He didn't do anything but *murder* them! Really, Frank, I'm beginning to wonder about *your* sanity!"

He made himself chuckle.

A mistake, discussing Silencer with her. With anyone.

He was the only one who knew the logic, the purpose, the motive behind each and every execution.

Not to say the sense of exultation and joy!

Lila went to the kitchen. This channel had something the other channel hadn't had—"An exclusive live telephone interview with Diana Woodruff, sister of the first murder victim, Carla Woodruff, who will be buried this Saturday." A picture of the first slut was flashed on the screen. "Right after this commercial message."

Lila returned with a tray—tea and Danish butter cookies.

The commercial ended and the newsman came on again, holding a phone. "I'm about to speak to Miss Diana Woodruff, who called me here at the studio just before the show. Hello, Miss Woodruff . . . Diana, if I

169

may. All of us wish to offer our sympathies on your loss."

"Thank you," the tinny, metallic voice replied. "I felt compelled to say something to your viewers after learning about the death of that seventeen-year-old child, coming so soon after the murder of a wife right before her husband's eyes."

"Yes, Diana, though unfortunately it appears the husband, Melvin Crane, either didn't see Silencer, or the shock of his injury drove the details from his mind."

"It *is* unfortunate, because the quicker Silencer is captured, the quicker a very sick man can receive help."

"Ah, that's a bit of a surprise, Diana. Most relatives of murder victims call for swift justice, *vengeance* if you will. And you're calling for a triple murderer to receive medical treatment?"

"The only justice here is to put him in a mental institution, and perhaps find out why his mind disintegrated, to prevent the same thing happening to more men, and their victims. Besides, there's no other possibility, as you, Graham, having been involved in reporting so many murders, must know. If captured, Silencer will plead innocent by reason of insanity, and who can deny his pleas?"

"You're right. But it makes my blood boil that he'll be getting away with mass murder!"

"Not the first time, is it, Graham? In New York, the so-called Son of Sam lives on, and will never face real punishment for his many murders. He says he took his orders to kill from a dog. I suppose Silencer will have a similar bizarre . . ."

Frank got up and went to the television. "Garbage," he said, and wiped his forehead. Hot tea always made him sweat. He changed channels and found a comedy rerun.

"About time," Lila said, biting into a cookie.

He joined her. They finished off more than a dozen. He was still sweating. He wanted to go out; to walk or drive.

What he really wanted was to find that Diana Woodruff!

A slut just like her sister, as he remembered reading or hearing. A nude dancer . . . or was that the Negro's slut? Well, either a nude dancer or one of those massage-parlor abominations. As for the victims being "innocent children" and the like, Silencer didn't make mistakes! The seventeen-year-old had been displaying her private parts from a street curb! The so-called *wife* had been involved in public perversions with a Negro! The Woodruff slut had actually begun to solicit him for immoral purposes!

And her sister, this Diana Woodruff, was equally deserving of Silencer's attentions!

Lila asked him if anything was wrong. "Your expression, Frank . . . you look so strange."

"I think I have a cavity," he said, probing a back tooth with his finger.

As she lectured him about having put off visiting the dentist for too long, he cautioned himself about Diana Woodruff.

Making plans that way, picking subjects that way, was not Silencer's style.

Pure and simple circumstance, happenstance, coming-upon-by-accident—*that* was Silencer's style, and the reason why he hadn't been and wouldn't be caught. Random subjects at random intervals. And for only as long as the bullets lasted.

Another reason, this, not to try and kill the Negro. It would be dangerous to deviate from the random pattern; there *could* be some sort of hidden police protection there.

The same might be true of Diana Woodruff. It was possible that the televised phone call was a ruse, a police scheme, meant to anger him with wild allegations, obvious insults, and so draw him to the slut, and into a trap.

With that, he put Diana Woodruff firmly from his mind.

With that, he returned to thoughts of Silencer finishing his work, retiring undefeated.

He smiled to himself.

Forever talked about, not like the unveiled Son of Sam, but like the mysterious Jack the Ripper. Marveled over. Secretly admired in certain religious, ethical, moral circles for his having cleansed the streets and frightened away many more abominations than he'd killed.

A legend in his own time, and in times to come!

He lit a cigarette.

Lila said, "Really, Frank! You promised to give them up. Or at least not to smoke in the house!"

He apologized. He considered taking a walk. But he was too comfortable, too relaxed. He put out the cigarette and enjoyed the comedy show.

Diana hung up the phone. She hadn't told the reporter where she was calling from. She hadn't made her plans to that point as yet.

She was at the Grecian Massage, at the front desk, with one other operator on duty. Dreena, a very tall, very black woman, was in a booth with a customer. She would leave at midnight, and Diana would be alone until eight a.m. Diana had come in two hours early, because there wasn't anywhere else she wanted to be.

Now she thought of how to let Silencer know where she was.

And how to repeat her taunts, her insults . . . though the reporters shouldn't see them as such.

A man killing women for what he thought good reason *would* see them as taunts and insults.

If she told the reporters where to find her, they might wonder why she was exposing herself.

So an anonymous caller would inform on her.

She picked up the phone again.

The door opened and two men entered—youths in their late teens. Hispanics in crisp slacks and colorful short-sleeved shirts. Swaggering and loud and full of Hey-baby's . . . to cover obvious nervousness, fear of rejection due to race. She'd run into this before, many times.

Perhaps it was lucky they'd interrupted her. She had

172

to learn patience in this game of catching a killer. She had to get Mel Crane's description of Silencer before setting herself up for him.

And she had to allow time to pass between media appearances, or else people might grow suspicious, and weary of her.

She rose. The shorter of the two youths, the louder and apparently the leader, looked at her quickly, guiltily, and said, "Just what we want!" He pulled out a wallet and flashed his money.

She nodded. "Have a seat, please."

"Hey," the taller one said, "we don't come for no seat, y'know?"

She stood there, and let them laugh, and let them look at her body in the mini-toga. After a while, the shorter one said, "Yeah, why not, a seat."

He sat down. The taller one followed his lead.

She said, "I'll prepare a room while you decide which one will go first."

The tall one laughed briefly. The shorter one said, "Yeah, okay, how much?"

"Twenty dollars for the basic massage. Anything else, we decide between us."

"Hey, a bargain!" the shorter one said, and turned to his friend and they slapped hands in the black fashion and went through their All-*rights* and *Yeahs* and all the rest of it. She said, "I'm Diana, and I'll be right back."

She left. She didn't have to prepare anything. She wanted to give them a moment to simmer down. At one time she had tried speaking Spanish, or inserting words like *hombre* and *amigo* in her chatter. It hadn't worked.

They wanted the same speech, the same treatment, everyone else got.

When she came back, they were sharing a joint. She said, "We can get busted, gentlemen. Not for the massage, for the pot."

The tall one muttered, "Sorry." He pinched it out with his fingernails and put it in his shirt pocket. He looked at the short one. "You first?"

173

The short one began to rise, then suddenly shook his head. "You found the place. You deserve first shot, y'know?"

"Yeah! First shot!"

She waited while they laughed and nodded and slapped hands. Finally, she reached out and took the taller boy's hand. She spoke to the shorter one. "Another girl is working here. She'll come out before I'm back. If you like her, you can go with her."

"Hey, no, I'll take seconds." And again the laughter, echoed only faintly now by the boy she began drawing away.

"Then don't let her joke you, or shame you, out of it."

"No way anyone can do that, y'know?"

In the back room, which she used because these were obviously first-timers, she collected twenty dollars in advance; then helped her client undress. He smelled marvelously of Old Spice, perhaps a pint of it. His body was scrubbed raw, it seemed. And he came before she had a chance to do more than grasp his sizable organ, or request the extra ten she usually got for masturbation.

He covered his eyes with his arm. "*Arrepentido*," he gasped; then, quickly, "I'm sorry, y'know?"

The *macho* could be painful at such times, so she kissed his cheek and told him he could come back in again, after his friend was finished. He nodded dispiritedly as he dressed.

"No extra charge."

That brightened him, a little.

"And we can spend a few minutes now, talking, before we go out to your friend."

That did it, and he smiled a big kid's smile and said, "Hey, you all right, y'know? I tell all my friends to come here."

"Thank you," she said. And thought of Larry Admer watching this, listening to this.

Diana Woodruff retained customers who had started this way, this young; who had followed her from parlor

174

to parlor. She had wanted to be a teacher, and sometimes felt she was.

Diana Woodruff wasn't ashamed of her profession, no matter what the straight world thought, no matter what Larry Admer thought.

And *that* was the big problem between them.

It had taken a dozen phone calls, and three conversations with Captain Cohen, who in turn had made a dozen more calls, but finally the Sunset Strip area had been beefed up by the transfer of six black-and-whites.

Larry had asked for an even ten patrol cars, but in this era of post-Prop Thirteen, he was satisfied. From now—midnight—until six a.m., the street people were going to be a lot safer than they'd been last night.

Tomorrow, the patrols would start earlier, at eight p.m., even though Silencer's M.O. indicated midnight on. They were going to play it safe.

And they weren't going to play pussy posse; weren't going to do a Vice Squad act.

In fact, the Vice Squad wasn't going to do a Vice Squad act; they'd keep hands off the hookers, pimps, junkies, dealers, gamblers, and assorted riffraff. Instead, they were going to watch for anyone who might be Silencer. Which added another three cars—unmarked—and eight detectives to the Silencer S.I.T.

Two of those eight were policewomen, and didn't have the comfort and relative safety of a patrol car. They walked the streets, dressed as prostis, netting would-be johns in a campaign that had drawn much criticism, but which the Chief felt he had to continue due to pressure from area businessmen. Now they would be putting their asses on the line in a different, more dangerous way.

If Silencer came across one of them, he might kill before her backup in an unmarked could jump in.

Of course, then they'd have him red-handed.

He rose from his desk, stretching, yawning.

A fucking long day, made longer by the news conference.

But things weren't going to be as easy anymore for

175

that psycho bastard; the odds were better now on their catching him.

A *little* better, he admitted to himself, as he went out to his car. Because surveillance was a sometime thing, and what he still needed was that snitch, that informer. Or that eyewitness.

Enough shop for one day.

Home to bed.

Where he tossed, wishing he was in Diana's bed.

TWELVE: *Saturday, August 5*

Frank had to wait in line about ten minutes, the savings and loan being crowded, as usual, on Saturday. And when he went to the first unoccupied teller, he saw the sign reading, "I'm in training to serve you—please be patient."

Carefully, he explained the situation. He had left his bank book with another teller two Saturdays ago, because his deposit hadn't been properly recorded due to the computer being inoperative. The teller said it would be mailed to him, and he would receive it Monday or Tuesday. "That was two weeks ago."

The trainee was a young black girl. She said, "Let me get Mr. Anvers, the assistant manager."

He then had to explain the entire situation over again, and to a man who didn't exactly inspire fiscal confidence. Mr. Anvers was in his twenties, bushily mustached, hairily handsome, and dressed in one of those flare-jacketed, pin-striped suits that seemed better suited to a disco than a bank. But then again, this Sunset branch of the S & L was constantly bringing in flashy characters.

Frank decided that once he straightened matters out, he would transfer to a bank downtown, where employees looked a bit more responsible.

Anvers stroked his mustache and spoke in a high, strong voice. "Have you looked carefully for the book, Mr. Breton?"

"Berdon," Frank said. "I can't look for it, since I never received it."

"I'll check the records, but we never keep a book more than a day or two. Are there any other members of your family who might have received it?"

"No," Frank said, feeling heat move up his body, toward his face.

Anvers smiled; a slick flash of teeth. "It's our experience that the book gets misplaced by a member of the family."

Frank had a sudden fantasy image of lunging over the counter and shaking the hirsute fool by the hair.

He looked down. "Please check."

"Of course. Mind stepping aside so the teller can handle another customer? Saturdays is bad for this kind of thing."

This kind of thing.

Glancing back, he saw that the line had grown even longer now, and that some of its members were looking at him with irritation.

He watched Anvers go to a bank of files. Search. Take out a white card. Go to a desk where an older woman with stiff-looking gray hair sat. Show her the card. Move his head toward Frank.

The woman rose and came to the counter. "I'm afraid we can't locate your book, Mr. Berdon. Our records indicate it was returned to the owner that same day, which was Saturday, July twenty-second."

"But that isn't so, or I would have received it two weeks ago. Besides, the teller said the computer wouldn't be working until the *following* day, at which time my book would be mailed."

"Which teller was that?"

Frank looked around and shook his head. "Another trainee. A blond young man."

178

She frowned. "Blond young man? I can't seem to place . . ."

"Maybe he wasn't blond! I can't remember exactly . . ." He stopped as he heard his voice climbing. "Just issue me a new book."

"We don't do that until you fill out the forms for a lost passbook. Then, in thirty days . . ."

"I did *not* lose the book!"

She gave him the same flash of teeth as Anvers had; from the same management-training program, Frank thought with rage. "Well, we try to satisfy our depositors, and rules were made to be broken. Just give me your receipt and I'll type up a replacement."

With a sinking feeling, he realized he should indeed have received a receipt for his book. "The teller was a trainee. He obviously forgot to give me one."

"And you didn't *request* a receipt before leaving your book?" She seemed incredulous.

Frank felt sweat trickling down his neck. He said, "Please . . . can't you understand that your bank has made the mistakes, not me? That you should correct these mistakes, not make it difficult and embarrassing for me?"

"We do all we can," she replied, suddenly stiff. "But without a receipt, you'll have to fill out the lost-passbook forms. Then, in thirty days, we will again mail your book to you."

"Again? Are you calling me a liar?"

She said, "Certainly not, Mr. Berdon," voice very cold. She stepped back from the counter. "If you'll go to the desk in front, I'll have our Miss Thomas help you with the forms."

He walked past the long line of people, all of whom stared at him.

He came to the desk with the young blonde woman sitting there. The older woman was bending close, murmuring to her. He flushed hotter, wondering what new infamies were being spread about his losing books and shouting and being unstable.

"Have a seat, Mr. Berdon," the younger woman said, smiling . . . but her eyes seemed to shift in worried fashion. And Frank wondered whether the gray-uniformed guard had actually moved from the door to a point closer to them, or whether it was his imagination.

He said, voice determinedly calm, "Really, it's annoying to be told you lost something when you never received it."

"Yes. If you'll just fill out these forms."

It took another fifteen minutes, and by then Mr. Anvers was there, holding a pink card and chuckling. "We seem to have made a little error, Mr. Berdon. I had the wrong card before. Your book was mistakenly mailed to the main branch, and when mailed back to us was somehow placed in the inactive file." Another cheery chuckle. "Computers, Mr. Berdon. They're marvelous, but not error-free."

"Can I have it?" Frank whispered, trying not to look at anyone, *afraid* to look at anyone lest his control shatter completely.

"It was perforated with a cancelled stamp. We'll have a new one typed immediately. If you'll sit down over there, I'll get you a cup of coffee . . ."

"Mail it to me," Frank said, and almost ran to the doors.

Outside, he began shaking with a terrible anger.

And not just against the fools in that bank. This sort of thing had been happening to him all his life.

Two months ago, the cleaners had lost a favorite jacket. He hadn't been able to present proof of value, and they'd given him a "settlement" of ten dollars for a "used garment," when the jacket had cost eighty only six months before.

Last year, he'd driven across an intersection on the yellow signal because a sanitation truck had been tailgating him, going far too fast for him to risk stopping short. And even though the truck had also gone through, the motorcycle policeman had given only *him* a citation.

It went on and on that way. Back to childhood. When he'd had toys stolen, and been accused by his father of losing them, even of throwing them away.

180

When he'd been bullied, cheated, ridiculed by other children . . . and sometimes ended up being the one punished by the teacher for "misbehavior" when he reacted against his tormentors.

And when it came to finding a partner, an ally against the world, he'd made the biggest mistake of his life—Lila.

Now his mother, the one person who had *ever* been correct, been fair, been loving to him, was in effect dead and gone.

He walked along Sunset, too shaken to risk driving, trying to lose the anguish, the mailed fist gripping his intestines.

"Hey, man, just in from Boston and need some help before I find a job."

He came to a sudden halt. Before him stood a short, slight youth with bushy hair and dark stubble of beard, dressed in dirty jeans and tee shirt, his hand extended, palm up.

"Just some change, man."

Frank stared at him, seeing everything he hated. He said, "Is it some sort of plot?" and reached for the thin throat.

The youth jumped back, shouting, "You crazy, fucking blimp!"

Frank snapped out of it, and dropped his arms. But he had to silence this scum before he triggered another loss of control. He said, "I'm going to call the police, right now."

"Fucking Scrooge bastard!" the youth muttered, but turned and hurried away. He looked back once, made an obscene gesture, and cut across the bank parking lot and out of sight.

Frank walked on, slowly.

No escape.

Wherever he went, there would be people.

And people, *all* people, were his enemies . . .

He told himself that was silly. He *knew* it couldn't be true. He'd simply run into a streak of bad luck. Mom's condition had shaken him; though his last visit to Cedars-Sinai had proven he was rising above it, mastering it . . .

He hurried home. To the back yard and the shrubbery and the only thing that eased the pain and panic.

Still, he felt close to the breaking point, and spoke to Lila about vacationing earlier than their usual last two weeks in December, when he closed the store for the holidays.

She said she would love a week or two in northern California but didn't see how they could get away, what with his mother's condition, and Martin, his assistant, not being capable of handling the store for more than a few days.

He had to agree with her. Which pleased her.

She began making overtures, kissing him, pressing against him.

He was repelled, but knew he couldn't put it off forever.

"I'm so depressed and exhausted," he muttered, then added, "Tomorrow." She nodded and said, "It's a date, Frank," and he wondered if he could carry it off and refused to consider what the atmosphere would be like if he couldn't.

There was the glaring bright summer sky. The rolling green swath, dotted by flat, ground-level tombstones. The minister intoning over the open grave. The five mourners, all that poor Carla could command: Diana, Larry, and the two women and one man from Carla's place of employment . . . the dress shop, that is. Her pimp, Diana thought, was either among the dress-shop people, or, more likely, hadn't bothered to come.

Earlier, there'd been a brief ceremony inside the theatrical church called the Wee Kirk o' the Heather, handled untheatrically enough by this same minister who'd been provided by Forest Lawn. Now the outdoors service was completed, and the minister took her hand and murmured his words of condolence. He strolled away, his summer-weight black robe flowing

182

behind him, and the others came up to say how sorry they were.

She looked into each face, but there was nothing to indicate that any one of them had directed Carla's career as a prostitute. And the man, who'd known Carla almost from the day she'd arrived in L.A., was the least likely candidate of all.

He grasped Diana's hand. They murmured each other's names, having met a dozen or so times over the years. He owned Variations Ltd., as he called his La Cienega dress shop, and was married. He was also the traditional older-man companion-lover that many young women sought, and that Carla had held to for almost eight years.

He broke down, his dark, handsome face crumbling as tears rushed from his eyes. He bent his head of thick, graying hair over her hand, mumbling, "Such a waste. Such a tragedy. How it hurts!"

She put an arm around him. She hadn't cried today, the entire funeral process seeming too unreal. But now, feeling Basil Varoda's pain, she leaned on his shoulder, weeping with him, trying to comfort him.

Finally, they separated, and he turned to join his two employees. She wondered if he knew that Carla had been whoring. She doubted it. Married or not, he didn't seem the kind who could accept such a state of affairs. Few men could.

Larry Admer stood a distance away. Despite her pain, Diana had to admit that his suggestion of Forest Lawn had been a good one, the least of evils. And also that he had helped her even more than she'd thought he would—by simply being there, watching her, taking her hand in the church, standing with her at the grave, even his tact in moving away as she greeted Carla's few friends.

But now he was moving to intercept Basil Varoda; moving in a way that made her remember he was a cop. Varoda tried to veer off in another direction. Larry caught his arm. The ladies were walking ahead, already on the path. Diana came up to the men, in time to hear Larry say, "I thought you'd retired?"

183

Varoda glanced at Diana. "Not now, please."

"Oh, she knows what her sister was doing. What she doesn't know is who did the pimping. And neither did I, until I saw you here, Varoda."

Diana said, "How can you say that?" and Varoda said, "You can't prove that."

"I don't want to. I've been out of Vice a long time." He let the man's arm go. "Mr. Varoda was a very successful pimp when we busted him five years ago. He made a deal with the District Attorney, copped a plea, and promised on pain of a very long stretch to get out of the business."

"I was never in the business. I've had my fashion boutique for more than twelve years. I simply got involved in helping a destitute woman . . ."

"Shit," Larry muttered.

Diana was angered by the obscenity, angered by his accosting this man who still had tears on his face, tears for her sister. Before she could express her anger, Larry said, "His income from his *fashion boutique* that year was over two hundred thousand dollars. I haven't seen the shop, but does it figure?"

She said. "No," and to Varoda, "It's not important any more, but just to tie up some loose ends for me, did you manage her?"

Varoda looked at Larry.

Larry said, "I can make a phone call and you'll be picked up for questioning before five o'clock."

"And released before seven."

"Not if you're a material witness in the Silencer case."

Varoda's expression changed. He said, "C'mon now!" And to Diana, "I'm not a professional. But I helped her when she insisted she was going to do it anyway. She wanted money. Lots. She was going to return to St. Louis and build her brother a mausoleum and take her mother away from her father and tell all her old friends she'd been a successful stage actress . . . such fantasy fulfillments. Except for you, I was the person closest to her, and I knew a bit about the

184

managing of professional ladies. I took nothing from her."

Larry smiled.

Diana said, "But your marriage?"

Larry said, "Five years ago, he was married to a nineteen-year-old bisexual who earned about two thousand a week, from women as well as men. That one still your wife?"

"We were divorced. I married an older woman."

"Probably twenty-one."

Varoda sighed. "I've told you what you wanted to know. Carla met my first wife, and she met my current wife. She understood my life style. We were very close, in our way." He looked at Diana. "She didn't want you to know about that part of her life. I said it was silly, holding back from someone who worked the massage parlors, but she wanted you to see her in a certain light. I honored her request for secrecy. I loved the girl in my fashion. We were together longer than I've ever been with any one woman. My grief at her death isn't any less real because of what you now know." He looked at Larry. "If you prick a pimp, does he not bleed? And no vulgar jokes, Sergeant, please."

"Lieutenant," Larry said.

"Congratulations. Can I go now?"

"Wait," Diana said, even as Larry said, "No."

"Did you see anything?" she asked.

Varoda shook his head.

"Have you heard anything at all?"

"Diana, I'd have helped, anonymously, if I knew anything."

"She was dead," Larry asked, "when you came to pick her up?"

"I didn't say I came to pick her up." But he allowed his eyes to slide away.

"You didn't bother to find out whether she was alive or dead, lying there on the sidewalk?"

Varoda's face whitened. "If I'd been there, I would never have left without first making sure she was beyond help."

Diana had nothing more to ask. Varoda said, "She

185

wanted you to have everything, but I suppose you know that?" His eyes slid to Larry and back to her.

"Yes. And about the deposit box."

"Ah. Then your loose ends are all tied up." He hesitated. "I suppose, Lieutenant, I can expect to be hassled by Vice?"

"If you goose a cop, does he not jump? On a bad guy?"

Veroda walked away.

Larry said, "He isn't all *that* bad, as pimps go. I'm not going to call Vice. Unless you'd like me to?"

She shook her head. "Carla loved him. Can we go somewhere and have a glass of wine?"

"Or two."

She took his arm. He bent and kissed her hair. "You did well today," he said.

Her heart moved. She didn't want it to move.

She said, "And after the wine, I want to sleep. I didn't get one hour last night." She didn't say it was because she'd worked, and planned her campaign to trap a killer.

He nodded. When they reached his car, he said, "I can wait. A hell of a lot longer than you can."

He sounded so sure, she was almost convinced.

THIRTEEN: *Sunday, August 6 and Monday, August 7*

The phone rang as she was clearing the kitchen table of dishes and the remains of her lunch.

It had rung several times since ten a.m., but she hadn't answered, guessing it was Larry. She wanted to put some distance between them for a few days. Now she went to the counter extension, thinking to plead illness, and to keep pleading it until Tuesday or Wednesday. After that, some other excuse would come to mind.

"Diana?"

She groaned softly; then said, "Hi, Mother! How's everything?" in the perennially cheerful voice she used on both her parents. They could rant and rave, weep and wail, and she would remain idiotically cheerful.

"How *can* everything be, with my son dead and buried and my daughters living thousands of miles away?"

Only *one* daughter living, Diana thought. *Two* children dead and buried. And how could she say such a thing to this weak, battered woman?

"And don't tell me," her mother continued, "that

187

you're not living in sin, both of you. Twenty-eight and twenty-six years old, you and Carla, and not married And not in a convent, so there have to be men."

It was an old line—the convent—and she responded as she always did, with a laugh and a, "We haven't found the right man yet, but we're still looking."

And Carla had done more than seventy-thousand-dollar's worth of looking. And would look no more.

"A filthy lie," her mother said, more bitterly than usual. "Carla won't even talk to us anymore, because she knows we don't believe those lies. She hasn't called for more than two weeks, and she used to call every Sunday morning. And when I called her, three times now, she wouldn't answer."

Not "didn't" answer; "wouldn't"—her mother's paranoid approach to her daughters, and to life.

"And you're to blame, Diana: leaving home without a word and enticing your sister to follow. Whatever happens is your fault . . ."

"Stop it!"

Why shouldn't she tell her parents what had happened? Why should she suffer alone when it was *they* who had made the home, the life, their daughters had had to flee? And flee to the special "careers" they'd chosen.

"Did you shout at me?" her mother whispered, shocked.

Diana gripped the phone and wanted to shout again to *scream*—because of that "whatever happens is your fault." Wanted to tell her both her daughters were whores, and one a dead whore to boot! Wanted to hurt her . . .

"Diana? Are you there?"

She took a deep breath. "We have a bad line, Mother."

"You shouted at me. You said . . ."

"I didn't shout. There are echoes on the line. I simply said you should stop worrying about us. Carla's away on a buying trip for her store. It came up suddenly, and she tried calling you one day, I don't

188

remember just which, and couldn't get you. I guess I forgot to call and let you know. I'm sorry."

"Why should you be sorry? You never call us, like Carla does. Just when will she be back?"

"You're going to be delighted for her, Mother. It could be *months*—four or five. She'll be staying in London, Paris, Rome, for long periods of time, finding and buying dresses and hats and all sorts of items for her store. And when she's finished, she's going to take a vacation on her own."

"I don't believe you," her mother said, voice sepulchral.

Diana was breathing hard, perspiring, and didn't know what else to say. "Its true, Mother." Her voice shook. "Honest."

"She went with a man, didn't she? She's on one of those *love trips*, that's what the magazines call them. She's having one of those dirty *affairs*."

"I've got to go to work now," Diana said, wrung out.

"Since when does a book store stay open on Sunday? If you want to get rid of me, say so!"

"This is Los Angeles," Diana said, weary of the lies on lies on lies . . . especially now that they were so pointless. "Some books stores stay open all week."

Carla said the two of you spent Sundays together."

"Yes. But now that she's gone, I'm making extra pay . . ."

"You want to hang up because some man is there, telling you to hurry. You're living in sin too, just like Carla. You'll both burn in hell for it, you know. Your father said that someday he's going to come to Los Angeles and walk in on both of you and expose . . ."

"Give Dad my love," Diana said, voice dull, mind dull. The worst that her parents could conceive of was infinitely better than the reality. "Take care of yourself."

"I'm afraid he would kill those men, Diana. With his bare hands."

Diana wanted to say, "Don't worry about it, Mother. He's a coward. Why else would he beat you?"

189

She said, "Goodbye."

Her mother said, "Wait. Did Carla say she'd write?"

"She'll be busy . . . but I guess a card or two." Maybe she could arrange with a mailing service to send typed cards from European cities. Or ask around if anyone in the parlor was going abroad . . .

She was groggy now. She remembered the coffin going into the earth at Forest Lawn. She had to get away from this voice, this woman, this victim who had done *something* to her and to Carla, or else why would they both avoid marriage, both sell sex?

She had never thought of herself as neurotically motivated, psychologically driven to the life she'd adopted, but this last week, learning the truth about Carla, looking into herself as she had since Carla's death, she wasn't sure.

"I'll pray for your souls," her mother was saying.

"Thank you," Diana said, and hung up. As she was leaving the kitchen, the phone rang. She ignored it. She climbed the stairs to the bedroom and lay down.

And covered her ears against the phone's continued ringing.

Larry let the ring sound ten times before hanging up. And just a few minutes before he'd gotten a busy signal. Put that together with his three earlier calls and it was plain that Diana simply wasn't answering.

Maybe it was for the best. As much as he wanted to be with her, what he needed today was a little action

He felt he was closer to changing their relationship to something more natural, more normal, but that it was still a tricky thing to accomplish. And being "closer" didn't mean that bedtime was anywhere in sight. Because of her job. Her goddam stinking job!

He paced his living room. He was off from work today, and edgy as hell. Gloria had cancelled out his visit with J.R. They were down in the Baja for two weeks.

He hadn't minded when she'd called him Friday, thinking he'd get to see Diana. But now he was alone. Now he was painfully aware that he hadn't had a woman since Roberta came over last Monday.

Six days. A long time between sessions for a man used to sleeping every night with a young wife; and after that was over, with a progression of willing girlfriends.

If they hadn't been willing, they'd been gone.

He went to the phone and dialed Roberta's number. She answered sleepily, and he said, "It's almost one and you're still in the sack?"

"Oh, it's you. The invisible lover."

He laughed. "Been real busy. Can I come over?"

"How do you know I'm alone?"

"Because your momma has a bad habit: she drops in to see her baby girl at odd times. That's why you always come here. But today I'll pick you up and we'll have lunch and *then* we'll come here."

"And then?"

"And then we'll watch the Dodgers on TV."

"And then?" She was beginning to lose some of that chill.

"And then we'll play gin."

She gave him her baby-voice giggle. "And then?"

"And then," he said softly, "I'll kiss you."

"You'd have kissed me long before then, sweet-thing."

"Yeah, but *where?*"

She sighed. "I've missed you, baby. Still love your little blonde 'Berta?"

This was the part he'd never been too comfortable with. This was the part that made him downright unhappy now.

But the bump in his pants wouldn't be denied. As that DI at Parris Island used to say. "When the head between your legs takes over, you'll lie to God Almighty to unload your nuts."

"You bet. I'll leave now, honey."

"Say it, Larry. You almost never say it."

"Love you, babe," he murmured. He hung up, exhaled explosively, and went to get his sports jacket.

The phone rang. He froze at the closet, thinking that with his luck it would be Diana and she'd want to see him.

191

And he wanted to see her, wanted to be with her.

And he wanted his cock up a woman!

He let it ring six times, and finally answered to stop the goddam noise. It was Roberta. "I'll come there," she said. "We'll eat later."

It was *much* later. Because she was turned on high, his fat-assed little blonde. Because her baby face twisted and her tongue licked every opening it could find and her tight box got him off swiftly. Then it took more than hour for the second go. After that, it was sweat and strain, twist and turn, grunt and groan, with pleasure so intense it was almost pain.

She came no less than five times. She was struggling to bring him to his third orgasm, riding him, saying, "Fuck-fuck-fuck . . ." over and over, saliva trickling from the corner of her mouth, eyes glazed, approaching her sixth orgasm . . . when he suddenly pulled out. When he said, "Jerk me off."

She stared at him.

He said, "C'mon! I'll use the vibrator on you!" And knew *why* she was surprised. Because he'd never asked for the hand when the cunt was there.

Who in his right mind would?

Who, except a man dying to capture *something* about the woman he loved. A woman who used her hand on anyone with the price. Anyone but the man who loved her.

There was no embarrassment about thinking he loved Diana. And there'd be no difficulty in saying it—he almost had at that Italian restaurant Thursday.

He said, "You're the highest paid massage-parlor girl on the Strip, and I'm a stranger in town, and when you take off your clothes and I see that dimpled ass, when I see that snatch, I want to buy, but you won't sell *that*. You're . . . let's get you a name. I once busted a hooker named Diana. You're Diana, queen of the masturbators."

She giggled. "Okay, I got it."

He was on his back and she was stroking him and she said, "I'm sorry, sir, but it's this way or no way. And the price is a hundred dollars."

"Oh, God, I want that pussy," he said, watching her fingers play with his glans. "At least kiss it, Diana."

Roberta kissed it.

"Suck it, Diana."

Roberta sucked it.

"*Now*." he gasped.

She pulled back and stroked hard.

"Diana, Diana!" And it was over.

And he felt *dumb*.

He rolled onto his side. "Let's take a little nap."

"Hey, I want the vibrator!"

So he had to finish her up. Then she said she was starved, so they had to wash and dress and go out to eat. And then she wanted to see a movie.

By the time he got her home, he was chain-smoking.

But he nodded to himself, thinking, "As long as it takes, Diana. As long as it takes."

Harold entered the lobby promptly at seven. Vivian rose from the couch and waved and walked toward him. He was just inside the revolving doors, and stopped and stared an instant.

She kept her confidence high. Other men had stared, and tried to catch her eye, as she'd sat waiting.

She smiled, and held out both hands. He took them, his eyes going over her, seeming surprised, perhaps even a little shocked. But he said, "You look better than ever, Vivian."

He did too. The graying look, the somewhat worn look, suited him even more than had his youthful look. The smile, the eyes, the voice were the same.

They went out to his car. They talked and laughed, and even though she knew she was spotting his carport girl more than twenty years, she felt she could *not* fail. Because she felt that sexy underwear sliding over her firm buttocks, between her full thighs. Felt her breasts touched by unfamiliar mesh, the nipples aroused by the friction, and by memories of Harold.

In the Jaguar, she used the visor mirror as he told her they'd be eating at the Brown Derby, "which I

193

thought you'd enjoy, since it's not only an excellent restaurant but an upper-class tourist attraction."

She said she'd heard of it . . . and saw her face, warm and delicate; her hair, auburn highlights stronger after her afternoon rinse and set, rippling to her shoulders; her breasts, pushing up over the low, wide neckline. Examined the clinging, black-and-brown dress, stylishly simple and more exciting than nudity. Was reassured and comforted by what she could see.

And was comforted even more by what she, and he, *couldn't* see; what he couldn't find in his Hollywood dates. And that was the years they'd had; the love that had brought them so close to a lifetime commitment. That was her sharing his generation, his experiences, *their* time in history. That was her education, her upbringing, her intelligence, her style. That was all the qualities his little girls couldn't provide.

While she *could* provide the sex, the excitement, the eroticism which were their only gifts to him.

But after a fine dinner, during which his conversation seemed to falter, and after a driving tour through Beverly Hills, Bel Air, and Holmby Hills, which he wanted to extend to the coast and Malibu, she realized he was avoiding a return to the privacy of his home.

She said she was tired. She said she wanted to see where he lived, "if only for a few minutes." She put him at ease, and he finally turned up Sunset Plaza Drive.

The house was more beautiful inside than out, and the night view was truly astounding.

But it was unimportant to her. What *was* important was Harold and Vivian becoming what they'd once been.

She did everything to make it so.

She kissed him and overcame his initial resistance and made the first overtly sexual move, pressing her hand against his fly. She drew out his penis and dropped to her knees while they were out on the deck with the city's lights spread out for miles below them. She sucked him, bringing a thickening, a stiffening to his lovely tool—who she had called his "bludgeon" in

194

the old days. She rose, grasping the bludgeon, looking into his face, *willing* him to grasp her rear, her breasts.

But he began saying things: about too many years having passed; about his illnesses having changed him.

She didn't argue the points. Words were useless now, and she undressed herself as she drew him to his bedroom. Words were unnecessary as she let him see the G-string panties and the mesh brassiere. And then, drawing off the panties, flaunted the garter belt and figured stockings and bare crotch. Turned and jutted her full rear at him, made fuller by those stilt-high satin shoes.

And the bludgeon hung at half-mast and she hurried him out of his trousers and onto her, gasping with passion . . . and with the beginnings of fear. Fear of the strained expression on his face. Fear of the weak response to the best that she could do.

She spread her legs wide. "Please, please, dear H, take me, take me hard!"

He began putting it into her.

She closed her eyes in ecstasy. "Bludgeon me, darling!"

But then her eyes opened. Because the bludgeon wasn't there. He had softened. He was raising himself, shaking his head, face no longer strained, but *angry*.

"You had no right to do this!" he said, and turned to his trousers. "Forcing yourself on me after seven years!"

In shock, she said, "Failure is no excuse for rudeness."

He whirled on her. "Failure . . . yes . . . because I need *young* women, truly sexual women, not aging . . ."

She said, "Take me to my hotel," and dressed and didn't look at him

In the Jaguar, she stared out the side window. He drove so fast she thought they would go over the cliff several times, and didn't know whether she feared or desired it.

She was hurting inside, as if cut by a scalpel. Bleeding inside with the shame of it all. Sick inside

195

with the knowledge that her long dream of love was finished.

And, as they approached the hotel, beginning to burn with anger.

Aging, was she?

They turned off Wilshire, and he drew to the curb. She opened the door. "Go home, Harold, to warm milk and medication and little whores—all the things dying men need."

She was on the sidewalk when she got his reply: a contemptuous flick of the eyes, from her head to her toes . . . and a low, extended laugh.

Which made her face flame. Which she had to top somehow.

But he was driving down the street.

He was gone and that insulting laugh rang in her ears and she couldn't live the rest of her life with it; with the memory of this evening ending as it had.

She had to change it somehow; win a victory; prove him wrong!

It took half an hour for another Ford to be delivered to the hotel.

At eleven-thirty, she was driving along Sunset Boulevard, still crowded, still rocking, this balmy Sunday night.

At twelve-thirty, she was sitting at the bar of a disco, watching the dancers, trying to get into the spirit of things, using martinis to drown feelings of distaste at the clownish costumes, the vulgar gyrations, the egocentric and juvenile dancers.

At one, on her third martini, she danced her conservative style of rock with a man about her own age—nice-looking and gentlemanly enough, but not what she was looking for. Because he wouldn't wipe out that contemptuous laugh, that word eating at her insides—"aging." Because she needed a real triumph tonight, a young "date" to match Harold's.

At one-thirty, sipping a fourth martini, beginning to feel loose and giddy, she saw the big youth coming toward her; the wide-shouldered, athletic-looking boy with a thick shock of blond hair, all-American, square-jawed face, and toothy, confident smile.

"Hey," he said, blatantly looking her over. "You like to dance?"

She slid off the stool and stumbled up against him. *"Ooops!"* she said, and held to his arms, feeling the hard biceps under the blue sports jacket. And as she pressed against him, felt something else growing hard. "Dancing's all right," she said, trying to control a thickness of tongue, "if dancing is what you have in mind."

"Yeah," he breathed. "Dancing's just the excuse to get to where it's at."

They hugged there, looking at each other, and he was like a steel spring under his jacket . . . and below the waist. Her head was really spinning now, and not just because of alcohol. The youth—perhaps twenty, but she wasn't going to ask—was rubbing his bludgeon between her legs, was looking down into her face, saying, "Let's split, right?"

"Yes."

"Wait. I'm with a friend. Can't just leave him here. We're teammates at UCLA."

"Football?"

"And baseball and track. Me, that is. He's just football."

"What else do you excel at?" Oh, yes, she was tipsy, going on drunk! And didn't care. Soon, she'd prove how wrong Harold was.

He laughed. "Lady, in a few minutes you'll find out. Don't go away while I'm getting my friend, huh?"

She didn't like that "Lady," and told herself not to be overly sensitive. "Your friend won't be coming along with us, will he?"

"Won't he?"

She laughed and said, "No, no," not being *that* tipsy!

"Well, let me tell him we'll be gone awhile."

She finished her martini while waiting, then he was back and they went to the parking lot and got into his car, which was a Buick, almost the same as hers back home. She said, "Love this car! Do you have reclining front seats?"

He said no, it was his father's, but that she didn't have to worry because he was a "car expert." And his right hand had pushed her dress up and his fingers were digging into that expensive G-string crotch and she was spreading and gasping and thinking, "Watch this, Harold! Aging, am I?" And her head spun and the world turned and she wanted fire between her legs.

He had parked. He was lifting her and telling her to turn and to move this way and that way. He was sitting under her, his trousers gone somehow.

She was straddling him, her panties shoved aside, hardness forcing its way up into her body. World turning and fire entering her vagina and see-this-Harold and the youth said, voice thick and changed, "Hump it, baby!" and she humped it and he had her breasts free and was sucking them and she wondered, briefly, if he thought them saggy. And then she was crying out in orgasm. And felt him collapse; felt sticky wetness trickling out of her, onto her thighs.

He was back behind the wheel, wiping himself with what looked like a towel. He tossed it to her, and said, "Always prepared, right, Momma?"

She said, "Yes, right," and didn't like that "Momma," but told herself it was just a colloquialism for sweetheart or honey that these youths used. And judging by what she was wiping from her thighs, he'd enjoyed her thoroughly.

Yet she heard herself asking, "How was it?"

He laughed. "I'll tell you after the second time around. After my buddy tells *me*."

"What?"

He opened his door and leaned out. He waved and she heard an engine start somewhere behind them. He said, "Just take care of him like you did me. Then you and I'll go again. Then you and Perry again. Then, if you say so, we'll visit another friend. Because that's one roomy cunt you got there Momma. It can handle the whole team." He reached out and flipped her left breast so it bounced. "Little silicone wouldn't hurt," he said, and laughed.

She said, "I have to get home. Drive me to my car."

By then a motorcycle had pulled up alongside them. Another athletic youth—dark and not quite as big as the blond—said, "All cool, Joe?"

She said, "Please . . . my car . . ." beginning to grow frightened, which helped clear the alcoholic haze a little.

Joe said, "Hurry up, Perry. She's about to pass out, but you can jump into her bottomless pit before she does."

She was trying to arrange her clothes, and reaching for the door. She was whimpering, because the pain and shame were back; she hadn't solved anything, she'd made it worse.

Joe was out of the Buick and Perry was getting in, reaching for her.

She got her door open and leaned sideways and fell to the pavement. Joe ran around the front of the car and said, "Don't be a stupid bitch!"

She screamed as loud as she could.

He said, "For Chrissake, you old cunt!" and a moment later the Buick drove off. She got up. She brushed at her knees, her clothes; then realized that the motorcycle was still there, the dark youth sitting on it. "It's after two," he said. "Hop on the back and I'll take you to my place. Otherwise, it's you and Silencer." He chuckled.

"Just tell me how to get back to Sunset Boulevard and that club. I don't know where . . ."

He drowned her out by starting his engine. He U-turned and roared up the sloping street, and was gone. She remembered something about that name, Silencer, but couldn't pin it down. And the street was empty and she was alone.

The dark youth was returning to the disco club to meet the blond youth. She would walk in the same direction, and perhaps come upon a cab.

She walked with difficulty on those stilt-high shoes, and unevenly because of the four martinis. She wanted to take the shoes off and sit down in a doorway . . .

but what if someone came along and saw her? Or she fell asleep and was found by the police?

She continued struggling up the street.

She heard a car, and hoped it was the blond youth relenting, coming to take her to the club. Or a cab, which she would stop if she had to throw herself in front of it!

But it was neither; just a car, passing by with a flare of headlights.

She reached a corner. She looked up and down the dark streets and there was no one to help her. She was exhausted. She was drunk and depressed and debased and near tears. And lost.

She wanted to go home. To New York. Tonight! She *hated* this crass, redneck town masquerading as a major city! She hated the people here! Even Louise had changed, and her children were noisy and uninterested in the books she'd bought them as presents. All they talked about was Disneyland and Magic Mountain and Knott's Berry Farm and Universal Tours and other obscenities.

She leaned against a wall. She took deep breaths, trying to clear her mind, to be reasonable about this silly business.

Soon, she'd get back to Sunset Boulevard. Then back to the hotel, to make arrangements for the first available flight out.

And she would never complain about Manhattan again.

Frank lay awake afterward, telling himself it had gone beautifully.

Lila slept flat on her back, mouth open, half snoring, satisfied finally, because she'd had two orgasms.

He'd maintained his erection this time.

He'd kept it in her for almost an hour, pumping away, the sweat running down his face and neck and sides, feeling her thick body turn damper, turn wet and slippery, as they went on, as she moaned and grunted and gasped, "Harder! Harder!"

Whatever she'd asked for, she'd gotten. Her bottom

squeezed and her anus fingered. Her breasts sucked as he'd pumped. Kisses and bites and whatever had been the request of the moment.

And he too had finally come.

But he didn't want to remember how!

He got up and went to the kitchen and put on the light. He made himself a sandwich with baloney and cheese and thick slices of sourdough bread and sweet pickle and mustard, and washed it down with beer.

He remembered the sandwiches his mother would make him when he came home from school or play, crying, defeated, which happened more often than not.

He remembered how she had looked in those long-ago days.

As he had remembered her in bed with Lila tonight, when he'd begun to turn cold at the heavy, doughy woman in his arms; the unlovable woman in his arms. And somehow had seen his mother, as she'd been thirty or so years ago, a slender yet full-hipped, full-breasted woman, with heavy, dark-blonde hair. Remembered how his father would pull her into the bedroom weekend afternoons, telling little Freddy to go outside, or to his room. And sometimes little Freddy, who in time had grown to where he wasn't quite so little, would tiptoe to the master bedroom and open the door a crack and see them.

He had blocked out his father.

He had feasted on his mother—on her warm whiteness and incredible roundness and vivid patches of hair under the arms and between the legs. And first masturbated that way, at their door, into his handkerchief, gasping his mother's name—"Rose!"—under his breath, as his father gasped it aloud.

He had known it was wrong, known it was something to add to all the other things for which he hated himself. And eventually felt such guilt that he had stopped. And forgotten it; forced it from his mind.

But tonight he had brought the memories back to help him through what was otherwise an impossible task.

Tonight he had in effect masturbated, remembering

201

his mother's body as it had been. Masturbated into Lila's body. And his mother was old and dying. And he was obscene, dirty, *bad* . . .

He ate another sandwich. He drank another beer. He was stuffed, and it was something else for which to hate himself.

He had to get out!

He had to exorcise the food, the memories, the dirty feelings, the guilt, the anguish.

God, God, he had to be cleansed!

He went to the bedroom for his clothes, and Lila slept on.

It was after two when he left the house.

Vivian had given in to the alcohol, the uncomfortable shoes, had sat down on a low brick stand, one of two bracketing the entrance to what looked like a four- or six-family dwelling. A few moments later, a young woman came by, and started violently when Vivian called to her.

She pointed ahead in response to Vivian's question about Sunset Boulevard, and hurried on, glancing back nervously. Vivian wanted to ask if there was any way she could call for a cab, but the woman turned into another house and was gone . . . and so was the opportunity.

She got up, to begin walking again.

And saw the man coming down the street. Perhaps from that corner house into which the young woman had disappeared.

Yes . . . she'd sent him out to help her!

Because this town had a lady killer and everyone was worried about him.

Silencer. That was where she'd heard the name. Silencer was the lady killer.

She walked toward the man, who looked at her and shook his head; a fat little man hurrying along annoyed that he'd had to come out to help a stranger. But all she'd ask him to do was to call a cab. The hotel could get the car tomorrow . . .

He said. "You can't walk around like that!" eyes darting down from her face.

She put a hand to her breast, and realized she hadn't gotten the brassiere back over the left one. And the dress was awry.

She stumbled and laughed in embarrassment. "Little too much celebrating."

"Whoring, you mean!"

He was right in front of her now, and she was about to tell him he had no right to say such a thing, when she saw the gun coming from under his jacket, when she heard him say, "I'm Silencer."

Things flashed through her mind: that she was a New Yorker and he didn't want her. That she was sleeping, dreaming, at home in Manhattan. That he was joking and it was inexcusable . . .

She lunged forward in a frenzy of terror and rage— rage at everything that had happened to her tonight. She reached his face with her right hand, clawing. She tried to scream.

But by then she was dead.

Frank stumbled back, clutching his cheek. She'd looked so drunk and dissolute, and moved so incredibly fast!

And she'd made a sound . . . begun to scream.

He turned and ran back up the street toward the corner and his car. Then he stopped running and put his head down and walked. Because if someone looked out a window . . .

A car came around the corner toward which he was walking. It moved slowly . . . and then it was under the street lamp and he saw the lights atop the roof. A police car!

He had to get away from that body!

His face was scratched and bleeding and the gun was under his jacket and they would know, they would take him, they would destroy him!

He came to the apartment-house entrance and turned left into it, seeing the gate and knowing that meant a courtyard or a pool area around which the apartments were clustered. If the gate wasn't locked, he'd be safe for a while.

The gate *was* locked.

He stood there, almost crying . . . and someone came up behind him. He turned, reaching under his jacket for the gun. The tall man said, "I've got it," smiling, nodding, eyes busy with the key and the lock. So that Frank was able to keep that left cheek away from him, and follow him inside, and turn to the right bank of doors when the tall man turned left. And move up a staircase to a second-floor landing and find another, shorter hallway cutting between apartments to a side stairway going down into an alley.

Where he sank to the pavement, back against the wall, and dabbed at his scratched face, and trembled like a frightened animal.

Where he told himself he should never have allowed himself the pleasure of that, "I'm Silencer," and would never risk it again.

Not that there was much chance he would *be* Silencer again.

He waited half an hour by his watch. He heard nothing outside: no sirens or voices or anything that would indicate a body had been found.

Of course, she had died in a dark place between street lights, and he believed there'd been a car or two parked at the curb, which would block the view of anyone driving by.

He went back up the staircase to the second floor and the short hallway, then across to the long hallway, and down to the courtyard and the gate.

Still no sound to break the early-morning silence.

He opened the gate and went out to the street. He didn't look toward the body. He turned left, away from it, and hurried to the corner and his car. Where he examined his face in the mirror and saw that the scratches were minor and had already stopped bleeding. It felt a lot worse than it looked.

Still, he was shaken and frightened as he drove to Laurel Canyon and then to the Ventura Freeway, both nearly deserted; then some thirty miles to Agoura and off the freeway west into Latigo Canyon, remote, barely inhabited because of its steep slopes of loose shale, its endlessly winding, rising, falling road, *utterly* deserted at this time of night.

He drove very slowly, very carefully along the dangerous road, which was illuminated by no lights but his own and the bright summer sky's.

He wasn't able to appreciate the bright summer sky.

He was back to what he'd always been, stripped of the armor of Silencer and the purpose of Silencer and (hidden thought but true) the glamour of Silencer. He was, again, Fat Boy, as his Marine sergeant had called him during that brief and futile time, that disastrous attempt to reverse a life of unmanliness, of cowardice and physical ineptitude. Fat Boy, who had been Fat Frankie in Valley High. Who had been Fatso in elementary school. And not just because of his weight— fatter boys had swaggered through those schools, respected—but because he was soft, he was scared, he was retiring.

He had his mother.

His face had stopped burning, and didn't look bad at all as another examination in the mirror showed him.

But he had to dispose of the gun.

The word "dispose" seared his mind as the drunken whore's nails had seared his cheek.

He reached to his hip and touched the cool metal.

He began to think more calmly.

He began to realize he wasn't in as much trouble as he'd first felt.

The drunken whore was dead. No one knew about him. As for the scratches, it shouldn't be too difficult to make up a story that would satisfy Lila—a cat leaping at his face as he bent; a minor car accident; anything reasonably plausible would do. Because she wouldn't believe him capable of being Silencer, even if he were to confess it!

And he wouldn't have to answer to anyone else, if he played sick for the few days necessary to heal the scratches.

But the gun would constitute a terrible danger, in

case anyone thought to suspect him. The gun alone could tie him to Silencer.

He would hide it. There were some large boulders down that last stretch of Latigo Canyon into Malibu. If he took a fix on the very first one over the last rise, he could bury the gun where he could find it again, if he ever decided to regain that armor, that purpose, that glamour of Silencer.

He came over the final rise before the plunge to the sea. He saw the boulder on his right, clear under the starry sky, perhaps fifteen feet high and equally large across the base, standing alone on a knoll.

He pulled to the side, his right wheels scrabbling over shale. He got out, carrying the flashlight from the glove compartment, and went to the trunk. He got a screwdriver from the tool kit, with which to dig, and the plastic bag, and walked to the huge rock. He went around behind it, and kneeled and looked and realized he didn't have to dig. The ground fell away from the rock in one spot.

He put the gun in the bag, wrapping the plastic all around it, twisting it, twisting it into a rope at the open end. He shoved it under the boulder, until he could barely reach it with his fingertips.

But he left a little twist of plastic extended toward the opening. So that someday, he could pull bag and gun and Silencer out again.

Assistant District Attorney Roger Vineland was a medium-sized man in excellent condition; a pleasant-faced man dressed in conservative suit-and-vest fashion, neatly mustached and with a rather short hair style in this day of hip attorneys. Dark and youthful and crisp, he had carefully orchestrated his appearance and manner over the years so that he now seemed eminently worthy of public trust, and was among the most highly-thought-of-assistants in the West Temple Street office.

He was still at his desk on Monday at six-thirty p.m., going over a photocopy of the Silencer file sent him by Lieutenant Larry Admer. He'd decided he wanted to read everything available on that madman—in preparation for an eventual indictment, he'd told Admer.

In reality, it was something more personal that was making him spend an hour of his own time, with Laura waiting dinner, with Chuck expecting to be taken to the movies at eight. A nagging sense of disquiet, of something still too vague to be classified as worry.

He'd been aware of the case from the first killing on the night of Friday, July 28th, before it became a media event: Carla Woodruff, a possible prostitute.

What had made him aware of a single homicide in a city that had more than its share was one that had preceded it, according to the Coroner, by less than two hours. A homicide outside the Silencer M.O., but—or so Vineland suspected—connected with it.

And with D.A. Roger Vineland.

But that was the most tenuous of possibilities, and he tried to mock himself for thinking about it.

He flipped to the front of the folder. Admer, quite correctly, hadn't included the file on the cab driver killed that same Friday night. But Vineland didn't need it; had already secured it from Captain Cohen.

The cab driver had been executed gangland style, and later turned out to be a Vegas casino dealer on the run from his employers.

Maxie the Mensch generally took care of such contracts out of his San Francisco headquarters. Except that the FBI had finally hung a rap on the Mensch—intimidation of a Federal witness—and he was out of circulation for at least two years. Still, Maxie's organization would continue to service its Vegas clients.

Maxie had bought an item from Roger Vineland thirteen years ago, when Roger had come home from Vietnam to find the good life. That item was a weapon that could be expected to stay in Maxie's organization indefinitely—unless some fuckup mechanic lost it during a hit. And unless someone riding in that cab picked it up and walked away with it and began using it to kill the kind of women he hated.

207

Vineland sighed, shut the folder, and rose from the desk.

The old sharpshooter was getting paranoid, he told himself. This was the thinnest kind of logic, hardly deserving of the word, based on little more than his long-time distaste for the way he'd had to finance his career.

And yet . . . if they caught Silencer, if they got that weapon and traced the serial numbers (which could be raised no matter what process was used to try and erase them), and if it was *the* weapon, they would find out it had originally been sold to the Company and that it had last been accounted for on a mission into the Annamese Cordillera. They would learn that one Roger David Vineland, then twenty-eight years old, was the lone survivor of the three-man assassination team, and that he had claimed loss of the Hi-Standard automatic with MAC silencer.

The psycho had killed again, early this morning, unless it was a copycat killing. They had found some indication that the victim had marked him—skin under her nails—so perhaps he would drop out of action, at least for a while. Possibly for good. Which was a pattern psychotic killers often followed.

There were hundreds of unsolved homicides in Southern California, many in multiple groupings under a suspected single perpetrator; thousands nationwide.

Which was, for once in his legal career, a *comfort* to Roger Vineland. But which still didn't dull the point digging into his composure, the point which eluded all logic, that logic being: the gun wasn't necessarily from Maxie's organization. And even if it was, it wasn't necessarily the one provided him by Roger Vineland thirteen years ago. And even if it was, it wouldn't necessarily be found.

And even if found, there was no proof that Roger Vineland had lied about not being able to reclaim it from the guide's body, due to hot pursuit of Viet Cong. No proof at all that he had brought it into the States . . .

He rubbed a handkerchief between damp palms.

208

That point, that goddam point threatening to pierce his heart!

If he ever had to answer questions about the gun, it would leak to the media as everything that happened in his office did.

And he planned to begin running for District Attorney as soon as his boss made public his coming retirement. Planned to be in that office in a year, at age forty-two the brightest of young hopefuls for eventual elevation to the Governorship. And, by Jesus, he had aspirations and ambitions to dwarf even that.

He had married a girl who was not only pretty, not only one hell of a lay, not only Phi Beta Kappa, but also the daughter of a state senator with national Republican Party connections. The Committee To Elect Roger Vineland District Attorney was already formed, and could be resurrected to become The Committee To Elect Roger Vineland Governor.

But one word, one grain of suspicion, linking him with that weapon, and he would never rise beyond this office . . . if indeed he could remain here.

He put the folder in his case and went down to his car. He drove toward Pacific Palisades and home. His even-featured typically Anglo face was again composed.

He would keep a close eye on the Silencer case. He had done what had needed to be done in 1966. Given the opportunity, he could do the same today.

BOOK TWO

BOOK TWO

FOURTEEN: *Friday, September 15*

Humming "Goin' Home," Mel Crane sat in the wheel-chair, waiting at the side door for his ride. Behind him stood the Chicano nurse with the big ass, whose bending and walking and stretching and turning had kept him in what could be called "high spirits."

Not that she'd done for him what Diana Woodruff had done.

He sighed. Diana hadn't done it much either, just twice that first week in August.

He knew that she might have continued to accommodate him, except that he'd continued to find excuses for not describing Silencer. And so that third and last time she'd visited him, in mid-August, when he'd tented his sheet for her, she'd smiled and said, "You're recovering so quickly, Mel, I believe you can reach it yourself."

And so he had. And so the tension hadn't been impossible.

But Diana had left that sunny summer day and not come back. Until this overcast fall day. And she was here only because he'd called and asked her to drive him home from the hospital.

The little orange Fiat convertible pulled up; the toy-like horn sounded; he turned to the nurse and said, "Well, Mom, can baby try walking now?" with some acid in his voice.

"Of course. It's the rules, Mr. Crane. You have to ride down in a chair, or else I get in trouble. Now you can skip and run; do what you want."

He rose slowly, using the cane they'd given him. He began to turn to her, but she came quickly around the chair to take the hand he held out. He said, "Goodbye, Maria. I'm going to miss your fussing around my bed." He let her see his eyes slip from her face to her hip, her bottom. He laughed as she flushed. "Ah, Maria, amor, amor!"

"You get too much amor, Mr. Crane, and you'll be right back with us."

"Can't ever get too much," he said, and turned to the Fiat, where Diana Woodruff stood holding open the passenger's door, looking like the queen of the Strip in boots and tucked-in tan denims and matching man's shirt, that great body making everything fit tight and juicy.

He walked carefully. He'd been practicing every day for almost four weeks now, using first a cage-like stroller that had enclosed and supported his body, then two crutches, then one crutch as his right leg lagged behind the left, and finally just the cane, pacing the hospital halls until the staff had nicknamed him the Galloping Black Ghost.

As for the jaw, they had removed the cast two days ago, and except for some pain in the mornings, in the joints, the hinges, it was fine, earning the comment, "Excellent recuperative powers, jaw and brain," this with a fatherly smile and a pat on the head from a thirty-two-year-old medical whiz-bang.

Except for a puckered scar under the left sideburn, where the bullet had entered, and five tiny pale dots—three in the left cheek, two in the right—where lead

214

fragments had exited after bouncing off bone, you wouldn't know he'd been shot.

He'd been very lucky all around said the whiz-bang surgeon and his two *colleagues,* as they called themselves, that band of bandits that had saved him and were now murdering him financially. The fragments of bone had either dissolved, were in the process of dissolving, or had worked their way out of his brain; while the lead fragments had never gotten in, most exiting out his open mouth and the rest through those five tiny dots. "Of course," a *colleague* had said, "there is always a question mark in recovery from brain damage . . ."

Though "brain" was not exactly the word to describe where most of the bone had lodged.

"Medulla oblongata," he explained to Diana, as she drove the short street to San Vicente, then turned right to head further south along the broad avenue toward his apartment. "Lowest part of the brain—really a thickened extension of the spinal column."

"You seem to know a good deal about it, Mel."

He ravaged her with his eyes. "Have I told you that I love you and want to spend my life serving you?"

"You left out," 'On hands and knees.' "

"That's a good position."

"What about the medulla oblongata?"

"It absorbed most of the bone fragments. Which could have meant real trouble, since the medulla setup holds the control centers for the heart, and for breathing, and for the blood vessels opening and closing and allowing blood to pass through. And I did develop a little trouble with my heartbeat—a crazy extra bump, or miss, once in a while. Gone now. Just like the paralysis, which came from two or three fragments that wandered off somewhere. Here's where the medics lose me with their explanations. But I think part of the midbrain was touched and damaged, and that hooks into the spinal column and controls what they call the motor reflexes. So my motor wouldn't work."

"Your motor was working pretty well in one area, when I last visited you."

215

"Yeah," he said, leaning toward her. "Funny you should bring that up."

"*Did* I bring it up?"

"Careful, baby, you're speaking to a sexually starved man." He paused; then leaned back in his seat. "You're angling."

"Of course. You know what I want."

"And you know what *I* want."

"I'd enjoy it, Mel. Let's make a deal."

He looked out at the streets. He hadn't seen them, been a part of them, in more than six weeks; had thought never to be part of them again. But his ability to feel pleasure was clouded by passion.

He hated to be an easy make, an easy deal!

Though what the hell, the fat fuck had stopped killing; had probably dropped out for good. That was a pattern these psychos followed, according to much of the reading he'd done while trapped in bed.

He said so, and added, "So you're not really getting anything for your end. And I do mean *end,* baby."

"You call it," she murmured. "But first, Mel, the description."

"I could make one up easy enough. I could hold back the real description for another bargaining session. If I *have* a real description."

"I know all that. But there won't be any more bargaining. You can take me, but only once. Either way, this is it."

"Except if I come to the parlor, right?"

She looked at him.

He sighed. "But that's business and this is special. So put some gas to it, baby!"

His place was dusty as hell. They opened windows and she changed the bedding and said that later she would go down to the basement with his wash. He looked in the refrigerator, which Greta, the old broad who lived with the manager, had cleaned out for him. He'd phoned and asked her to stock the place with fresh groceries, but no luck. She and the manager were alkies, and when they tooted, goodbye work and promises.

Diana said to relax: she'd go to the nearby market and bring back an assortment. He grabbed her as she went by. He held her in his arms and stroked her fine body and kissed her sweet neck. He socked it between her legs, and she moaned a little, but then she drew away. "See if you can write down your description of Silencer while I'm gone."

When she returned a half-hour later, he had the fat fuck down pat, in pencil sketch as well as words. And was proud of himself when she said, "That's really good, Mel! You're a natural artist!"

"I also got rhythm," he said, sitting at the kitchen table and sipping his first beer in four months. He didn't tell her he'd taken lessons through the mail for almost a year, thinking to be first an artist, then a cartoonist. It hadn't worked out, and he'd finally given up. But he *had* drawn that woman on the matchbook cover easily, and handled all the early lessons . . .

She was taking off her boots and denims. She put the boots back on—Strip smart, all right!—and took off her blouse and brassiere. Her knockers were big and hung a little, naturally. Her ass wasn't nearly as big as the Chicano nurse's, but it was showgirl ass, French ass as they used to say in the old days—swelling out, not broad in the beam.

He finished his beer as she put away the groceries wearing just her boots and panties. He got up and went to her and put his arms around her from the back and ground his erection into her and cupped her breasts. He sighed deeply, a desert wanderer about to drink his fill.

She said, "In a minute," and he loved the tremble in her voice. She was a good chick. She plugged into her partner's feelings. She was trembling because he was trembling. And he hadn't forgotten the part about his being black, because some chicks, even the hard-core pros, never forgot it. While other chicks, like this one, didn't seem to know it.

He had a second beer, and after the vacation from alcohol it bombed him out. His legs got weak and he just about made it to the bedroom, where he fell onto

217

his back, head swimming, afraid he would blow the whole thing.

He didn't. Because she gentled him and undressed him and massaged him and kissed his face and told him he was a beautiful man with a beautiful penis.

He thought he would bang her once, hard as he could, then ask for head, then go up her creamy white butt and stay there as long as she could take it.

It didn't turn out quite that way. After he was pulsing hard, he took her in his arms and they kissed and she brushed the head of his tool with her fingertips and he stroked her body and it went on until the flick of her fingers threatened to get him off. Then he climbed between her legs and they smiled at each other and he slid in and worked awhile.

And found he was too weak, was panting too hard, was running out of breath and strength.

He admitted it, flushing hot. She said, "I like being on top anyway," and climbed on him and within moments he was breathing strongly again, going strongly again, feeling strongly again.

She went into orgasm, or a hell of an act, bending all the way over and pressing her breasts to his chest and gasping his name. She was so beautiful, so sexual, so exciting with that twisted look on her knockout face that he came right after her, gasping more than her name because his way was with obscenities and "big-assed-cunt" and all the other stuff learned from Tijuana Bibles, the little dirty comic books which were the sex manuals of his youth.

When he finished, he apologized, thinking she might be upset, as some chicks were.

She said, "Upset? Over those *exciting* words? I want more!"

After they sixty-nined a while, he asked if he could do her ass.

She said, "If you really know how. Otherwise, it's hell."

He chuckled, "It's my thing," and went to the bathroom for the baby oil.

When he came back, she was on her hands and

218

knees, bottom stuck way up in the air. She looked terrific, but he said, "No. The way you were before, riding me."

He was aching, throbbing hard again, just from looking at her, which at his age was a hell of a compliment, if she but knew it.

She got on him and they did it awhile and it felt so good he could have forgotten the back-door job. But grasping that beautiful bottom, he remembered and took the baby oil from beside the pillow and squeezed some onto his fingers and worked one, then two into her rectum.

She grunted, and her eyes closed, and he guessed she didn't really dig it . . . but then again, despite the porno shit, few women did. Beth-Anne had, because she'd liked a little pain, but only if she could watch herself in a mirror.

And why was he thinking of Beth-Anne now, allowing her to creep into his mind, getting in the way?

He told Diana to reverse her position, rear to his face.

She did, and he substituted the head of his penis for his fingers. She grunted again, and he slid the shaft easily into her rectum, drawing her down onto it rather than shoving himself into her. It gave her some control, and she paused once, adjusting, before giving in to the gentle pressure of her hips.

Finally, he was totally sheathed. He said, "You do it, baby," moving his fingers around to her front.

She rode him, first very slowly, with an occasional grunt, then strongly, and at the end with violent plungings, her hand pressing his fingers deeper into her vagina. He almost blacked out at his orgasm, made even stronger by her own wailing, grinding conclusion on his fingers.

After they showered, he got into his bathrobe, lay on the couch, and watched as she dressed. Then she got the laundry together. He sat up. "You don't have to do that."

"I said I would." She left with the basket.

He smoked a cigarette, feeling first terrific, then a little sad, then empty.

Terrific because his body had really needed this session.

Sad because this fantastic fox wasn't going to be back; she'd told him so, and she did what she said, as with the laundry.

Empty because he was remembering the woman he'd married, the woman much closer to him than Diana could ever be because she was so much more *like* him.

Diana came back, the wash neatly folded. She put it away and said, "Anything else?"

"Yeah. Drop around tomorrow for another deal. I'm trading my right arm."

She didn't laugh. She came to the couch and kissed him.

He said, "I should have given you that information more than a month ago."

She shrugged. "He stopped more than a month ago."

"So you didn't get much out of our swap, did you?"

"Unless he begins killing again." She went to the door. "And I got you, Mel. Goodbye now." She hesitated with her hand on the knob. "Can you think of anything more to tell me?"

He shook his head. "Forget him, Diana. He's gone. Your sister and my wife are gone. Life goes on."

"I intend to go on, too. But if he *does* reappear, I've got some ideas I'd like to try." She paused. "If you ever find him . . ."

"I'll take care of him myself, as you would."

"Yes. So that's it. Business concluded." She waved, and was gone.

He lay down. Time to start thinking of making bread again; getting his business moving again. He owed twenty percent of one hell of a hospital bill, that being the part his health insurance didn't cover. It amounted to almost two thousand dollars, and hospitals were noted for using the most modern medical techniques while you were inside, and tough collection agencies when you were outside. He had to begin scrounging right now.

Unless he could get Admer to release his five grand.

The lieutenant had shown a great deal of patience during his questioning sessions. In fact, he hadn't been around in two weeks. At that time he'd said, "You may have lost your bargaining position, Melvin."

Could be, with Silencer gone.

But they hadn't filed any charges on that dusted pot. They would eventually have to give back his money, even though Admer had called it "evidence," smiling broadly, the bastard.

If he gave him the description he wanted, he might get the money.

Though that would be cheating Diana out of her deal. She'd traded for the information. If it suddenly appeared in the media, she'd have been taken.

He could always give Admer a phony description . . . but that would be dangerous if they found Silencer and Admer decided he'd been fucked.

No, he would just have to keep quiet. He didn't want to help the cops anyway, because it was still possible the killings would start again. And if they did, he could still catch the fat fuck himself.

But how he could use those five G's!

He went to his armchair and the phone table beside it. This is where he would sit for hours, doing business. Now he took out his wallet and found the card Admer had given him. He dialed and spoke to a desk sergeant and waited. "Lieutenant Admer? Mel Crane. I got out of the hospital today."

Admer said, "Congratulations."

"Thank you. But the bill is a monster. I had three doctors, including two brain specialists. I need my money."

"If they released you, you're well. If you're well, your memory must be working again. Want to tell me anything about your assailant?"

"Lieutenant, I've told you what I know!" He gave his voice the proper ring of frustration, easy enough when thinking of all that bread locked away. "I can't

221

tell you any more! I shouldn't be punished for *not* knowing something, should I?"

"How about for possession of narcotics?"

"Christ, I'm the victim here!"

"As Patty Hearst said."

"Did you ever think I might be telling the truth?"

"Sure. And if you were an ordinary citizen . . ."

"White, you mean?" It was worth trying to lay a little guilt trip on the man.

Admer chuckled. "Shit, the mayor's black. If you were an ordinary citizen, you'd get your money no matter what I thought. But you're a dealer. We both know that. I don't know what level, and frankly I don't care. I do know that I can hold back on you as long as I like."

"And how long will that be?"

"Maybe forever. Or until you risk bringing a court action. At which time the D.A.'s office will decide whether to fight it because of the drugs found in your possession, or to release the funds. Only one way to find out."

Mel didn't reply.

"You'd need up-front money for a lawyer on a case involving drugs. No hope of a contingency deal, until *after* you got the money, when he'd grab a third to a half. And it could take years."

"Thanks for the advice," Mel said, chuckling, keeping it light, holding back rage. The old hatred of cops, bulls, fuzz, *pigs,* rose in him; the hatred born of parental training by a whore mother and a pimp father and brother. The hatred even more basic to a black child and teen-ager of thirty-five years ago, when the white arm of the law had come down heavily and often in the New Orleans ghetto. But he knew better than to hang up, as he would have on an ordinary honky. "I hope you'll change your mind, Lieutenant. I'm really hurting for money."

"And I'm hurting for a suspect to four murders."

Mel said, "Goodbye," and waited for the cop to hang up first. Then he went to the bedroom and dug under the mattress. He found his little red-leather book and returned to the phone. Where he began making calls, first to his suppliers, especially the old broad who worked in a major pharmaceutical warehouse.

He tired quickly. He had to quit before he'd made even a dent in his list of customers. He said, "Later," when one chick wanted to deal ass for Valiums.

Much later. He wasn't nearly back to normal.

He slept and dreamt of Beth-Anne and awoke with rain pelting the window. Rain in September! Like they said, the Ice Age was returning!

The apartment was cold. He raised the thermostat, and still felt cold.

He had a sandwich and coffee, and got back to the phone, vowing to forget everything but bread and broads.

Frank had bought the Little League Special, a small wooden baseball bat, the first week in August, after an incident convinced him he needed protection. He'd been driving along Pico, on his way home from work. A Lincoln sedan had shot out of a side street without regard for the full-stop sign on the corner, and swung in front of him. He'd managed to slam on his brakes in time, and blown his horn in anger. At which the driver of the Lincoln, a seemingly mature man with neatly cut black hair, had gone berserk. He'd slammed on his own brakes as Frank began driving again, and Frank had almost run into him. Then, when Frank tried to pass him in the open right lane, he swung violently into that lane.

Frank had blown the horn again, long and loud, as was his right, and a mild enough protest over such irresponsible behavior!

The other driver had then swung his vehicle across *both* lanes and leaped out. He was running and his face was wild, mad . . . and Frank reacted instinctively, as instant panic dictated. He stamped down on the gas, heading left for the double yellow line, to pass in the opposite lanes. The madman was in his way, and Frank hesitated for one split second, wanting desperately despite fear—perhaps *because* of it—to make the man pay for it, to strike him down and leave him a bloody puddle in the gutter!

But he'd moved the wheel the inch or so necessary and come around the madman's car, and sped off, leaving Pico and taking side streets in case of pursuit.

He'd stopped at a sporting-goods store a few minutes later for a ball bat. And he kept it on the floor in back, swearing not to run if such a thing happened again but to smash, to kill!

There had been another, though milder, incident just last week. Two boys in an old convertible had tailgated him on a side street where there was no room for him to pull aside and let them pass. They'd blown their horn again and again, and he'd finally reacted in anger, gesturing "Go away" out the window. When he reached the corner and was able to pull right, one had jumped out and tried to reach in the window to strike him. He'd thought of rolling the window up quickly and trapping the boy's arm inside, then getting the bat and coming out to beat them both senseless. But he'd simply jack-rabbited away, turning off the side street, heart pounding with fear. Later, he'd eaten too much and grown nauseated and been unable to help Lila with his mother.

And he'd realized that the bat was no good. That a hunting knife he'd considered buying was no good. That even a regular pistol, available in any gun shop, was no good.

Realized, as he had ever since hiding it in Latigo Canyon, that only the long automatic was any good for him. That he needed to be Silencer again, and not just for the pleasure, the incredible release and joy. Needed it to survive, to stay sane.

But it had seemed too dangerous. Still seemed too dangerous as he considered it this rainy afternoon, driving home to take Lila out to dinner. Because he'd had quite a time explaining those scratches on his face.

Lila had surprised him when he'd returned at four that Monday morning from Latigo Canyon. She'd turned on the lamp and sat up in bed and begun ques-

224

tioning him. And for a moment, he'd been too startled to think.

He hadn't expected to answer any questions until eight or nine, maybe later if he could keep his face hidden in the bedding and tell her he was ill and to call Martin at the store for him.

But there she'd been. And he'd stammered and turned quickly to the bathroom and locked himself inside.

The scratches hadn't looked that bad. He'd washed his face and searched the medicine cabinet and found Lila's bottle of Hideout, a medicated makeup for occasional blemishes. After using it, he felt he could risk facing her long enough to get his pajamas, jump into bed, and turn out the lamp.

He'd done that, but she'd said, "Your face, Frank. What happened?"

"Damnedest thing. Took a ride, and then a walk . . ."

"How long have you been gone?"

"About an hour," he offered tentatively.

"I've been up almost two, Frank!"

"Well, perhaps two. I didn't keep count Lila. I was driving, and then I walked through Beverly Hills."

"At this time of the morning? Are you losing your mind?"

Safe in the darkness, he'd turned to her and found her hand. "I was too excited to sleep, dearest. Our lovely night. Our renewed love . . ."

She'd softened, but returned to the question of his face.

"In Beverly Hills," he'd said, "I bent to tie my shoelace. There was a cat on the lawn and it jumped out at me and scratched my face. Only then did I realize there were three kittens almost at my feet, and you know what they say about a nursing female being the most dangerous animal in the jungle."

"I know what they say about roving husbands being the biggest liars in the city!"

Still, he'd gotten out of it—though the matter had come up once again, two days later, as they'd been reading the *Times* in the living room. He'd been flip-

225

ping through the auto section, looking at the ads, wishing he could buy something new and sporty, when she'd said, "You know, Frank, that woman killed by Silencer Sunday night had skin and dried blood under her fingernails. It says here," and she began to read from the paper, " 'It is believed that her attacker was marked on either the face or hands. Anyone having information or suspicions should contact his local police or sheriff's department.' "

He'd chuckled. "Are you saying I'm Silencer?"

She'd looked up at him, and nodded, and for a moment he'd gone cold inside. Then she'd begun to laugh. And laughed and laughed.

He'd pretended he was laughing with her. But inside he'd no longer been cold; he'd been burning hot. Because she thought it impossible that he could kill a flea, not to say a human being. Because she thought him incapable of any manly act. Because she thought him a worm, a fool, a coward . . . all the things he had indeed been until the night he'd picked up that gun and become Silencer.

They'd had a long laugh together. She'd wiped tears from her eyes. He'd wiped rage from his heart . . . and dreamed how good it would be to draw the gun from his waistband and put it to her face and say, "I'm Silencer." And see the fear, the horror, well up in her eyes.

He'd held to that daydream for a week, and it had helped.

But then had come the driving incidents. Then had come his mother's release from the hospital.

Now it was clear he couldn't live this way much longer. Because five weeks without the gun, without Silencer, was a pain-filled eternity!

He pulled into the driveway and cut the engine and sat there a moment, listening to rain pound the metal roof, gathering his strength. It had never been much fun coming home to Lila and Mom. But with things the way they now were, it was pure hell.

He got out and walked inside. Lila was in the kitchen, slumped at the table, drinking coffee. She looked up and shook her head. She said, as she'd said almost every day of the past ten, "We've got to put her in a nursing home. I can't take it."

He didn't bother with his own litany of: "She'll get better. You'll see. Can I do the wash for you?" because he no longer needed it. He'd been forced into something today that would solve those problems, while creating new ones, financial ones.

That Dr. Herrera had been right. Mother did things in her bed—urinating, defecating, vomiting. Mother forgot the people around her. Mother wept in the late hours of the night, cried out in pain, sometimes in childish rage.

Mother was driving them crazy . . . and yet, the alternative was something he still could not face.

Putting her away to die with strangers.

So today he had a surprise for Lila, a present that would have to take the place of all the presents he might have bought her for her birthday in November, and for Christmas, perhaps for years to come. That would also have to take the place of their annual two-week winter vacation, because there just wasn't enough money for both.

He had hired a full-time practical nurse. Mexican. With experience. With some English, so his mother wouldn't be totally lost. Who would come early in the morning and leave late in the evening, Monday through Saturday.

The agency said he was fortunate they had found Mrs. Flores.

Yes. But she cost a hundred eighty-five dollars a week, and that wasn't fortunate, no matter what the agency said about "bargains." That was backbreaking.

Still, Lila would be delighted.

He went to his mother's room. She was dozing. The stench was controlled by constant cleaning and bathroom deodorants; Lila was, if anything, *too* meticulous a housekeeper.

He looked at his mother, as he did at least once each day, and murmured, "I'm home, Mom." He went back to the kitchen to wait for Cousin Meg to come sit

227

with Mom. And to plan the way he would spring his surprise on Lila.

He would tell her about the nurse during dinner. He would do it over a bottle of wine, and she would celebrate by drinking most of it. It would send her to bed early, so that later *he* could celebrate.

By driving to Latigo Canyon and finding that boulder and resurrecting Silencer, no matter what the risk.

When the phone rang at three, Diana expected it would be Larry, asking where they would meet this evening. They'd seen each other five more times—on Friday nights, because she'd been taking Fridays off. It was a relationship that had grown strained as she continued to remain physically aloof, and as he—or so she guessed—began to realize she would not come around simply in the course of time.

She went to the phone, sighing, dreading the conversation. Not that she dreaded *being* with him. On the contrary: there was a distinct pleasure, a strange titillation, in this platonic but far from sterile friendship.

More titillating, in fact, than most of her sexual experiences, including the one with Mel this morning. And the black man had been good; was a lover of professional caliber, as was she.

But that was the ordinary. That was what she could get anytime, anywhere, most especially at work six nights a week. What Admer could also get.

She no longer wondered why she didn't give him what he wanted. It was a game, a contest of wills. And when they were together, the game excited her.

But when they spoke on the phone, the element of excitement was missing, and the last two times he'd been cold, subtly accusing, quite unpleasant. She felt that the time was fast approaching when he would turn on her in some way.

She expected it would involve Carla's deposit box. Because she couldn't see his allowing such a handle, such an area of vulnerability, to remain unused forever. Not when he knew he could get either money, or her body.

She wondered which she would give him, if and when the time came.

She preferred it to be money, because of the victory it would represent—her resisting the cop's importunities, even at the cost of a piece of her future.

But then again, she knew herself to be extremely cautious when it came to finances.

She raised the phone, saying, "Hi," prepared to handle Larry Admer.

Her mother said, "Diana?"

Diana had to reset her mind; dig in for this unexpected and different kind of verbal battle.

"Yes, Mother, good to hear from you!"

"Good to hear from me? It's been over a month! And I called the last time too!"

Diana maintained the determinedly cheerful voice she always used on her parents. "Has it been that long? Well, time flies, as they say. Everything all right in good old St. Louis?"

"Where's Carla?"

"Hasn't she written?" Because one of the parlor girls had accepted an airline pilot's invitation for a long weekend in France and promised to send a typed card from Paris. "She said in a card to me she had."

"She wrote you? In her handwriting?"

"No, Mother. Typed. Carla has a new toy—one of those cute Italian portables. She's using it for everything! But didn't she send you . . . ?"

"One postcard. Thursday. Not even signed. It isn't like her."

"Oh, well, she's busy and having fun and you'll just have to forgive her." *Because she's rotting away by now, Mother, and the man responsible is gone, unpunished . . .*

"I don't forgive either one of you! The Bible says honor thy father and thy mother. You two *ignore. . .*"

"How's Dad?" Diana interrupted, not sure she could maintain the lightness of tone much longer.

"How do you expect him to be, with such children?"

"Grateful," Diana said, "that we bother to remember him at all."

"What did you say?"

"Have to go now, Mother. Goodbye."

The phone rang again a moment later. Diana picked it up immediately, prepared to tell her mother everything. Prepared to share that burden of grief and guilt she'd carried alone. "Yes, what is it!"

Larry Admer said, "You sound ready for a fight. Which is, I guess, what you could call our dates." He tried to take the curse off his words with a chuckle.

She drew a deep breath, and sat down. "Then don't bother."

"Is that what you want me to do, stop bothering?"

With no more Silencer, with nothing to be learned from the police, her original motive for seeing the lieutenant was gone. If she answered his question with a yes, it could prove interesting: precipitate that squeeze with Carla's money as the lever. Force her to pay, or come across.

She'd hesitated while thinking, and he suddenly said, "I was kidding."

"So was I."

"I'm not so sure."

And this was the part, with his voice growing tense, that she wanted to avoid.

"Can't talk now. I have someone here, girlfriend from St. Louis. Pick me up at eight."

"Sure it's a girl?" This time even the chuckle was tight, sweaty, angry. "Sure it's not one of your classy Strip friends—a pusher, a pimp? Maybe Carla's pimp, who dropped around to renew an old friendship?"

"Eight," she repeated, and hung up before he could say anything more.

Larry Admer got up from his desk, walked to the high metal cabinet and yanked open the top drawer, A-to-E. He pulled the file on Baker, slammed the drawer back in, yanked open the third drawer where the P's were, and pulled the thick file of names he'd lumped under "Phony." He stamped back to his desk and threw down both files and said "Goddam fucking shit!" And he didn't mean the false confessions that kept coming in on Silencer. It was his just-concluded phone call he meant.

Marv Rodin, who was out in the bullpen, tapped on the door. "You calling, Lieutenant?"

"No," Admer said, and muttered, "I'm *crawling*," sick of Diana Woodruff and the idiot game he was playing with her. A massage-parlor whore, and she barely kissed him goodnight! Marv had been right, treating her the way he had the night of her sister's death. If he'd done the same, he'd have fucked her a dozen times by now, and forgotten her!

Instead, he wasn't sleeping well, wasn't working well, was short-tempered with everyone. Even with Roberta, when she'd said she was "tired of playing that massage game and being called Diana." Sensed something, little Roberta had. Felt used, and abused. And he'd told her she would play the game or get the hell out.

Luckily, she'd wept and stayed. Then he'd apologized, and played the game *she* liked: that she was a suspect in a murder and even though innocent was being brutalized by the sadistic police lieutenant who forced her to bend over a chair, shoving his penis into her while making her kiss his badge.

Goddam game bugged him! But he would play it, to keep her playing his. And he would watch his temper from now on. He couldn't afford to lose Roberta, his sexual outlet, his escape valve.

He tried to read the rapist's file . . . and admitted something to himself: that he had to be even more careful not to lose Diana. Because his weekly meetings with her were the core of his existence.

Frustrating, they might be. But also full of joy! Eating with her, talking with her, touching her hand, kissing her briefly, drinking—sometimes heavily—as she sat and watched, all this made up a strangely powerful nether-life, unreal, yet more important than anything he could grasp, control, own, fuck!

Tonight it would happen again. And tomorrow he would take out the *un*joyful part on Roberta's willing body. And call her Diana . . .

The phone rang. It was Roger Vineland. "You'll have to release Leon Baker. We can't make a case."

"Jesus!" Larry exploded. "He confessed to three rapes in the Hollywood area alone, and we know he killed that thirteen-year-old!"

"Easy, Larry." Vineland sounded surprised, and annoyed. "You and I don't play this kind of game. He refuted the confession, and there's no possibility of a conviction without it. Since when did we start getting personally involved?"

Larry said, "Forget it," and reached for his Camels. Might as well smoke now; he wouldn't when he was with Diana.

"Keep him under surveillance," Vineland said. "Be patient, and you'll get him yet."

"No way," Larry said, lighting up. "He's got the message. He'll leave the area, like Silencer did, and start up somewhere else."

"Do you have reason to believe Silencer started up somewhere else?"

"No. Just making a point."

"That case interests me. I hear you had another confession today. Any possibility it's legitimate, or that it's based on knowledge of legitimacy?"

"None at all. A man about sixty who says he's the reincarnation of Jack the Ripper. He certainly has *that* case down pat. But when it comes to Silencer's M.O., he hasn't even bothered to learn what's in the newspapers. He insists the reason there was no noise was that he used a knitting needle through the heart."

"How many confessions have you had so far?"

"Nine. Every time the media does a recap on the story, we get a few more."

"I wonder what happened to the real Silencer? He had a surprisingly short career for that type of killer, one that successful, wouldn't you agree?"

"Not really. Four victims, that we know of, is a respectable score. As for why he stopped—he was probably scared off by a combination of things. The last victim, Vivian Garner, fought him and marked him. Then there's the heavy concentration of personnel we put on the street that week. And the recovery of his one surviving victim, Mel Crane."

"Did Crane ever give you a decent description?"

"No. He might not have one to give. Then again, he could be going for personal revenge. Or just hate cops more than killers. I wish you'd consider filing on the marijuana."

"Not good P.R., Larry. He paid that minor debt with a bullet in the jaw. Has he made a formal request for his money?"

"No. And as I told you, I want to keep it for a while longer. It's the only hold I have on him, if we don't file a drug charge."

"The day he comes in with a lawyer is the day we release his funds."

Larry said nothing.

"And even without a lawyer, perhaps another month . . ."

"Fine. And we'll lose the very last possible lead to Silencer's identity. Leaving us with another unsolved. Dammit, we're being *buried* by unsolveds!"

Vineland was silent a moment. "You should consider marriage, Larry. It would brighten your outlook."

"I did consider it once. It fucked my outlook."

Vineland said goodbye.

Like Neil Diamond, Linda Ronstadt, Mick Jagger, and others, Burn Digger lived in a big house in Malibu. Even the man Burn called King of Kings, with an enormous admiration and envy bordering on worship —Bob Dylan himself—lived in Malibu, in a rambling, onion-topped mansion that no one could price since a remodeling job alone had cost two and a quarter million. And like all these, Burn made money, quick money, and spent it, large amounts of it, because, as he told Chez, fondling her ass that first time in his bedroom with crashing surf beyond the glass wall and his voice and guitar coming with ear-splitting intensity from the eight speakers in the opposite wall, "Who the fuck knows when it'll end?" And he'd torn the dress right off her and torn the panties down her

233

legs and fallen on his back and begged her to urinate on his face.

Stunned, she'd muttered, "It'll ruin the rug."

He'd shown her it was just a cheap removable hunk of carpeting over a rock-studded concrete floor. "Like Keith Moon's bathroom," he'd said. "Rocks for a rock star, right?"

So she'd done it. It had given him the steam to make it straight, in bed. And so had begun her three years with The Digger. And during that time Keith Moon had died and lesser-known musicians had died and at the heart of it all lay the life they lived, these millionaire junkie children.

At twenty-six Chez—born Betty Anderson, and forget the Father Knows Best cracks—had been a wise old lady compared to the twenty-four-year-old Digger and most of his friends, even the ones that had managed to live to forty. Now she wasn't quite as far ahead of them, the life they all lived having worn her down. Now she was twenty-nine, just two months and eleven days away from the dreaded thirtieth birthday. Now The Digger wasn't just balling other chicks, which he'd always done on occasion; he was bringing them home with him. And waiting, with that soft, endearing smile on his lean, Aussie face, for her to blow her cool so he'd be saved the trouble of asking her to split.

Maybe The Digger was worried she'd get a lawyer and base a case on the Lee Marvin precedent, where a live-in girlfriend had sued for the same financial rights as a wife. And maybe Chez would do just that.

But she wasn't ready yet. Hadn't given up yet. Despite the teen-aged redhead with the big boobs doing the pissing the past week. Despite Chez's being banished to the guest room. Despite no real contact with The Digger for close to a month. Because when it came time to go calling on his peers, Burn still relied on his Chez for a little style, a little grace. She was a long ways removed from Bennington, Vermont, but some of the style, the grace, had endured, and here in L.A., especially among the rockers, they were at a premium.

234

She supposed she shouldn't have left her job as assistant to the producer of two top-twenty TV programs, half-hour situation comedies called "contempo-humor" by the status-seeking staff. The money had been fair, and she'd been learning, and eventually they'd have wanted her to be their token female script consultant, or associate producer, or even director.

But The Digger had poured on the bread. The Digger had poured on the sex and glamour and travel and concerts and parties. And snort and acid and anything else she might have wanted . . . but here she'd read the dismal record of their lives, and except for an occasional joint had remained the straight, the square. And driven The Digger home in his white Corniche convertible more often than not. And gotten the doctor to him, and the private ambulance, that time he'd almost O.D.'d on mainlined H. (And became as spoiled as the rockers themselves by a level of affluence and self-indulgence unknown to artists in other media.)

He couldn't do without her, she thought, brushing out her black hair in the guest bathroom.

He would come around, once the jail-bait redhead returned to junior college and her Motel Management course. Or after Chez dug into the cow's purse and found her home phone number and placed an anonymous call to a father who might indeed know best.

But that was tacky, and probably not necessary, since Burn wasn't taking the redhead out tonight; he was taking her. And they were going to the one place every rocker would go, if he could: to the exclusive night spot above The Roxy concert hall on the Sunset Strip. To producer Lou Adler's "living room." On The Rox, a very private club with between forty and fifty members, and The Digger one of them since last spring. Where names like Elton John, Rod Stewart, Alice Cooper, mingled with guests whose entry depended not on money but on accomplishment—writing novels, making movies, dancing ballet (but only if they were *cool*). Once the buzzer opened that second-floor door, you were *on,* you were being judged, you lounged around in couches and big stuffed chairs and listened

235

to your peers and superiors; and when you spoke you made sure it wasn't dumb.

That's why The Digger wanted his Chez with him. That's why he had wanted her even when they'd done the B-group spots like The Candy Store and The Rainbow. And that's why he would *always* want her, return to her, when the new hots wore off, which never took too long.

And that's why she kissed his cheek when they met in the round living room crammed with so wild a mixture of furniture that even after three years it made her wince. That's why she forgave his calling back to the master bedroom, "Keep it nice and moist for the Digger, baby," and merely smiled at the answering, piercing giggle. That's why she accepted his long silence . . . if you could call it that, since he blasted his voice from the Roll's quad speakers when, before, he'd kept the volume down in deference to her taste.

But he had a wicked surprise for her. And it proved, finally, that he wasn't just fooling around, bringing the redhead home, and that no amount of patience and understanding would do any good.

"Take the car," he said, as the parking-lot attendant opened the door for her, as he opened his own door to the dampness of a recently ended shower. "Go to Gary's place." Gary was his keyboard man, and lived way out in Encino. "Bring him and his chick to Ivy's." Ivy's was a B-group bar in a C-group neighborhood near the airport, run by an Australian whom The Digger had known in Melbourne. "I'll be along in a few hours and we'll have dinner."

She was shocked. She said, "Think it through, Burn. You're going to On The Rox without me?"

He was unwinding his long, rawboned body from behind the wheel. He stepped out and straightened. "Learned to walk at six months. Learned to talk a little later, like last month. And I *do* things, y'know? I write and sing my own songs. You bullshit, and it's becoming a drag."

She wanted to say, "You'll love my book, *Toilet*
236

Habits of The Digger!" She wanted to jump out and slap his face!

But Bennington girls didn't act that way. Besides, it wouldn't mean anything to him.

He walked off. She slid behind the wheel and backed out to Sunset. So he didn't love her anymore, if he ever had. But he loved his Rolls Corniche.

She would arrange for him to spend a few days looking for it.

She drove west to the first corner and turned left into the side street. She breathed heavily, fighting back the sense of loss, of panic, because what was she good for any more? She was The Digger's girl. How could she face an average job and average men when she'd helped handle finances of over a million a year, shared a life lived on concert stages amidst shrieking, idolatrous fans, sometimes fifty, even a hundred thousand, at a time? How could she settle for "gatherings" with a few friends when she'd managed parties that rivaled descriptions of those the Roman emperors had thrown, with at least as much wine, women, and song?

Being The Digger's girl ruined your palate for normalcy.

She made a few more turns, her vision becoming clouded as tears welled up. She parked in the darkest spot on the darkest street she could find, her back to the glow of light rising from the Sunset Strip, where The Digger was at ease among the mighty . . . without her.

She cut the engine and slumped in the deep leather seat. Then she turned the ignition back on to activate the stereo, and slid in his latest tape, "Digging The Digger," which was outselling all of his five previous albums. *Rolling Stone* said it would go platinum, and the title single was already first on the charts.

And she no longer had any part in it. He was the doer and she was the hanger-on. Clear now, where before she'd thought herself a loved and valuable partner.

She listened to the tape, the sound low. She was thrilled, and driven to heavy weeping, by his acid voice

237

and stark rhythms. And fell asleep, willing it as the only way to escape her misery.

Lila hadn't been as pleased with his hiring the nurse as Frank had thought she would be. "I really look forward to our Christmas vacations," she'd said. "Now we'll never get away." And she'd begun drinking the Burgundy he'd ordered, less as a celebration than as a narcotic for her disappointment.

But after finishing two-thirds of the quart carafe, she'd cheered up; begun to see the tremendous advantages; had finally said, words slurring, "You're right, Frank—the only thing to do. Know you want to get away too. Giving up your vacation to help me . . ."

He'd talked her into an after-dinner brandy, and when she'd gone to the ladies room, weaving a bit, poured more than half his into her glass.

So that she'd dozed in the car, and been ready for bed when they'd gotten home, even though it had been only nine o'clock. So that she'd been fast asleep by nine-thirty. So that he'd been on his way to Latigo Canyon by a quarter to ten.

Now it began to rain again, heavily, and the fast-moving schedule slowed down. Not that he cared. Knowing he would be Silencer again gave him infinite patience. He drove carefully along the Ventura Freeway, listening to soft music, watching the substantial Friday-evening traffic for drunks, for trouble, feeling he again had good reason to stay alive.

It was ten-thirty before he entered Latigo Canyon, and twenty more minutes before he reached that last downgrade to the sea. And here there was no traffic to speak of.

Just one car, a BMW had come up behind him, and the kamikaze driver had roared around him, impatient with his careful pace on the rain-slick road. He'd hoped to see the car fly off a cliff, but had settled for recognizing the boulder.

He crouched behind the huge rock with his flashlight, and at first wasn't able to see anything in the gap

238

between earth and rock. Then he realized that the rain could have washed the plastic twist further back, so he put his hand inside and began to feel around. He found the bag in short order and drew it out. He stood up, saying, "Here you are!" and laughed and hurried to the car. Where he pulled off the wet, muddy plastic and dropped it on the floor in back.

He checked the long automatic: it was dry and apparently unharmed.

He sniffed the barrel. The gunpowder aroma was still there, and he hugged the cold metal to him like an old friend, like a lover.

After a cautious U-turn, he drove toward Agoura and the Santa Monica Freeway. He put on the all-news station, listening to the crises abroad and the problems at home . . . and it was all old-hat, all boring.

But soon, Silencer would be back! Soon, the news would be exciting again.

He could confuse them by going to another area entirely.

Agoura, for example, which he would reach in a few minutes.

But what if they failed to see it was Silencer?

No, he wouldn't take any chances. Besides, Agoura might not have what he wanted . . . at least not flaunting itself on the streets.

He would return to the Sunset Strip. It belonged to him. They would be sure to recognize his work there. Then, if he felt it was getting dangerous, he would go someplace else to use the four bullets that would remain after tonight. But not far. Hollywood Boulevard. Another street of blatant women in sexually revealing costume; of whores; of breasts and buttocks.

He realized something, and was shocked, surprised.

He had an erection.

He'd never reacted that way before when thinking of those women. He still hated them, despised them . . . but he remembered the one with the Negro, her big breasts hanging free as she sucked on his penis. And the youngest one, with long blonde hair, and plump legs spread apart as she sat on the curb, with the whiteness of thighs ending in a dark joining as he drove slowly by. And the last one, older but dressed so that the lush body was clearly displayed . . . and one heavy breast almost completely exposed.

And the very first one, saying, "Why don't we go to your place?" and the back of her hand brushing his fly as if by accident. But her smile, her brazen eyes, her tight skirt emphasizing her bulging bottom . . .

He was breathing quickly.

He wondered what the one with the Negro would have done if he had offered her a chance to live?

Done what she'd been doing to the Negro. Done anything he'd asked for!

And the others. On their knees. Begging. Mouths open . . .

He turned up the volume on the radio. He made himself listen. He was sweating and opened the window, despite the driving rain. He tried not to think of using the next one before punishing her.

And finally ended the excitement with the sobering thought that the rain was now a downpour and there might not be anyone on the street to use *or* punish.

They went to their usual Malibu seafood restaurant. He drank a good deal before dinner, and she looked out at the storm-swept sea; looked through the rain-spattered window, and the world was dark, grim. And turning back to the man across the table, saw more darkness, more grimness.

They ordered. He had oysters, and while eating, said, "I must be crazy. They're supposed to be aphrodisiacs."

She dipped a shrimp into horseradish sauce. "It's a myth, Larry. There are no aphrodisiacs."

He was looking at her, that strong face not as strong as she would have liked. His lips moved a moment before anything came out. "How about the mind as aphrodisiac? How about thoughts, dreams? How about normal desire, blocked?"

She tried to let it pass, but he suddenly snapped, "Answer me!"

240

She looked up. "All right. I don't know exactly why it's so, but I prefer not to deal sexually with you. Not until certain things change."

"Silencer caught?"

"Yes. And other things. My mind. Your mind. When it feels right, Larry, and not before then."

"How do you know it won't feel right if you don't try it? All those men at the parlor! You said you were going to quit, but almost every goddam night you're at the parlor! How the hell can you justify denying me when I care, I really . . ."

"That's business," she said, wearily. And thought that the unpleasantness of their phone conversations was moving into their meetings. "If we have to go through this all the time, then we might as well not see each other."

He stared at her. Then he said, "Fine," and the way he said it, the hard and heavy way he said it, made her stop eating.

She wasn't surprised when he continued with "I overlooked untaxed income for a friend. If we're not going to be friends, I think you should either declare the contents of Carla's deposit box, or share it."

She answered calmly, "Declaring it will probably mean losing it as illegal income. I'd rather share it, if you can subdue your official instincts."

"I've subdued far stronger instincts with you." But his voice was changing; losing the hardness, the heaviness, becoming less certain. Then he said, "I'll give you a better deal, Diana. Sex with me, and keep the money."

She couldn't help laughing.

His face reddened. He half-rose, glaring. "That's a hell of a lot for a massage-parlor whore! Half that deposit box means about thirty-five thousand . . ."

She nodded and raised a placating hand. "I didn't mean to laugh. Not at you." She couldn't tell him the laugh was one of triumph, at having guessed that he would make this very move . . . which justified her viewpoint of men and women and their relationships. "I don't blame you at all."

241

He sank back down, but he was still flushed, and he called to a waitress at a nearby table, "What does it take to get a drink around here?"

The waitress took his order, while a few people stared. He stared back, stared them down. "Last time I eat in this fucking dump! I like steak . . ."

The waitress had broken all records getting him his double vodka on the rocks. He murmured, "Sorry, miss," and, "bring another."

He would be falling-down drunk soon. He'd drunk a considerable amount on their other dates, but never this much. He'd been a benign inebriate, and capable of driving.

This time he might be different.

"Don't worry," he said, finishing his drink as the new one was placed on the table. "I'll be gone as soon as you give me your decision. The money, or you."

His voice was dull now. She sensed how much he disliked what he was doing. And it touched her, a little. The man would never have asked her for money if she had treated him, as he'd put it, normally. And he probably didn't think to take a dime from her even now, since he wouldn't expect any woman to give up half a fortune for a few sex encounters, especially "a massage-parlor whore."

She said, "How long would you want to have me?"

He spread his hands, trying to look unconcerned . . . but his eyes blinked rapidly. "Oh, say our weekly date, for a year. That's fifty-two meetings. About seven hundred dollars a meeting, not bad, right?"

She didn't bother checking his arithmetic. "A full year," she murmured. "I'll have to think about it."

He stared, to see if she was joking. Then he flushed again, made a laughing sound, looked down at his oysters. But he didn't eat anything more, while she had a full dinner. Instead, he drank.

She had to help him out of the restaurant.

In the car, he lay against the door, mumbling, "She's gotta think. Tough decision. Thirty-five thousan' to fuck the beast. Massage-parlor whore's gotta think." He choked on laughter.

242

He was almost out by the time they got to her home. She struggled to half-carry him inside, and he fell on the couch and was instantly asleep.

She removed his shoes and covered him with a blanket. Then she turned out the lamp and went upstairs to bed. But not to sleep. Her recent work schedule had made her a night owl. It was only eleven. She would read, listen to the radio, relax.

She didn't have to consider the choices Larry had offered her.

There was no longer any point in holding onto him.

Not that she wouldn't miss his company . . . in a way.

But the fierce joy of being able to tell him that the "massage-parlor whore" preferred giving up thirty-five thousand dollars rather than submit to his force play couldn't be denied!

Besides, it wasn't her money. It had cost Carla her life. To hell with it!

And then, too, there was the hidden thought, the strong thought, that comforted the other side of her nature; the side concerned with holding onto every dollar:

He was still that lieutenant of police who had sought to impress her in Carla's bank; the one who might not be able to take the money, no matter what he'd said in the heat of rejection, under the influence of many stiff vodkas. The man she would bet on to walk away into the sunset, an all-American hero to the last.

He refused to go into his Vietnam war experiences, which only made her more certain that he'd been a dedicated soldier—as likely to take money from a woman as John Wayne.

She'd always loved John Wayne.

She closed her book and lay there, listening to soft music on the radio. She was aware of the ambivalence of her feelings toward Larry Admer.

But that twice-repeated "massage-parlor whore" stayed with her, and she could hardly wait for morning when she would wake him and say: "We can go to the vault now."

243

*　　*　　*

Chez didn't know where she was for a moment. Rain drummed on a metal roof and water ran down a sloping window and she was cold.

She heard Burn's voice and sat up and rubbed her eyes. And remembered the dismal details leading to her being alone in the Rolls on a dark side street off Sunset Boulevard.

The dashboard clock read ten minutes to twelve. She'd been asleep more than two hours. Now she had to get a cab and return to Malibu and pack everything she owned, every last piece of clothing and jewelry The Digger had given her, that she'd earned in his service—and how much did you charge for being pissed on, literally? Had to drive her Toyota to a motel; then make plans to find an apartment and a job and a man and a life . . .

It was too much to handle without a little help. She leaned to the right and opened the glove compartment and found the cigarette holder. She unscrewed what was normally the replaceable filter section and drew out a joint. She hoped it wasn't laced with angel dust, because PCP tended to send her out too far, too fast, but she didn't let the possibility stop her. She put the joint into the holder and used the dashboard lighter and inhaled deeply.

It wasn't easy to tell straight from laced marijuana, and she smoked for a few minutes before feeling the sudden lightness of head.

She said, "Oh, wow," and thought to stop smoking, and thought of The Digger, and took another long, sipping drag. Giddiness, and an accompanying hint of nausea, told her it was indeed laced, and heavily.

But maybe this time she would get the good high Burn and many of his friends got from dusted pot. Maybe she would fly to happy land and be able to make it through this dismal, rainy night and do what had to be done to walk away from The Digger.

She was looking at the windshield, at rain running down in crooked, crazy patterns . . . and one pattern grew thick and snake-like and turned a watery cobra head to stare balefully at her.

"Bad trip," she said aloud, just to hear her voice, to shake the sudden panic, and she dropped the cigarette holder on the floor and closed her eyes.

She breathed deeply, steadily, telling herself she would *not* have another nightmare experience . . . like the first time two years ago with PCP; which was the last time before this; which she'd sworn would be the last time forever. That was the time she'd try to run into the ocean.

"Imagination," she said. "People smoke it every day. The Digger. Gary. Bob the drummer. Hundreds. Thousands! Little kids! *No problems!*"

She heard herself screaming at the end. She tried to stop and breathe. And the miasma of burning PCP filled the car and she was choking and had to get out into the air to stop the bad trip.

She tried to hold her breath. She couldn't find the door handle. She began to cough and began to pour sweat and ripped at her raincoat. She got the coat open but kept coughing and sweating and the snake was on the windshield and she knew it was getting bigger and bigger even though she wouldn't look there.

She struggled and squirmed and got out of the coat. She felt a little better, and began tugging at the dress, because without it she'd feel better still.

Again she tried to open the door, but the handle had dissolved in the rain and run down onto the floor.

She knew that was nonsense and laughed and found she couldn't stop and lay back and kicked at the door and got out of her dress, her beautiful dress, tearing the seams and popping the solid silver buttons and finally running out of strength and just lying there, shoes against the door window, gasping, laughing, full of fear and anguish.

The Digger was still singing:

"Don't be my buddy, baby, soulmate.
Go your own route,

245

Sing your own poem,
Tempt your own fate . . ."

She'd been there when he'd first put it together; been there when he'd recorded it; heard it a dozen times. And never known he'd been writing it for *her*. And she should have known, since everything he wrote was based on his own small circle of people, his own level of experience.

Now nausea was rising and she had to get out. She had to wash her body in the rain and breathe clean air. Now she kicked at the door with her high heels, battering it, pounding it, and found the hysterical laughter rising along with the nausea.

The door opened.

Her legs still up, her body clothed only in her shoes and pantyhose, she laughed without being able to stop and tried to make out the shadow in the open doorway. She felt chill, wet air wash over her and felt the nausea recede and sat up, unable to shake the laughter, but grateful for freedom from this $100,000 prison.

The voice said, "Look at you!"

She leaned forward into the healing chill and wetness, trying to speak through the laughter to the shadow, to the voice, both of which were probably no more real than the snake on the windshield. "Hey, man . . ."

As panic and nausea receded, so did the laughter. She saw him clearly, and heard him say: "I'm Silencer."

She remembered that from somewhere. Silencer. A new group? Single act?

Not bad. Catchy. Maybe he needed a Girl Friday.

She said, "Can you use me?"

He came closer. He pushed and she was going back and he was inside. He was real, maybe. Fat and funny-looking and she began to laugh again.

Her bare breasts were being manipulated. Her crotch was being rubbed. Her mouth was being kissed.

She turned away, laughing, saying, "God, what a trip!"

Her hand was holding something, was being made to move on something.

She looked down. She saw the stubby penis.

She looked up. She saw the gasping mouth.

She pulled her hand away. "Don't care if you're real or not. Get out. Disgusting . . ." And had to laugh again at the face growing twisted and white.

He waved a black wand. She began to ask if he was a wicked warlock, a fairy demon. But he tapped her on the forehead and her trip was over.

FIFTEEN: *Saturday, September 16*

She'd lived alone ever since her mother had left, saying
she couldn't take "the crazy hours, the crazy life."
Hortense Laver didn't mind. Her mother had been too
unreal. Which was to say, she'd been too far removed
from Hortense's very real fantasy life.

Not that Hortense recognized the fantasy as such, all
the time. But even when she knew she was playing a
part, she didn't worry about it, wouldn't stop doing it,
preferred it to the terrible, grinding bore that life had
become after *Chief Shut-In* had been cancelled; after
she'd stopped going to the studio every morning to play
the part of the bedridden, L.A.P.D. Chief's main assistant, "a crisply attractive and mature blonde who
came up through the ranks as one of Southern California's finest policewomen, to finally become senior
among Chief Shut-In's three active helpers," as the pilot script described Mamie Belfont.

A year now since the final segment had been shown
on network television. And with the reruns on a local
channel every weekday evening, she was typed, she

was blocked from network parts. It was different for the star, Jeremy Chalk. He'd done a movie-of-the-week, and his new pilot was being advertised in the trades for a second-season premiere. Not so his "three assistants"—they would have to wait a while longer to escape the stigma of typecasting.

Hortense was just as glad. She'd been ill at ease doing *Hollywood Squares*, and the role, she'd had in *Cloisters*, an experimental play put on by a Santa Monica group, had left her with the feeling that she was out of place playing a young dance-hall queen. Not that she felt too old. At thirty-four she still had the face and the body to handle mid-twenties roles. It was more that she felt the part to be a betrayal of the person she'd become during *Chief Shut-In*'s six successful seasons. Felt as she had on *Hollywood Squares* that she was demeaning herself somehow; or demeaning Mamie Belfont, who had been far too dedicated an officer to do such foolish things . . . except, of course, in the line of duty.

Felt, quite seriously, and also comfortably, that she and Mamie were one and the same. Watched herself on *Chief Shut-In* each evening at five, reinforcing the knowledge that *this* was her real self; these were in effect home movies. Mamie Belfont was her name and Hortense Laver an old and discarded identity.

But sometimes—more times than she could tolerate when Mother had been living with her—she'd been made to feel that she was abnormal. So Mother had to go. So now she was alone, except for Daisy, her housekeeper, whom she'd received, along with the beautiful Benedict Canyon house, that first year of *Chief Shut-In* when Adam had grown unreasonable about her career. It had culminated in his shouting, "I'm sick of marriage to a sexless cop who takes an *Ironsides* rip-off for a way of life!" So they'd been divorced. He'd given her a great deal more than Daisy and the house, of course, being one of the wealthiest realtors in Southern California, but then again she'd never wanted for money, not from earliest childhood. It was true relationships she'd lacked.

Her father had been a successful Anaheim pharmacist with three large stores, and much too busy for his only child. Her mother had been equally busy as owner-manager of a fashion boutique in Westwood Village. The two had met in Palm Springs, and Mamie, then Hortense, had been conceived that first passionate evening, as her mother had confessed—or rather bragged.

A liberated woman, Mother. Quite active with other men, both before and after Father's lingering death by cancer. A woman who understood, and forgave, almost every human foible, especially in herself.

But not able to understand about Mamie Belfont refusing to die along with the show.

She had left two weeks ago and was traveling in Mexico with a "gentleman friend" some twenty years her junior. Good luck to her. Mamie didn't approve of such affairs, didn't approve of affairs at all, actually, but she had more important things on her mind.

Like the failure of law enforcement to solve "a glut of sexually heinous crimes," as Chief Shut-In had once put it. Several rapes of young women in Hollywood. A rape-and-stabbing in Studio City. And, of course, those frustrating Silencer murders.

Chief Shut-In had solved a similar case, involving a psychopath who'd killed women he considered prostitutes. Actually, four of the seven victims had been perfectly moral: three with husbands, one a UCLA co-ed. Mamie had disguised herself as a rather flagrant hooker and begun walking the streets—the Hollywood area, in this case, on and around Vine.

As luck would have it, she'd made contact with the killer the very same night that Blake and LeRoy, her co-detectives, had been delayed in the special ambulance that carried Chief Shut-In wherever he was needed. Someone had tampered with the ignition, this a corollary of a sub-plot, and placed Mamie's life in awful danger. The killer was an ex-boxer abandoned by his mother, his wife, and a series of girl-friends, who'd cracked and become Mister Clean, as

251

he signed himself in lipstick on his victims' foreheads.

Though he'd disarmed Mamie of her service revolver, she'd fought him, using every trick of judo and karate learned during her years on the force. She would have been able to defeat an ordinary man, but Mister Clean's years in the ring made him too much for a woman. It was only the mechanical wizardry of LeRoy, the black detective, the Grand Prix level driving of Blake, her handsome blond admirer who almost, but not quite, paid her court, and the superb marksmanship and steely nerves of Chief Shut-In himself, who at the last second fired a shot from the speeding ambulance to snuff out the killer's life, that saved Mamie from being strangled.

Marvelous case!

And Hortense-Mamie was certain that if Mother hadn't been here, interfering with everything she did, Mamie would have gone out and trapped Silencer the same way. Now he'd disappeared.

She was watching television, and flipping through the trades at the same time. Daisy had gone to bed in her quarters over the garage at her usual hour of ten. It was one o'clock and the movie ended and Hortense-Mamie stood up to switch channels to a late talk show.

But she stopped with her hand outstretched. A news roundup had come on, and the announcer's opening story had grabbed her attention:

"While police are cautious in classifying it as the work of Silencer, a young woman found shot through the head in a car parked near the Sunset Strip seems to fit this killer's style. And while the victim was partially unclothed, early reports indicate no signs of sexual molestation, nor were the victim's valuables taken. Which adds up to the return of someone Los Angeles hasn't missed."

That was all, and she switched to the talk show. She finished *The Hollywood Reporter,* and began turning the pages of *Daily Variety*. But she wasn't listening or reading. She was thinking of Silencer, hoping that tomorrow the killing would indeed prove to be his.

After awhile, she climbed the stairs to her bedroom and went through the wall-length double closet, assembling a costume. Then she walked into the study, used the key on the oak cabinet, and took out her snub-nosed .38 Detective Special, the very gun she'd used on *Chief Shut-In*.

Then it had been either empty, or held blanks.

Now it was loaded with live ammunition, the protection needed by a woman living alone. Now she would remember the instructions given her those first weeks on the show, when the cast had gone to the Angelus range to fire their weapons under Sheriff's Department supervision. Now she would realize a year-long ambition to get back on the job . . . though, sadly, without Blake and LeRoy. And especially without her father figure, mentor, confessor, near-God: Chief Shut-In.

When Jeremy Chalk, who'd played the part but at first not lived it, not taken to heart the Chief's almost saintly character, asked her to go to bed with him, she'd refused for the very best reason in the world: "It would confuse me, Jeremy. It would make your role and my role a lie." He'd laughed, but he'd been drinking and she'd forgiven him. And after the show had zoomed into the Top Ten, he'd become a lot more like the Chief, at least during working hours.

She pulled back the stubby revolver's slide-catch and pushed out the cylinder. She checked the five chambers, and each held a bullet. She snapped back the cylinder with a flick of the wrist, doing it quickly, with confidence, as Mamie often had before going into action.

She put the gun away and got into her flannel pajamas. In bed, she closed her eyes . . . but couldn't sleep, feeling the blood course through her veins, feeling her pulse pounding, feeling *alive* as she hadn't for more than a year.

Tomorrow night, she would begin the search for a killer, a solo assignment, not the first of Mamie Belfont's career. And when she found him, knowledgeable though she was about the psychologically unbalanced, he would either surrender or she would pump those five bullets into his body with as little remorse as he had shown for his victims.

As Chief Shut-In often pointed out, "Our Mamie's one tough cookie!"

Diana was reading when the classical-music program ended and a newsbreak came on. And she learned that "Silencer has probably killed again."

She turned the radio dial to the all-news station, where a moment later she heard the Silencer item, phrased a little differently, but with nothing new added.

She shut off the radio and got out of bed. She changed from her favorite sleeping garment—an old, comfortable cotton nightgown—to a wisp of diaphanous black lace that Carla had given her last Christmas "for that special guy, when you find him."

She put on high heels, went downstairs, and found the "special guy" sleeping on the couch. Because with Silencer back, she would need the lieutenant again. And she was about to lose him. And there was only one way to heal the rift.

She bent and shook him. "Larry."

He was on his back and moved and groaned, but he didn't awaken.

Two hours had passed since they'd returned from the restaurant, long enough for him to have regained some degree of sobriety.

She kneeled and rubbed his face with both hands. He opened his eyes. She bent and kissed his mouth. "I got lonely, honey."

He cleared his throat. "What?"

She kissed him again. "I accept your deal." And now that she had a *reason* for making love to him, now that it was business, almost like the parlor, she began to grow excited.

And it was more than the parlor, and she was beginning to tremble in anticipation of satisfying his long, built-up need, her own long, built-up curiosity.

He pushed himself back, half-sitting against the arm of the couch. "Once a week for a year?"

"Or twice or three times for as long as we both want to."

He put his feet on the floor. "Can I have some coffee?"

She walked to the kitchen doorway, where she turned. He was looking at her: at her legs and thighs in the shorty nightgown; at her breasts and bottom in the see-through lace; finally at her face. "Another dream?" he muttered.

"Why don't you go upstairs and shower? I've got a wraparound towel-robe hanging on the door that might do you."

He rose unsteadily and made his way to the staircase. She entered the kitchen and loaded the electric coffee machine. Then she went to the hall closet and got into a coat. It was a chilly night to be near-naked.

As soon as she heard him coming down, she took off the coat. She poured two cups of coffee, moved two chairs close together, sat down in one.

He came in, wearing her half-sleeved robe of white terry cloth—the tie-belt just about keeping it closed around him—and black socks. He said, "One laugh and you're dead."

Actually, she didn't find him funny. The robe, which was long on her, showed his legs from the knees down; muscular, hairy legs. His arms were thick, corded, with blue veins running into heavy-boned wrists. His shoulders pulled the terry cloth open at the chest; a deep chest. And he rubbed a head of hair still damp from the shower and smoothed a bristly mustache.

She patted the seat beside her.

He came over, but took his coffee standing.

When she said, "Sit down, Larry," he said, "Don't think I better."

She tugged his hand. He sat down; the belt gave way and the robe parted. She saw his thighs . . . and the dark knot of genitals. She didn't give him a chance to draw the robe closed again, leaning into him, murmuring, "Kiss me."

He kissed her. It was too gentle for this moment, and she reached down between his legs. "*Kiss* me!"

His penis swelled and his kiss intensified. He bent her head back and his hands moved over her breasts. Suddenly, he rose, drawing her up with him, then picked her up, one arm under her knees, the other under her shoulders, and carried her at a stumbling run toward the stairs.

She was thrilled, thrilled, sucking at his lips, biting at his mustache, thinking she was insane not to have done this a month ago.

Halfway up the staircase, he paused, gasping, "Christ, weak in the knees."

She reached down and caressed his genitals, and he was still rigid.

He leaned against the staircase, shifting her in his arms. "Diana, wait, the booze . . ."

She squeezed his penis. "Big! A real cop's club! Use it on me, Lieutenant!" And twisted her head to look down at it, and jerked it a few times, burning for it.

And felt the spasm, as she'd felt it so many times at the parlor.

He let her down instantly, groaning deeply: "Finish, baby!"

She hated him!

And hated herself—her "magic fingers," as one long-time customer put it.

But she turned into him, lifting her nightgown with her free hand, jerking him off into her belly.

After which he sank to the stairs, sitting there, head down. "Sorry," he muttered.

She said nothing, still holding her nightgown waist-high, the other hand cupping low on her stomach to catch the semen.

He looked up. "Hey, it's no different than most of your customers, right?"

She walked to the landing.

"Diana."

She turned. He was smiling. "You're really mad at me? You really wanted to make it? Not just the deal?"

She said, "Let's get some sleep."

He rose and began to walk downstairs.

"Up here," she said, and went through the bedroom into the adjoining bathroom. Where he joined her, and they both washed. She made a production of it, rubbing the washcloth not only over her stomach but between her legs, her buttocks. She saw him watching in the mirror, and figured he'd be ready in a few minutes. She walked out, kicking off her shoes.

He followed. "This is the last time I drink like a fool. Not since I found out a Jody had my girl did I put away so much, so fast."

"A Jody?" she asked, getting into the king-sized bed.

He went around to the other side and slipped out of the bathrobe. He had a wide, muscular body, quite hairy, with just the beginnings of a belly. "Jody, a man's name used in a Marine marching song. It became the term for anyone who took a grunt's woman."

"A grunt?" she asked, as he turned his back and sat down at the edge of the bed to remove his socks.

"A soldier. Rifleman. The guy who takes the hills and wins the wars . . . only we didn't."

She wondered if he was finally going to talk about Vietnam.

"I guess you felt wrong about being there?" she prompted.

He stopped moving, his back still to her. "Wrong?"

"Well, most of us were against that particular war. The big bully picking on the little kid, you know."

"The big bully with both hands tied behind his back, feet hobbled, trying to butt with his head and getting kicked in the nuts by a very tough little kid, *you* know."

He sounded really upset. She said, "Get into bed."

He stayed put. "What was wrong about our being there was that no one here gave a shit. What was wrong was that we were stumbling around catching hell and being called murderers by everyone from Jane Fonda to Doctor Spock . . . neither of whom, I'd

257

guess, has ever had to catch hell for his country."

"Larry, I'm sorry I asked. I didn't realize it was still so fresh in your mind."

"It isn't." He paused. "Maybe sometimes, like when I drink." He turned to look at her. "Isn't it possible that we were as honestly motivated as the ones burning their draft cards? With much more on the line, risking much more? And look at what Vietnam has done in the last few years—Cambodia, the boat people. Isn't it possible we were as right as North Vietnam was?"

"I don't know," she said. "I wasn't political as a student. I'm not now."

"Same here," he said. "But it had nothing to do with politics. It had to do with something more important—keeping your family alive. That's basic to a society. Keeping one's family alive. And we were your family."

She realized he was shivering, sitting there naked, and she reached out and tugged his arm. He quickly laughed, said, "A load of bullshit," and rose to sweep back the covers.

She wanted to say, "Not bullshit," because he'd touched her with that "Keeping one's family alive." Because she understood it, having lost half of her own.

He was in bed with her now, but kept his distance. He was shy with her, the ex-Marine, the tough cop . . . and she liked it.

And also understood it, since she'd kept him at arm's length for more than a month.

"Hold me, Larry."

He moved over and took her in his arms, fumbling to get comfortable, finally sighing and touching her cheek with his lips. "I know you don't feel the same," he whispered, "but I've got to say it."

She didn't want to hear it . . . and she did.

"I love you." His arms tightened. "Jesus God, Diana, I love you and I can't stop and it doesn't make any difference what you do because I'll just go on loving you!"

Her pulse quickened. It had been a long time since

258

she'd allowed herself to be in a position to hear such words. Years. Back to St. Louis, even.

She stroked his shoulder, his hip. She kissed his chin, his lips. She wanted to reawaken his passion because her own needed satisfying. But waited for him to make the overt moves, the sexual moves, this time.

And waited, and waited. And realized his breathing had fallen into a steady, rhythmic pattern.

He was asleep, the bastard!

Then she laughed, seeing the humor of it, the poetic justice of it.

She considered masturbation. And decided to wait until morning, when he could demonstrate his love.

But in the morning, she awoke to his hand shaking her shoulder, his voice saying, "Gotta go, Diana."

He was standing beside the bed, fully dressed.

"What time is it?" she mumbled.

"Early. I have to call in when I stay away from my phone. There was another Silencer murder last night." He paused. "You heard it on TV or radio, didn't you? Before you woke me?"

She tried to clear her mind. "I heard a brief news item . . ."

"You should have told me."

"They weren't sure it *was* Silencer at one this morning."

"They are now. Ballistics got a break. The bullet went through the victim without disintegrating, and lodged in thick leather upholstery."

She sat up. "Can't you stay for breakfast?"

He was staring at her. "I wondered why the sudden change of heart. Now I think I understand. You'll do anything to help avenge your sister, won't you? To encourage this particular police officer . . . ?"

"No change of heart," she interrupted sharply, the old combativeness reasserting itself. "I told you I needed time to think over your deal. I didn't say it had to be a *long* time."

"Right," he said, and nodded, as if to himself. "My deal. It'll never be more than one deal or another for

259

you, will it? Keep the money, or get revenge, or . . ." He shrugged. "Your line of work is your way of life."

He turned and left. A moment later, she heard the front door open and bang shut.

"Right," she muttered, and forgot the vagaries of love and concentrated on the solid reality of hate. Hate for the man she'd never forgotten for one minute, never forgiven for one second during his six-weeks' absence.

The news conference was the biggest, noisiest, most disorganized ever for Larry Admer. A real circus, overflowing from the parking lot, with literally hundreds of onlookers and cars jamming the street. And the newspeople screaming at him, at each other, but most of all at the tall, lean man who handled the madness with calm competence.

Larry realized that rock star Burn Digger was used to larger, noisier, probably more dangerous crowds than this one, but still admired the younger man's poise, especially in the face of some of the questions being hurled at him.

He described his relationship with Betty "Chez" Anderson as "a real good friendship." Said the car-park boy's judgment that they'd "had a fight" a few hours before her death was "the kind of drama people look for in these cases." Shook his head ruefully when asked to explain why she would park off the Sunset Strip when she was supposed to go to Encino. Didn't bother answering at all when a question from the mob was distasteful, such as the woman's voice screaming, "There's a rumor you and Chez had a child. Where is it now?"

When that was followed by, "Or an abortion. Could you comment?" he turned to Larry and in a voice too low for the newspeople to hear, asked if he could leave.

In an equally low voice, Larry said he'd been free to leave after the routine questioning session. "You didn't have to let yourself in for this."

"Can't turn off the media, Lieutenant. Not in my business." He grinned. "But man, I hate the mothers!"

On the strength of that, Larry ran interference for him through the parking lot.

They reached the street, where a limousine and burly driver were waiting, and a different type of crush began, one comprised mainly of fans.

Larry left The Digger to cope on his own, and made his way to the station house. Half a dozen patrolmen, and Captain Cohen, stood in the doorway, watching the insanity. Cohen drew him aside.

"We just got word from Parker Center. They're assigning five more detectitves to your task force."

"They had thirty or forty men on the Hillside Strangler *task force,* and a lot of good it did them."

Cohen ignored him. "Plus a high-ranking officer over you."

"You know, I have a friend in Oregon, a big political fish in a small pond. He offered me the job of chief of a small-town force. Run my own show, he said. Twenty men and four good-looking women, and almost nothing for them to do except give traffic citations."

"I'm the high-ranking officer."

"When do you think you'll make an arrest, Captain?"

Cohen frowned at him.

"That's what they keep asking *me.* Now they can ask you."

"No, Larry. They'll still ask *you.* Because all I'm going to do is look into your office each day after lunch and belch."

"Don't you do that now?"

Cohen chuckled and ambled away.

In his office, Larry decided he was lucky in his captain. He could have had Blue Balls Cochran, who was almost as bad as the officers dreamed up by ex-cops turned writers. Cochran's trouble was women. At fifty, he was obsessed by young women. He could barely restrain himself when a meter maid walked by. But restrain himself he did . . . and it led to one of the

261

most frustrated personalities in all of law enforcement.

As Cohen once said, "Since Cochran can't fuck ass, he kicks it."

Larry Admer was beginning to understand Captain Cochran in a way he never had before.

Still, his own frustration was going to end, at least in the purely physical sense. Six weeks was long enough to wait on a virgin, much less a massage-parlor girl! A deal was a deal, whether it was based on her pushing him to work harder at solving her sister's case, or wanting to keep all the money in that safety box. One thing he had to accept, swallow, digest—it wasn't based on love, nor would it ever be. And that was fine with him. Or would be, once that deep ache went away.

The phone rang. It was Vic Chasen, one of his men, calling from the Coroner's office.

"It's official now, Lieutenant. She wasn't laid, and no one shot a load into her ass or her mouth. No semen on her body. No sign of sexual activity of any kind."

"Any explanation for her wearing only shoes and pantyhose?"

"Maybe the joint on the floor. It had heavy elements of PCP."

"Get me the guy she was smoking with and we'll find out."

Chasen gave the boss a chuckle—something Larry had always refused to do, even with hard cases like Cochran. After Vietnam, kissing ass had not only seemed indecent, but irrelevant.

"Have you dusted the Rolls for prints, vacuumed thoroughly, examined it inch-by-inch for anything that might help us?"

"Sure, Lieutenant." Chasen sounded insulted. "I was going to ask if we could take out the seats, the stereo equipment, the panels, really tear it apart."

"Why would you want to do that? You think Silencer hid his gun in the door? Put his fingerprints under the upholstery? Shot his load into the radio?"

Another perfunctory laugh. "The PCP, Lieutenant.

262

That junkie musician might have a stash somewhere."

"I didn't realize this was a drug bust, Vic. I thought it was a murder investigation."

"Well, as long as we can nail him for that dusted joint . . ."

"But we can't. It was his car, but he wasn't there. He was in a private club, seen by some two dozen people, at the time the girl was smoking and being murdered. We could nail *her* for the joint."

Chasen didn't laugh this time.

"That's a hundred-thousand-dollar car, Vic, belonging to a man who can raise considerable hell, if he wants to."

"Who'd listen to a rock freak over a police officer?"

Larry sighed. Unlike Captain Cohen, he didn't have the patience to conduct lectures on changing times, or on the political muscle generated by people who frequented On The Rox. He didn't like dope, he didn't like dopers . . . but he liked what he'd seen of The Digger. He wasn't a one-track mind, a one-track cop.

"Forget the car. We'll hold it awhile, but we're not dismantling it. Anything unusual from the coroner?"

"Unusual? Same like the others, mainly. Powder burns, so the gun was either touching or very close to her skin. The bullet passed through her brain—in through the face somewhere and out the back of the head, you'll get the details in the written report. The rock freak'll have to change his car's carpeting—she bled like a fucking pig. The bullet's in good condition and Forensic's made a matchup with the other Silencer bullets and fragments. No doubt about it: whoever killed the four other cunts killed this one."

Larry said, "You're a natural poet," and hung up. He lit a Camel, his first since taking Diana to dinner yesterday. A record of sorts. But it only served to make this cigarette taste better than any of the others.

The phone rang. Assistant D.A. Vineland's voice said, "So our friend is back. Have you been informed that your S.I.T. is being upgraded to a task force and increased by six men?"

"Five."

"Well, the loss of only one man is a victory. Another victory is keeping the group in the family, firmly under your control."

"You know about Captain Cohen too?"

"My good man," Vineland said, obviously enjoying himself, "I arranged it."

"You're taking a hell of an interest in this case, including working on Saturday."

"Ah, you noticed."

"According to the movies I see, you're doing it either because you're Silencer and you want to keep tabs on our progress, or else you want to be Governor."

Vineland laughed, a little too quickly. "I often work Saturdays. Sundays too. As for Silencer . . ." He paused. "It's an important case. You solve it and you make captain. I prosecute it and I become D.A."

"We blow it and we become shit."

"Not *we*. If I blew the case in court, yes. But right now, it's all *you*, Lieutenant."

"How can you be sure you'll be assigned the case, if we nail him?"

"I've already been assigned the case. Second in command, you know. What will soon become public knowledge is that the D.A. is stepping down due to poor health. So do us both a big favor, Larry. *Work* on it."

"Night and day," Larry said.

He hung up the phone, lit another Camel, and dialed Diana's number. She answered sleepily. "When do we consummate the deal?" he said.

"Friday, my day off."

"I don't want to wait that long. I'm taking Wednesdays off from now on—just one day, until Silencer is caught. I want you to change *your* day off to Wednesday."

"I'll try."

"*Do* it. Or forget it." It had taken some effort of will to be that hard with her, and it took even more to hang up. Then he waited an eternity . . . until the phone rang; until she spoke.

"Larry, don't be that way with me. Don't turn from supplicant to tyrant. I'll keep my end of the deal, but . . ." She paused, and her voice dropped. "But let's try and make it something special. You want that, don't you?"

He suspected her motives, still. But he also loved her still. "Yes, I want that." He took a deep breath, and exhaled anger and rejection. His voice softened. "Give me all of Friday night. Until the next morning."

"Yes."

After that, it was easier to get back to the file cabinet. All those unsolved crimes. And the mounting toll of death and destruction in the city. . . .

Eating a cottage-cheese salad, and watching the five o'clock news, Diana was appalled by the carnival atmosphere and riotous exhibition put on by the media and bystanders during the news conference in which first Larry Admer and then Burn Digger answered questions about the murder of Burn's girlfriend—because she was planning to let herself in for the same thing by phoning five television stations, two radio stations, and two newspapers, to give them anonymous tips as to where Silencer's first victim's sister worked. A juicy little side angle—the suspected whore-victim having a sex-masseur sister—to go with the revived story. Should get them all down to the parlor tonight.

She'd been waiting over a month to do it. But now she realized that if only half her calls had the desired effect, there would be too many cameras, too many reporters. What she wanted to say could be lost in the resultant confusion.

Also, she'd be finished as a media event in just this single interview.

She changed channels, watching until she caught the same news conference on the two other networks, each of which had a somewhat different point of view, playing up the reporting technique of its own particular star.

It was six-fifteen before she turned off the set, having decided how to handle her interview.

Just one network for this one night.

Just one newsperson: Wyona Wise, the most popular on the early news shows. The brightest of them all. And a woman, capable of being sympathetic to another woman's point of view.

She sipped coffee and thought it through. She would have to act surprised when confronted at the Grecian Massage. Embarrassed at being photographed there, caught *in flagrante delicto,* as it would seem to Ms. Wise. Indignant at being insistently questioned. And finally resigned; after which she would present her point of view of Silencer as a sick, pitiful degenerate rather than a monster.

And hope that most of her remarks made it to the tube; reached Silencer with her message . . . and, just as important, her location. So that he could find her. So that she could find *him.*

She stood up and went to her purse. She checked the photo copy of Mel's sketch—the fat face, the narrow-set eyes, the high forehead. She had copies in her car, raincoat, several jackets, and the two mini-togas at work.

She then went to the counter phone to resume the operation she'd begun six weeks ago, when she'd called a newscaster and spoke to him and his audience. And, she hoped, to an enraged Silencer.

She dialed and asked for Wyona Wise. As she waited, she made a mental note to buy something she disliked, that she'd put off even thinking about for as long as she could. Something she had to go out and get right now. Something she would need after tonight; certainly after tomorrow night, when the rest of the media would show up at the parlor.

A gun.

Chris gave Mel the big embrace. Jerry leaned over the bar to shake his hand and ask, "Champagne and brandy, shaved ice, tall glass?" The girls he'd known when his wife was dancing here at the Pink Club came over to say sorry-about-Beth-Anne and how-you-feeling-baby?

Nice. Even though Chris had been fucking Beth-Anne right up until the night she'd been killed. Even though Jerry worked at every cunt he could make from behind that bar. Even though half the girls were bi-sexual and most of the others straight lezzie and Beth-Anne had tasted just about all of them.

Only Chico, the fag lighting-and-music man, hadn't given him the horns, Mel thought. And smiled to himself, because it was the way the game was played here on the Strip. And Chico had tried to suck his dick one drunken night, so everyone had an angle. On Wilshire Boulevard the angle was business, screwing the other guy for big bucks. Here it was screwing, period.

A new girl with small jugs but an ass that more than made up for it was doing a set on the stage. Knowing where her strength lay, she kept her back to the audience most of the time.

The audience wasn't much this early in the evening—maybe half-a-dozen dudes at the bar, another half-dozen at the tables in the big, square room which was kept as dark as possible. Mel always said the darkness was to hide the food, but he ordered a Pinkburger and salad. And he told the topless waitress, Kelly, a bi-chick who hooked on the side, to give his best to Bootsie, the cook.

"Bootsie's gone," she said, looking down at her silicone-steady boobs, admiring them. "He was busted for dealing smack."

Mel shuddered. Heroin was a heavy rap. "He wasn't a dealer. He just used, occasionally. Did they plant on him?"

"I don't think so. He was importing with a merchant-seaman friend of his. They had a kilo coming down from Frisco. The friend was followed, and when he made the delivery to Bootsie, narcs broke in the kitchen door and nailed them both. We were closed for three days while Chris was investigated. Didn't you hear about it?"

"Had other things on my mind," he muttered. *In* his mind, would have been more accurate. And he was wondering if all those things—those particles and fragments of lead and bone—were actually gone. Because he had one hell of a headache; his neck was stiff; his right hip and leg ached for no damn reason. All fucked up, and out of the hospital just a day and a half.

He asked about the new cook. Kelly said, "He's really good, Mel!" So he stuck with his order.

He nursed his champagne and brandy, watching the big ass rotate in the spotlight. When the girl finished. he gave her his patented little whoop of approval. Which made most of the other customers look at him, some with less than true love for the nigger lusting after white meat.

Yeah, he knew the routine. Racism, baby, as American as apple pie and baseball, and don't you forget it, because it wouldn't forget you.

But fuck 'em! Mostly tourists, and what did tourists know anyway? He'd been king of the Sunset Strip with a gorgeous chick, sometimes two, on his arm and in his bed every night. He'd whooped in every club, including those on Santa Monica and La Cienega, and five or six years back there'd been *dozens* of them, man. Like the Class Act, where he would bring money and cunt together just for the fun of it. Favors, baby, and they'd been returned in other ways.

Tonight he was meeting someone who owed him a few.

A very unpleasant someone, William Dessio Jr., called Little Billy Balls. Not because he was small, and not because of anything unusual about his testicles, but because he was six-two, wide as a house, and had balls for any action on God's earth, including murder. Mel was going to remind Billy of all the quim he'd shoveled his way those bygone halcyon years. He was going to bring up the names of mutual friends in Vegas. He was going to ask for one big favor in return for the many little ones.

268

Billy arrived as Mel was finishing his burger and salad, and said, "Is it safe to eat in a cunt heaven?"

No how've-you-been. No glad-you-recovered. Just sat himself down on the red-leather bench beside Mel, making it creak, and called out across the room to where Kelly was at the bar, "Double Scotch, chesty, and move it."

She looked around, annoyed. Mel shook his head, making sure she saw it. And Chris, who was not only manager but bouncer, with the youth and muscle Beth-Anne had dug, quickly moved to her and whispered; then called back, "Nice to see you again, Mr. Dessio. A double Chivas, on the house."

Billy said, "Thanks," and turned to Mel. "You look like shit."

"It's the life I lead."

"That Silencer fuck's for real, huh?"

"Until you blow him away for me."

Billy was big, but his face was *enormous*. It seemed two-feet square. Only the eyes were small. Still, you couldn't miss them when they fixed on you . . . like a snake's.

Mel finished his champagne and brandy. He wanted another, but decided that since he not only looked like shit but felt like it, he'd better not. He put down the glass and let Billy stare at him. He began to feel sick to his stomach, and wondered if the new cook was really as good as Kelly thought.

Finally, Billy said, "Are you asking me to do a contract? I charge, Mel. It's gone up to two grand, for a friend."

"You owe me," Mel said, looking into the snake-eyed gaze. "Just this once."

Little Billy Balls always made quick decisions. Mel knew he would either walk out, or say yes.

Billy said, "Give me a name, an address, a picture."

"I'll give you a drawing. But I don't have the name and address of the man who killed Beth-Anne and shot me."

Billy laughed. His drink came and he looked at

Kelly's breasts and said, "Honey, you ever hurt anyone with those bowling balls?"

She'd gotten the word and bent to wipe at the table, pushing them in his face. "Couldn't hurt a big man like you."

Billy put out his tongue. She giggled and quickly straightened, looking around. Touching the girls was a no-no, something the vice cops used as an excuse to close up clubs.

Billy pulled out his wallet and gave her a twenty and a card. "Let me hear from you, chesty."

"You can count on it." She went to another table.

Billy raised his glass, said, "*Ciao*," and tossed off the double. "Well, at least I had a laugh and met a cunt." He began to rise.

Mel said, "You can do it," knowing quite suddenly that Billy couldn't. Knowing that he'd been dreaming of easy revenge, amateur revenge, as he'd accused Diana Woodruff of doing. This to help him through the endless hospital days.

Billy sat back down. "I don't know you anymore. You were one of the smart spooks. Champie said you could've been right up there in the Vegas ranch operation if you'd wanted to."

A ranch operation was whore houses. Mel was almost sorry he hadn't gone from Champie's New York turf to his Nevada action. Would have saved him a lot of trouble, like losing a wife and getting a hole in the head.

"Yeah," he muttered. He felt ashamed. And still, he couldn't help asking, "Isn't there *any* way? The organization's so big."

"If we had that kind of smarts," Billy said, taking out cigarettes, "we'd make deals with the government." He smoked a while, watching a very beautiful Oriental girl dance in white boots and cowboy hat. "You need money, Mel?"

Did he ever. But he always said no to racket money, because that was repayable in services. And he said it now.

270

Billy said, "See you," and walked out.

Mel decided on another drink after all.

Kelly served it bubbling cold and with a smile, but it didn't taste too good this time. He left it unfinished and got up.

Or tried to get up.

Because, somehow, his right foot got tangled with his left leg and he fell over on his face and lay there, wondering what the hell was going on. Then he vomited into the carpeting and lost consciousness.

Later, he woke up on the couch of Chris's office and Doc Byrnes was there. Byrnes was a top-notch GP out of Beverly Hills, but about eighty years old and retired and available only to the employees of the particular nude club he happened to be visiting. He visited one or another almost every night. The girls he would treat for colds, or sprains, or hemorrhoids—preferably hemorrhoids.

The men on an emergency basis only.

"So, Melvin," the thin old man said, sitting beside him. "You got out of the hospital a little too soon."

Mel began to sit up, but stopped when the pain hit his head. He groaned and lay back carefully . . . just like after the shooting. "I was in six weeks, Doc. They were sure I was recovered."

"They couldn't be sure. Not with the brain. They could be hopeful."

Mel began to nod, and stopped. "What do you think I should do?"

"Go back to Cedars-Sinai, Melvin."

"Christ, I'd go nuts! And I'd run up my bill even higher! How can I make money to pay for what I already owe if I'm on my ass?"

"I don't know. I'm through with all that." He stood up. "I'm going back to the club to watch something I'm not quite through with." He smiled, showing his neat gray dentures. "Keeps me alive, Melvin. I hope you find something that does the same for you."

Lying there, eyes closed, Mel began to sweat. And the room wasn't hot.

He tried to calm himself.

He sat up, very slowly, and it was all right.

He stood up, just as slowly, and it was fine.

He walked to the door and everything worked and he thought that maybe it was just the hamburger, just the booze.

But in the parking lot, he tripped over nothing and sprawled on the blacktop, scraping his knees.

He got up and brushed himself off carefully. Water had puddled from yesterday's heavy rains. He'd slipped. That was it. He'd go home now and change his soiled trousers and go out again. He'd visit a few more clubs and see a few old friends. It was only nine-thirty; much too early for bed. And he'd had enough TV in the hospital to last the rest of his life. What he wanted was *people!*

Including a cute new chick.

Like the doc said, to keep him alive.

He got in the car and drove home.

He climbed the stairs to his second-floor apartment and went to the bedroom. He opened the closet and selected fresh clothing. But then he turned away, holding his head with both hands. "Please, please, don't start this shit again!"

He felt hot and got out of his clothes and lay on top of the blankets. He closed his eyes and told himself he would sleep and when he awoke it would be better. But then he got cold, terribly cold, and even after covering himself couldn't warm up.

He lay there, shivering, unable to sleep, unable to stem a growing horror.

They were waiting in the Grecian Massage parking lot when she drove in at eleven-thirty. She saw the van and the movement behind it, but acted as if she saw nothing. She parked near the entrance and got out . . . and they were running across the near-empty lot, three of them: Wyona Wise and a cameraman and a man with lights which flared on and blinded her.

She flung an arm over her face and made as if to head for the parlor.

The cameraman blocked her path, moving side to side, filming her as she tried to get by. She ducked her head and made an end-run. As she expected, the light-man blocked her.

"I'm Wyona Wise. We want only to give you a chance to say what's in your heart after the brutal murder of your sister. You phoned one of our colleagues five or six weeks ago and said certain things. Now that Silencer has killed again, we're offering you the chance to comment more fully."

Voice low, Diana said, "How did you know where to find me?"

"We have our methods."

"If you'll meet me Monday, somewhere else, anywhere you choose . . ."

"I'm afraid it has to be here and now, Miss Woodruff. Just compose yourself and we'll begin the interview."

Before Diana could argue further, Wyona Wise directed camera and lights onto herself and gave her usual introduction; then turned to Diana, the camera and lights swinging with her. "Miss Diana Woodruff, sister of Silencer's first victim, is herself a possible victim of this determined destroyer of women since she works in a massage parlor off the Sunset Strip. She has previously expressed herself in public regarding the man who has killed five times in this very area . . ."

Diana stood quietly, resignedly. When Wyona Wise held the microphone out to her, she said, "I've never felt that the man you call Silencer is responsible for his actions. Far from being a 'determined destroyer of women,' he's helpless in the grip of a sickness that controls him like a puppet. Not that he's unique in this. The way our society views women—and I don't mean just women who work at jobs like mine, but women in general—makes many men feel they can act violently toward them and get away with it. These men might actually be a majority in our culture, considering the vast numbers of wife beaters . . ."

She went on this way, and all the time she was

aware that Wise hadn't given the *name* of the massage parlor.

But she completed her statement without including it. Not only because it would have to be stuck in, gratuitously offered, but also because a Diana Woodruff truly surprised at her shameful job would try to hide it.

With more reporters coming tomorrow, someone was bound to let it slip. So she nodded as Wyona Wise thanked her, and went on into the parlor.

She relieved Lola, a new girl claiming to be French but quite obviously of Mexican stock, and said, *"Adios, hermana."* It earned her a supposedly puzzled look, and she shrugged.

She got into her mini-toga, checking the inside pocket for her folded photocopy of Mel's Silencer drawing, and settled down with a paperback copy of *Patterns of Culture,* wondering if it would hold up for her after ten years.

Someone came in. She marked her place and began to rise. Then she sank back down. It was Wyona Wise's lighting man, short, broad, middle-aged. He said, "I figured as long as I'm here . . ." He grinned.

"Are your friends waiting for you?"

"No, I'll get a cab."

"Expensive, if you don't live nearby."

"Well, Saturday night and all that."

"With the hundred I charge, it'll be *quite* a Saturday night."

"You only live once."

"But extravagantly, on an expense account."

"I guess I could try to write it off."

"Definitely, since you're on a story: Inside the Grecian Massage, a special report by the staff of the Early News."

He shook his head. "Now how could we report anything like this?"

"I'm not sure. But I reserve the right to refuse service to anyone."

"You know, we deliberately held back on giving the name and exact location of this place. If you

274

don't want every weirdo in Los Angeles coming in here . . ."

She picked up the phone.

He walked to a chair. "Don't be foolish. Wyona wants this."

Diana dialed her own number and spoke to the continuing ring: "Arthur, I need some help." She hung up and opened her book. Before she'd read a paragraph, he was gone.

She sat there, thinking. This was only the beginning; the curiosity seekers were yet to come. And among them, she was sure, would be a sprinkling of irrational types, perhaps even dangerous types.

She could ask Arthur for a bouncer. But that might inhibit Silencer if he scouted the place. And the bouncer would report on all the nut action to Arthur, who would then transfer her elsewhere.

She shrugged. She would have to face the psychopaths alone. Until that one, fat, fortish psychopath showed up.

She concentrated on remembering what she'd said during the interview, and what she'd left out. Plenty that she'd left out, she realized, and took pad and pencil from the desk and began making notes.

Tomorrow, she would say that those who wanted to execute Silencer had to realize he wasn't capable of premeditated murder; that he could act only as his insanity moved him to at a particular moment.

That he probably fell into the classic woman-killer mold: inept with women all his life, finally impotent, until now all he could do with one was kill her.

That she advised women to carry weapons: that simply showing a knife or gun would terrify Silencer, a basic coward who dared not attack his physical equals and so turned on women.

She reread her notes, and nodded, satisfied. If anything could make him plan her murder, and reveal himself to her to prove he was unafraid and sexually competent, this would.

Which could add up to his losing his strongest plus

—his element of surprise. He would become vulnerable to someone waiting; someone hunting him . . .

Which reminded her, and she went to the back room and the locked closet where she kept her purse. She removed the purse, and from it the gun she'd purchased earlier this evening.

It was a caliber .25 ACP Colt automatic, just four and a half inches in length, a so-called Lilliput or Ladies' Pistol, that fit easily into purse or pocket. It was nickel-plated, light even when fully loaded, and she was able to extend it, aim it, and not feel any strain.

The gunshop salesman had suggested she fire at a target "to familiarize yourself with the characteristics of this basically short-range weapon, and to develop good marksmanship."

She cared nothing for its characteristics, beyond that it could kill. And the range, for her, would be very short indeed, precluding a need to develop good marksmanship. She would empty its six-shot magazine into Silencer's face and chest from just inches away.

As for all the safety instructions, she'd listened politely, accepted the NRA booklet, and asked the salesman to load the automatic. She'd paid, taken the boxed gun and extra ammunition in the heavy brown paper bag, and left. In her car, she'd removed the gun from the box, and slid the manual safety to off. Now it could be picked up and fired. Now it was instantaneously lethal.

She'd tossed the bag, box, pamphlets, and extra ammunition into the Fiat's trunk and driven off. She would use the weapon only once, or not at all.

Now she walked to the front of the Grecian Massage and pulled back a corner of the window drape. No life in the parking lot. And Wyona Wise and her interview wouldn't be on the air until tomorrow. So no chance of Silencer coming here tonight.

Still, she got a hand towel and wrapped it around the gun and put it in the desk drawer. She would carry it with her when she took a customer in back. She could carry it with her when she drove home, ate in a restaurant, went to the bathroom. From now on, it would be with her always.

Hardly aware of her thought process, she wondered what Larry's reaction would be if he knew.

SIXTEEN: *Sunday, September 17*

Hortense-Mamie slept until three in the afternoon, and for the first time since the show had been cancelled, felt as if she'd earned the rest. Because she'd been patrolling the murder area from midnight on—the time the Coroner estimated Silencer's most recent victim to have died.

She'd mapped out, driven to, and then covered on foot, three distinct sections off the Sunset Strip. The first, marked by Fairfax Boulevard on the east, had side streets on the north as well as the south side of Sunset. It had taken about an hour to cover, sauntering along as a prostitute would.

The second, marked by La Cienega on the east, was in the hills area, which meant that there was very little in the way of streets on the north side of Sunset, but a large section on the south, running all the way to Santa Monica Boulevard. This included three streets where Silencer had struck. And this was where she had sauntered more slowly, more tensely, hand close to her open purse and her gun.

The third and last section ran from San Vicente west to the sign reading "City of Beverly Hills."

Altogether, about four hours of walking. And almost no women on the streets, especially strange for a Saturday night. Silencer had frightened them away . . . all but Mamie Belfont.

A good night's work, she'd felt, and slept the sleep of the just. And at three-forty-five p.m. got into her swimsuit and ran downstairs, humming the theme from *Chief Shut-In.* Daisy was dusting in the living room, and said, "Good to hear you happy again, Horty."

She wanted to say, "Call me Mamie," but didn't. Predictably, it would upset the aging housekeeper, who wouldn't understand how one could live a role, become a character. As mother hadn't. As Everett Cole, who'd played Blake, hadn't the one time she'd let down her guard with him. That was three months ago when he'd come to dinner with a Jeroboam of excellent French champagne and she'd drunk too much and allowed him to kiss her, to fondle her breasts, to maneuver her up to her bedroom.

Where she'd called him Blake and told him she'd dreamt of making love to him ever since he'd saved her from the Revolutionary Tribunal's abduction squad.

He'd pulled back and looked at her, and she'd gone on to say she owed him so much—including her beauty, when he'd flung the pillow across the room at the acid-thrower. "I know it's shallow, Blake, but I couldn't have tolerated being scarred and ugly."

He'd begun laughing drunkenly.

At that point, she'd realized that he'd never taken on the finer qualities of Blake; that he was just another silly, lecherous actor killing time with any available woman. And she'd made him leave.

She went out to the pool, which she kept at a tepid eighty-six degrees. She hadn't been swimming the past month, but now she felt vigorous, purposeful, and dived in and began counting laps.

When she grew tired, she floated, looking up at the clear sky, thinking she would begin her patrol earlier tonight.

She swam a little longer, then went upstairs. By the time she came out of the bathroom, it was almost five o'clock. She went to the dresser and the portable television. Then she got into bed and settled back against the pillows.

"And now," the voice-over-logo announced, "another *Chief Shut-In* adventure."

Mamie clapped her hands ecstatically when she saw that it was one of her stronger cases, almost a solo, during which she'd returned to college to trap a campus killer.

Mel awakened to the sound of the phone. For a moment he didn't know where he was; began calling for the nurse to answer for him.

But then the events of the past two days flooded in on him and he lifted himself on an elbow and reached to the night table.

"Melvin? That you?"

He said yes and cleared his throat. "Who's this?"

"Lieutenant Admer. You know that Silencer's back, don't you?"

"I'd have to be dead not to know that, Lieutenant."

"I thought it might stir your memory a little, get his face clearer . . ."

"No, I lost all memory when I lost my money." He chuckled to show he was only fooling.

"Could we arrange a trade?"

Mel was silent, unwilling to admit, yet that he *had* anything to trade.

"You think about it, Melvin. I can have your money released tomorrow afternoon, if I want to. Goodbye."

Mel looked at the digital clock. "Jesus!" he exclaimed. It was almost five, and the light in the windows proved it couldn't be a.m. He'd slept from about ten last night to five this afternoon. He'd slept nineteen fucking hours!

He began to get out of bed, and stopped. His head was spinning. But at least it didn't ache like it had last night.

He sat still a moment, then put his legs over the edge of the bed and onto the floor.

Another moment's rest, and he stood up.

The room seemed steady enough, so he went to the bathroom and got into his robe. And vomited.

The nausea had come on him so quickly he'd barely made it to the sink, which was only a step away.

He got into a hot shower, and told himself the new cook at the Pink Club was related to the Borgias.

But he was frightened.

Still, he was able to dress, have eggs, toast and coffee, and keep everything down. Then he was able to get on the phone and make a few contacts, including one named Idy who danced at Nude Village in the Valley. Black chick, and he didn't usually dig black chicks, but this one had lots of cream in the coffee and a real good head—for both head *and* conversation. So when she said, "It's brokesville, man, and I'd really like some pot," he suggested she drop over later on and "we'll work it out."

He made a few more calls, a few sales with deliveries or pickups set for tomorrow. And while it was brokesville for him too, he'd received a pound of reefer and other assorted goodies in the form of pills yesterday afternoon, some of it owed him from before he'd gone into the hospital, and the rest on his good credit.

He'd be a few hundred to the good by tomorrow night, and breaking even with his bills by week's end.

But that didn't include the hospital bill.

It *could,* if he called the cop and said he had Silencer's description for him.

He thought of Diana Woodruff and her deal, and shrugged. Sometimes you couldn't give exclusive rights to a friend. Pressures of economic reality, baby. Besides, like old Melvin, she was daydreaming; she'd never be able to use that description . . .

The phone rang. It was Doc Byrnes. "Are you all right, Melvin?"

Funny, the doc and the cop both called him Melvin. Almost no one else had since his momma had dropped dead while showing someone up a long flight of stairs in the New Orleans cat house she'd run.

"Sure, Doc. Last night was just something I ate. Bad hamburger meat."

"Ah. Then you feel normal today?"

"Perfectly. After I threw up one more time and got that food poisoning out of my system."

"No headache? No dizziness? No impeded mobility? No torpor?

"No headache, Doc. Dizziness—I'm always a little dizzy when I get up. Impeded mobility—I guess my falling twice last night, but I had a few drinks. What's this torpor?"

"Sluggishness. Reduced physical power and activity."

"Got a girl coming up in a few hours. I'll let you know after that." But even as he chuckled, Byrnes said, "Periods of reduced consciousness, which could be masked as sleep."

"I always sleep long."

"How long did you sleep last night, for example?"

Mel decided to get some free medical advice, "Maybe nineteen hours."

"Ah. And there was dizziness on awakening? And nausea?"

"Yeah. So do I make sure my life insurance is paid up?"

"Melvin, go back to the hospital. You might be showing signs of brain-tissue trauma; perhaps deterioration."

"So if I did, it would go away? Lying there at a hundred bucks a day is better than lying here?"

"Surgery may be indicated."

Mel realized he'd shaken his head violently, because it radiated pain. "I'm not ready for that, Doc. But thanks for giving a damn."

"Consider it, Melvin. Your life is really all you have; all any of us have."

Mel went to the bedroom and the closet and the chest where he kept his dope. He took out a bag of grass and got papers from the dresser. His hands shook, but he finally rolled a joint and lit up. He went back to the living room and his chair and the phone. He got busy with his numbers.

Tomorrow he would call Grinch, whom he'd thought never to call in all his life. Grinch dealt only in the hard stuff—cocaine and heroin. The stuff that brought the heavy raps. The stuff Mel Crane basically disliked, disapproved of, feared.

People thought coke was safe. And maybe it was, for those who sniffed once a week at fashionable parties. But the real users, those who snorted every day, and sometimes put it into their veins, had sores in their noses and twitches in their eyes and bills that could be handled only by the finance companies, and later by stick-'em-up. As for heroin, it was big casino, end-of-the-line, and don't let any of the smiling young users and their hip morality deceive you. They aged, and rotted, rapidly.

But the contact with Grinch was worth a grand a week, minimum.

And with "torpor" closing in, what did he have to lose?

Except he still wasn't sure it *was* closing in. And there was the cop willing to trade for his five grand . . .

He was about two-thirds down on the joint and beginning to feel mellow. He swiveled the chair around and leaned over to the TV. Six o'clock; time for the Sunday news with Wyona Wise, a tough but well-built piece of plastic. Mel watched her mouth which never stopped moving and thought of sliding his dick between those thin lips and chuckled and sucked at the roach . . . then lost the fantasy and the hard-on.

Diana Woodruff had been nailed at her parlor last night. An anonymous tip.

What a miserable break! Not only would the Wise broad do a number on her, it would bring down all the other camera freaks. The snitch was probably one of the parlor girls, someone who had it in for her.

The interview began, and he put down the roach and listened "with the whole head," as his daddy used to say. He began to get a feeling.

When it ended, he murmured. "You set yourself up, didn't you? And what you said . . . it'll drive that nut wild." He got to his feet. "It's not bad. It could work."

Which meant that any time now, the fat fuck could come after her.

He walked around the room. She had the description and the sketch. But it was still second-hand knowledge, and she wouldn't be as sure, as *quick*, as Mel Crane.

It could cost her.

But even that wasn't what was bugging him.

The fat fuck hadn't done nearly as much to Diana Woodruff as he'd done to Mel Crane. Hadn't done nearly as much to *anyone*. Because Mel Crane had not only lost his wife, Mel Crane had a headache and torpor and a growing suspicion that he was dead. Or a vegetable.

He was suddenly tired, and went to the bedroom and lay down.

He'd have to do without the five grand. He couldn't give the cops the description now. Because it was important that Diana's plan work. It was important that she, not the police, spring the trap on Silencer.

So that Mel Crane could kill the bastard who had killed him.

Simple, right?

Except he had to figure out how to get to Silencer before Silencer got to Diana. And he wouldn't be cheating her—probably saving her life.

If her plan worked . . .

He dozed awhile. He woke and remembered that Idy was coming over. He went to the bathroom and washed his face with cold water. He still didn't feel like balling, but refused to give in to the feeling.

He dressed in good threads and hung a silver medallion around his neck and got into shoes with four-inch heels because Idy was a tall one.

He wanted a drink, but remembering last night's "impeded mobility" decided against booze.

He waited for Idy, and thought of how to cut himself in on Diana's trap. Only one way, really. *Be there* when the fat fuck came . . . which could be anytime, or no time.

He'd have to begin staking out the parlor, the one just off Sunset, about a block from La Cienega, if he wasn't mistaken about that piece of parking lot shown in the filmed interview.

He'd check it out. He'd watch the tube at eleven for a repeat of the interview. Then he'd hit the street, because the fat fuck might also recognize that parking lot. Because it could come down *tonight*.

The doorbell rang. He went to answer it, flashing his patented Mel Crane grin. And thought he'd have to dig out the old Smith & Wesson .38, dust it off, and hope that after seven years it wouldn't blow up in his face.

Larry shut off the television.

Roberta said, "Why'd you do that?"

"My eyes are tired. Remember, I worked a full day."

She nodded. "Y'know, the massage-parlor hooker they just interviewed—didn't they call her Diana, the name you like me to use when we play that game?"

"I didn't notice. Want a beer?"

She said no and hugged her knees. She was curled up on the couch, wearing his pajama top and nothing else. Which had been fun about an hour ago. And which had promised to be fun again, later.

But he'd just seen The Mouth interview Diana, and he didn't feel like fun anymore. He felt like *kicking* whoever had blown the whistle on her!

Though she'd taken it well enough. Talked her head off, in fact. Bullshit psychology about Silencer being more to be pitied than hated.

Which wasn't like the Diana he knew . . . yet *was*, since she analyzed everything to death.

Roberta was asking him to "come here and snuggle." He said he was going to the john; then sat on the closed toilet seat to get a little thinking time.

And understood what had bothered him about that interview.

It was what Diana *might* have said, discussing

286

Silencer objectively, if her own sister hadn't been one of his victims.

Of course, she'd had a camera stuck in her face, a microphone stuck in her mouth, and a nightmare of confusion and embarrassment . . .

Hell, he was upset because soon everyone would know where she worked. Including all sorts of psychos who could bug her. Including Silencer.

He'd have an officer survey the massage parlor at least once each night, just on the off chance. And tomorrow he'd have his Vice Squad back, and his five extra detectives. Tomorrow his task force would be reactivated and Silencer would find it harder to kill unnoticed.

A *little* harder, because Vivian Garner, the last victim before Silencer's vacation, had been shot with a hell of a lot of cops in the Strip area.

On that cheerful note, he walked out of the bathroom and back to Roberta, but not to snuggle. He said he was exhausted, and reminded her he had to work six days a week until Silencer was caught, including weekends.

She grumbled, but finally got dressed. And since she'd come in her own car, he was spared driving her home.

But there was a long I-love-you-love session to be endured before he was alone.

He called the station and arranged to have an undercover man check on the Grecian Massage.

"Tomorrow, right?" Sergeant Mines said.

"Tonight, Sergeant." Then he had a beer and a smoke and brushed his teeth and went to bed. He kept his mind off Diana; deliberately off Diana. Yet just before he fell asleep, with his consciousness and its defenses down, he thought, every guy watching the tube will want that beautiful woman. And once they find out where to go, who knows how many will actually buy her . . .

He slept. He dreamt. About being back at boot camp. About marching and singing in cadence:

"Left, left, left-right-left

Ain't no use in goin' home
Jody's got your gal and gone

Ain't no use in feelin' blue
Jody's got her sister too

I'm gonna get a three-day pass
I'm gonna whip old Jody's ass

Left, left, left-right-left."

Then he was in 'Nam, still marching, still singing, the lines of grunts no longer drill-field smart but straggling as they moved over the high road between rice paddies. And a Marine whose name he had forgotten, who'd died by a sniper's bullet through the lungs, was hicupping blood and cursing because his girl had gone with a Jody.

And Corporal Lawrence Admer cursed along with him because Diana was also going with a Jody. Or a dozen, a hundred, a thousand . . .

After the longest half-hour of her life, Diana broke away from the crowd of at least twenty newspeople and fled into the Grecian Massage. Even then, two men tried to follow her, including the big newscaster she'd always disliked on the air—the one who'd been a football player. He'd put his hand on her hip as she'd turned away. "Baby, wait, I've got an idea for an *Enquirer* article." She'd simply shaken her head and left, thinking he and the *Enquirer* belonged together. Now she had to lock the door against him and another reporter.

Dreena, the black girl, said, "You should ask Art to send you to another place. Those reporters are doing a job on you, honey."

Diana shrugged, but she was trembling inside. Three television stations, the two all-news radio stations, and a newspaper had sent people here tonight. And while some were restrained, other, like the ex-football player, were detestable!

Too much, she thought, and said, "It pays to advertise."

The knocking continued at the door. The football player's voice called, "It's illegal to discriminate against any kind of customer."

Dreena said, "That so?"

Diana shook her head, and asked about business.

"Normal Sunday. Slow. But it'll pick up for *you,* Diana! You gonna get all sorts of shit. Why not switch to Santa Monica or the Valley?"

Diana said she didn't want to lose her steady customers. But of course, she had to stay where Silencer could find her. And tonight they had used the name of the parlor and even located it by street. Tonight they had pinpointed her.

The knocking stopped. The football player called, "Try you some other time, Miss Woodruff."

Dreena said she'd been in a booth with a repeat customer when the commotion began in the parking lot. "We came to the front and looked out. The minute my client saw all those cameras, he jumped into his pants and ran out the back, carrying his shirt and shoes." She giggled. "Never even asked for a refund; I hope I don't lose him."

"I'm sorry," Diana murmured, pulling the heavy drape aside and looking out. The vans and cars were leaving, en masse. Still, she decided to keep the door locked for at least an hour.

Dreena left by the back door, which was always locked, and Diana saw her come around by the alley into the parking lot. And saw the man and woman appear from the street and hurry toward her. The man carried a still camera; the woman a side-slung tape recorder and club-like mike.

Dreena leaped into her Chevy, slammed shut the door, and obviously locked it too. Because when the man tugged at the handle, it didn't open. Dreena gunned the engine and sped around in a circle and out to the street.

The couple came up to the parlor door and rattled the handle. The woman said, "We'll pay well for an exclusive interview—how you and your sister came to be involved in this kind of work. Childhood and adolescent influences . . ."

Diana went to the back room and lay down on the table and tried to relax. And found she was crying.

Quite suddenly, she knew that "this kind of work" was approaching its end.

They repeated the whore's interview at eleven. Frank watched it carefully, trying to find landmarks in the background to tell him where it had taken place. He might want to stroll by there one evening. He might want to give her the chance to meet the "sick, helpless puppet" face to face.

She seemed genuinely upset at having been traced to her house of ill repute. Which weakened his suspicion that it could be a police trap.

The interview had been taped the night before and consisted of the same pseudo-psychological nonsense she'd babbled about a month ago, after he'd punished the young slut exposing herself on the street curb.

He tried to laugh it off, but it finally became too much.

He left Lila and went to his mother's room, supposedly having heard something, but actually using movement to rid himself of rage. The filthy slut, standing in front of that masturbation parlor and spouting nonsense! Why would they allow such a . . . a *criminal* to speak to thousands of people!

His mother slept. He returned to the living room and told Lila he was going for a walk.

"At eleven-thirty? With a madman like Silencer in the neighborhood?"

He didn't debate her choice of labels. He said, "I'm not female, or a prostitute, so I have nothing to fear."

"He shot that black man, didn't he? Maybe he shot that cab driver too, no one is sure."

He was sure, and he said he wouldn't be long and went out to the driveway. He turned toward the street;

then he heard music in the house on the left, past the fence to the south. Rock music. Very loud. And lights blazed from several windows.

Surprising. His neighbors were an elderly couple, childless . . .

But then he recalled Lila saying they had sold the house and were moving soon.

"Soon" had obviously arrived.

He began walking, trying to ignore the noise. But it infuriated him! And depressed him deeply. Because now even his home was being assaulted by his enemies, the people who liked that kind of music, the people who humiliated him. As Chez Anderson had, with rock music coming from the Rolls's cassette player . . .

He turned quickly from the street toward the back yard. He got the gun from behind the bush and hurried to the car, stripping off the plastic bag and jamming the long automatic under his belt. He got behind the wheel, moving carefully so as to accommodate the weapon on his left hip, and started the engine.

As he began backing out, Lila came through the door, waving, calling, looking upset. He knew she wanted to ask where he was driving to at this time of night, when he'd said he was taking a brief walk. But he couldn't stop. She would come to the window; she might see the gun.

So he waved back, called, "Starving . . . sorry . . . diet killing me," and kept going.

As he pulled around into the street, she put her hands on her hips and glared.

Well, another pleasant scene in the making. His life was full of them. His home life consisted of a deteriorating human shell, a whale, and neighbors who blasted rock music at eleven-thirty at night.

But he had four bullets left. Four more moments of triumph. And then, perhaps, enough satisfaction in retiring undefeated to carry him through this ugly, poisonous world.

Gale Corinth was twenty-six and had black hair, good legs, and small, high breasts. She was dressed the way she liked to dress, in an above-the-knee mini that was years out of style but that suited her looks, and her insides. She also wore a snug, bulky sweater for this not-too-warm evening, and moderate heels on a jazzy, funky shoe that looked like a spike but wasn't, allowing her to swing along, covering considerable ground comfortably. Which was important to her profession.

She walked the streets, and screw Silencer who was keeping her friends and competitors indoors. Because she could handle anyone—john or freak—the Strip could throw at her.

Because she was a he.

She did a hell of a business with her hormone-induced tits and skilled mouth and tight ass . . . and, if the client wanted it, with her seven-inch penis. Because she—and she felt like a woman just about all the time—was a transvestite with a man's genitals, who could play any sexual role imaginable with a male, and quite a few with certain types of females.

She had a moderately strong-featured face, framed by crisp hair cut short, pixie-fashion. She was pretty in an exuberant, humorous manner, and humor was a big part of her bag. Humor was almost always the leadoff to a hell of a wild party for her customers, and many had told her they'd never loved as hard, come as hard, enjoyed themselves as much.

Repeat business, however, was rare. That was the culture, baby; that was the prejudice. So she lived off the one-timers, and a few steadies. But she still lived well. Because after the shocked client had grabbed a lot more under her mini than he'd expected to, she would spring her famous line: "Don't you want something *different,* honey?"

Most did. Most were married, looking for new nookie to chase the boredom, the growing-cold blues. And since she'd already allowed them to kiss her, to fondle her, to realize that she had everything *else* they wanted, they were almost always hooked.

Because she assured them, and they sensed, that she was a woman. A beautiful, sensual woman. A woman who handled their genitals in such a way that they couldn't say no . . . even when she sprang the bite, a cool two hundred, only rarely reducible to a hundred-fifty.

Some, of course, ran. Those who stayed around to satisfy their curiosity—and they were the vast majority—also satisfied their lust as never before. And paid with a smile.

There were always the deadbeats. There were always the losers trying to get a freebie, telling her, as one hardhat dude had, "Fuck off before I kick your sick balls."

After she'd used her little leather-and-buckshot sap on his head, his teeth, and both kneecaps, she'd found he was carrying twenty-five dollars, total. So she'd taken his watch, his ring, and his wallet. At home, she'd examined the pictures of a worn-looking woman and two kids, and mailed his wallet to the address on his driver's license, along with a perfumed note in her feminine hand:

"Darling Vince: You left these on the dresser. Love you, honey. Yours, Hotsy."

And addressed the envelope to "Braubacher," his last name only, giving it a good chance of reaching the wife while Vince was in the hospital nursing his bruised skull, broken teeth, and fractured knees.

A vindictive bitch, Gale Corinth, and proud of it.

A tough bitch, Gale Corinth, and no one would rip her off . . . or put a gun against her head and blow her away. Because she still had all that muscle she'd built up during a childhood and adolescence as a he.

She was working the side streets between Sunset and Santa Monica, dark and empty, but wise johns knew where to look. She preferred the Sunset Strip itself, because it was a quick hustle there. But mostly it was difficult because of Vice Squad coverage, and tonight it was impossible because of all sorts of plainclothes—a predictable reaction to the killing of Burn Digger's chick. Cops always showed after a murder, narcs after an O.D., and hookers after everyone calmed down.

She stolled along, eyes busy checking doorways and

293

cars where a horny john might be waiting. She hummed a Digger number, wishing she could meet him, hook him on her action, get into that fast-moving, big-money crowd. Word was he dug the golden shower. She would drink champagne all day and piss on him all night.

She heard a car behind her, saw the lights hit the street, turned her head, and smiled pretty. But also opened her little beaded purse so she could get the six-inch blackjack in case she needed it. And it wasn't just for Silencer. There were a hell of a lot of psychos in this town, especially in this area, and a girl had to be ready.

The car pulled over. She hoped for a Rolls, a Mercedes, one of the other good imports. Hard to tell a Cadillac from a Chevy these days, especially at night . . . and this *was* a Chevy, and far from new. So she figured money-up-front, if possible, and smiled at the darkened interior and walked slower, with more hip roll.

The man's voice said, "You available?"

She said, "You a police officer?" and tinkled delicate laughter . . . but waited for an answer because if he said no, and later turned out to have a badge, she could claim entrapment.

The man in the car didn't answer. She called, "Bye, officer!" and turned and walked the other way, so he'd have to U-turn.

He got out instead and came after her. She whirled, hand in her purse. He stopped and said, "You have a right to be nervous." He reached under his jacket, and came out with a wallet and flashed a badge.

"Silencer could have one of those, couldn't he?" she said.

"This isn't a bust. Just get off the street. We don't want any more of you girls hurt."

She said all right, and he returned to his car and drove off. She knew he'd be back, so she went along until she found a two-story apartment house with an open gate and entered the courtyard and waited there.

Sure enough, the cop cruised by in the opposite direction.

When he was gone, she came out and continued the way she'd been going. She was okay as long as she stayed on this street, because he had other streets to cover.

She kept walking south and approached the lights of Santa Monica Boulevard. This area was almost solidly gay—aggressively liberated gay—and she would find no business.

She crossed the street before reaching the corner and turned back, walking north. She thought of Fasty and his heavy equipment and his indefatigable lovemaking. And figured that if she didn't score within the hour, she'd forget tonight. Because her beautiful baby was at the pad, snorting some snowy-white and watching the tube and working up an appetite that only she could satisfy.

And professional or not, transvestite or not, she was young and deeply in love.

Sure enough, the cop ordered by in the opposite direction.

When he was gone, she came out and continued the
way which had been going. She was what-if-ly fashions as she
stayed in this field, because he had other streets to
cover.

She kept walking south, and approached the intersection Mattis Boulevard. The area was almost completely deserted. Ghostal sea—and she would find
no buildings.

She stopped the car at standing the corner and
turned to do writing each. She thought of Harry and
his expressions and his imperturbable forbearing.
And figured that if she didn't, sore within the time
she'd rather not get breakfast... and maybe she'd
be had, so once going chores, chite and watching the
chite and working out an appetite that only she could
indulge.

And premonition? or not... remember... if not, she was
young and deeply in love.

SEVENTEEN: *Monday, September 18, a.m.*

It was twelve-thirty and Gale Corinth paused to check her watch by a streetlamp. She'd been hitting the pavement for more than an hour. Time to go home.

But Jesus, she needed the bread. She'd been extravagant on clothing, and on a gift for her man—a not-so-little gold spoon with a ruby-chip in the handle on a heavy gold chain, to wear around the neck, to use when he was snorting. She needed a score tonight for rent and groceries and Ludes . . .

The car came toward her on the opposite side of the street, and slowed. A face looked out at her, male, and she waved and called, "Hi! I'd really appreciate a lift! My car broke down!"

He was by her. She stopped and waited. And murmured, "All *right!*" when she saw the headlights swinging around in a four-corner turn.

The car came back and pulled to the curb. Another old Chevy—goddam town was full of them—and she would have to go for money-up-front. But since this was the first bite all night, she would hook him with a little action.

She bent to the passenger's window. The driver leaned across and rolled it down. He didn't look anything like a cop, and she decided to skip the entrapment question. She said, "Thanks for stopping. My name's Gale. Can I get inside?"

He said, "I'll get out," and did something to his clothing on the left side, the side opposite her; then reached under the seat. Hiding his wallet, she figured, which made him smarter than he looked. Fat face and short fat body, and when he got out and walked around to the sidewalk, he didn't improve any.

"Do you really need a ride?" he asked.

She bellied up to him. "Cute little feller," she murmured, and pinched his cheek. "I sure do need a ride. Climb on, sweetness, and give me one."

He wasn't smiling and he didn't look turned-on, so she rubbed against him. "Don't be shy, honey. Use your hands."

He lifted his arms. He put a hand on her bottom and one on her breast. He did it stiffly, like some sort of machine, and she began wondering if she didn't have herself a problem here: a man who was afraid of sex; who failed at sex. That kind pulled all sorts of shit, including asking for refunds.

She slid a hand down to his fly. No problem there, and she glanced around. The street was still deserted, so she opened the zipper and put her hand inside. He gasped. She said, "Let's go to a hotel where I can suck it and you can stick it in me!" She stroked his stiff dick, heard him gasping, figured it was time to make the deal. "Two hundred. *Now*." If he was out hunting pros, he'd have enough, or close to it, on him. If he wasn't, she'd better find out.

The man nodded.

Almost always, they said it was too much and tried to bargain. So she got suspicious. "You've got it? Let me see."

"All right. But first . . ." His voice was so hoarse, she could barely make out the words. But she knew what he wanted. Which meant it was time for something she preferred to do in a hotel room, but that she'd often done on the street, in doorways, in cars.

His hand was under her dress.

Her purse, with blackjack, was hanging in the crook of her left arm, and she raised that arm a bit to be able to get at it more easily. Because once in a while a prospect reacted badly, got violent.

Fatso didn't seem the violent type, but you never could tell.

She moaned a little, squeezed his cock, and felt his hand moving up her thigh. She always reacted to a man's aroused organ, and to a man's hand approaching *her* organ. Which made this life of hers not only profitable but fun.

Her tool was stiffening. She raised the purse higher, ready to jerk her right hand from his fly. The fat man was panting, murmuring, "Yes, yes . . ." And then he pressed his hand between her legs.

His head jerked up. She said, "Surprise, darling. I can do anything you've ever dreamed of. I'm a Roman orgy in myself. That's why I'm expensive."

His hand was still pressing. Her tool was beginning to throb. He kept staring into her face, and she kissed him lightly on the lips. "Is it a deal?" she whispered, and tickled his balls and felt she had him.

He slid his hand inside her panties and felt around her penis and testicles. He had a hot, soft, plump little hand, and it was shifting her into high.

But he still looked shocked; hadn't answered her; hadn't okayed the deal. So she said, "All right. One-fifty. For the whole night. For that *fantastic* hand of yours. That baby-fat hand . . ."

He moved so fast she cried out in shock.

His hand *tore* away from her crotch, ripping the panties. He jumped back from her. And ran around the front of his car and got inside.

She said, "Just say no!" and turned toward Sunset, where her car was parked near Doheny. A long fucking walk after a nothing night. And now she was horny . . .

She heard footsteps. She turned, opening her purse. He was walking around his car, onto the sidewalk;

299

walking toward her. He was adjusting his jacket and staring at her, *glaring* at her, and she considered kicking off her shoes so as to be able to move properly.

But Christ, he was such a soft little cherub, such a marshmallow. And maybe that wasn't a glare; maybe it was determination she read. Maybe he'd gotten his wallet and was going to pay . . .

"Degenerate filth!" he said, voice shaking. "I never ever *dreamed* of such filth!"

She'd had enough. She didn't have to kick off her shoes; didn't even need the blackjack to handle this fatty. But just to play safe, she decided to put him beddy-bye.

They were about ten feet apart when she took a long step forward, whipping the blackjack from her purse. At the exact same instant, he opened his jacket with his left hand and with the right removed something from the waistband. Did it quickly, smoothly, as if he'd practiced. Brought up his hand, and what was in it stopped her cold; froze her in place.

Long and black and unlike any gun she'd ever seen.

Before she could say, "Easy," he said, "I'm Silencer," and something hit her forehead. Hit harder than her father's fist had when she'd told him she wouldn't live out his fantasies and play high-school football. And *why*. Hit and exploded her marvelous, something-different life away.

Frank could hardly drive, he was trembling so. And muttered, "No, stop it!" when he remembered holding that penis, which had felt enormous; the only one besides his own he'd ever touched.

He'd held it only because he'd been surprised, expecting a woman, and suddenly . . .

But he'd known it was a man from touching *outside* the underwear.

Known and should have jerked away then; not put his hand *inside*.

"I was stunned! I didn't know what I was doing!"

He was shouting now, driving much too quickly, swerving from side to side on the narrow street.

He slowed. He was approaching Sunset, and he didn't want to travel on a main street.

He saw a driveway and used it to start his turn. He drove back to the corner and turned left, toward home. He put on the radio and blasted his thoughts with music, the very rock music he hated. He refused to remember excitement.

Yes, *normal* excitement, when he'd thought he was dealing with a normal prostitute; a woman. And *that* was the excitement that had continued for a few brief seconds afterward.

But he could still hear the words, "I can do everything you ever dreamed of," spoken in that sweet, husky voice; could still taste the lips that had touched his as he'd felt the male organ through that silky underwear. And had reached inside to grasp the penis, the testicles . . .

"Shut up!" he screamed at his inquisitor brain. And realized he was holding the gun; was raising it to his head.

He laughed—a hysterical giggle—and shoved it under the seat.

No one would ever know he had put his hand inside that degenerate's shorts. No one would ever know he had thrilled to the feel of that throbbing penis. Because he had killed the degenerate.

He was calming rapidly. He was beginning to think of tomorrow, and the news media. "SILENCER IS BACK!" the headline had screamed in one Sunday paper, and a more sedate "FIFTH SILENCER FATALITY" had shared equal billing with the foreign crises in the other.

They would have their sixth fatality. There would be news conferences and editorials and it would be Silencer this and Silencer that and he would read and watch and listen and enjoy.

But how much more satisfying to let them know it was Frank Berdon!

The thought had just popped into his mind. And of course he *couldn't* let them know; not and go on

301

feeling satisfaction. Little satisfaction in being executed, or locked up for life!

Still, it was a daydream to dwell on. The media using his name, his photograph, and everyone who had ever humiliated him thinking, *God, he could have killed me!* And searching for him. And he disappearing, free of Lila and Mom, knowing he had defeated a world of enemies.

He stopped himself.

Dangerous fantasy.

It was enough to use his remaining three bullets and retire, as he'd planned.

He thought then of Diana Woodruff, and how satisfying it would be if one of those bullets could go into *her* head!

But that too was a fantasy, and he would forget it. Besides, he didn't know where to find her. And asking questions about a victim's relative, departing from his purely random killings, could bring disaster.

No, he would use his remaining bullets as he'd used all the others.

He would use them quickly, too, because there was bound to be a build up of police in the Sunset Strip area as time went on.

Perhaps another execution tomorrow.

Perhaps even *two* tomorrow!

In any event, an end to Silencer's killings in the next few days.

He was at the house. He was entering the driveway. The lights next door were still on. And when he went into the back yard to hide the gun, he heard the music still playing. At ten to one in the morning.

But it didn't bother him as it had before.

The mind picture of that degenerate's skull exploding was driving every negative feeling away. He walked into the house with head high, smiling, thinking that he had been strong and passionate tonight, and had the degenerate been a woman, he might well have sexed her right there, before killing her.

And that among the next three whores was bound to be the experience he was looking for.

302

(And Diana Woodruff was Silencer's enemy and Diana Woodruff was as beautiful a whore as could be found and oh the games he could play with Diana Woodruff, fired by hate and lust combined; the games before that final game of sending her to join her sister in hell!)

He was standing in the kitchen, locked into the fantasy.

He realized that it had gained considerable hold on him. That he had better finish with Silencer before it drove him to disaster . . .

The lights went on and Lila said, "Let's hear your explanation. Televison comedy is nothing compared to your explanations, Frank."

He chuckled. And thought that another enormous satisfaction would be killing *her*. The game here would be telling her he was Silencer, and making her believe it with a bullet in the head.

"No scratches tonight? No cat defending her young in Beverly Hills? And eating at IHOP's or Norm's, a few blocks away, took you an hour and a half?"

"I wasn't interested in a coffee shop," he said, and walked toward the bedroom. She stepped in front of him, and he said, "Drove downtown to Little Tokyo and had a fantastic Japanese dinner."

She stared at him. She was wearing a nightgown, and bursting out of it. He suddenly reached out and squeezed her left breast. She jerked back, said, "What sort of vulgar nonsense . . ."

He simply had to get rid of the passion, the fire, the semen filling his testes! He put his arms around her, grabbed her enormous rear, said, "Get your fat ass into the bedroom!" And walked her backward, through the door, across the room, while she gasped and stumbled and almost fell.

"Not like this! You know I hate violence!"

He threw her onto the bed and yanked up her nightgown and tore at his trousers.

"Frank, *stop!*"

He leaned forward and slapped her face.

She wailed . . . then went still and quiet. And left

303

the nightgown up over her trunk-like thighs, her heavy bush of genital hair. He had his pants and undershorts off. He flung himself on her and pulled her breasts and buttocks and said, "Put it in, bitch!" She spread docilely and put it in and moved with him. Then they both moved frantically. Then she cried out in orgasm, and slowed. He said, "Hump it, damn you!" and grabbed her bottom with both hands and spent himself into her.

Immediately afteward, he got up and went to the bathroom. He showered, and when he came out got right into bed, turning his back on her, eyes already closing, mind already fogging.

She whispered, "I don't know you anymore. You frighten me."

He liked that.

"What did you really do tonight?" she asked, still whispering. "What did you do Friday night, when I drank too much wine? What did you do all those other nights, a month or so ago? That night with the scratches?"

He'd almost been asleep . . . but this brought him back. This he didn't like.

"What?" he said.

"Those nights that match . . ." she began. And stopped and muttered. "Nothing. Goodnight."

He couldn't believe she had actually been drawing a connection between him and Silencer; between her contemptible husband and a mass murderer.

And realized he should have expected it, anticipated it, done more to prevent it by hiding his movements from her more carefully. She knew when he'd left for his "drives" and when he'd returned. Not in every case and not in every particular . . . but enough so that she could draw that parallel if it ever occurred to her. The one person in all the world who could do so . . . and it *had* occurred to her.

He lay there, eyes blinking into the darkness.

He wondered if she was lying the same way, firming up her suspicions, her conclusions.

304

Tomorrow, when tonight's murder was reported, she would have still more to suspect, to conclude.

And there were three more killings to come.

If the last of them could be Lila. If it could be a Silencer killing, on the street, late, with the body not being found until morning. If he could say they'd quarreled and she'd stormed out and he'd thought she'd gone to her cousin, a friend, somewhere to spend the night. If he had by then rid himself of the gun, they wouldn't have any reason to suspect him.

And even if they did, they would have no proof. And would never be able to find proof. Because the only proof was in the gun, and in Lila's mind. And both would be gone forever.

He would think of it.

He still felt he wouldn't have to do it—that once Silencer was finished, Lila would reject her suspicions.

She hadn't even been able to voice them properly tonight.

By the time she got around to it, everything would be over.

Still, he had that option, that plan. And even if things went wrong, there was always that fantasy of being known as Silencer; running away and starting over again somewhere else . . .

He felt fine, in full control, unafraid of any of the possibilities. He felt stronger, surer, than he had in all his life. And fell into a sweet, heavy sleep.

Mel sat in his car across the street from the deep parking lot, and from the Grecian Massage behind it. Diana's Fiat convertible was parked near the door . . . but he was no longer watching car or door, or thinking about the five customers who'd entered since he'd arrived here at eleven-forty. It was now two-fifteen, and for the past hour, a strange-looking hooker had been prowling the area.

She was coming back up the street again, out of the darkness, climbing toward the Grecian Massage, and toward Sunset Boulevard half a block further north. He watched her in his side-view mirror, then turned in his seat to look back and across the street, following her progress.

He couldn't figure her out . . . though there was nothing *that* different about her. Her clothes . . . well, too good, maybe. Slit skirt and low-cut frilly lace blouse and natural leather boots with big, wide heels. Sexy, sure, but in the wrong way . . . not obvious enough, *cunty* enough for a Sunset Strip hooker. Also, her face: composed and haughty; society or career-woman style . . .

But maybe the strangeness wasn't in her. Maybe it was in *him*. His aching head, which ached worse than ever. His right leg, which felt numb and leaden. His eyes, which burned . . . but that was because he was exhausted after balling Idy and being out here two and a half hours.

Time to take off. Silencer didn't kill this late. And Mel Crane wanted his sleep.

Then he shook himself, stretching, trying to come alive. Christ, he'd slept nineteen hours! He should be able to go until noon, at least.

But that was the old Mel; the pre-August-first Mel.

Oh, how he wanted to see that fat fuck! How he wanted to get him somewhere and make him beg and then kill him, slowly, putting one bullet in his big gut, then watching him bleed and squirm . . .

The strange hooker had paused near the entry to the parking lot, resting, and he didn't blame her. She'd been walking almost continuously, up and down the long street. He thought he'd seen a car pull over further along, in the darkness, when she'd been somewhere in that area. But she'd come walking back up again.

He couldn't see her failing to score, even if her price was high. Because she was the classiest if not the youngest.

She was glancing at him. He decided to check out his feeling, his old-pimp instinct. He waved out the window. "Hey, baby, you available?"

She hesitated, and that was Clue One.

She didn't turn on the smile, and that was Clue Two.

But she finally began to cross over.

Clue Three was her walk, right out of a lousy movie; a hip-swinging, shoulder-shaking burlesque routine that had him fighting back laughter.

Still, when she reached the car, when he finally saw her up close, he confirmed that she was a blonde knockout: super-cool, super-Anglo, and if he hadn't had Idy a few hours ago, and if he didn't know there was something wrong here, he'd have tried to score.

"Hello," she said.

He said, "Hey. What's your rip?"

She blinked. He said, "Your price." She said, "Of course—fifty dollars." He said, "Fantastic. Inflation hasn't reached *your* cunt, has it?" She not only blinked this time, her head jerked. He nailed it home: "I want my cock sucked until I come. In your mouth. Then a second go, in your asshole. I'll pay extra for the ass-fuck only if I come again."

Clue Four: She stood there, trying to answer, her face brick-red. She was either a phony, or an amateur— a housewife trying to get out of some sort of financial hole.

If she was a phony, that meant a cop.

But he'd never seen such a misinformed, naïve cop.

She finally spoke. "Can't tonight. Perhaps tomorrow."

"Why not tonight?" he asked, and looked more closely at that great face, and felt he'd seen it somewhere before. Maybe she *was* a pro; maybe he'd run into her in a club; maybe she was just dumb and delicate.

She took a step backward. "Meeting someone." Her right hand fiddled with the clasp of her purse, and he thought: a cop for sure, because that's where the badge and gun would be. An undercover cop he'd noticed around the Strip.

He nodded slowly.

She backed another step. "I'll be seeing you, hand-some."

He was glad when she finally walked away.

307

Because he could turn his head and let the laughter out.

He reached for the ignition. Well, maybe Silencer was dumb enough to take such bait. Maybe even a normally hip john wouldn't see anything wrong in her. But she wouldn't fool *any* street person.

He drove toward the Strip. He'd stop in somewhere for a nightcap, check out a few chicks, rap with the bartender.

But he felt a tickle of nausea deep in his gut. And that headache wouldn't let up.

So he told himself it wasn't smart to leave the car and his .38 alone so late in this neighborhood. Someone could break in; maybe even a cop, checking for Silencer.

With logic on his side, he was able to head home without admitting to himself he was weak and sick.

But a few blocks later, he felt things going wrong, coming apart, in his head, in his body. And began to shake uncontrollably in the right arm, the right leg.

He pulled to the curb and smoked a cigarette, holding it in his left hand. "Easy," he whispered, as if it were panic alone that had caused the sudden attack.

After a while, the spasm passed and he went home. He got into bed and began falling asleep. But it felt more like it had during those early days in Cedars-Sinai; more like passing out cold.

He fought it. He thought of Diana Woodruff. His stakeout wouldn't be worth shit if the cops were also there.

Of course, the cops didn't know what Silencer looked like.

If Silencer showed, and backed off, no one would think to follow him. Because Diana would be inside, where she couldn't see him. And any cop—not just that Ritzy dumb blonde—would have to have something specific to go on, like an attack on Diana.

So it was still up to Marvelous Melvin to pay off for Beth-Anne and the others. And for himself. Because as he let go of consciousness, as he allowed the darkness to grab him, he knew his time was running out.

308

*　*　*

Mamie-Hortense went right to her car after the black drove away. Her face was twisted in disgust and anger as she drove the silver Jaguar along Sunset and into a neighborhood of lush greenery. Beverly Hills and the Sunset Strip were so very close to each other, and yet worlds apart.

As far apart as that obscene black was from her sweet, dependable LeRoy, a family man with a grammar-school-teacher wife and ambitions to become an attorney and eventually a judge who could benefit his race with all sorts of legal services and programs. Who without being subservient managed to provide them all with the occasional meal they ate in Chief Shut-In's Hollywood Hills mansion, an old and extremely moody place that harked back to the days of silent films.

Who chauffeured the chief around, rolled him on his specially equipped table, and by implication, bathed and dressed him. All with quiet good nature, dependability, and a recognition of his good fortune in being in a great man's employ.

And who *never*—dear Lord, not even by glance!—showed sexual awareness of any of the female characters, certainly not of Mamie. Not because he felt . . . well, racially restrained. Chief Shut-In was totally unaware of race, color, religion. In fact, one episode revealed he'd been about to marry a Jewish girl back in his youth, when her family had aborted the elopement. Later, she'd been murdered and the chief had used Mamie as his main operative in solving the case.

But this low-bred black tonight! The utterly revolting things he'd said! Not even her being disguised as a prostitute justified his language! And she couldn't believe that white prostitutes—certainly not all of them—automatically accepted black customers. So he should have proceeded carefully, until she'd revealed whether or not he was acceptable.

She fervently hoped he would find a sex partner and busy himself with her for some time . . . at least long enough so that he wouldn't bother Mamie Belfont during the next few critical nights.

But later, at home, she got a hunch and dug out her file on the Silencer Case—newspaper clippings, mainly—and found the smudgy wedding picture of Mel Crane and his murdered wife, Beth-Anne. The obscene black in the Mustang *could* be Crane. In fact, the longer she examined the picture, using a magnifying glass, the more certain she became.

Which brought up a new and exciting possibility: that Crane had the Grecian Massage under surveillance because he believed, as Mamie did, that Silencer would come after Diana Woodruff, and wanted to exact personal revenge on the murderer.

This gave Mamie even stronger positioning! Now she could watch Crane as well as the massage parlor. If and when he reacted, she could stop him from his vigilante action and get Silencer herself, for the law. Unless Silencer, or Crane for that matter, resisted. Then one or both might learn first-hand how tough Mamie Belfont could be. And she wouldn't mind teaching Mr. Foul-Mouth a severe lesson!

As for how Crane had learned Diana Woodruff was at this particular massage parlor, he had probably used the same method Mamie had. She'd checked every parlor in the Sunset Strip area with a parking lot large enough to be the one in which Diana Woodruff had been interviewed. Driving up and down the side streets, heading west, this had been the third possibility. She had recognized a tall cypress against a corner of the building, and then the little Italian convertible, both of which had showed in the TV interview.

She reached home, showered, and went right to bed. She was going to need all the rest she could get, all the strength she could garner. Because the case was growing more complicated. Which invariably meant that the climax, the *crunch* as LeRoy put it, was fast approaching.

Diana unlocked the door at two a.m., not only because there hadn't been any activity out in the parking lot, but because Arthur had called to say he was dropping over "to show a new chick around."

She was relieved that she would have company against the expected increase in kook-customers; though only the Wyona Wise interview had run today, and the parlor hadn't been named. Still, anyone who knew the Sunset Boulevard area could figure it out from the film clips.

She'd begun reading, when the door opened. It was too soon for Arthur, and her hand moved to the desk drawer and the little automatic. A middle-aged man entered, short and plump, and her heart began to pound. But then she saw the heavy, faded-brown hair and the large eyes. Then she saw that the face was wrong for Silencer.

Besides, he turned to someone outside and said, "It's all right, dear. There are no men present," and a small, dried-up woman entered.

The man closed the door. He said to the woman, "Yes, that's her," and to Diana, "You're Diana Woodruff."

Diana rose. The man looked at her body in the mini-toga. The woman, who was dressed in a frumpy plaid skirt and sweater, flushed to the roots of her graying hair. "Yes," she mumbled, "that's her."

So they'd seen her on TV. So they'd gotten some sort of idea how they could revitalize their dull sex life. Because the woman didn't look anything like the kind who came here for threesome turn-ons and kicks.

Diana would allow a woman to watch a massage, to kiss or fondle her man while it was going on, but nothing else. And she charged both partners equally, which discouraged such action.

Tonight, she would gladly have forgone all charges, all business. But she was here and they were here and she said, "Just what do you have in mind?"

The man, who wasn't dressed any better than the woman, in a baggy brown suit and dingy, open-necked shirt, said, "It's what we have in our hearts that's important, isn't it?"

Diana grew more cautious, and sat down so as to be closer to the drawer and the gun. "Just what do you have in your hearts?"

311

At which the little woman suddenly screamed, "God! The Lord Jesus! That's who we have in our hearts! Not the Devil, like you!" She took a book—a Bible, Diana realized—from her purse and raised it over her head. "Let yourself be smitten with the Word! As our leader, The Lord's Sea Marshal, has written, 'Strike the Evil Ones on the head, twice, and twice again!' "

Diana recognized that reference to "The Lord's Sea Marshal." He was the bearded, messianic leader of one of Southern California's more fanatic religious cults.

She opened the drawer, saying, "No way."

The man, meanwhile, was locking the door with the turn bolt. He then opened his jacket . . . to draw out a cat-o-nine-tails which had been fastened to his shirt. He stripped white surgical tape from the short wooden handle, saying " 'And the Whore of Babylon shall be whipped naked for her sins.' Thus spake The Lord's Sea Marshal."

They advanced on her, with book and whip. The man said, "Be docile now, whore, and ye shall be cleansed." He was sweating on his forehead and upper lip. "Remove your garment."

The woman glanced at him. "It's not seemly . . ."

"Quiet, woman! Strip, whore!"

Diana slipped her hand inside the drawer and grasped the gun. "I think your husband would enjoy seeing me naked. Was it your idea or his that you come here tonight?"

"You damned temptress!" the man shouted. He stepped up to the desk and raised the whip.

Diana drew the gun and fired as close to his left ear as she dared, which wasn't very close. And the gun made a surprisingly small sound. But he screamed and darted to the door, where he fumbled frantically with the lock.

"Use your book on *him*," Diana said to the woman.

The man had finally gotten the door open, and turned as if to say something more. Diana aimed carefully at his chest. He jumped out, running before he hit the blacktop.

The woman walked slowly, glancing back fearfully. Diana lowered the gun. The woman said, pleading, "Let me strike you with the book. Twice, and twice again, as the Lord's Sea Marshal instructs. Just lightly. To save you."

Diana shook her head.

"You don't look like a devil. Not even like the Whore of Babylon." She left.

Diana went to the door and locked it. Arthur would have to knock. Everyone would have to knock, at least until she calmed down.

She began searching for damage, for some sign of the bullet, and found a small hole in the molding above the side window.

She returned to the desk and put the gun away.

She was almost glad the religious nuts had come ... because now she *knew* she could use the gun.

A short while later, she let Arthur and a very young-looking girl into the parlor. The girl had long red hair, startlingly blue eyes, and skin almost as fair as an albino's. She was big-chested, big-bottomed, and her legs, though plump, wouldn't be bad in really high heels.

When Arthur questioned Diana with lifted eyebrows, she said, "You'll do well here, Brenda." Then couldn't help adding, "If you're of age."

"Twenty-one," Arthur said quickly, and the girl said, "I got papers—ID and birth certificate."

Diana nodded, smothering a smile. The Strip was loaded with phony papers, and this girl was barely eighteen, if that.

She locked the door again. Arthur said, "Lots of shit coming down?"

"Not really. Just playing safe until the TV interviews stop running. That means another day or two." She reached for the lock again. "But if you'd like it open—"

"That's all right. I'm going to instruct Brenda in massage technique, and I don't want to be disturbed anyway."

"Have fun," Diana murmured.

Brenda said, "I did regular massage in a health

313

club. But I figured I might as well be paid for what they kept trying to put in my hand. Arthur says I could make five hundred a week right off."

"At least," Diana said, looking her over.

The girl smiled. "Wanna come with us and help?"

Another bi or les, Diana thought. The business was full of them, as were the nude clubs. She said, "No, thanks," and Arthur said, "Diana is our resident virgin. Yet she handles more men than anyone in my parlors. More, maybe, than anyone in town."

The girl said, "That's *weird*."

Arthur took her hand. "Well, you'll just have to settle for me and my little joy stick." They walked into the back, laughing.

Diana sat down with her book. A moment later, Arthur called, "Hey, c'mere for a minute, Diana! You just have to dig this!"

She'd been asked to "dig" Arthur's scenes, his new girls, his "well-hung" friends, for years, and always said no. She began to say no again . . . when the doorknob rattled and a male voice called, "Hey, you open for business?"

She didn't answer, trying to decide whether she was or not.

"Diana Woodruff there? I'll pay fifty, maybe more, for Diana Woodruff."

She spoke in a gruff voice. "No such woman here. And we're just closing."

"You know where she works?"

"Maybe Garden of Venus on LaCienega."

"Yeah? Hey, open up and let me see what you look like."

"Closing," she repeated.

But the doorknob rattled, the voice kept calling, and she left the front room for the back.

Arthur was on the table, trousers and underwear down. The redhead stood over him, nude except for her medium heels. She had remarkably pink genital hair, which Arthur was curling around a finger. She was kissing his belly and playing with his penis, which wasn't half up.

314

"Well," Arthur breathed, seeing Diana in the doorway. His penis swelled and rose. "At last." He pulled Brenda's head to his rigid organ and held a hand out to Diana. "Baby, you owe me."

She nodded. For the Quaaludes. For paying her the very top rates. And most of all, for his good humor, his lack of sexual blackmail, over the years.

She came to the table and kissed him. He gasped and moaned, then pushed Brenda's head away. "I want to grab this one chance with the resident virgin. Help her out of her toga, hey, Brenda?"

The readhead said, "You bet!" and found the zipper and worked it down the back. She got the toga off, accompanying this with a few gentle strokes of breasts and thighs, and one soul kiss pressed between the buttocks. She then helped Diana onto the table, and onto Arthur. She fed Arthur's penis into Diana, whispering, "Oh, God, am I gonna love working here!"

Not if it depended on *her,* Diana thought. Because this was simply a payoff. Payoff Number One.

On Friday would come Larry's turn and Payoff Number Two. Different, perhaps . . . but still, only a prelude to departure.

And if her plan worked, sometime soon would come Silencer and a different kind of payoff. After which she would leave Los Angeles. She could travel, or go home . . .

Sexual frenzy was wiping out her thoughts. Arthur was a skilled cocksman; he was working himself up into her, working deeper and harder. And Brenda was kissing her breasts, biting her nipples, stroking her body, digging her fingers in alongside Arthur's penis, doing things Diana had never allowed, except for that one time with a bayonet at her throat. And there was no longer time for plans, for payoffs, for anything except the burning tide, like lava filling her vagina.

Payoff Number One lasted quite a while. And was so successful that when Diana said she felt a little too shaky to stay on alone at the parlor, and a little afraid of going home alone, Arthur followed her all the way to Malibu in his Caddy. Where he walked her to the door and showed a type of sensitivity that Bible thumpers could never match. That Larry could never match. Of course, it was in his field, his speciality—sex.

"I get it. A sign-off. You going to let me know when you split?"

"If I can."

"No sweat either way." He bent and tenderly kissed her cheek. And cupped her groin. "You could've gone without paying the tab. Now we're even. I appreciate it, baby." Another tender kiss, another feel of her groin, and with a regretful shake of the head he was gone.

She had to laugh a little. She'd been in the business almost nine years, but Arthur Dumont was still a rare creature.

Larry never did get to sleep, though he returned to bed at about three a.m. At three-ten the phone rang and he was told another Silencer killing had taken place.

He was at the scene—Corwell, almost exactly halfway between Sunset and Santa Monica—at four, and approached the group of officers and civilians standing around the woman's body.

Except that one of the civilians, an ambulance attendant, said the body *wasn't* a woman's. "Opened the clothes up to check for body wounds, and guess what. Maybe he was coming from a costume party?"

Larry bent and examined the face, the shape of the body. "No, a transvestite with possible medical changes. And from the way he's dressed, a hooker."

He asked for the responding officers, and spoke to two uniformed men. He then spoke to John Vieress, the third member of his original S.I.T. on the Carla Woodruff murder, a high-school basketball star who at six-four had been too short to make the UCLA varsity. He'd gone to the police academy instead, become a fine cop, and was now an excellent young detective. If Larry had been asked who, among his men, was most likely to make it to lieutenant and above, he'd have picked the lanky, good-humored Vieress. Who again proved his mettle.

"Any witnesses?" Larry asked, looking toward the corpse.

"Two," Vieress replied, leaning against a car and chewing gum.

Larry's eyes snapped to him. "You're kidding. That psycho hasn't killed yet where anyone but a victim was present."

Vieress pointed at a man in a raincoat-over-pajamas talking to chunky Marv Rodin, who was taking notes. Beside him stood a woman in a winter coat over a long nightgown. "When I arrived, I saw them at a window. So I went over. It seems they were there earlier and saw what they took to be a couple making out on the street. Actually it was the male witness, Mr. Anthony, who couldn't sleep and was at the window. When the sex began getting interesting, he woke his wife to come see. So they both saw the man go to his car, come back, and kill the woman. Or the transvestite."

"They hear anything? Voices or gunshot?"

"Neither, Lieutenant, and they should have heard the gunshot. So it was Silencer, all right."

Larry said, "Way to go!" and turned to the witnesses.

Vieress said, "It's not all that good. Look across the street to the high-rise building. Third floor. Fifth window from the left. That's where I spotted them. That's where they were."

Larry muttered, "Quite a distance." He looked about thirty feet south, to the nearest streetlamp. "Not too much light, either." He looked up at the sky. "But a bright sky."

"I'd say it's brighter now than it was at twelve-thirty, twelve-forty."

Larry stared at him. "You mean they saw the crime committed at twelve-thirty and didn't call in till around three? Or did someone fuck-up in calling me?" And then he remembered that Vieress had said he'd seen the couple at the window, questioned them, and only then learned they were witnesses.

317

"Don't leave me guessing!" he said, voice heating up.

Vieress stopped leaning on the car. "Sorry. Someone else, a Mr. Roth, leaving for his early shift at a trucking firm, reported the body. Mr. and Mrs. Anthony didn't realize they'd witnessed a murder. They watched the couple clinching, guessed there was some heavy petting going on, and then saw the woman fall and the man drive away."

"But the woman didn't get up."

"They couldn't be sure of that. I went up to their apartment and looked out the window. That car there blocks their view of anyone flat on the pavement. Besides, they went to bed as soon as the man drove away."

Larry turned to look at the couple. The woman was now talking to Rodin. "Maybe they got ideas of their own from the clinch on the street."

"Could be, Lieutenant. Though they're not that young."

"No one's that young compared to you, Johnny-boy."

Vieress grinned. He was twenty-five and looked even younger. The story was he'd been carded a few months ago while undercover in a bar.

"So what've we got?" Larry asked.

"They agree that the man was a little shorter than the woman, maybe two inches. They'll measure her at the coroner's, but I'd say she's five-nine or ten in her heels. That means Silencer's about five-seven or eight. They don't agree about much else, but I managed to get a consensus on the following: Silencer is short, and chubby-to-fat. He wears a regular suit—at least slacks and a jacket. He doesn't wear a hat. He drives an American car, maybe a dark color, maybe not. It could be a Ford or Chevy. But it could also be a Plymouth . . ."

"Yeah, or anything else. What about the license plate?"

Vieress shook his head. "It was parked wrong for them. And they didn't think to look."

Larry's hopes were being dashed. "You didn't men-tion hair; whether he was bald or blond or what. How about distinctive walk—limp or something? You don't have to be close to see those things!"

Vieress was shaking his head. "Maybe Marv will get more. You know how sometimes the more they talk, the more they remember. And we'll have them into the station tomorrow. And again in three, four days, to see if time doesn't stimulate their memories."

Larry looked at the third-floor window across the street, and at the middle-aged couple, and said, "I'm going home. I'm sure you'll find a bullet, or fragments, to match Silencer's."

"We already found a pretty good fragment."

"And I'm sure you'll be here bright and early," Larry continued sourly, "to canvas the street, both sides, every house, for other witnesses."

Vieress was nodding. "Right."

"And I'm sure we'll be just where we are now, which is fucking nowhere, when he dumps his next corpse on us!"

Vieress cleared his throat and examined his shoes.

"Christ, won't the son-of-a-bitch *ever* make a mistake!"

The group around the body was staring at him. He said, "Do your goddam jobs!" Marv Rodin smiled a little; Larry met the smile with a glare. Then everyone got busy, looking everywhere but at him. Except for Rodin, who kept smiling.

He felt the way he had the last time he'd been with Diana in the Malibu fish house: blocked, frustrated, put upon, enraged. And wait until the fucking news conference later today!

He walked to his car, and drove toward Laurel Canyon. He smoked a Camel and listened to some music.

Friday would help. Diana would help. Even if he was only getting a small part of the total woman . . .

Which made him light up another cigarette.

Frank and Lila had an early breakfast together. He chatted about the store and the possibility that they might yet be able to take a few days off around Christmas, despite the expense Mother's nurse represented.

An expense beginning today, in fact. "Almost nine," he said, checking his watch, smiling. "The hour of your deliverance."

She'd been remarkably quiet. *Delightfully* quiet, he would say, except he now had to judge any change in her normal behavior by what it could mean in terms of her suspecting him of being Silencer.

Though in the bright light of a balmy morning, such a suspicion seemed highly unlikely. As for his killing *her,* that not only seemed unnecessary, but dangerously stupid.

Still, it *was* an entertaining daydream. As was the concept of killing the loud-mouthed Diana Woodruff.

Lila was sipping coffee. She looked at her cup, her hands, the wall clock, anywhere but at him.

He said, "Honey, was I too rough last night?"

"Is there any doubt about it?"

"I'm sorry. Love is sometimes violent." He got up and came around the table to bend and kiss the nape of her neck. He fantasized putting a bullet there, slanting it up into her brain, seeing the top of her head erupt.

He felt heat infuse his genitals. He put both hands over her breasts and bent around to kiss her mouth, controlling the urge to tear at those fat tits, to bite for blood at those tense, resisting lips.

"Frank, please, the nurse will be here any minute!"

"Just put your hand . . ." He was opening his fly. He was going to have her stroke it, then jam it into her mouth and come! He was full of fire, frenzy, strength!

She jumped up, knocking over the chair and shoving him away. "You said you were sorry for being so rough, and now you're doing it again!"

He came to her, uncaring.

The doorchimes sounded.

Lila had her hands outstretched against him. "It's the nurse! Get hold of yourself!"

He already had. He zippered his fly, righted the chair, murmured, "I really want you, Lila. It's a reawakening of our love. It's what we've both wanted."

She was walking away from him, toward the hallway to the front door, her big rear rolling under her loose skirt.

And he saw her falling, the pieces of brain flying out of her shattered skull. Saw her big ass quivering as she lay freshly slaughtered. Saw himself ripping off the skirt and jamming his rigid member into that still-warm pile of meat . . .

He was gasping, he wanted it so!

And he knew he had to control the fantasies: killing Lila; killing Diana Woodruff; allowing his identity as Silencer to be known. *Dangerous nonsense*. He had to get his inflamed imagination under control.

But his sexuality—that he would allow free rein.

How marvelous his newly found passion was! It had *never* been this wild, this strong! And it was all due to Silencer; to his approaching the point of becoming a legend.

Just three more victims. Random killings as all the others, despite the delightful daydreams. Then he would be safe forever. Then he would become the man he'd always wanted to be, immune from the imbecilic insults and violence the world imposed. Because he could ignore it, knowing what he knew, knowing who he was and what he had done! Could turn a blind eye and deaf ear on it all, smiling, forever smiling. And would be passionate enough, sexual enough, *sure* enough to handle not only the whale, but attractive women, many of them, on the side. As strong men did. As would be his right, his prize . . .

Lila was back, introducing him to a small, round woman. "Mrs. Flores."

They all went to Mother's room, which smelled like a freshly used toilet.

Mother was crying like a child with a full diaper.

"Why is the cleaning lady here?" she sobbed. "It's not Thursday yet, is it?"

He soothed her, and spoke to Mrs. Flores. "We didn't get the chance to check her this morning. I assure you it's not always like this."

But of course it was, and he saw from Mrs. Flores's face that she wasn't too happy about it.

What did she expect to do for a hundred eighty a week, be a genteel companion?

He excused himself, saying he had to get to work.

Lila also excused herself, after showing Mrs. Flores the linen closet and the guest bathroom. She said she had to go shopping.

They left the house together, and Lila turned immediately to her car. He said, "No goodbye kiss?"

She pecked him on the lips. He turned away, acting rebuffed. She said, "Frank . . . I need time. To adjust to certain changes. Your personality . . ." She didn't finish.

He said, "Yes. The stress of dealing with Mother. But now that Mrs. Flores is here . . ."

"I don't think she'll last long. Did you see her face?"

"She'll adjust. It's her living. How many Mexican women earn this much money?"

"She's a trained nurse, not an illegal alien, Frank!" This was delivered with her old snap and combativeness, and made him feel better. Yes, everything would return to normal, once he got the three remaining victims out of the way.

He went to his Chevy, thinking of the radio, the newspapers, and later, the TV newscasts. Marvelous prospects for a marvelous day! And to cap it all, going out for what Lila would accept as his nightly drive.

True to his word, Captain Cohen had been sticking his head into Larry's office each day about one, one-thirty, whenever he returned from lunch, if not to belch then to be almost as brief with an "Okay?" and an immediate withdrawal.

Today, however, he stepped through the door and sat down beside the desk. Larry looked up from the file on Gale Corinth, twenty-six, real name Gabriel Cherney, real sex male. Though "real" in this case meant only what lay between the legs, not what went on in the mind.

Nothing new had developed. The two witnesses were practically worthless, though he had already held a news conference and given out that general short-stout description, for all the good it would do.

"Didn't hear your belch, Captain."

Cohen wasn't in a smiling mood. "The couple that saw Silencer, the Anthonys, a few other people on the street when you arrived—the ambulance team, another civilian, even a cop who shall remain nameless—they were a little surprised at your manner, your choice of language."

"Why the fuck would that be?" Larry asked innocently.

"You used obscenities. In front of citizens."

"Slipped. Won't happen again."

Cohen nodded. "You on top of the phone-call log?"

"The tips have been too far out with no basis in fact. We've checked a few. Crap."

"You see how many have poured in since the last two killings?"

324

"Vic Chasen's in charge of phoned tips. We've got over seventy, all told."

"I've spoken to him. It doesn't appear he's taking them too seriously. Forty-one since the Betty Anderson killing alone."

"I'm aware of them, Captain. Look at the log yourself if you want to see the quality of the tips. Almost all from neighborhoods abutting Sunset Boulevard and the murder areas. All but two from women who want us to question their neighbors, brothers, boyfriends, husbands, who've been out late on the nights Silencer has killed. Who've had their faces scratched, or have been acting different in some way since about the time of the murders. Acting badly to *them*. Revenge stuff, Captain."

Cohen nodded and began to get up. "Just playing superior officer."

Larry said, "We return every single call. We ask if there's a long weapon in the house—a silenced gun. We ask if there are bloodstained clothes that can be examined. In only three out of all those complaints did we get answers that justified sending an officer to the residence. In one case there was a long weapon, a sawed-off shotgun. Seems this timid type was having trouble with a competitor in his ice-cream vending business, panicked at threats, and decided to carry the thing around under his jacket for protection. It would sound like a cannon. The D.A.'s considering an illegal-weapon charge, but he's harmless. In the other two cases there were bloodstained items of clothing. One was a guy who'd been punched in the nose in a bar. The other was animal blood from picking up a dog struck by a car."

Cohen was standing now. "How about today's log?"

"You never give up, do you, Captain?" He lifted the phone and got Vic Chasen. He wrote on a pad, and said, "No, Vic, I don't think they're worth shit. Pardon my indelicate language." He hung up.

"Funny," Cohen said, and Larry knew that that particular line of humor was finished.

"Three more calls since midnight." He checked them

off on the pad. "Mother reporting a son. But the son hasn't been seen in two weeks. Guess she wants better action than Missing Persons is giving her.

"A woman reporting her husband." He looked at this one a moment longer. "Nights out match. Personality changes—has grown more violent, to the wife. Scratches on his face night of the Vivian Garner killing, before Silencer's vacation." He shrugged. "But no weapon reported. We've had this much several times before, and then it turns out the nights don't *really* match and the scratches are either on the wrong night or perfectly innocent." Still, because of the Captain's presence, he again picked up the phone. He dialed and waited.

Cohen said, "As long as you're on top of it."

Larry said, "Mrs. Lila Berdon?" He paused. "When will she be in? No. No message."

He hung up. "Hispanic maid, I guess. I'll try again."

"Why not leave your number?"

"C'mon, Captain. What if the husband calls instead?"

Cohen said, "I'm retiring just in time, right?"

Larry grinned.

Cohen said, "But I'm not gone yet. And I hear you're putting the massage parlor where that Woodruff girl is working under full surveillance."

"Part-time surveillance," Larry said quietly, and cautiously. Someone had been talking about him again. "A man checking it for half an hour at a time, maybe two, three times during the night. We don't get started until tonight. I might let up after a week . . ."

"And a Vice Squad woman assigned to drive by when the man isn't on duty, so that you're giving that one parlor almost constant coverage, this at a time when we need every officer moving around the *entire* area. What's your justification for this?"

"Diana Woodruff is the sister . . ."

"I know. And you've been dating her, haven't you?"

Larry stared at him. "Have *I* been under surveillance?"

"You were seen by an off-duty officer at a Malibu

restaurant. When I checked your duty roster for to-night, I guessed the rest."

"I don't buy that, Captain. Someone decided to play tail. Someone who knows Diana Woodruff. You wouldn't brace me on one sighting and so much guess-work."

Cohen just stood there.

Larry remembered the first night he'd met Diana. Remembered Marv Rodin manhandling her, insulting her . . . and how he'd come down on Rodin and kept him far away from Diana, on the very fringes of the case, in fact. Also, Rodin had been present last night when he'd let off steam to John Vieress. That smile . . . and they hadn't been talking much lately.

Maybe it was paranoid, but he decided to try a shot in the dark.

"Remember when Marv Rodin was brought up on charges for slapping a topless dancer?" And knew from the way Cohen turned abruptly that he had his sneak, his spy, his shoo-fly.

"He was acquitted," Cohen said, and walked to the door. "Don't make vendettas, Larry. You've been too emotional about things since this case started. Or since you met Diana Woodruff."

Larry half-rose. "She's been shooting her mouth off about Silencer on radio and television, and how do we know he won't go after her? How do we know she doesn't *want* him to go after her? It's a reasonable assumption . . ."

"She shot her mouth off six weeks ago and he didn't go after her. He's had all that time and never deviated from the random-victim pattern, no matter what she wants, no matter what amateur revenge game she might be playing. There's nothing reasonable at all about the way you're handling the Grecian Massage and Diana Woodruff."

Larry sat down, knowing he was at the thin edge of being bounced off the case. Which could mean a nota-tion on his record about "emotional instability," or "al-lowing personal involvement to impair judgment." He'd seen it happen to other men. They'd then rotted at the rank they'd reached, and in some cases had been pressured into early non-pension or part-pension retirement.

But there was one thing he couldn't and wouldn't tolerate, and that was a spy on his own S.I.T. He said, "You might be right, Captain, but . . ."

Before he could continue, Cohen said, "So might you, Larry. Do some spot checks each night on the Grecian Massage. I'd hate to be responsible for a friend of yours getting hurt."

Larry was disarmed, and muttered, "Thanks, Cal."

"But just for a few days. After that, she's to be treated no different from any other Strip person. That means no individual tails, no personnel devoted to her protection." He opened the door.

"Mind telling Detective Rodin to step in, Captain?"

Cohen muttered, "Should I guess why?"

"I'm transferring him the hell off my S.I.T. I know the days when a cop could casually shoot off either his gun or his mouth are gone, *but no knives at my back!*"

Cohen stared at him. Larry met the look. On this point, he'd go down to the wire.

Cohen finally said, "*I'll* do the transferring, Lieutenant," and went out.

Larry wanted to get Rodin in anyway. Wanted to call him a sneaking son-of-a-bitch and come around the desk and pound his fucking face . . .

He was standing. He was shaking and sweating.

He sat down once again. Emotional instability wasn't far from the truth. Personal involvement was putting it mildly.

God! He needed Friday! A dozen Fridays!

And went to lunch, refusing to think—again, again!—of what would be missing from Friday.

Just to get *that* part of her out of his system . . .

Mel slept late again, until almost four, and called the whiz-bang medic who'd handled his case at Cedars-Sinai. He wasn't at his office, so Mel left his number with the answering service and walked unsteadily to the bathroom and took a long, hot shower.

He came out and dressed, feeling better, but only a little. The full line of crap was back—headache, lingering sickness in the pit of the stomach, dead feeling in the legs—both of them now. And something else he'd thought he'd left behind—brief, recurring periods of sleepiness. *Heavy* sleepiness. So that in the next two hours, while making and eating breakfast and trying to get the phone working, he took three quick naps. And finally ended up sitting in his big chair, head down, half-out, waiting to tell Dr. Gerfield he was finished.

The phone rang. It was a chick wanting Ludes. He said he had them, and to drop by.

"Can't play house, Mel. Got my main man in town."

"That's cool. Bring cash instead of gash."

A while later, the phone rang again. He roused himself, and it was the cop. "Well, Melvin. You still need that money?"

Mel smiled a little. "No, Lieutenant. You can keep it." And he didn't bother being polite. He just hung up.

Nothing to worry about anymore. Not bills or cops or chicks.

Just one worry—Silencer. *Get that mother!*

The phone rang. It was the whiz-bang medic. Mel said, "You know, Doctor, you struck out with me." And he told him what had been happening.

"You'd better come right into the hospital, Mr. Crane. Tomorrow morning, the latest."

"And what happens then?" he asked, feeling as if he'd rehearsed this with old Doc Byrnes.

"Tests . . ."

"You told me you took, and I quote, 'every conceivable test.' You told me you did, and I quote, 'everything that could be done.' You said I'd either make it as I was, or I wouldn't make it at all."

Gerfield cleared his throat. "That was then. Now we've got to fight a new battle. And we can't do it on the phone. Come in tomorrow."

"I can't afford it."

That stopped the good doctor for a moment. "Your insurance . . . ?"

"Can't afford the twenty percent." And when there

was another moment's pause, he said, "Let's wait a week, Doc. If I can't make it by then, you can bring me in by ambulance. And I'll beg from ward to ward." Or he'd make a deal with Lieutenant Admer.

"I'm going to have my nurse call you every morning and evening at ten. If you don't answer . . ."

"I don't get up till noon, and I don't get home till one or two, on slow nights." But that was the old Mel Crane, and he added, "You can try."

"You don't sound as sick as you say you are, Mr. Crane."

"I'm not," Mel said, and they said goodbye. And he wasn't as sick as he sounded. He was sicker.

He went to bed, setting the alarm for nine in case the impossible happened and he slept another long stretch.

Frank was home at five-thirty, and went to his mother's room, which was fresh and clean. She lay quietly, staring out the window at the fence on the north, and beyond it at the old apartment house, so many of which dotted the streets off Sunset Boulevard.

It wasn't at all like living next to a high-rise. These two- and three-story houses were more like small motels, invariably built in a U around a court, garden, or pool.

This one was two stories, twelve apartments somewhat run-down but remarkably quiet. Quieter, in fact, than their new neighbors in the single-family dwelling to the south. The music had been blasting as he'd walked up the driveway. And he'd seen a motorcycle out front.

Perhaps he'd sell. Perhaps he'd get enough with the inflated property values to buy something close to the sea. He'd always loved the sea . . .

But it wasn't *he*, it was *they*. He and Lila and Mom.

He said, "Hello, Mom."

For the first time in almost a week, she responded rationally. "Hello, Frankie. How's business?"

He was delighted, and sat down at the edge of the

bed. "Picking up, Mom. You know, you're really looking great today! Mrs. Flores is doing you good."

"That woman insulted me, Frankie."

He took her hand. "I can't believe that. She likes you. She's going to take care . . ."

"She said I was filthy. She said it when she was changing the bed. I heard her say it under her breath. *Sucio*, she said. And later, *mugriento,* when I couldn't control gas. She didn't think I understood. She doesn't know I had Mexican maids since I was a bride. I don't want her here anymore, Frankie."

He stood up, embarrassed. "Well, I'll speak to her." But he wouldn't; didn't dare.

"I hate her!" his mother suddenly cried out. "Get her out of this house!"

"She's gone for the day. Tomorrow will be better, you'll see."

"*Hate* her!" his mother said . . . and farted mightily.

He hurried from the room, and his mother called, "I'm sorry. I can't help it. I have no privacy . . . can't go to the bathroom . . ." She began to cry.

He came to the kitchen. Something smelled good, and Lila said it was lamb stew and yankee beans. He rubbed his hands together. "I'll go wash up!"

She said, "You have time. It won't be ready for about an hour." And then: "Mrs. Flores left at four. She's supposed to work from eight until five, or nine till six, her choice. I don't think she's happy, Frank."

"It'll be all right," he said, unwilling to face more unpleasantness. He went to the living room. Time to watch the news shows. He'd already enjoyed the newspapers and the radio. He hadn't been bothered by those so-called witnesses, the Anthonys, who'd seen him from across the street and three stories up. "Short and stout," the police said. "Wearing a suit and no hat. Driving an American sedan."

He'd chuckled. Some description! They'd have to arrest half a million men!

What *had* bothered him was the interview with that idiotic prostitute, Diana Woodruff, though he really didn't know what she'd said. He'd turned off the radio

331

the instant she'd begun speaking. He'd turned the *Times* page past quotes from that same interview. He would keep turning her off, refuse to read what she said, refuse to watch her on television. And that way remain unbothered, untouched . . .

But the moment the set warmed up, her face sprang out at him. And her words bit into him:

". . . not going to get death, or even life, because he's not capable of premeditated murder. He can act only as his insanity moves him to act at a particular moment . . ."

". . . classic woman killer, sexually inept all his life, probably impotent by now . . ."

". . . any weapon, even a knitting needle, would probably scare him off. He's a basic coward . . . doesn't dare attack a physical equal, only unsuspecting women . . ."

He was sitting hunched over, feeling actual pain: cramps deep in his stomach. He was trembling with the need to *do* something about the way she was insulting, smearing, reviling Silencer. He had to cut her off . . . and yet he sat there, watching, listening, hating. Because cutting her off here, at his TV set, would leave her talking to the rest of the city. Because only by sexing her, demeaning her, and finally killing her would he really cut her off. And then the media, and through them all the people, would realize how wrong she'd been.

God, God, he wanted to go to her tonight! And knew it was stupid and dangerous.

He changed channels. He watched the foreign news, wiping his mind clear of Diana Woodruff. Until suddenly she was back, talking on this channel, insulting Silencer on this channel . . . and on yet another channel he turned to.

He shut the set off and went to the bathroom and began choking, retching.

He didn't throw up. With an effort of will, he stopped it, refused to allow the whore to make him sick.

Or to make him do anything foolish.

He washed. He lay down and rested. Lila called him. He went to the kitchen and had a marvelous dinner. And had seconds. And wiped out the stewpot with slices of sourdough bread.

Strangely enough, Lila said nothing. Even when he went to the refrigerator and got the apple pie they'd agreed to save for a before-bedtime snack. Even when he finished both large slices left in the tin.

She sat quietly, sipping coffee, looking into her cup, raising her eyes only when he spoke to her, replying mainly with nods, yeses, no's.

He said, "Another Silencer killing last night."

She nodded, eyes on her cup.

"And I was out. My God, do you really think I'm Silencer?" He laughed.

She also laughed, nervously, and looked up and said, "I didn't really . . . I mean, Frank, I was just being emotional after you, well, practically *raped* me."

He laughed harder. "Am I going to have to rape you again tonight?"

She smiled, and he didn't quite believe her smile. "If you skip a night or two, I'll capitulate gracefully."

What she was saying was that she didn't want him touching her tonight, or tomorrow night. Maybe for as many nights as she could manage. Which was quite a switch.

She said, "As for your being out last night, or on some of the other nights when . . . well, you know, those women were killed—as for that, you go walking or driving just about every night, don't you."

He said, "Yes. As I will tonight. Drive and walk and get rid of this enormous dinner!"

She sipped her coffee. She murmured, "Want company?"

"I'd be delighted!" he said. And felt he could outplay her here, because she couldn't stand walking. A block was her limit. He'd take her out and walk her a quick block and she'd go home and he'd be free for his drive and walk and execution. Maybe two of them. And by tomorrow night, the night after, certainly by week's end, he'd be through with Silencer. Through

333

with him in terms of being safe from capture. But never through with him in terms of memory, of satisfaction.

Except for that damned Woodruff whore!

He stood up. He stretched. "Seven-thirty. Want to watch a little television?"

She said she would clean up the kitchen first.

He watched a quiz show. It ended and she still hadn't joined him.

He walked to the kitchen. She was at the table, sipping another cup of coffee. He said, "You're becoming an addict. Are you nervous about something?"

She got up and went to the sink. She emptied the cup and rinsed it. "Just about Mrs. Flores staying on."

She returned with him to the living room, where they watched a police procedural show. "They find clues," he said. "They make suspects talk. They catch crook after crook. If it were only that way in real life."

After a moment's pause, she said, "What makes you think it isn't?"

"Our theft-insurance rates, for one thing. Our unsolved crime rate, for another."

"Oh."

"Silencer," he said, "still doing exactly as he pleases."

She said nothing.

He smiled to himself. Soon, her suspicions would die from lack of anything to feed on.

The show ended at ten, and he shut off the television. "Let's go for that walk."

She nodded. "I think I'll wear a sweater."

He said he'd get it for her, but when he returned from the bedroom, she said, "I forgot your mother, Frank. It's not right to leave her alone."

"Not even for ten or fifteen minutes?"

"No, Frank." She paused. "Is that how long you'll be gone?"

He laughed. "Only when I'm with you. You know *my* walking capacity. Think I'll try Beverly Hills again." He turned to the hallway. "Don't wait up if you're tired," he said and strolled out jauntily.

He'd already prepared the gun, putting it in his attaché case, and the case in the Chevy's trunk. He had to be more careful from now on . . . about Lila, that is. Had to take the chance of keeping the gun in the car so as not to risk having her catching him in the back yard, at the bushes, where she could later search and find the one thing that could destroy him.

At least for the several days remaining.

Frank had been driving for almost an hour, and he'd actually spotted *two* possible victims. Yet he hadn't stopped. And now that he analyzed his feelings, he understood why.

Random killings of strangers was no good any more. Silencer had changed, evolved, matured. He needed *meaning*, personal satisfaction, in his remaining killings.

Diana Woodruff . . . one of the three final victims . . . or the final victim who took all three bullets. In her filthy groin, her filthy mouth, and only then, after much richly deserved pain, in her head.

Yes! He *wanted* that . . .

He suddenly realized where he was, and pulled sharply to the curb. Without consciously planning it, he'd driven to Grover Street, where Diana Woodruff worked.

He looked around. He was in a dark spot, unobserved, safe.

He smoked a cigarette, thinking calmly, rationally.

Despite all the killings, and the supposed witnesses, no one knew what Silencer looked like. He was absolutely safe. He could walk past that parlor, walk *into* that parlor, and no one would know who he was.

If there were other girls, other men there, he could hire Woodruff for sex and enjoy her, knowing her execution had simply been postponed.

If there was no one there and some way of isolating himself with her, he could punish her with the extra bullets, after first using her for sex.

And if he had to do it quickly, on threat of being interrupted, he could kill her and be out in about a minute.

However he did it, she would die with the words, "I'm Silencer," in her ears. Possibly tonight.

Of course, he wasn't unaware that the police could be having the parlor watched, hoping he would walk into a trap.

But they didn't know what he looked like either.

He flipped his cigarette into the street. He began to think of other ways, clever ways, intricate ways, as opposed to the quick, simple method Silencer had used until now.

Finally, he got out of the car and began to walk, uphill, toward Sunset Boulevard, two blocks away. Toward the Grecian Massage, a block and a half away.

Mamie had been patrolling the streets around the massage parlor for twenty minutes before the Mustang appeared. She checked her watch—eleven-thirty—and made a quick entry in her notebook, something the Chief insisted on so that full reports could be submitted to his old friend, the District Attorney.

The Mustang parked further south this time, further into the darkness, and she realized why when she caught the glint of glass, then saw the binoculars at the black's eyes.

She passed by him on the opposite side of the street, the parlor side.

He waved.

She crossed the street. "Hi, handsome."

He smiled.

"Got a cigarette?" she asked.

He extended a pack through the window. She took one, held it to his lighter, and blew smoke in his face. "I'm Val," she said, using one of her cover names. "And you?"

"Mel."

She smiled. *Clever Mamie!*

"You don't seem to be doing any business," he said.

"Oh, I had two tricks before you showed up. A gold mine, this street."

"Overflow from the parlor, I guess."

She nodded, grateful for the absence of yesterday's obscenities.

Then he said, "How about me?"

"Well, I'm an old-fashioned girl. Southern-raised."

"You don't sound it. I'm New Orleans myself. You sound native Californian."

Which she was, but she shook her head. "Still have a bit of trouble with . . . well, you know, mixing the races, sexually."

"Then fuck off, redneck cunt!"

She felt as if she'd been punched in the stomach, but fought for self-possession. "It's . . . understandable, isn't it?"

He turned from her. "I don't know who or what you are, but get off my case."

"*Your* case?" she snapped, having had just about enough abuse!

He laughed sharply, unpleasantly. "My *back*, lady cop or whatever you are. I'm breaking no laws sitting here."

"I'm not a cop," she said, hating this *person* for doing what no one had ever done to Mamie Belfont before—blown her cover. "And I have no interest . . ."

But he was turning in his seat, looking back to where she now heard footsteps.

"Ah, a customer," she said, and began to walk back across the street, glad to break contact, knowing she'd made some serious errors handling him. The script had been unusually weak here!

Then she saw the stout man walk under a lamppost, and heard the black exclaim, "*Thank* you, up there!" By the time she looked back at the Mustang, the black was getting out. With a large pistol in his hand.

She was in the middle of the street when he called, "Fat Fuck! It's Melvin Crane!"

The stout man immediately turned and began to run.

She was trying to decide how to handle this sudden plot twist—whether to arrest the black, who *was* Crane, for carrying that weapon; whether to follow the stout man on the assumption that he was Silencer—

when Crane sprinted past her. And stumbled and dropped the gun and fell to his knees.

She had her own gun out now, and came cautiously closer.

Crane was holding his head with both hands, rocking a little, crying a little. She was shocked to see blood trickling from his mouth, his nose. He said, "Jesus, stop, stop!"

She bent to him. "Crane. It's Detective Belfont. Is that man Silencer? Did he wound you somehow?"

He looked up at her, his face twisted. "Yes . . . Silencer. Get him!" And fell over on his side.

She immediately began to run toward that street light where she'd last seen the stout man. Because Melvin Crane would know Silencer.

She reached the lamppost and ran past it . . . but the street was empty as far as she could see. She kept going, pausing to glance into alleyways, doorways. She kept her gun ready. She wouldn't give up! Not with the climax so close!

She reached the corner. She paused, undecided . . . and thought she heard something, a car door closing, across the intersection and further south on Grover.

She began running again. She watched for headlights.

If he was making his escape by car, she could shoot out his tires . . .

She heard someone. "Miss, over here! A man with a gun . . . Quickly!"

Someone she couldn't see. On the other side of the street. Calling on Mamie Belfont for help.

She began to cross over . . .

Mel knew he should stop and explain to the dumb lady cop what was happening. But he couldn't stand her redneck guts, act or not, and the fat fuck was running, running fast. The fat fuck was getting away, because Mel Crane didn't have good legs anymore.

He knew he'd been dumber than the lady cop for not waiting a moment longer, for not dry-gulching Silencer. But the fat fuck had paused about twenty feet past that street light, as if about to turn back. The fat fuck had been there, clear as day, and Mel had been unable to believe in his good luck; had flipped out; had jumped the gun.

Still, he was sure he'd be able to put a bullet into him when he passed under that light again. Watched him turn and run, and ran too, and prepared to aim and empty his gun . . .

Something exploded in his head. Lights went wild behind his eyes and thunder roared in his ears and he was on his knees. He put his hands over those roaring ears and begged God to stop it. Because he knew what was happening. Because he didn't fear death nearly as much as he feared becoming a vegetable. Or letting the fat fuck get away.

He spoke to the lady cop, telling her to get Silencer.

He fell over, everything getting very dull, very numb. He wept, because he didn't want a lifetime in that hospital bed.

He prayed for death and grew number, duller . . . but with consciousness.

Someone else was there: a man's voice saying he was a police officer and had been watching from the corner. Mel brought him into focus. Undercover Vice, because he looked like a healthy wino. Flashing a badge. Asking if he'd been shot "by that hooker."

He tried to tell him the hooker was also undercover. He tried to send him after her and after Silencer. But his tongue, his vocal chords, wouldn't work anymore.

There was another, massive explosion in his brain, and he felt his heartbeat turning ragged. And despite mortal fear of death, was grateful.

Mamie Belfont stopped crossing because a car was coming. She stepped back and tried to see in the lights of the approaching vehicle just who had called her. And as a van went past, did see a shape in a car on the other side. A head . . . or a headrest?

She again began crossing, the gun firmly in her hand, though pressed against her hip so as not to alarm any civilian. She said, "Is that you in the car?"

He said, "Keep low, for God's sake! He was running from you! A stout man with a gun! Somewhere on this side!"

She went into a crouch, and ran toward the cover of that parked car.

She reached it, and the window was open, and the voice spoke from inside. "I know you. You're the actress from *Chief Shut-In*."

It was dark, but she was able to make out a white male face. She was confused now, because he'd called her "the actress from *Chief-Shut-In*."

Not Mamie Belfont.

But, of course, she *was* an actress . . .

He said, "I'm Silencer," and the gun pressed between her eyes and there was no time to bring up her own gun. She wondered if this was when the Chief would make his appearance and save her and there'd be a long-moment-of-unspoken-thanks-in-Mamie's-look. Then cut and commercial and fade-in for epilogue and explanation.

The cut came: The sudden ending of picture, of sound.

But no commercial. No epilogue. No explanation.

The screen was dead.

NINETEEN: *Tuesday, September 19*

Because of Larry, Diana was able to leave the Grecian Massage at one a.m., while it was still full of all sorts of people, mainly police and still-arriving radio and TV newspersons.

But *before* Larry arrived, she'd been thoroughly humiliated. Mainly by a shabby man with drawn gun who'd burst in while she and Dreena were with clients. An undercover officer, he'd said, and made them all come into the front room, at gun point, she in her mini-toga and Dreena and the two customers in almost nothing between them.

A near-hysterical officer, she'd guessed, who'd raged on the phone that "the fucking spook got knocked off right outside his car, and the broad who did it—I think she did it, but I was up at the corner—she ran south and by the time I figured out what happened and followed and looked around and found her, she had a bullet in the head too!"

He'd hesitated when Dreena begged to be allowed to dress, and the customers begged to be allowed to leave.

He'd stopped hesitating the moment Diana added

341

her plea to theirs. "Damn it, you knew Crane was outside, didn't you, Woodruff? You're the reason all this happened . . ."

She'd said he was being ridiculous and that she was going to get into her street clothes. She'd turned away, and he'd yanked her back brutally. "You're wearing enough!" he'd shouted. "You're not leaving my sight! You others—get dressed!"

He'd obviously been trying to blame her for what he'd felt was going to be seen as an enormous failure—allowing two people to be murdered while he had the scene under surveillance.

She'd gauged his need to strike out at someone, and sat down at the desk, remaining very still.

The customers had run out the back door, but Dreena had returned to face the music with Diana. Mainly because if the police asked, Arthur would give her name and address.

So Dreena had been lucky, been dressed in a skirt and blouse when the other officers and the newspersons began pouring in. The willowy black girl had wept anyway, because she didn't want her folks to know. "Please don't take my picture!"

Diana had tried to huddle inside the mini-toga, the revealing wisp of pink lace, and felt the many eyes on her and felt the lights on her and the cameras . . .

Larry had arrived. And immediately told her to dress. And for an instant she'd loved him!

When she'd come out of the bathroom, he'd had the undercover officer backed into a corner. What he'd been saying had been composed almost exclusively of profanity, and promises of reassignment to "fag toilet patrol."

He'd stopped, because the reporters and cameras and mikes were turning to her again. He'd led her past them, saying, "Miss Woodruff was not a witness to tonight's events," and seen her to her car and said, "Go right home. I'd send a man with you, if I wasn't under strict orders not to. I'll call, so no stops on the way!" All of which made her feel that Payoff Number

Three was going to be a real pleasure . . . and maybe something more than a payoff.

By then she'd known that the ambulance crew hadn't been able to find any wounds in Mel Crane's head or body, and pending a coroner's report were assuming he had died of natural causes.

By then the woman who'd been shot in the head had been identified as Hortense Laver, a TV actress who seemed to have been playing the part of real-life detective, and who apparently had found Silencer.

Anyway, Diana was on her way home now, through with it all. Through with Silencer too, she imagined. Psychotic he might be, but stupid enough to risk a second entrapment on Grover Street? Unlikely. He'd killed seven times . . . *eight,* if it turned out Mel had died of that head wound he'd received in August. And was still free as a bird.

She came to the turnoff where Sunset ended at the shore, and headed right toward Malibu. There was still some traffic; Sunset and Pacific Coast always had a few cars. Tonight they comforted her. Tonight she didn't want to be all alone on the street.

Didn't want to be all alone in the condo, either, she discovered, once she shut the door behind her. Not that she was frightened of anything specific. She had the gun in her purse. She would keep it by her, at least for a while longer. It was more that she felt an emptiness in what had once been her home; a lack of reason to stay on here; a need to find purpose elsewhere.

She would wait out another week or two at the Grecian Massage, just in case Silencer was crazier than she thought. She would see Larry Admer; was beginning to *want* to see Larry Admer . . .

The phone rang. She answered it, pleased, not caring *who* it was. Even an obscene caller would get a cordial reception!

It was Larry.

"You all right?" he asked.

"Fine. Are you all through there?"

"Not yet. But you are."

"What does that mean?"

343

"That it's too damned dangerous for you to work in that place anymore. Silencer killed that actress just a block away! And the Grecian Massage will become a magnet for increased nut-action. Don't tell me you haven't had a few hairy experiences already."

"Nothing, really," she said, unwilling to tell him of the religious-fanatic couple. And there'd been a tasty few earlier tonight, one of whom had begged her to allow him to put a toy pistol to her head while she masturbated him. Another who had been impotent and hoped that having her call him Silencer and plead for her life would help him copulate successfully. A third wanted "the TV star to masturbate."

She'd sent the toy-gun addict packing, with the help of one of her regular customers; had gotten rid of the second one herself; and as for the third, he'd paid a hundred dollars and she'd used Dreena's vibrator, faking an orgasm because the parlor had become a far-from-fun place for her.

"Business as usual," she said.

"I don't believe that. I can close down the Grecian Massage . . ."

"Please don't," she interrupted. "Give me a few more weeks. I'll quit on my own. I just don't want the girls and the owner to suffer because of me. And I don't want to make decisions under pressure. Let me slack off, come to my own natural end in this business."

"Do you really mean that?"

"Yes. As for Silencer, he's not crazy enough to bother me after tonight."

"Well . . . can I come over?"

She wanted to say yes, but suddenly was exhausted, drained by the night's events. "We have our date on Friday. We'll have other Fridays. No pressure there either, Larry."

He said, "Right," and she said, "Thank you," and he said, "I know all we've got is a deal, but I can't help worrying about you." She was silent, and he spoke again, voice very low. "I'm your very special john, Diane." He hung up.

She put the phone down slowly. She was left with a

sweet, sad feeling, but told herself that when she finally split, his natural prejudices would help him get over "the massage-parlor whore."

The phone rang again as she was in the kitchen, eating yogurt from a container. It was Arthur, and he wasn't happy about what was happening to his Grecian Massage.

"I'm closing it down for a while," he said.

"But everything's cool. Why lose money . . . ?"

"Nothing's cool! You want to work, switch to the Valley Delight. I'll give the other girls notice."

She said she would lose her regulars and the other girls would lose their incomes and some of them had families to support and it wasn't fair. "And what more can happen, Arthur?"

"Who knows! Maybe someone from *Battlestar Galactica* will zap the whole block!"

She spoke quietly. "Close one day for a cooling-off period. Open Wednesday and see what happens. Any problems you can close again."

"I don't know . . ."

"And real late, before I lock up, you and Brenda can drop in."

Arthur was silent.

She asked if it was a deal, and he said yes, and she returned to her yogurt.

A lot of trouble for just a few more weeks of what was almost certainly spinning her wheels, wasting time trying to entice Silencer to come after her. But she was now the only person who had any idea of what he looked like. She had to try; had to convince herself before giving up.

She decided she would get up earlier than usual tomorrow. That she would visit the offices of the real estate firm a mile north on Pacific Coast Highway and put the condominium up for sale. That she would trade the little Fiat convertible in on a good-sized station wagon, not only so that she could take most of her possessions with her, but also because it would better suit the climate in St. Louis. And on the day she finally left L.A., she would visit both her bank and Carla's.

She would put all that undeclared cash into a suitcase and drive straight through, night and day, so as to put it into another vault.

She went upstairs to bed. She tried to think of anything else she should do in preparation for going home.

Going home. It made her smile. She wondered if Mom and Pop would be happy to have her back. Perhaps not at first, but in time . . .

Half asleep, she wondered if her old friend Jeannie still lived in St. Louis. And her first love, John Kleiser. And if Axel Mandel was still involved in amateur theatrics at Washington University . . . if other old friends and lovers and acquaintances were still around.

She dreamt of herself as she'd been before her brother's death, before the move to L.A., before entering the massage parlors, before Carla's death.

And they were all different Diana Woodruffs . . . leading to today's Diana of the closed heart and cynical mind.

In her dream she wept because she didn't want to be today's Diana. Because today's Diana couldn't go home and live happily ever after.

Frank was having a fine day at the store. Nathan Koler of Koler Tax Consultants walked in and without having to be sales-pitched bought *four* Olympia electrics. Asking for the discount, of course, but it still netted Frank roughly two hundred dollars.

Not that he hadn't been unusually cheerful even before that. Martin had finally asked if "Mother Berdon" was feeling better, thinking that would account for Frank's humming and smiling.

Frank had said yes, much better, but he'd been thinking of last night, and still was. Of the Grecian Massage and the series of events that had taken place nearby. Events that had turned out perfectly for him: Silencer had proved he could improvise, could react quickly to take advantage of any possible situation.

Mel Crane was dead "of a brain hemorrhage caused by a wound received in August at Silencer's hands," according to this afternoon's radio news. Which was delightfully satisfying! Which wiped out his one failure!

The TV actress was "murdered, police assume, as she chased after Silencer, whom both she and Melvin Crane apparently spotted outside the Grecian Massage . . ." And that had been great fun: recognizing the phony hooker at the last minute; killing the celebrity fool!

Also, the police were being criticized, because they'd actually had an undercover man at the corner of Sunset Boulevard, "who failed to provide quick medical help for Crane, or to protect Hortense Laver. Silencer must be laughing today . . ."

As indeed he was! (Though he'd also sweated, briefly, thinking how *close* the police had been.)

And exulting! Talk about killing two birds with one stone: he'd picked up two victims with one bullet! And while not all the newscasts, the newspapers, had begun counting Crane yet, a few had. Which placed Silencer's record at an incredible *eight!*

Immediately after finishing with the actress, he'd U-turned and driven to Santa Monica Boulevard, and then into Beverly Hills. He always thought well when driving through those dark, quiet, tree-lined streets. And he'd thought well last night, parking several times for leisurely cigarettes.

He'd kept his radio tuned to the all-news station, and had begun thinking of the very last thing the police would expect Silencer to do—return to the scene of the crime. But if Crane were taken away, no one there would know Frank Berdon was Silencer. And even if seen, Frank Berdon would be only one of several, maybe many, motorists and pedestrians who were bound to have gathered to gawk. And if he came up on Sunset rather than Grover, and parked near one of the late-nightclubs or restaurants . . .

A news flash had come on: "Melvin Crane, wounded by Silencer six weeks ago, is dead tonight outside a Sunset-area massage parlor . . ."

He'd turned south then and there, leaving Elevado for Bedford, and had driven to Sunset. He'd turned east and headed back toward the Strip. And had heard the second news flash about Hortense Laver.

It was twelve-forty when he drove sedately by Grover Street, taking a long look at the Grecian Massage.

A legal four-corner turn a short distance further along Sunset, and he was moving back on the north side of the street, parking at a meter near the Hillside Topless, still going strong, as could be concluded by the sight of a large group of Japanese tourists being escorted inside from their bus in the parking lot.

He'd now been able to see down Grover, through his open driver's-side window, to the parlor and the parking lot which was full of police cars and media vans. And to the street where cars were also parked, people looking out of them or standing beside them.

After intense examination, he'd spotted what he was looking for: there in the lot, amidst all those vehicles, all that hustle, had been the little foreign convertible he'd seen in the newscasts. Diana Woodruff's convertible.

Within ten minutes, the convertible had pulled out of the lot, and he'd started his engine. It had come up to Sunset, and he'd seen it was a light-colored Fiat. It had made a full stop, then swung across the east lanes and into the west, so that all he'd had to do was pull away from the curb and he'd been behind it.

Marvelous! He'd considered her as good as dead, Silencer's ninth and last victim, since he would use the remaining two bullets on her.

He'd followed the Fiat all the way to Malibu, staying well back at times, coming up close at other times, experimenting, enjoying himself, seeing Woodruff's dark head occasionally, seeing it clearly when he was one car removed from her at a stop light, remembering the things she'd said about him . . .

But he hadn't been quick enough when she'd pulled to the curb before a stretch of townhouses, and jumped from the Fiat and run up the path to a door. He'd barely slowed, barely considered where to park his own car, when she'd been safely inside.

Well, perhaps not so safely if he'd decided to knock and enter.

But that would really have been pushing things. And no necessity for it. There was always tomorrow.

He'd walked up that same path and read the address and returned home. It had been after two, but Lila had been awake, and murmured from the bedroom darkness, "So late, Frank."

She'd been wrong. For all that had happened since he'd left the house, it had been very early indeed . . .

Now he allowed Martin to leave at four as a mark of celebration. And thought that tonight might see a true celebration—a city-wide media event—the conclusion of Silencer's historic work!

He closed at five and drove home, staying cheerful despite the rush-hour traffic, refusing to notice the boors, the drivers without manners, the teeming motorized animals that, if he could, he would eliminate with one atom bomb!

He pulled into the driveway at five-forty, and heard the music blasting from next door. He looked around to see if anyone was watching, then gave them the finger, jabbing it viciously at their windows. And went to the trunk for his pacifier, his tranquilizer.

After touching the long automatic, he went into the house . . . which he soon determined was empty. *Really* empty, because his mother was gone, her bed made.

He finally noticed the sheet of paper taped to the refrigerator:

Frank: Mrs. Flores called this morning to say she was quitting. She got another job. I called the employment agency, but they said it would be difficult to replace her. Seems she told them about the job conditions here. So I'm doing the only sensible thing, and I'm sure that once you see how pleasant Oakdale Nursing Home is, you'll agree that Mother will be better off. I don't know exactly when I'll be home, as there's much to do, especially since they were kind enough to take her without notice. Though I did talk to them last week. Have something to eat. Relax. We'll talk soon. Lila.

" 'Have something to eat! Relax. We'll talk soon'!" He heard his own voice, shouting; realized he was pounding his fist against the refrigerator.

He got the wine and poured a water glass full. He was shaking. She'd done this to his mother! Without even one word of discussion! *His mother!*

He took a swallow of Burgundy. Then he looked at the large glass and poured the rest back into the bottle. He couldn't afford to dull his wits in the slightest. Because of what he had planned for tonight.

And because of what he was now thinking of adding to that plan.

He opened a can of tuna and toasted two slices of bread, normally an *hors d'oeuvre* for Frank Berdon. But he couldn't finish.

He went to the living room and put on the television. He watched the local news. He saw Crane and Hortense Laver carted into separate ambulances. The announcer listed them as "victims seven and eight," and Frank tried not to think of his mother, tried to enjoy what he was watching.

Laver's co-actors on the old *Chief Shut-In* show expressed shock at her death. One said, "She was having identity problems since the show ended. Maybe before. Remember, she was Mamie Belfont for six long seasons—six years, in effect. And she was such a dedicated actress, throwing herself into the part . . ."

There were shots of Diana Woodruff in a revealing whore's outfit that quickened Frank's breath. And she remained blessedly silent, turning away from the microphones, giving no interviews this time.

But then they showed a rehash of her last interview, along with comments from an in-studio psychologist, a so-called "criminal expert." And the damned old fool agreed with the whore! *Agreed!* And the film clips went on and the psychologist went on and Silencer was being defamed on the day he'd lost his mother and he screamed, "Fucking trash!" and leaped up and kicked them.

The tube exploded. He jumped backward and almost fell over his chair.

He'd put his foot through the screen, through the picture tube. He'd ruined that beautiful set.

It was the whore's fault. It was also the whale's fault.

He went to the kitchen where he wouldn't have to see the broken TV and sat down and went over his fantasy of killing Lila.

Getting her out of the house, onto the street, somewhere out of sight, so that she wouldn't be found for quite a while, preferably not until daylight. So that he might even have to find her himself. So that he would have time to get Diana Woodruff and complete Silencer's work with two major triumphs in one night.

Oh how that prospect thrilled him!

He began refining the fantasy, turning it into a plan.

Lila had to be killed right outside this house, as if Silencer had intercepted her as she'd walked to her car. She had to be killed in her own back yard . . . where Frank Berdon, the husband, might have to discover her if a neighbor or meter reader or one of the children who occasionally trespassed from the apartment house didn't. Where Frank Berdon, the husband, certainly wouldn't kill and leave his own wife! Ridiculous concept! Suicidal concept!

Tomorrow, when they questioned him, when they tried to be suspicious of the husband because that was the first one they suspected when a wife was murdered, he would weep, he would blame himself. They had quarreled over his breaking the TV and she'd gone out in a huff and he'd assumed she'd gone to her cousin, perhaps a friend, to spend the night. And, God, now his beloved wife was dead. Ask anyone, they'd had a good marriage. Had only each other. Ask anyone, he'd never been with another woman; not the faintest whiff of suspicion connected with Frank Berdon.

And so on. And while there might be a little unpleasantness, being brought down to the police station

351

and the like, it would be a Silencer killing with a Silencer bullet and Diana Woodruff would also be a Silencer killing and what did Frank Berdon, loving husband, loving son, respected businessman, have to do with such things?

Especially since the only proof was in Lila's mind, and in the gun, and both would be gone forever. Lila in a well-tended grave (he would certainly see to that). The gun deep in the brush at the bottom of the wildest part of Latigo Canyon, where it would never be found. And if by some miracle it were, he'd have wiped it clean and it would lead nowhere; certainly not to him.

He went out to the driveway and backed his car to the street, where it wouldn't be blocked by Lila's Toyota.

He got the attaché case from the trunk and walked into the house. He took the gun from the plastic bag and put in back into the case. Then he took the plastic bag to the bathroom and cut it into strips with his nail scissors and flushed it down the toilet.

Putting the scissors down, he thought of something, thought ahead, and picked them up again and went to the little service area off the hallway where the washer and dryer were. He found the nylon clothesline and cut two lengths of about two feet each, and then cut down the middle an old towel Lila used for dusting and took one of the halves.

He put the sections of rope and the piece of towel into the case, behind the flap, where it wouldn't interfere with the gun, and put the case under the table. His preparations were completed.

He began to feel good. He began to feel hungry. He finished the tuna and toast and poured a glass of milk and found a sugar bun, somewhat stale, and ate it anyway. He promised himself a plate of spaghetti and much wine when he returned from dealing with Diana Woodruff tonight.

He made excellent spaghetti, ask Lila . . . while you still could.

He found that thought amusing. He was still laughing when he heard Lila come in the door.

He stopped. He sat somberly at the kitchen table. Her footsteps hesitated in the hallway, and he smiled to himself. She was afraid of him. And how right she was. She should run. For her life.

She came inside. He looked up at her. "You shouldn't have done it without consulting me, Lila."

She went into explanations. He watched her lips move, her arms wave.

He answered her. But not violently. And saw how relieved she was.

She asked if he'd eaten. He said yes, a little.

She asked if he wanted anything more.

He said coffee perhaps. And some of those frozen-dough cookies she baked in the oven.

She rushed to accommodate him. She kept talking. She said his mother was "going to love being with her contemporaries."

He asked if she'd been happy on her arrival today.

"Well, it's the first day. She was a little upset. She wants to see you. But I think you should give her a week to adjust, Frank."

He nodded. He would see her tomorrow. He would comfort her. He might even tell her the tragic news about Lila. He wondered if she would smile.

Then he could take her home . . . but he doubted he would. A man and wife could handle a sick mother. But a widower? A man alone?

No. And the deed was already done. He would leave her in the nursing home. He would have his new life, his freedom . . . and soon new women.

He smiled. Lila noticed. "You're really taking this well, Frank! I've been so confused lately. You've been staying out so late. And Mother's deterioration has upset me. All sorts of things . . . some of them illogical, I guess."

"You mean thinking I might actually be Silencer?"

She laughed nervously.

He nodded. "I was out a long time last night."

"So were a lot of other men," she said quickly. "And no one *really* knows what happened with that

353

black, that crazy actress, both running around with guns. *You* certainly don't have a gun!"

"Of course not. What would I want with a gun?"

"And while waiting for the paper work to be done at Mother's new home, I read in the *Times* that the police have received almost a hundred calls from women believing their relatives and friends—mainly husbands, by the way—to be Silencer. Because of absent hours and scratches." She laughed. "The same things that were bothering me. Not that I *really* thought . . ."

He chuckled.

She began serving the coffee and cookies.

He said, "I never worried about it, honey." She bent and kissed his cheek.

"I know how enormous a drain on *you* Mother has been," she said. "I know how much you love her. I think that's why you were so rough, so irrational, at times."

"Never again," he said, eating a cookie, that kiss infuriating him. *How dare she! After carting his mother away! After kidnapping the old lady from her home, her son!*

It was eight and quite dark outside when she cleared the table. She asked if he wanted to watch television. He'd forgotten he'd broken the set, and rose quickly. "I want to walk. With my wife. Never again alone. Only with my wife. So she won't get paranoid about me."

She hesitated, and he knew that despite all her rationalization, she was still worried about him.

"I've had quite a day," she said.

Yes! he thought. But it would end soon.

He took her hand. "It's important. It's a new beginning."

She said, "All right."

He reached under the table with his free hand and got his case. "Might as well put it in my car for tomorrow." Then they walked down the hall and out to the driveway.

The rock music from next door had stopped. The

354

windows were dark. Lila said, "Have you heard those new neighbors of ours?"

He nodded. "I was thinking we'd move soon."

"Well, we'll have to discuss *that,* Frank!"

"Of course," he said. "Careful discussion." While disposing of a human being, the most important human being in his world, had required only a whale's quick decision.

She was turning toward the street. He said, "Remember that bush in back that was dying?"

"The yard is your department, Frank."

"The one I was watering in the dark?"

She suddenly laughed. "Yes. How is it?"

"I'll show you." And still holding her hand, he turned left and walked quickly toward the back.

She tried to resist. "You can show it to me in the morning!"

"I've got a flashlight in my case. It'll take just a minute. I'm proud of that bush." He kept walking, kept tugging, and she would have had to literally dig in her heels to overcome the momentum. And they were past the windows and off the blacktop and walking in darkness, on grass.

"Right there," he said, pointing. "The lilac."

"I can't see . . ."

"Just bend down a bit, and I'll get the flashlight."

She bent. He put the case on the grass, opened it, and drew out the gun. She said, "This is ridiculous. Are we going to walk or not?"

She had straightened and was turning. He placed the gun against her forehead and said, "Not."

She made a strangling sound.

"*I am* Silencer, whale."

The strangling sound reversed. She was sucking in air, her mouth opening.

He would have liked to mock her a little, torment her a little. But that intake of air meant a scream was coming. So he pulled the trigger.

Her head snapped back with a wet, splatting sound. She farted, louder than Mother had, and fell over. Her body thumped on the grass. And lay still.

There was a foul smell. Perhaps more than gas. Perhaps she had defecated.

The thought pleased him: that she should die in the filth his poor mother had to live in. He was also pleased by that strangling sound, that brief glint of horror in her eyes.

Well, little enough after what she had done.

He put the gun back in the case and walked briskly out to the street and his car. He didn't bother with the trunk. He put the case on the seat beside him, and drove off.

He doubted that the massage parlor would be open, or if it was, that Diana Woodruff would be back at work so soon after what must have frightened her badly. But he would check anyway.

The Grecian Massage was dark, the parking lot empty.

He headed for Malibu.

He remembered how she had left her car last night: jumped out and hurried up the path, not bothering to lock the Fiat's doors.

Of course, she'd had a bad night. She might normally lock her car.

He didn't worry about it. A way would present itself. Silencer hadn't failed yet. Lila had been victim number nine. She'd found out how clever Silencer could be.

So would Diana Woodruff. And (extra added delight) she would round out Silencer's score at a perfect, incredible *ten!*

She'd accomplished much today, Diana thought: listing the condo for sale and buying new luggage and pricing station wagons. She'd also bought some clothing, sedate St. Louis–type clothing . . . at least as her parents represented St. Louis.

Her body was luxuriating now in a hot, soapy tub. Later tonight her mind would luxuriate in a rich mixture of Bach and Updike, something for which she hadn't had the attention span since Carla's death.

And she would eat well too, if within her caloric

and nutritional guidelines: Manhattan chowder, broiled salmon, brown rice, and a split of Montrachet.

But before food, music, and literature would come something that might not be too pleasant. And she left the tub and used towels and hair dryer and tried to plan the call she was going to make.

Finally, she sat at the edge of her bed, dialing area code 314 and her parent's number, wondering what she would say if presented with something like, "We saw that Silencer business on TV. We know about Carla. We know about you."

The phone was ringing at the other end. She was breathing hard . . . and she *hated* the feeling of fear, of guilt, of sweaty tension that only her mother and father could give her.

And suddenly remembered the time difference, two hours. It was after ten there and her parents went to bed early on week nights, sometimes as early as nine.

She almost hung up, and her father's voice said, "Hello?" in that furry, irritable way that indicated he indeed had been asleep.

"It's Diana," she said helplessly. "Did I wake you, Dad? I'm sorry if I did. I wanted to speak to you and Mom. Should I call back tomorrow?"

And hated her groveling, her trembling, her anxiety.

"It's Diana," her father said away from the phone, and her mother's voice said clearly, "Is she all right?"

Which broke a dam. Which stopped the self-hatred and brought a sudden rush of tears. She gained control. "I'm fine, Dad. How are you?"

"Okay. We ever going to see you and your sister?"

"Carla's still in Europe. But I might be in St. Louis in a few weeks."

He again spoke aside: "She says she's coming here in a few weeks." Then: "Your mother wants to talk to you. I'd like it fine if you came home."

She wanted to ask if he meant for a visit or for good. But one reasonable conversation didn't make a life . . . and she could never forget the beatings he'd given her mother. She said, "I'll be speaking to you again, Dad. Take care."

357

Then her mother was saying. "About time you paid us a visit. Nine years is long enough, wouldn't you say?"

She said yes, and wanted to answer that her parents could have come to Los Angeles. She and Carla had invited them often enough, especially Carla, who had worked out a sightseeing extravaganza that covered the entire state and parts of Oregon on the north and Mexico on the south.

"Heard from your sister again?"

"No, Mom. But we'll talk about it when I get home."

"What's to talk about? Honor thy father and thy mother . . ."

Diana dialed nine as her mother was speaking. Her mother said. "Hello? What's that clicking noise? Can you hear me?"

"Line's gone bad," Diana said softly, and continued dialing.

"I'm going to say goodbye," her mother shouted.

"Bye, Mom. I'll call soon."

It had gone better than she'd expected.

She used the phone again, to make a reservation for dinner for ten o'clock. Claude, the captain, said, "For one, Miss Woodruff?" and she said, "Yes," and he said, "I'll see to your table."

She would miss her Malibu fish house and her table over the water.

She would miss the sea-view condominium.

She would miss the warm winters.

Anything else?

Well, that cop, perhaps, because he had persisted so . . .

She went downstairs and put a cassette in the stereo and picked up her book. Dimly, in the background, she heard the hum of traffic, and behind that the muted sound of the sea. Occasionally, a car started or stopped close to her home, and that intruded a little more strongly on her consciousness. But time passed beautifully.

With a start, she realized it was nine-thirty. She had to rush through dressing and run for the car. Because they served until eleven and that table of hers was prized by many. If she wasn't there on time, the captain would have to give it away.

She unlocked the Fiat's door, jumped inside, started up, and pulled away with a scream of burning rubber.

She reached the restaurant at ten after ten, and had to park quite a distance from the doors. She wished they had valet parking on weekdays as well as weekends, but then again, the self-parking was a money saver that many of the parons appreciated.

She came into the anteroom short of breath. The captain was at his podium station. Also present were five or six couples waiting for tables.

The captain smiled. "This way, Miss Woodruff."

Her table was set and waiting, the only empty one she could see.

She sat down. The sea glittered and crashed on two sides. She said, "This is *very* nice of you, Claude."

He ducked his head in a little bow, and handed her a menu. "May I take Madam's order myself?"

He'd never done that before. And this holding of the table on such a busy night . . .

As she opened the menu, she felt his eyes, and looked up. He smiled again. He was looking at her in a way she recognized, but had never seen in this place. His eyes were slipping over her breasts, down to where her leg showed through the long, slitted skirt.

She gave him her order. He went away, and returned shortly with her half-bottle of Montrachet. He opened it and poured the taster portion, and all the time he smiled and all the time his eyes worked her body.

After she'd said, "Excellent," he bent close and murmured, "Miss Woodruff, I wonder if you would be willing to give me your phone number? I've long admired you—your taste, your intelligence, your beauty."

She sat there, thinking she could scratch this restaurant from the list of things she'd miss in L.A.

"I was watching television . . ."

"And you know where I work."

359

He nodded, his smile dimming a bit at her tone of voice.

"Then you don't need a phone number."

"I was thinking that since we've known each other so many years . . ."

She stood up. "We haven't *known* each other, Claude. We've conducted business, I purchasing, you selling. When you come to the parlor, our roles will be reversed. But we still won't *know* each other."

She found ten dollars in her wallet and put it on the table. He said, face red, "That isn't necessary."

"Yes it is. *I'll* demand payment."

She walked out, not too quickly, smiling at the bartender when he smiled at her, seemingly calm and self-possessed. But when she reached the darkness of the parking lot, she said, "Dear God," and shook her head savagely, as if to negate what had just happened.

And immediately afterward told herself she was over-reacting. She'd handled literally thousands of men at various massage parlors over a nine-year period. So what if a waiter wanted her phone number?

But of course, it was much more than that. It was her private life and her professional life coming together and leaving her no place to hide.

And that included her car, she realized an instant after getting behind the wheel. Because she felt something, smelled something different . . . and on turning her head to the back seat, looked into the barrel of a gun. And beyond it, at a round face that Mel Crane had sketched for her.

He'd been upset at how quickly she'd left her home and driven away. He'd barely grasped his case when he'd realized he wouldn't be able to get to her in time, not even from his parking place just twenty feet behind the Fiat.

But she hadn't driven far, and he'd been able to turn into the restaurant parking lot, after driving by to make sure there were no attendants. Had there been, he would have parked on the road and waited there.

The lot was large, and though all the spaces near the

restaurant had been taken, there'd been plenty of room further south. And when he'd checked her doors this time, they'd been unlocked.

He'd glanced in and seen the small back seat and even smaller floor area—but large enough for the short time he would spend there.

He hadn't entered the car right away. He'd walked to where the lot ended in a narrow stretch of sandy soil, beyond which was another paved section and a business of some sort, closed and darkened.

He'd walked to the sea-side of the sandy strip, where it led down to a rocky beach. But first there was a section of knolls with clumpy scrub grass. First there were shadowy hollows . . . and he'd known where he would take her.

He'd assumed he had plenty of time while she ate her meal, but glancing around to make sure no one was observing him, he'd seen the woman come out of the restaurant. And though she'd been a distance away, and though only minutes had passed since she'd gone inside, he'd moved swiftly to the Fiat, gotten in back and snapped open his case.

He'd been uncertain that it was Woodruff until the moment she'd gotten inside. After which he'd risen from the floor to touch the gun to her forehead.

Now he smiled at her. Now he heard her gasping breath, and imagined he could hear her pounding heart . . . but perhaps that was his own.

She said, very low, "Can I ask why?"

He had the rope for her hands and feet and he had the towel for her mouth, but instead of using them he did something he'd never planned or fantasized. Thinking how to answer her, remembering what she'd said about him, he suddenly smashed the side of her head with his gun.

She sagged sideways on the front seat. He bent over her. She bled a little from the left ear; she moved her head. He revised his plan, which had been to make her drive the hundred or so feet further south to the end of the lot, and then tie her wrists and lead her down to the knolls, the shady hollows. Where he would tie

361

her ankles and gag her. And play with her awhile, with her breasts and bottom, undressing and enjoying her, perhaps sodomizing her, perhaps removing the gag so she could use that foul but lovely mouth.

Now she couldn't drive. Now *he* had to.

He got out, and there were people entering a car perhaps fifty feet closer to the restaurant. But they talked and laughed and never glanced his way.

He shoved her further over, still holding his gun, and his free hand pressed her bottom and clutched it briefly.

He got behind the wheel, jamming the gun under his left thigh, and realized the key wasn't in the ignition. He had to move her again, pulling her purse from under her. She began to moan, and he didn't want to hit her again and perhaps ruin her for his games. He searched the purse and found a small gun and a wallet, but couldn't find keys.

He was sweating heavily. Where were the damn keys? Such a small thing, and he didn't want sweat, he didn't want fear because that wasn't Silencer's way!

He was about to search the floor when he thought of how he always carried an extra key in his wallet.

He searched her wallet and found two keys in a side flap; one slid into the ignition.

He threw the small gun and the wallet into the back and started the Fiat. It had a shift stick. He hadn't shifted in years, not since trading his old Plymouth coupé.

Her legs were in the way and she was stirring strongly now and he said, "Don't move!" He shoved the stick forward and exclaimed as the gears ground loudly. He remembered to clutch then, and got the car moving forward, jerkily, and drove it around toward the sandy strip.

She was beginning to sit up now, and he stepped on the gas and the car lurched forward. He had to slam on the brakes to stop from crossing into that sand, where someone might think the car was stuck and come from the parking lot to offer help.

He stalled, which was all right. He grabbed his gun

and got out and ran around to the other side and opened the passenger's door. She was sitting up. He put the gun against her head and said, "Walk in front of me."

She got out, staggering a little, moaning as she shook her head, saying, "Please . . ."

He moved her in front of him. *"Please?* Are you *afraid?* What do you have to fear from a contemptible psychotic coward who's also impotent?"

"Death," she said, and stumbled as he directed her to the right, down the long hill toward the knolls. "I'll do anything to live."

He didn't want her talking, making sense.

Only *he* should talk! Only Silencer should make sense! Because Silencer had waited through nine killings to talk, to make sense, to play, to enjoy!

He shoved her as they reached the knolls. She went headlong, rolling. When she stopped, she quickly sat up and turned herself to face him. Her dress was high and her legs, her thighs, gleamed white.

He *loved* the sexual frenzy coming over him! Just standing there, looking at her, he was stiff and throbbing! And now he would tie her, gag her . . .

His attaché case. It was back in the Fiat.

"Damn you! Spoiling things! But I *can* plan! I *can* premeditate! And I can change directions, improvise, too!"

She moved. He leveled his gun. Only one bullet, and he wanted that to go into her head, after his pleasure was over. But if he had to, he would shoot her now; would do the best he could with her wounded, dying, or dead body. Then if it were necessary, he would strangle her in the sand.

She was pulling the dress up around her waist. She was pulling down her panties. She was staring at him, at his gun. She was terrified of him, of Silencer. He had nothing to worry about, nothing to sweat and tremble about. She was his plaything, until he laughed in her face and destroyed her.

The sexual frenzy returned as she opened her thighs, leaning back on her elbows. She whispered, "Please,

please," her voice shaking. The frenzy increased as he came closer, looking at the white fullness, the black joining.

He put a hand to his belt buckle. She spread herself wider, shamelessly, lifting her arms. Her eyes looked up at him. Again she said, "Please," begging for her life, trying to trade for her life.

But he suddenly wasn't sure it *was* terror he read in her eyes or voice. Suddenly suspected a trap in those full thighs, that black joining, those lifted arms.

Because how could he lie between those legs, make love to that dark joining, and still keep her under threat of instant death?

The gun to her head, yes . . . but there was too much movement in coitus. There was awkward positioning in getting atop her and in her. There were opportunities for her to *do* things.

"Get on your knees," he said.

"Please, please . . ." The arms, the eyes, the black joining beckoned. And threatened.

"Your knees!" He leveled the gun at her chest instead of her head, needing a larger target from this distance.

She scrambled, and he laughed as she knelt.

"I'm Silencer," he said, taking two steps forward to stand directly in front of her. He turned the gun and put it against the top of her head, left side, slanting down and right, so that the bullet would course through the brain more completely than in any of his other victims.

"No one has heard that and lived," he said, full of laughter, full of triumph, because this one had thought to trick him, trap him, destroy him first with that little pistol, then with arms and thighs and black joining. And here she knelt!

He opened his fly with his left hand, Silencer's cleverness, Silencer's triumph, adding to his desire.

He pulled out the stiffness, the throbbing hotness. She opened her mouth without being told, and he said, to be more clever still, "Do it well and you'll live."

She did it well and his eyes closed in ecstasy. He

364

soared, soared, and approached orgasm swiftly, and prepared to put the bullet into her brain at the same time.

The moment he stopped moving toward her, Diana knew she had a chance. At least to take the animal with her. Because he wasn't a total maniac; wasn't out of control. Because he saw the danger in those legs, those arms, as she'd hoped he would; as she'd tried to reveal to him with narrowed eyes and too-anxious plea.

Now she knelt with his organ in her mouth.

Now she experienced the full measure of what her life in the massage parlors had brought her to: fellating her sister's murderer. Moving her mouth up and back along the length of his penis; pausing at each stroke to nibble at the glans as a good little cock-sucker should.

Her head still radiated pain and she wasn't sure she could move quickly enough at the right moment . . . which she tried to anticipate with her lips and tongue. Wasn't sure she could do what she had never done before; what no woman she'd ever heard of had done before.

He gave a soft cry of pleasure, the first he'd allowed himself, and she felt the first, tiny spasm in his penis.

She jerked her left hand up, grabbing at the gun, his hand, anything to move that barrel from her head. And bit down directly behind the glans, behind the head of his penis. Bit as hard as she could. Kept biting, biting, going against every human instinct, screaming deep in her throat as she did.

She heard *his* scream; then had the gun. She felt him lunge, explode, erupt, leaping upward and backward.

Yet she still held him in her mouth. Part of him.

She choked on his blood and spat the piece of meat from her mouth and vomited. But didn't turn from where he lay, face down, clawing and screaming into the sand. Weaker screams now, barely audible above the crash of surf.

She was still retching, and wanted to run. She was sick and had to go home. And scour her mouth and body and brain of this vileness.

365

But she couldn't leave him like this, even though she had lost the fierce determination to kill.

She came closer. His face and hands dug into the sand and the screaming was a whimpering and the dark stain spread under his middle.

She looked at the gun. She wasn't holding it properly. She put her finger inside the guard and on the curved trigger. She bent and touched the thickened, extended muzzle to the back of his head. He never noticed. She pulled the trigger and felt the gun jerk. He stopped clawing.

She dropped the gun, and thought vaguely about fingerprints and forensic medicine and evidence that might lead to her. She wanted to leave for St. Louis. She didn't want police and publicity and more chance than ever of her parents finding out about her and Carla. And especially about *this*.

She got her panties on. She looked around and found her left shoe, which had fallen off when he'd shoved her down the hill. She picked up the gun and walked to the water's edge and turned left, walking further south, away from the restaurant, to where the rocks decreased and the beach began. To where she'd once walked with Larry.

He'd have to do without his payoff.

She stooped and got a handful of wet sand and rubbed it, scrubbed it, over the entire gun, especially the handle, as she'd once read in a mystery novel. She kept sand between her hand and the gun as she continued walking.

She saw the wooden pier and went out on it, to the end, and looked around. She seemed to be alone and unobserved. If she wasn't, there was nothing she could do about it.

She threw the gun as far out into the ocean as she could, and returned to her car.

She found her purse, and the key still in the ignition. She looked for her wallet and gun, and found them in the back, along with his attaché case. She took tissues from her purse and used them to pick up the case by the handle and drop it out the window. Then she drove home.

She waited when she saw the couple leaving the townhouse two doors away . . . and later, in front of her bathroom mirror, was glad she had. Because she looked like Dracula after a hearty meal.

She brushed her teeth and gargled with mouthwash and scrubbed in the shower.

She threw up again. And brushed and gargled again. And told herself, "You *won't* think of it!"

After which she began packing; as much as the Fiat would hold.

Larry kept himself under tight control as he took a seat n Captain Cohen's large corner office. Assistant D.A. Roger Vineland sat beside him, both of them facing Cohen's desk. Control was necessary, because he knew now that Diana had split Los Angeles, and he hated the bitch for leaving him twisting slowly in the wind of his desire, for failing to live up to even that minimum, physical payoff . . . which would have been *something*.

But control; control was absolutely necessary to prove that he was an officer in charge of an investigation, trying to tie up important loose ends, perhaps catch a vigilante-killer.

He'd made a mistake Friday, breaking down Diana's door and conducting an illegal search. One of several mistakes he'd made on this case, culminating in losing his cool with Captain Cohen Saturday morning.

They'd found Frank Berdon's body a little past eight a.m. Wednesday. At first Larry hadn't been informed, since the corpse was out in Malibu and no immediate connection to the Silencer killings had been made.

But a meter-reader had found Lila Berdon's body at

ten the same morning. And that one had brought him up against a hell of a mistake—"ignoring," as the brass put it, the call she'd made about her husband, Frank Berdon. Only one of over a hundred such calls, of course, but Captain Hindsight was in command.

So they'd begun looking for Frank Berdon, and that had led to the Malibu body and the Coroner's office. Once they'd gotten past the excitement of that "genital wound," they'd found the bullet in the sand; it matched the bullet that had killed Lila Berdon and all the other Silencer bullets.

Larry Admer was pretty sure who'd been blowing Frank Berdon on that beach.

No answer to his calls. No answer to her employer's calls. No one knowing where she was. The crime scene being so close to her favorite restaurant. It all led to only one logical reconstruction of the crime.

Frank Berdon waiting for her. Taking her to the beach. She getting the better of him. Then shooting him. Then leaving.

But why hadn't she called him? He'd have helped her. He'd have kept her out of it. Didn't she know that? Didn't she understand that deals notwithstanding, he couldn't help loving her?

But that had been before. Now he hated her guts! Because he'd still hoped she would come back on Friday, at least call, at least say goodbye and "See-you-someday."

She hadn't. He'd done a bit of drinking that afternoon and gone to her place and kicked down the door. He'd searched her closets and they'd been empty and then he'd really ransacked the place, determined to find an address, a phone number, a photo of another man she'd been hiding somewhere, making a fool of him . . .

He'd been interrupted by two uniformed officers with drawn guns, and the neighbor who'd called them, looking in from the hall. He'd learned that his badge wouldn't work in cooling the whole thing, because of that neighbor and the patrolmen knowing he might file a complaint.

Which he had. Which a real-estate company also

370

had, saying they were responsible for Diana Woodruff's property until it was sold. Which had then gotten to Captain Cohen, who'd said he would try and cool it if Larry paid for the door.

Fine, and he had, and then he'd made what was a logical request, a perfectly normal request by an investigating officer: send out an All Points Bulletin on Diana Woodruff. Homicide was a reasonable assumption, and he'd given his scenario of the Frank Berdon killing, including the evidence of her being seen in the restaurant, and being a natural target for Silencer after what she'd said on television.

That had been Saturday morning, and Cohen had been sitting just where he was now. He'd frowned. "Homicide, Larry?"

He'd quickly retreated. "All right. Make her a material witness."

Cohen had shaken his head. "You're being emotional about that woman again. I see no evidence on which to issue an A.P.B."

And Larry had lost control, shouting that it was his case and the woman had disappeared at a crucial time. "And it has nothing to do with my personal feelings!"

"I didn't say personal," Cohen had replied quietly. "I said emotional." As Larry had tried to continue, he'd raised his hand. "We've got Silencer. No doubt about it any more. Those prints we lifted from the Rolls's seat on the Betty Chez Anderson case—thumb and forefinger—they're a strong match to Berdon's. Berdon's wife's call, and her being murdered, and the timing of Berdon's own death. By someone he tried to victimize, obviously. By person or persons unknown, Larry, not Diana Woodruff. And then there's his Marine record."

Larry had winced at that. The bastard had actually been a Marine, in combat in Vietnam. He'd been rated UNSAT and discharged, after killing two South Vietnamese villagers. And the circumstances—the villagers had been found naked in each other's arms. They'd been making love when a patrol of grunts had sprung a surprise search for snipers: "Private Berdon mistook movement in a shadowy corner for enemy activity and opened fire, killing the couple . . ."

But no time to think of that now. Now he had a chance to get the A.P.B. and bring Diana Woodruff back to Los Angeles. She liked to give television interviews? She'd have her chance on *this* killing! Her name and face would become world-famous: "The woman who bit Silencer's prick off!"

She liked to con police officers? Well, once he got her here, he would throw at her every possible charge he could dream up, starting with homicide and going through unlawful flight and the various forms of suppression of evidence. He'd get her on *something*. And later there'd be that undeclared money . . .

He wiped sweat from his face, his hands, and put the handkerchief away. He had to be cool. He couldn't blow his top again. *Cool!*

On Saturday, Cohen had finally agreed to submit the question to the D.A.'s office. If Vineland gave an informed opinion that charges of some sort, any sort, could be filed, Diana Woodruff would be sought for return to Los Angeles. Larry had worked all Saturday night and half of Sunday bringing the Silencer file up to date, and tacking on the Woodruff memorandum. He'd kept the memorandum short, but ended with what he'd felt was a clincher:

"She is probably the one person who can tell us where to find the silenced .22 caliber handgun used by Frank Berdon. She may even have it in her possession." Which a would-be political star wouldn't be able to resist.

He'd driven to Vineland's home Sunday at six p.m. and delivered the file to him personally.

Now he lit a Camel and glanced at the youthful-looking Assistant D.A., who had given the file to Cohen some ten minutes ago. They'd been waiting while the captain skimmed it.

Cohen closed the folder. "I've seen most of this before. The memorandum is well-phrased, but I'll reserve my opinion until you give yours, Mr. Vineland."

Vineland's voice was cold. "There isn't the slightest

possibility that our office would consider filing felony charges against Miss Woodruff. Nor would we concur in any harassment of this woman, who has already suffered the loss of a sister."

Larry stood up. "What the fuck's wrong with you!"

Vineland also stood up. "Captain, I agree with you completely. Lieutenant Admer is pursuing a personal vendetta and should be removed immediately from the case. You're the commanding officer of record anyway. Just take over and close it out."

Larry felt the blood pounding in his temples, and stepped forward, fists clenching.

"*Admer!*" Cohen said. Vineland stepped back, left hand going out, right hand rising in karate chopping position.

Larry's body sagged. "I'm sorry." He saw his career going down the drain. "I really didn't feel my request was that unreasonable, but I can't argue with two expert opinions." He sat down again.

Cohen said, "Mr. Vineland, I hope you'll remember Lieutenant Admer's long, excellent record before you make any reports or statements."

Vineland went to the door, where he stopped. "I've seen officers caught up in similar situations—prostitutes and various offshoot types getting their hooks into them. Ethical men, honest, law-abiding men, are sometimes easy prey for this kind of woman. But it doesn't mean the woman can be sought, cavalierly, for a major felony."

Larry kept his head down, his mouth shut.

Cohen cleared his throat.

Vineland didn't continue, but neither did he leave. Larry finally turned in his chair. Vineland said, "You'll be fine, Lieutenant."

"Thanks." Larry smiled for the bastard. "Though I might be due for a vacation."

"You are," Cohen said. "I've checked."

Bet you have, Larry thought wryly.

Vineland came back to the chair, and Larry rose, and they shook hands. "We're going to nail plenty of 'em between us," Vineland said in his best campaign style. He waved, and was gone.

"Who *was* that masked man?" Larry muttered, sinking into the chair.

"You've got accrued vacation time of . . ." Cohen was checking a pad. "Thirty-nine days."

"Listen," Larry said. "I know you were against the A.P.B. But was I really as far off base as Vineland seems to think?"

Cohen hesitated. "He was a little emotional himself. But let's get back to your vacation. I've cleared you as of today."

"No. I've got the Dellinger-Carter case."

"Either that, or medical suspension."

Larry grinned. "Thanks for the vacation, boss. I'll take J.R. to Hawaii. Or Baja. He'll keep me away from the broads."

He stopped by the office for his carton of Camels, then went out to the parking lot. A network van was just rolling in. The Mouth jumped out and ran across to him as he reached his car. "Just five minutes, Lieutenant. We've learned that Frank Berdon was a Marine, and since your bio also lists Marine service . . ."

He said, "You know, you'd make a hell of a lay, if you'd only shut up."

He got in his car. She was staring at him. As he began driving off, she said, "I do shut up, for certain men. Call me sometime."

He laughed. Might as well, he thought. What he really wanted was gone forever.

374

EPILOGUE

The Thursday before Christmas, Larry Admer went shopping for J.R. He considered picking up something for Roberta, but their relationship was just about finished now. She'd wept about his "coldness" too many times. He'd stopped playing the I-love-you-love game. He'd taken to using the massage parlors out of the county once in a while. Hell, sex was sex and the other thing was mythology. In that Diana had been right.

It was a nice time of year, mild and pleasant. Even though this was the rainy season it hadn't actually rained in a week, and the forecast was for clear skies and low-seventies temperatures. Still, all the snow freaks were heading for Lake Arrowhead, Big Bear, and the higher elevations.

As for him, he'd be going to the party Captain Cohen and his wife threw every Christmas Eve: a goddom feast with more booze than any of the captain's men would feel comfortable drinking under his watchful eye. A generally quiet affair, where you didn't feel you had to have a date.

Early Christmas day, he'd go over to Gloria's and

give J.R. his presents. He'd shoot the breeze with her husband, Roscoe Green, who after a while would say that they were expected for big doings at his socially prominent family's "estate." Larry would kiss his kid, peck Gloria on the cheek, and take off, feeling low as shit, as he did every Christmas.

And this year he'd have to fight hard, with booze and maybe a pickup, not to think of a girl he still dreamed about. A cheating bitch whom he could have found through that real-estate firm, through the moving company that emptied her condo, through the post office that forwarded her mail. Whom he could have followed on that thirty-nine-day vacation of his back in September. Whom he could have found at any time since . . . had he been willing to risk his job.

But the job hadn't been the real reason he'd failed to at least satisfy himself as to her whereabouts. Once the pain of rejection had faded, once the rage had passed, he'd felt that if she didn't care anything about him, there was nothing to be gained by knowing her.

Silencer was forgotten. A new mass murderer, this one concentrating on skid-row alkies, was horrifying and entertaining the city. But he was none of Larry's business: Lieutenant Admer wasn't getting the big cases anymore.

He drove down the ramp to his apartment-house garage.

He wasn't getting the big cases, and he wouldn't make captain. Not without Cohen writing a hell of a recommendation, which wasn't likely, and not without coming up with a media sensation, even less likely.

The bitch was responsible for most of that too. The bitch had cost him.

There was a car in his parking space—all the spaces were numbered by apartments—and he smiled grimly in anticipation of writing his first traffic citation in years.

He parked in the adjoining space and got out. The offending car was a station wagon, a new model but dirty as hell. Missouri plates.

Maybe someone who didn't know the rules in L.A.

apartment houses. Maybe he'd give them an hour's grace.

He started walking.

A woman was sitting on the little bench beside the elevator, smoking. For a moment his heart leaped . . . but Diana didn't smoke. And she didn't dress in such drab, Monkey Ward–style clothing.

He came closer, and she raised her eyes.

She put out the cigarette in the sand urn. She looked worn, tired, a lot older than when she'd left.

"How come you're smoking?" he said, to say something.

"I'll stop soon, now that I've left childhood behind, now that I'm back in sunland, funland." She smiled a very weak smile.

"You went home, huh? It didn't work out?"

"That's putting it mildly. Sorry I took your parking place. I was at your station and spoke to Captain Cohen. He's really nice. He gave me your address and your apartment number. You're not in the book."

"Too many bad guys like to wake a cop at night, tell him off anonymously."

"No bad girls?"

"I *give* them my number."

"Captain Cohen says I made trouble for you. He says he's retiring and wants to leave you with a chance of promotion. But he doesn't know how because of your attitude."

"He's an old Jewish momma," he snapped.

She looked down.

He sighed. "Cohen's okay."

She stood up. "Well, do I stay or do I go?"

His heart was banging away now. He was afraid his voice would choke off in his throat. "Do what you feel, lady. And forget the deals."

"I feel like staying."

"Then get your car out of my parking space."

She nodded, and began to walk past him. "Later," he said, and pressed the button for the elevator. "Going back to the parlor?"

"No. School. I'm a rich bitch, remember?"

The elevator opened and two small children ran out, followed by a teen-aged boy. "Jesus!" he yelled. "Can't you wait even ten fucking minutes!" Then he saw Diana and flushed. "Hey, sorry."

Later, in the apartment, she imitated the boy. "Jesus, can't you wait even ten fucking minutes?" she said.

The answer was no, like the children running to Christmas excitement.

He was stripping off the drab clothing. He was revealing the goddess he'd dreamed of, wanted, hated, loved. He fastened his mouth to her breast, and she began to say something else, began to laugh, but stopped and sighed and lay slowly back on the bed. Because this was no joking matter. This was the most serious business in the world. Larry Admer and Diana Woodruff were coming alive again.

When they were naked, she tried to draw him up to her face, her lips. But he murmured, "No, have to," and meant he had to exorcise the multitude of men she'd had, so he kissed her belly and skipped down to her thighs, her knees. He kissed her feet, as she protested, weakly, that she hadn't washed. He was beyond caring about such things. This was a rite of rebirth. This was religion.

His face went between her legs. He made her laugh convulsively, and then moan.

She finally got him up to her face. They finally kissed, and again there'd been no time for washings, no thought of the scentings and cleansings and chemical niceties.

She wanted to go down on him. He allowed her to, but his real need lay in going into her body, not being stroked and sucked. Later, maybe, when resurrection was completed and games began.

For one instant, as her mouth caressed his penis, he thought of what she'd had to do on that Malibu Beach, and wanted to ask about it.

But he knew he wouldn't, knew he would wait for the day when, if ever, she would tell him.

He was too close to orgasm and said, "I want in!"

She rolled over and he mounted her and pounded her and she murmured, "Male chauvinist pig," and kissed him, kissed him. Until neither had breath for kisses. Until both gasped, faces twisting in the near-pain of sexual ecstasy.

He lay quietly beside her. She put her hand on his penis. He said, "How about a little rest?" She looked at the stirring, lengthening tube of flesh, and said, "Certainly." She rolled over, presenting him with her goddess ass, and said, "Night."

He grabbed that ass. He ground himself into it. He got her on her hands and knees. And they loved.

The next morning, at breakfast, she told him she could help him recover Silencer's gun. "If it's of any use to you."

"Along with my new attitude," he said, leaning over to kiss her hand, "it could be worth a captaincy."

"Then let's drive to Malibu."

On the way, she was absolutely silent. He kept trying to make conversation, kept trying to get her to smile. Finally, he said, "You're not worrying that I'll bring you into it, are you? I'll get the divers by citing an anonymous phone tip."

"I know. It's just going back there. It's just remembering things. Everything. Carla . . ."

He felt that they would have plenty of time for talking. Years for talking. And allowed her her silence.

On Saturday morning, two days before Christmas, Roger Vineland was in the bosom of his family. He and his wife sat in his study, outlining the social functions she would conduct on his behalf, as soon as he announced his candidacy for the position of District Attorney of Los Angeles in the special election.

She was called out by the maid, and Vineland stretched in his big leather chair behind his big, Morocco-topped desk. The announcement would be made the day after Christmas, at a Watts charity bazaar his father-in-law had arranged for that express purpose.

379

People had been urging Roger to announce ever since D.A. Allen had undergone his kidney transplant, but he'd continued to watch what was going on at Cohen's station house, continued to worry about Silencer's automatic turning up.

The worry had decreased, however, over the past four months, until now he was ready to move.

He stood up, thinking back to those stark days in the Annamese Cordillera. Thinking back to previous assignments: to hunts, to kills, to dangerous and, yes, thrilling assignments. It all had a rosy hue now, those memories. It was the old-soldier syndrome—the reliving of battles, the forgetting of blood and mud and pain.

But he *did* remember the blood, the target's blood, and not without pleasure.

You had to admit it, the CIA had been the best intelligence organization in the world at that time. And talk about building men . . . if you made it in the Company, you could make it anywhere, including the White House!

He paced about, full of enthusiasm and energy, waiting for Laura to return. He heard voices and the door opened and ten-year-old Chuck ran in, saying, "I'll bet it's in the garage, in that tool cabinet you keep locked."

He said, with some severity, that a boy had to learn patience to become a man. The presents would be his after dinner on Christmas Eve, and not a moment sooner. But then he smiled and hugged his son. Just as Laura came in with a large brown envelope.

"What's that?" he asked.

"From a Lieutenant Admer."

He opened it and inside was the Silencer file wrapped in blue ribbon with a big red bow on the cover.

Chuck said, "See, you get *your* presents early!"

Roger pulled off the ribbon. The bow went with it and underneath he saw the stamped black lettering: CASE CLOSED.

He still didn't understand . . . until he opened the folder and saw the hand-written note:

Dear Next D.A.:

I once disappointed you with my work on the Silencer case. But here's your Christmas present, in time for one hell of a media announcement. We've got the gun! It's on its way to the FBI labs and not just because of the Federal laws on silencers. They'll be able to raise those filed serial numbers, and we may get ourselves a fat-cat source. So enjoy! My best to your family.

Lieutenant Lawrence Admer.

Roger sank into his chair. Laura was asking him what was wrong and Chuck was complaining that he should "get at least one present early like Dad got," and he tried to think, tried to tell himself the odds were still against it being *the* gun.

But his world was shaky now, where a moment ago it had been rock solid.

Laura's voice kept probing at him—"You're so pale, dear"—and Chuck was whining, pleading, and he suddenly shouted, "For the love of God, can't I have a moment's peace!"

Laura stepped back, her face tightening. Daddy's little girl wasn't used to being shouted at. He wondered how she would feel visiting him in San Quentin.

She took Chuck's hand and they left the study.

The sharpshooter was alone . . . but still not at peace.

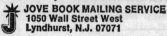